The House of the Edrisis

Middle East Literature in Translation
Michael Beard and Adnan Haydar, *Series Editors*

For a full list of titles in this series, visit
https://press.syr.edu/supressbook-series
/middle-east-literature-in-translation/.

The House of the Edrisis

~ A Novel ~

Volume Two

Ghazaleh Alizadeh

Translated from the Persian by
M. R. Ghanoonparvar

Syracuse University Press

The original Persian of this novel, *Khaneh-ye Edrisiha*, was first published
in two volumes in Tehran in 1991 by Tirazheh Publishers
and in one volume in 1998 by Tus Publishers.

Thank you to the S&B World Foundation Inc. for their generous
financial donation to the publication of this volume.

First Edition 2025

25 26 27 28 29 30   6 5 4 3 2 1

For a listing of books published and distributed by Syracuse University Press,
visit https://press.syr.edu.

ISBN: 9780815602941 (paperback)
9780815657200 (e-book)

Library of Congress Cataloging-in-Publication Data
Names: 'Alīzādah, Ghazālah, author. | Ghanoonparvar, M. R.
(Mohammad R.), translator.
Title: The house of the Edrisis / a novel by Ghazaleh Alizadeh ;
translated from the Persian by M. R. Ghanoonparvar.
Other titles: Khānah-'i Idrīsī'hā. English
Description: First edition. | Syracuse, New York : Syracuse University Press, 2024. |
Series: Middle East literature in translation | Contents: v. 1. The house of the Edrisis:
a novel, volume one — v. 2. The house of the Edrisis: a novel, volume two.
Identifiers: LCCN 2024013714 (print) | LCCN 2024013715 (ebook) |
ISBN 9780815602897 (v. 1 ; paperback) | ISBN 9780815602941 (v. 2 ; paperback) |
ISBN 9780815657194 (v. 1 ; ebook) | ISBN 9780815657200 (v. 2 ; ebook)
Subjects: BISAC: FICTION / Cultural Heritage | FICTION / General | LCGFT: Novels.
Classification: LCC PK6561.A414 K4313 2024 (print) | LCC PK6561.A414 (ebook) |
DDC 891/.5533—dc23/eng/20240730
LC record available at https://lccn.loc.gov/2024013714
LC ebook record available at https://lccn.loc.gov/2024013715

Contents

Translator's Foreword

The House of the Edrisis by Ghazaleh Alizadeh (1947–1996) is one of the most discussed and critiqued novels in postrevolutionary Iran. Even though some aspects of the events in this novel generally recall the Bolshevik Revolution in Russia, and although the locale of the story is the city of Ashkhabad (in English spelled Ashgabat after 1991), the capital of Turkmenistan in Central Asia, for many Iranians the story alludes to the Islamic Revolution just over a decade earlier in their own country. In other words, such readers' assumption is that by disguising the time and locale of the story, which is about a revolution, and for the most part avoiding the use of Islamic names for the characters in the story and using Persian and Russian names instead, the author successfully avoids the scrutinizing eyes of the censors who would shun any criticism of the new Iranian regime in any form.

The House of the Edrisis is populated with a large cast of colorful characters, almost all of whom are described in meticulous detail, whether in regard to their behavior and exterior actions and appearance or their inner thoughts and emotions. Even more meticulous is Alizadeh's description of nature, of plants, flowers and trees, of birds and animals. Nearly all of the events of the story occur in the house of a declining aristocratic family, who have by the beginning of the novel lost much of their affluence. In fact, the main character of the novel is the house itself, including its courtyard and garden, which are also described in exquisite detail.

Like all revolutions, the revolution in this novel has resulted in the overthrow of a regime most people had regarded as tyrannical, and, as often occurs in revolutions, the revolutionaries have evolved into tyrants, and the regime they have established has become even more despotic than the one they have replaced. This is perhaps the main reason that this novel has appealed to its Iranian Persian-language readers, since they have viewed the story as a grim reminder of the events that had occurred recently in their country. What seems to have been overlooked by most readers, including critics, is the sardonic outlook of Alizadeh regarding the revolution, perhaps any revolution—an outlook she expresses by making skillful use of subtle humor, employing a combination of the elements of black comedy, farce, melodrama, slapstick, parody, irony, and tongue-and-cheek statements of the narrator and the characters.

The author's choice of Ashkhabad as the locale of the story of an ostensibly socialist revolution that results in the rule of a despotic regime is not random or accidental. The city, the original name of which in Persian is Eshqabad (i.e., "the city of love"), was a part of the territory of Iran (internationally known as Persia before 1935) until the late nineteenth century, with more than one-third of its population consisting of speakers of Persian. Alizadeh's city of birth, Mashhad, in northwestern Iran, is the closest major Iranian city to Ashkhabad. The same is true of the author's choice of an aristocratic mansion as the stage of her theatrical story of a revolution. She was born in a wealthy and cultured family and grew up "in a house with a pool and lawns, full of flowers, willow and cypress trees, and box-tree shrubs," similar to the house of the Edrisis, and, similar to what occurs in the novel, Alizadeh's house was also confiscated after the Islamic Revolution and occupied by squatters.[1] All of these and other factors in a way justify the choice of Persian along with a number of Russian and Turkish names for her characters. Interestingly, Alizadeh intentionally avoids identifying the religious faith of most of the

---

1. Ḥasan Mir'ābedini, "ALIZADEH, Ghazaleh," *Encyclopædia Iranica*, //www.iranicaonline.org/articles/alizadeh-ghazaleh-writer (accessed 16 October 2017). Mir'abedini also provides a succinct biography and assessment of Alizadeh's literary output.

characters as Islam in a city with a majority Muslim population; the only characters whose religion is specified are Christians. By doing so, she also sidesteps providing any direct link between the characters of the novel and the Muslim population in the Islamic Republic of Iran, a diversional tactic so successful that *The House of the Edrisis* became the recipient of the award of the best novel of Twenty Years of Fiction Writing by Iran's Ministry of Islamic Culture and Guidance in 1999, six years after the author took her life.

Critics have generally praised Alizadeh for her masterful use of Persian. In harmony with the type of characters she creates, at times she employs a highly sophisticated diction and prose style, and, on other occasions, she utilizes vernacular slang and colloquial expressions. I have tried to render her diction and style as faithfully as possible. While in the socialist revolutions, including the Bolshevik Revolution in Russia, the term "comrade" was used as a form of address by the revolutionaries, in Iran the Islamic revolutionaries employed the terms "brother" and "sister" for the same purpose. In this novel, Alizadeh uses the Persian word *Qahreman* as an honorific of the revolutionaries. In this translation, I have rendered it as "Hero." The original Persian of this novel, *Khaneh-ye Edrisiha*, was first published in two volumes in Tehran in 1991 by Tirazheh Publishers and in one volume in 1998 by Tus Publishers. Since the latter edition, which I was initially using, suffers from carelessly missing pages and misplaced passages, I have based this translation on the 1991 two-volume edition, which was published when the author was still alive.

Given the large number of characters and names that may be unfamiliar and difficult for some readers to remember, I have provided a list of the most important characters with brief explanations at the end of this volume.

I am grateful to M. Mehdi Khorrami for scanning many missing pages and sending them to me. As always, I am most indebted to my wife Diane for laborious editing of this translation. Finally, I would like to express my great appreciation to S&B World Foundation Inc. for its generous financial contribution toward the publication of this volume.

The House of the Edrisis

PART 3

Ashkhabad

Chapter 1

The sky opened up before sunset. Vahab was cheerful. He picked up a bamboo chair and sat under the shade of the walnut tree. In the soft sunlight, the dewdrops were evaporating. The house was quiet and uncrowded. He leaned his head against the back of the chair. He closed his eyes. He felt that his circumstances were vacillating. That which had become stable in him was hanging by a hair.

Mrs. Edrisi, Leqa, and Yavar were not like they were before. Aunt Leqa walked around in front of the men's eyes and played the piano without any concern. She would squat down alongside Teymur and pull out the weeds from the flowerbed. She would shake the wet laundered clothes, spread them on the clothesline, and put clothespins on them. She would run on the lawn with the children, and she would teach them songs. She had forgotten the past frames and structures within which she lived, but that was nothing to be regretful about.

Grandmother would mockingly tell the secrets of the family to Rashid and Kaveh. She took out an exquisite tablecloth—a combination of embroidery and lace, with scalloped edging—from the closet and spread it on the table. The Heroes adorned her highly praised handiwork with stains of tea and grease. She would pick flowers from the flowerbeds and put them in Sèvres porcelain vases, which were trampled on under the hands and feet of Qadir, Showkat, and Borzu. Hero Rashid would tell everyone that he had found a new grandmother, and the elderly lady would confirm it.

Yavar would not leave Kukan's side. He had even decided to learn tailoring in his old age. They would take out expensive fabrics from

3

the bottom of trunks, spread them out on the table, and cut them crookedly with a pair of heavy scissors.

Kukan had sewn a roomy pair of pants made of Bukhara silk for Yavar. The old man had set aside his old clothes, and he even went into the streets in a velvet vest and flower-print trousers. While ironing them, the tailor had burned the trousers, leaving behind an eye-catching yellow stain above the seat of the pants.

Yavar was at the beck and call of Showkat. He would pour tea in tea glasses with silver tea-glass holders, place them on an enamel tray, and bend down before Showkat and Borzu, offering them tea.

Showkat had hung the charcoal portrait of Grandfather upside down. The twisted tips of his mustache were pointing at the ceiling. She had stuck donkey-blood-red sequins on his eyes. Yavar paid no attention.

Vahab himself was not unaffected. The dominant presence of Roxana would dissolve the distant dream of Rahila like sugar cubes in hot tea. It would mix them up, the personality of the latter would diminish the radiance of the former, and Rahila's aristocratic face and smile would fade away with Roxana's laughter. Rahila's foggy eyes seemed to light up like a fire in Roxana's scorching glances, but Rahila's dignified figure scattered in the wind, and the entangled components, the dust and particles, fell into order in the body of Roxana.

When Roxana talked, Vahab would remember his mother, the small inn in Tbilisi, the woman burning with fever in a disorderly bed. In the Edrisi family, Vahab's mother was the first and the last person who did not fit the structures and frames. Roxana would sit on the veranda and fabricate dreams. The scent of the vines wafted around her body. In the humid afternoon air, the leaves on the trees did not move. The girl would gaze at the landscape of the city gate. Carts and carriages were going toward the capital city, leaving behind some dust. The city was too tight for her. The local young men bored her. That is, until Vahab's mother entered her life. Roxana's father did not know it. She probably imagined the man who had left as a merciless husband. Rana often told lies, and gradually came to

believe them. She was fascinatingly deceptive when she spoke, and
Roxana had a receptive mind. She was the one who taught the girl
how to gamble with her life, the illusive passion for which she lost all.

Vahab half opened his eyes and stroked his forehead. Was his
mother a loser? Or was her short unsuccessful flight, compared to
the tedious lives of the other women of the house of the Edrisis, some
sort of success? In the face of death, she suffered a harsh punishment.
With regret, she returned and remained in bed to her last breath. At
midnight, she would wake up startled, yelling and trembling. She
could not bear to look at the light. She buried herself in a dark abandoned room. They had cut her feathers, but in the end, she flew. He
was seeing his mother's life under a new light, from another surface
of the prism.

The women of the family, from one end to the other, were sub-
missive and victimized. Luba, Mrs. Edrisi, and Rahila all accepted
their destined fate. They knew neither the precipices nor the depths
of suffering, love, and death. A clan of beautiful and talented women:
white morning glories that bloomed on the ancestral pond and, after
a while, withered. Their fleeting glory did not run deep. Their suffering and pride were due to their being young and naive. The family's
past was crumbling before Vahab's eyes. No grandeur remained of
the line of fairy-like women who had walked for years between columns; had held their big blue, gray, or black eyes toward the light;
and had suppressed their sighs. Dejectedly, he thought: Had Rahila
stayed alive, what advantage would she have had over the others?
She would have probably become Moayyad's wife, walked in his palace between seven windows like a shadow clad in white with her
small nimble feet in satin shoes, come down circular stairs, talked to
the servants, worn pearl and diamond necklaces at banquets, gone
to summer quarters, and, at most, ridden a mule. Alongside rivers,
she would have sat surrounded by the scent of savory staring at the
cascading water, and she would have had some children who would
run around her in straw hats. That would not have been so bad, but
it was completely removed from the dream of the perfume of the
Kashmir valleys and bazaars of India and the tracks of caravans. He

concluded that Rahila's death at a peak that was moving toward her downfall was a blessing. But his mother, despite her humble origins and family, had a more stable strength and essence than the fragile morning glories. She was a manna bush, a stem of wild violets. She walked along precipices, but she remained faithful to her own essence to the end. Despite her resemblance to Rahila, Roxana belonged to the species of his mother, Rana. Now, after so many years, the memory of the mother was blossoming in the son's mind, and he was beginning to understand the smoldering of the wild violet. The legacy of Rana's loneliness continued in Roxana. He missed her: she would stand alone under the branches of the jujube tree and smile with half-closed eyes, a woman at the end of the road.

Nothing would make Rahila happy. Her melancholy stemmed from egotism. Roxana was cheerful, even though a swallowed weariness resonated at the bottom of her laughter. More realistic than the sorrowful eyes of Rahila, who was always perking up her ears to find some shelter on the earth and in the sky. Tied to unfulfilled expectations, disappointed passion, Roxana looked at the marsh, the pond, and saw the fleeting fire. She would not utter what needed to be said, and most likely there were thoughts that she herself feared. Vahab was gradually coming to understand how the woman could lie outright. In her ceaseless effort, she was not in pursuit of any benefit. The water had risen over her head, and her hopelessness was at such a height that it disparaged sorrow. Vahab was ashamed of his previous suspicions, his placing the burden of his conscience on the shoulders of Roxana. He got along with Showkat, Qadir, Borzu, and Haddadiyan, more or less. There was a valley between him and the Heroes, but Roxana would fly above the valley and distort the boundaries. Vahab feared the House of Fire, flags, and slogans. Crowded lines made him feel stifled. The deluge of the crowd was his constant nightmare. On the other hand, Roxana had come along with that same deluge. The receded river had tossed its pearl straight at him.

He held his hand before his eyes. The sun was still shining, and the bees and butterflies were flying around him. He scratched his nose and thought that his perception of Roxana might all be a delusion. Regarding people, he sometimes was drawn to exaggeration. He would scrutinize perceptively, and was often disappointed. Nevertheless, he was unable to overcome the ebb and flow of his imagination.

On Saturday morning, Roxana had gone to the House of Fire with Haddadiyan and Showkat, and she had not returned. A shadow fell on Vahab. He opened his eyes and began to stand up.

Yusef rubbed his hands together. "She hasn't made a peep."

"Who?"

"Roxana." He sat down and whispered: "From among the friends of Hero Qobad, a few are in the House of Fire. They brought the news."

A rustling sound was heard. Hero Qobad was putting the tip of the crutch on the grass and coming forward. Yusef got up in a hurry. The old man raised his hand and his lips moved. "Don't start a ruckus!" He turned his back to them, walked away, and at the end of the garden, sat on a stone slab.

Yusef picked a flower from the flowerbed and, smelling it, whispered: "He is still involved." He jumped over the boxwood, went to the edge of the reflecting pool, and put his face in the water.

Yunos came down the stairs, waved to Vahab, entered the lawn, and gazed at the sun. "Such weather!" He turned to Vahab. "Let's go for a stroll!"

They went away from the flowerbed and stepped onto the gravel road.

Vahab lost his patience. "Yunos! Hasn't Roxana come back?"

Yunos shook a branch. Dewdrops sprayed on his hair. "Roxana is like water."

Vahab grabbed his sleeve. "What does that mean?"

"Have you ever seen water stay in one place? It either finds a hole to get through or it evaporates."

"Has she now opened a hole?"

"She knows her own business. At the equator, sometimes the water of the springs evaporated to the last drop. The leaves of lotus and bamboos, heaps of Baghdad flowers, orchids, and cockscombs went behind the warm fog. The earth would shake, the wood would crackle just like a boiling samovar, the springs would bubble, and the tribal people would beat the drums and dance half naked until the steam would subside."

Vahab stroked his damp forehead. "Let me see! What am I reminded of? It's not just one or two things, it's a thousand things!"

"That's exactly your problem. Confusion! Make a singular face of her!"

Vahab suddenly stopped. "I can't! Thinking about her makes a world blossom in my mind."

Hero Yunos pushed a pebble back and forth with his foot. "What were you reminded of right now?"

"The cemetery behind the church, a tombstone at the side of which a yellow flower has bloomed. Roxana is looking at the flower. This look stays with her. Now she has the same look regarding the world."

Yunos started to walk. "If a woman has this look and a person does not fall for her, undoubtedly, he is an idiot."

"Yunos! Have you ever fallen for anyone?"

The man's left eye sparkled. "Yes, the magical string of words, images that flash only once in the dark. To hunt them, I sit in ambush day and night. Sometimes they come on their own, and I begin to tremble. Before they assume a material form, there is no way to be saved."

"What images?"

"It makes no difference—an empty glass, a passing smile behind a window, the growth of a seed in the crack of the earth, a streak of light on the fuzz of the forearm of a sleeping person, hedges under the rain, or a termite making a furrow inside an old piece of wood. Single images are not important—existence is a combination of all of them, the making of a harmonious world in the face of chaos, the unison of sounds, the music of creation."

Vahab looked at the chunks of pink clouds in the late afternoon sky. "Then when did you live?"

"I used to climb up to the peaks, look at the roaring white water of the river, and sleep on the grass. The shadow of the clouds moved over the valleys. I grew old when I was five years old. Now I have no age. I used to consider the revolving of the earth and time as futile. Later on, I came to believe that futility is meaningful. Every relationship goes back to its origin—otherwise, it will be annihilated." He crossed his arms over his chest. "I make a new design from virtual faces, from the shadows of the lantern of imagination. I set my heart on that perfection."

Vahab stared at the ground. "Hero Yunos! Tell me why I go this way and that chasing the shadow of Roxana?"

"Don't ask me! I am distanced from such passion. Have you heard the story of Jonah?"

"Yes, the storm and the belly of the whale."

"What does the belly of the whale mean?"

Vahab contemplated. "Some sort of solitary confinement."

Yunos laughed out loud. "They are not comparable. In solitary confinement, the ends of your strings are linked to the world. Recollections of memories, a chat with the guard, the sky behind the window. But there, in the belly of the whale, there is no memory. It is the silence before creation, the absolute loneliness of the Creator. Once you step on the earth, you are a thousand years old. You fall asleep under a squash bush. The images on the canvas surround you. Every human being moves with the wind, swells up, becomes hollow. Alas! The sounds have gone far away, but the silence of the sea has remained within you."

The burning flame of his left eye made his face frightening. A polar chill began blowing toward Vahab. The heaviness of the burden of that man was moving beyond his ability. He stepped back. "I am afraid of you!"

Yunos sank his hands into his pockets. "An error again! I have not learned silence. Engage in your amorous imagination!"

"It is not love! A longing that is nested deep within, a thin rope that I grab."

Yunos looked into his eyes scornfully. "Compared to Roxana, you are the thin rope! You might even be afraid of her!"

Chapter 2

Leqa opened the window. The air was fresh. She picked up a handkerchief and wiped the dust off the picture of the female saint. She saw her face in the mirror: swollen eyelids, the vague lines at the corners of the eyes connected to the yellowish temple, wide cheeks that quivered with the movement of the head. She turned her back to the mirror. She thought: Had she been deprived of the beauty of the girls in the family? Even Vahab had managed to have some charm, shining eyes, and a pleasant face. The formerly scrawny young man had acquired some remote resemblance to Rahila. Why had she not perceived this resemblance before?

She stepped out onto the interior balcony. Her mother was walking back and forth alongside the balustrade slowly, her hands in her pockets, deep in thought. Leqa said hello. The elderly lady nodded, ran her hand over the balustrade, and blew off the thin layer of dust. Leqa blocked her way. "Again, you didn't sleep? Your eyes are sunken."

The elderly lady knit her brow. "Do you expect an old woman like me to be a symbol of vibrancy?"

"Why do you stay awake at night? You will get sick."

"Later on, I will go to sleep for good. While my head still moves, let me stay awake in compensation for the days that were lost in sleep and weariness."

Hesitantly, Leqa asked: "Doesn't Vahab these days resemble Rahila?"

"He resembled her from childhood. He withered after her death."

"What a pity he has grown out his hair. He talks like Yashvili. I have lost my fondness for him."

"Well, you could also talk like Rashid!"

Leqa was enraged. "Mother! That is shameful."

The elderly lady shouted: "If Rashid is not to your liking, how about Hero Showkat!"

From the end of the dark hallway, Showkat's voice was raised. "Who was calling me? I heard my name."

Leqa took refuge in the garden and sat on a stone slab. On the previous day, Showkat had dumped a pile of clothes before her feet and ordered her to wash them. The odor of dirt and sweat rose from the fabric. Leqa had tossed them into the reflecting pool and stirred them with a big stick. Laughing boisterously, Torkan and Kowkab had brought a washtub and taught Leqa the ways and techniques of washing clothes. After clawing at the clothes for an hour, the skin of her hands had begun to get numb and feel like pins and needles. Showkat had kicked Leqa's handiwork into the reflecting pool and shouted: "You fat piece of filth! Let one of your shitty hands know what the other one's doing!"

She had twisted Leqa's arm hard. Leqa had held her cracked hands before Showkat's face. "Watch the strength of my fingers on the piano keys!"

With the strike of her whip, Showkat broke a branch from the aspen tree and walked away in solid steps.

A hand touched Leqa's shoulder and a large piece of bread was extended to her from behind her neck. There was a piece of cheese inside the folded bread. Leqa looked back. Hero Kowkab smiled. "They have sent it from the House of Fire. Today is the anniversary of the mountain feast."

Leqa bit into the bread and cheese and chewed it. She swallowed it hastily and inquired: "What is the mountain feast about?"

"A reminder of the day when the first shot was fired on the mountain."

Leqa nodded. "So, they brought the cheese for Qobad."

Kowkab's brow knotted. "Hero Qobad didn't even touch it."

Leqa ate all the bread and drank a sip of water from the spigot. She held her head toward the sky. "My fear of Showkat made me eat too fast!"

Kowkab patted her on the back. "She went to work. She now has a lot of enemies in the House of Fire. They say she's not standing on firm ground. Today, they brought a ton of clothes. They want them washed and ready before sundown."

Torkan and Pari came to the garden with baskets piled up with clothes. They walked bending over, pressing the heavy loads on their bellies. They put them on the edge of the reflecting pool and stretched their backs.

Pari scratched the tip of her nose. "The smell of medicine makes me want to throw up."

Torkan flicked her finger on Pari's cheek. "Don't get yourself upset this early in the morning!"

She filled the washtubs with water and set them side by side. All three sat down.

Hero Pari told Leqa: "You rinse them."

Limping, Rokhsareh was coming. Her big belly was quivering under the pleats of her dress. Her hanging breasts swayed like a pendulum. She raised her tired body toward the breeze like a banner of victory. Her thick brown stockings slid down from her knees and fell around her ankles. "What are you doing, girls?"

She did not make a distinction between Leqa and the rest. The sole daughter of the Edrisi family had so settled into her new position that, even in her own eyes, she was considered a washerwoman.

Rokhsareh sat down and complained: "I always separate the white clothes from the colored ones. Where I worked, this was what they did."

Torkan raised her left eyebrow. "Where did you work?"

Rokhsareh took a look around. "In a really big house, like this one."

All the other four women followed the direction in which she was looking. Mirroring her, their eyes also widened, as though, by what she said, a white building had sprouted before them. It even looked unfamiliar to Leqa's eyes. She bit her lip and frowned.

Rokhsareh whispered: "Carriage and stable, hot milk and fresh cream! When they had parties, the house was lit up like daytime. The women's skirts looked like sugar cones, because they had wire underneath. When you looked from a distance, it was as though colorful flowers were going this way and that way on the lawn. The young and the old took off. The master had three daughters, like rosy red apples. The sons-in-law wore swords. At their wedding celebration, the first one gave me a gold coin." She paused. "It was spent on doctors and drugs."

Hero Kowkab gazed at her. "You sly fox! You've hidden it somewhere."

Torkan grabbed Rokhsareh's wrist. "Tell us the truth!"

Rokhsareh burst into tears, sobbing loudly and intermittently. Sounds like a chicken before it dies spun in her throat. The corner of her lips had foamed up.

Leqa sheltered her with her wide chest. "Stop the tears! We believe you."

Hero Torkan protested: "What business is it of yours? She's got to fess up!"

Rokhsareh crawled forward and hit her head on the runoff gutter of the reflecting pool. A thin stream of blood began to trickle down from the roots of her hair.

Leqa scratched her own cheeks in concern. "She's going to get herself into trouble."

Torkan held up her chin. "Don't put on a show for us!"

Rokhsareh wailed: "After forty years of labor, I have saved one coin." She shook her crooked hands and calloused fingers in front of them. "I've got ailments from head to toe. I have kept my coin like it is my child, for a rainy day." She ripped her collar and punched her bony chest with her fist. Her dark dry breasts shook like raisins hanging from a pest-infested cluster of grapes. "Look at my body! All my weight is water." With her cracked nails, she split the back seam of her skirt, took out the coin, and put it on her palm. "You can have it! Take it!" Saliva ran down her chin. "You can change your clothes, but bad lack is with you to your last breath." She struck her forehead. "May mud cover my fate that is written on my forehead!"

Kowkab closed Rokhsareh's fingers. "It's yours! You keep it!" She pushed Rokhsareh's hair under her scarf. "Change the hiding place of the coin! We've all seen the back seam of your skirt. The devil could tempt us," she said as she drew an arch in the air that enclosed Torkan, Pari, and Leqa.

Rokhsareh smiled, tossed the coin into the air, and gazed at it spinning in the sunlight until it landed on her palm, inside a familiar hollow space. After having been with her for a long time, it was as though it were a living being. The woman's eyes were covered with a curtain of tears. "Why didn't you say that first? You almost scared me to death."

Hero Kowkab frowned. "Because your heart and tongue were not the same."

She put the coin into her pocket. "Aren't you going to tell on me?"

Kowkab put her hands on her hips. "No! We aren't spies." She looked at Leqa suspiciously. "At least, not Pari, Torkan, and me."

Leqa's cheeks were on fire. She stared at the ground and acknowledged the judgment of the women about her. She pulled on the fringes of her shawl and hummed a song.

Hero Pari stood in front of her. "Don't be offended! We don't know you that well."

Leqa covered her face with the shawl and ran toward the stairs.

Hero Torkan went after her. "Come back! Don't be mad at us! Times are bad."

She brought Leqa back by force.

The middle-aged old maid sat by the reflecting pool runoff. "I hate even looking at Showkat, because she is two-faced, a cheater, and a liar. Early this morning, she made my heart skip a beat. She hit my ankle with a stone."

The women stared at her mouth suspiciously. She turned red and closed her mouth.

Rokhsareh scratched the split in her earlobe. "The master was three times the size of Vahab. He constantly recited poetry. Every evening, he ate four skewers of kebob."

A shooting pain ran through Leqa's protruded navel. She swallowed.

Hero Pari picked up a lump of earth from the flowerbed and licked it.

Rokhsareh exhaled noisily through her nose. "My precious kids died." She leaned against the back of the bench and stretched her legs. "The sun is nice!" She rubbed her knees. "I always see a herd of kids together. I don't understand who is who." She pulled on Pari's skirt. "Where is your husband?"

Pari wrung out a pair of pants. "He left and hit the mountains. No trace of him." She handed the pants to Leqa. "Take them and rinse them! Up to three months ago, I was wandering around waiting in lines. I became friends with everybody who had lost someone. I would go from this department to that. They never give you a straight answer."

Hero Kowkab was kneading the clothes, and the smell of disinfectants scattered in the air.

Torkan picked up a stalk of hay from the manure fertilizer in the flowerbed, wetted it with her saliva, and stuck it on her eyelid. "It's fluttering, a bad omen."

Leqa tossed the washed clothes into the water. Clusters of bubbles foamed up from the depths of the reflecting pool. Pajama pants puffed up and the legs got entangled. The air gradually exited from small holes, the pants seats went up in the air and spun in an entire circle. Shooting pain ran through the middle-aged old maid's spine, her stomach contracting, and she diverted her eyes from that scene. She picked up a sharp stick and poked the clothes. She took them out, poked them with the tip of the stick, and spun them in disgust. She rubbed her navel and grumbled under her breath.

Torkan came to side of the pool. "Why are you poking the clothes? They'll get ripped." She took the thorny stick from Leqa and threw it away. She struck Leqa's chest. "Step aside!" She rinsed the floating clothes and wrung them out. Her small hands concealed astonishing strength. Embarrassed, Leqa looked at her own hands. Her wrists were wide and her fingers long, but, instead of strength, it was as though molted wax was circulating in her veins. She would get tired just as she would start, and begin panting. Hero Torkan hung the clothes and put clothespins on them.

Rokhsareh was sitting under the clothesline, water dripping on her head and face. She scooted forward toward the runoff gutter. "There's one thing I like, quickness and cleanliness." She turned to Torkan. "Like you, I also could not rest and be calm. After washing a mountain of clothes, I would pick up the broom. The lady of the house would raise her voice, 'Rest a bit, you are tired, woman!' All day long, I went up and down the stairs so much that at night I would collapse like a corpse."

Torkan straightened her back. "Did you have fancy dinners, like pilaf and things, every day?"

"They were openhanded. The master went hunting and brought deer and wild goats. I wouldn't eat it. It's a bad omen. It was for them. They were uprooted and became refugees. Do you also have two kids?"

Torkan nodded. "Aslan and Shirin."

Rokhsareh's nostrils quivered, as though she could identify the children by how they smelled. "Shirin? The one who's sick?"

Hero Torkan became angry. "Shirin isn't sick! Don't make up stories!"

Rokhsareh dipped the tips of her fingers in the water. "Children aren't loyal. As soon as they can take care of themselves, they go their own way. Look at the sorry situation of Teymur!"

Torkan shrugged her shoulders. "His son might come back."

Hero Kowkab wiped the soapsuds from her cheek. "Someone who leaves will never come back, like my damn husband. Like I had eaten donkey brains, I would put on my shoes and go looking for him inch by inch in—I'm embarrassed to say—brothels, taverns, and opium dens at the end of the city. That dead dog had turned into grass and was eaten by goats. Now, if he comes back, I'll spit in his face."

Teymur was shaking off the dust from the boxwood leaves.

Hero Pari dumped the dirty washtub water in the runoff gutter. "Come and sit with us, Papa Teymur!"

Torkan pulled on the old man's sleeve. "You must be tired! Sit down on the bench!"

Teymur took a deep breath. "I turned over the soil in one flower-bed. If I plant seeds, they'll grow. I wish we had flower seeds."

Leqa looked at her mother's window. "We do, but they're old."

Teymur's eyes sparkled. "Seeds of what flowers?"

"They were sent to my mother a few years ago. In the pictures of them, they look pretty."

The old man scratched the back of his neck. "If they germinate, I'll make the garden look like paradise."

He rubbed his hands together and put his rough fingertips on his lips. Leqa took the rinsed clothes from Kowkab and hung them on the clothesline. Teymur sat down on the edge of the bench and lit his clay pipe. "With my hands, any flower and plant grows, if they aren't poor seeds."

Torkan lifted her head. She shook a moth-eaten tank top. Gray dirty water sprayed in the air. "You have to get permission."

The old man's eyes darkened behind a curtain of cataracts. "Do you need permission?"

Torkan bent her head over her shoulder. "Without permission, you can't even wipe your nose."

Hero Teymur hooked his fingers together. "I have planted flowers and plants as far back as I can remember. Now, are you telling me, you mangy dog, go put your tail between your legs and sit waiting for death?"

Hero Kowkab took a few steps, bending down. "They might want to level the garden and plant wheat."

Leqa went on her knees. "What about the fruit trees?"

Kowkab gazed into the light. "I'm a village girl. I was raised among fruit trees. What a waste! There is no rhyme or reason to the orders from the House of Fire."

Teymur touched the patch on his trousers. Water from the reflecting pool sprayed on his face. It was the fault of Leqa's inexperienced hands. The old man dried his face. "The palace of the former governor has become the Central House of Fire. It scares you to death, black from top to bottom with red windows and an onion-colored gable roof. I went there. I went with four other gardeners to prune the cypress trees. Going close to the palace was prohibited, but we could see the governor on the stone veranda in the sun on the red throne. We could hear music. We couldn't tell who was playing it. They said it was the governor's three daughters. No one saw them. It was rumored that they looked like birds with red beaks, and that they flew over the city after midnight. The people in the city shut their windows, even in the heat of summer."

Hero Torkan jumped up. "Oh, don't tell us any more! It scares me to death. What happened to them?"

Hero Pari hissed: "Shut your mouth! These rumors are just superstition. Humans don't have beaks. They had made up tales."

Leqa leaned against the tree. "Because the prince, the governor, was so bloodthirsty. My mother said that he ordered three hundred young men to be buried in a wall in one day."

Rokhsareh looked at Leqa and Pari with a demeaning smirk. "I was a daredevil. One night, I made a bet to sleep on the roof. That's how you are when you're young. I said to myself, to hell with it, the worst thing is that they'd come down to gouge out my eyes with their beaks. That's nothing, I'll run away. There was moonlight. I spread my bedding near the ledge of the roof. All three were flying together. They were as big as people, and they were glittering from head to toe. Wherever they passed, all around them would get dark. I felt the world was spinning around my head. I ran downstairs, and fainted in my room."

Torkan's hands became weak. Her teeth were chattering softly. Hero Kaveh appeared at the top of the stairs. The women all screamed.

Frightened, Kaveh went back to the middle of the hallway, stood under the faint light, and looked into the oval mirror.

Hero Pari came to the edge of the stairs and wiped her hands on her skirt. "Hero Kaveh, forgive us! It's their stupidity that's to blame. They make up such nonsense tales that it makes smoke rise from your brain. If the spies report it, we're done for."

Kaveh rubbed his chin. "I haven't shaved for three days. I have grown stubble. I thought that was why the ladies screamed."

Pari smiled. "Who would be paying attention to your beard?"

Kaveh's face contracted and wrinkles appeared between his eyebrows. "Yes, times have changed. I have changed as well. Women used to pay attention to the way I looked and dressed. I remember thirty years ago, in late afternoons, I would go for a stroll in the National Park. I would hold my shoulders back and look off at the horizon. Women liked dreamy men. They wanted a man who understood the tenderness of their spirit. I was an expert at this. What a calamity! They would put their heads on my shoulder and cry like spring showers. I still have no idea where they got all those tears." He walked down the stairs, looked at Leqa, and with the tip of his toes, tossed a small pebble into the flowerbed. "Yes, crying was fashionable in those days. Now, apparently, they prefer the strength of the arms." He raised the corners of his lips. "I have never liked women who look like men. In the old days, women had tender hearts. The good old days! The world was bright and tender." He looked at the sky and waved his checkered handkerchief as a sign of adieu. "Oh, fragile beloveds, where have you gone? Instead of those oriental eyes, cheeks flushed from coyness, slender waists, and silky hair, a he-giant comes wearing a yellow dress just like armor, and shows her coquetry with knives, daggers, and revolvers."

Leqa picked off a leaf from a tree, put it between her lips, and a long whistle resonated in the air. Several birds flew off the branches. Kaveh's cheeks turned yellow. The last spark in his eyes was extinguished, and he felt that he had stepped into a cold world forever. Stooped over, he went toward the bench and sat down beside Teymur.

Hero Torkan sniffed. "No sign of the cologne smell. Now we can breathe."

Kaveh took a cigarette out of the chest pocket of his jacket. "It's running out. I need to be thrifty." He broke the cigarette in half, struck a match, puffed, and sent the twirling smoke among the branches.

Teymur lifted his head. "Has anything happened?"

Kaveh opened his arms and flicked the wood with his finger. "I wish it would! Days come and go monotonously, pushing me closer to old age and death." He turned to Leqa. "And you have given up playing the piano!"

Leqa pulled a pair of trousers full of soapsuds out of the water, wrung them out, shook them, hung them on the clothesline, and secured them with clothespins.

Kaveh looked at the ground. "Do you prefer this job?" Leqa rubbed her hands, wrinkled by the water, together. No sound could be heard except the sound of the splashing and splattering of the clothes in the water. "What were you talking about?"

The gardener sank his fingertips into the strands of his beard. "About the Georgian governor, and his three daughters who flew at night and who had red beaks."

Kaveh laughed and began to cough. He pounded his knee with his hand. "Red beaks? What nonsense! I had seen all three"—he pointed to the oak tree—"from this close."

Rokhsareh's mouth was left open. "So daring! Weren't you scared?"

"On the contrary, I was intoxicated! We were coming back from the war with the Turks. I was a cavalry officer. I wore a white uniform with gilded epaulettes. On my chest, a row of medals, wearing a sword at my waist, and a shoulder belt. I had a dog whose name was Blanche. It would eat rice cookies out of my hand." He pulled up his shoulders. "I hate wars. I do not comprehend the purpose of being killed or killing others. Everyone is a human being, wants to stay alive, and take a nap under spring sun by a wheat field. No one in this world has the right to take away the gift of life from another.

Well, we were young and inexperienced. We made a lot of mistakes. Who doesn't?"

He stared at the sky. Hero Rashid came into the garden through the small door. Shading his eyes with his hand, he approached the reflecting pool, tired and sluggish. He dipped his face into the water and then leaned against the elm tree. The color had drained from his face and his eyes were sunken. He pressed his hand to his mouth.

Hero Kowkab grabbed his arm. "What calamity has fallen on your head?"

Rashid opened his eyelids halfway. "I was standing in the middle of the bales. All of a sudden, I felt dizzy and collapsed on the ground. They gave me permission to come home. Hasn't Borzu come back yet?"

Hero Kowkab took the young man's pulse. "No, you don't have a fever. Did you have something bad to eat?" Rashid shook his head. "Then you must have had a heatstroke. Borzu will come back at sundown. If there's any sweetened endive extract in the house, drink some mixed in a glass of water and go to sleep."

"No, I feel better in the fresh air."

Leqa looked at Rashid. He looked like a sick child. His over-powering physical energy and the beating of his veins were gradually diminishing in his lost eyes and pale face. The smell of his body, the scent of a broken branch. She walked closer to Kowkab. "Yavar has endive extract."

Kowkab smiled. "May you have a long life, my girl! Go and get it quickly!"

Leqa went to the entrance hall. She thought about how hard the poor young man worked. All day long, he moved the bales this way and that. He rolled around in dust in damp basements. And then what did he eat?

She entered the kitchen, opened the cabinet, took out endive extract, made a beverage with extract and water, put it on a tray, and came out.

Her mother bent over the balustrade. "For whom are you taking the sweet drink?"

Leqa smiled. "Hero Rashid. He got dizzy at work."

From the glass windowpanes, a blue ray shone on the elderly lady's eyes. For a moment, the color of her eyes became aquatic, like the sea, and flared up like those of Hero Qobad.

Leqa went to the garden. Steam was rising from the washed clothes, sending the warmth of life wave by wave toward her. She was even fond of Kaveh. His gray hair, the banner of old age and loneliness, wandering in the air like its owner, blowing in the wind.

She gave the glass to Rashid. Sunlight passed through the cut crystal, filling the light liquid to the brim with colorful prisms.

Hero Rashid held the glass up and looked at everyone. "Please have some!"

Kowkab said: "Drink it!"

Rashid drank the beverage and sat next to the elm tree.

Hero Kaveh coughed. "We did not finish the story of the three daughters." He wiped his nose with his handkerchief. "Yes, after the war against the Turks, the prince invited the commanders to the palace, ten people. The news of it spread everywhere. The governor never would open the door of his palace to anyone." His cigarette went out. He took the matchbox from Teymur, lit the cigarette, and raised his left eyebrow. "They entertained us on the vast lawn behind the cypress garden. It was late summer. Before sunset, they had arranged a royal banquet. Roasted pheasant and partridge, calf shanks, fish kebob with chestnuts, sheep testicles, goat cheese and Caspian Sea caviar, hot cinnamon and saffron cookies, a large bowl of rainbow-colored pudding, and aged red wine. They brought everything from the palace. We were allowed to go up to the apple orchard. The flower-beds were filled with flowers." He grabbed Teymur's arm. "Flowers from everywhere in the world. They had brought bougainvillea bushes from Benares and planted them under the arbors covered with silk. Each bush spread like an umbrella, ruby, violet, saffron, purple, and lotus. From behind the flower petals, you could watch the sky. In an octagonal flowerbed, they had planted black roses."

Teymur's eyes became dreamy. He nodded in agreement, turned his clay pipe upside down, and the ashes dropped and were carried away by the breeze. "I had seen black roses in the botanical garden of Khwarazm. Dewdrops wouldn't stay on them. I wanted to get some cuttings—they said they wouldn't bloom in this climate. Of course, every plant sets roots in its own soil. Humans are like plants—they die in exile." He bit his index finger. "My poor boy!"

Kaveh flicked his cigarette butt into the water. "Teymur, humans are not all the same! Some are by nature like water—if they stay in one place, they become putrid." He put his finger on his own chest. "I, for one, go to sleep at night thinking about traveling. My heart yearns for warm regions, Zanzibar and Morocco, camellias and Iberian trees. The hot sun of the sand deserts returns the energy and enthusiasm of youth to you." He gazed at the mass of yellow leaves in the corner of the flowerbed. "No, it is futile!" He pushed back his disheveled white hair. "The final voyage!"

The clay pipe fell out of Teymur's hand. He picked it up and examined it. It was cracked. He licked it. "So, tell me about the governor's garden."

Kaveh scratched his forehead. "How far did I get? Sweet pilaf of Kashmir?"

Hero Teymur swallowed. "Tell me about the flowerbeds."

"He had a pair of Indian servants. They wore brocade tunics woven with gold. Purple turbans covered their heads. On the top of the folds and pleats of the turbans, two red rubies as large as fresh jujubes. These servants waited on the governor. The bejeweled handles of their daggers glittered. After drinking a few cups of pear spirits, we became jovial. The Georgian governor was pacing around the flowerbed restlessly, like a caged black tiger. They brought him food on a solid gold tray. He took a bite and pushed it aside in disgust. He would clench his jaws, his eyes would darken, as though he was being tormented by a horrible pain. He approached us and asked about the situation of the war, but he did not listen to the response. They brought a crystal bowl filled to the rim with water, purple flower petals floating on the top. He dipped a flower-design silk handkerchief in it and wiped the grease from his black agate-like mustache. They handed him a mirror. Wrath and hatred flamed up in his eyes. Perhaps he was tempted to issue the order for his own murder. He smashed the mirror on the ground. He kept lions in the courtyard behind the palace. The roaring of ferocious wild beasts was his lullaby."

Hero Rashid put the glass on the stone of the runoff gutter. His bluish lips moved. "My grandmother said that the soldiers of the Georgian governor had killed her brother on the charge of rebellion. He was not an outlaw rebel, he was a quilt maker."

Kaveh twisted his mustache. "Around sunset, the windows of the palace were lit up. From the end of the black building, we heard the sound of the *kamancheh* and *santur*. The governor sat on his inlaid ornamental throne and closed his eyes. The legs of the throne were made of gold in the form of the claws of a lion. From between his closed eyelids, teardrops dripped down his cheeks. I was a daredevil. I took off my boots under the table and tiptoed toward the sound of the music. I went behind the window and peeked inside. The fragmented reflections of three girls with black hair quivered in the mirrorwork on the ceiling and the walls. One of them was playing a *kamancheh*, the second one, a *santur*, and the third girl had her hand under her chin, listening. Black silk curtains were fluttering in the late afternoon breeze. Around a room with five sashed windows, they had arranged purple cushions with gold embroidery. A fire was blazing in the fireplace. The girls were bending over the instruments and playing with a passion that made one's heart rip open. I thought about how I could rescue them. The kamancheh player lifted her head. I saw her burning eyes." He lit the second half of the cigarette. A thin vein began to palpitate on his forehead. "Thirty years have passed, but the memory of her beauty still makes me weak in my knees." He constantly moved his hands as he spoke. "How can I describe her? The offspring of fairies! It was as though the features of her face were carved out of marble, her lips, lustrous rubies. She had a teardrop ruby necklace around her gazelle-like neck. A purple dress hugged her delicate body tightly. What could I say of her eyes? Those of the gazelles of Khotan, bright and tearful. She dropped her eyelids and plucked the strings of the instrument. The flames in the brazier cast a shadow on her cheeks. I wished to drown myself forever in the blackness of those eyes. I heard footsteps, a guard approaching. Quietly, I ran behind the Judas trees and went into the cypress garden. The governor's eyes were still closed. Nighttime came. The banquet came to an end. We left. I could not sleep for a couple of months. The memory of the eyes of that young girl would set my being on fire, like two pieces of glowing charcoal. In deference to the rubies of her necklace, I never again looked at pomegranate arils."

Rokhsareh sighed, her lips quivering. Kowkab, Pari, and Torkan rinsed the washbasins. Leqa hung the last piece of clothing on the clothesline. Hero Rashid turned on the jetting fountain.

Chapter 3

There was a downpour in the late afternoon. Under the shower of rain, the gable roof was raising a ruckus. Vahab was sitting under the arbor. Clusters of violet jasmine were falling from the branches. There was a soft knock at the door. Vahab jumped up, slightly opened one of the doors, and looked through the narrow gap. Roxana was standing under the awning. He opened the door. She walked in and squeezed her wet hair. "Good thing you're here. I don't want to see anyone else."

Vahab looked at her soaking-wet clothes. "So, do you intend to stay out in the rain until morning?"

Roxana moved her toes in the cotton shoes. "Where should I go?"

"To the stable."

The woman smiled. "Your old place?"

Alongside the aspen trees, they walked to the end of the gravel road. Vahab opened the wooden door. The cows turned their heads toward the light.

Roxana jumped on the platform, sat on the pile of hay, and leaned against the wall. Her teeth were softly chattering.

Vahab took off his woolen jacket and extended it to Roxana. "Put this on until I bring some clothes!"

"What kind of clothes?"

He put his hands in the pockets of his trousers. "Whatever I can find. Does it make any difference to you? Of course, I can't go into Rahila's room—everyone will be watching."

At the door, he shifted hesitantly from one foot to another. He was afraid to leave Roxana by herself, as though her presence was

not real, it was ephemeral. He turned around, approached the platform, and placed his hand under his chin. "You are my everyone!
Mother, father, brother, beloved. Sit right here! I will be back!"

For him, the world was summed up in the semi-warm stable.
Roxana turned her head toward the window.

Vahab ran the length of the garden and entered the entrance
hall. Qobad was leaning against the column. Vahab went to his own
room, opened the closet, wrapped a pair of black trousers, a blue
shirt, a pair of long woolen socks, and a pair of white shoes—a memento from the bazaar in Jammu—in a silk handkerchief and held
it under his arm.

He went down the stairs. Someone called to him. Terrified, he
turned around. It was Qobad. "When did she come back to the
house?"

Vahab dropped his head. "Her clothes are soaking wet."

Qobad moved his crutch and a fly flew.

Vahab ran under the downpour, stepped inside the stable, and
closed the door firmly. Roxana was still looking at the outside. She
looked like a statue.

The man slid the clothes toward her. "Here! Consecrate my
clothes!"

He walked out of the stable and stood under the dripping umbrella of the maple tree. In the hubbub of the rain, he heard the woman's voice. He entered the stable and rolled a rock behind the door.

Roxana was standing on the platform, her hands in the pockets
of the black trousers. The blue shirt cast a shadow on her pale face.
She raised her right foot. "The only thing is, these shoes are too big."

Vahab climbed on the platform.

Roxana sat down. "Talk! Warm me up with your voice! Take me
to the dawn of life! You have your mother's tone. When you talk, I
become ageless."

Vahab knelt and looked into her eyes. "Tell me where you come
from. Why don't you resemble anyone? Why do you resemble everyone? I see you everywhere—in the drops of rain, between the rose-
buds, an apple that falls from a branch. It is as though you are within

me. I have even cried for you, because you are lonely. You are a child, and, like Venus, you have frozen sparks!"

Roxana's eyes were clouded and dust was pouring on her.

Vahab whispered: "Why do you conceal your soul from me? Why are you afraid?"

The woman turned toward the window. "No, it is useless. You will disappoint me. With the passage of time, you will become like the others, a part of the world of apparitions. As I reach out to the air, your glance will become hollow. You will crumble little by little. I can no longer bear seeing destruction, disintegrated components, the eyes of dead fish. I am shivering to my bones. I hate the cold. All my life has passed in the polar cold. You will not know me—you are after the shadow of Rahila!"

Vahab touched her sleeve. "Don't turn your face away! On the day of your arrival, beside the flowerbed of tuberoses, you displayed ancient faces, people, images, and forms. That power, that plurality, frightened me. It was as though your veins burned in fire, and from the ashes of each spark, another ember arose in flames. That fire- work was too much for me to bear."

Roxana leaned against the adobe wall and stared into Vahab's eyes. "Why am I distant from you?"

"It is quite simple. You don't see! The outside world has no path to your soul. You have severed ties with the world!"

Roxana picked up a fistful of hay. "I have made so many mis- takes that I cannot endure the weight of my own body. I have gone from one city to another in pursuit of insignificant dreams. I have spun on the stage like a windup doll! For art? I don't think so! I wanted them to like me. No, they did not like me. I dissolved in the midst of the odor of makeup, wig glue, and the dust of the curtain. I lost my simple innocence. When I looked into the mirror, I did not recognize myself. Characters fabricated by the minds of others had swallowed my everything: Masha, Hedda, Irina, Julie, Antigone. Then where had I gone? They dried up my roots. They cut my links with life. I became a floating thing. There was no safe corner. With- out exception, everyone lied. The shadows of hypocrisy, gender and sexuality, and money darkened my surroundings. I took refuge in the church. I visited the prisons. To them, I was a mockery. The moment I walked away, they would burst out laughing. Poverty might weaken one's emotions. Priests surrounded me. They had the best food and wine in my house, but their only objective was to rip me off. The intellectuals who were enamored with art and the geniuses of the age were only seeking my body. They called this feeling love. They would send baskets of flowers, jewelry, even books to the backstage. I wouldn't touch the pricy ones. But I wasn't that innocent either. I wore fur coats and Parisian dresses. There was loathing behind my smile. The more the number of acquaintances, the more I understood the meaning of corruption. Now, from a distance, I think they were also weak, without will, and victims. A bunch of windup dolls, we were spinning in vain around an incomplete circle. We were not much different. We were all growing in deceitfulness."

Vahab clenched his teeth. "Then what about Marenko? Was he innocent?"

Indifferently, Roxana waved her hand in the air. "That issue was different. I was dependent on him. When we were away from each other, I felt like I was missing a wheel. The world looked empty to me. In a crowd, my eyes were searching for him. He was humorous and passionate, and in his own way, a bookworm. But he showed off more than he knew. He embellished ordinary talk. Other than himself, he did not see anyone. He would mention other poets with sarcasm, disparagingly. In parlors and restaurants, he would stop in front of every mirror, his eyes filled with self-praise. Among his supporters, he created an Olympian image of himself, but, secretly, he demeaned the people. His famous smile was the good tidings of the rising of the sun. Occasionally, something would get in his head. He would pack up his suitcase and set out. On the table, he would leave a sheet of paper, which he had carelessly ripped out of his notebook, on which he had written a few passionate sentences to justify the attraction that dragged him toward the forests of Ukraine, in order for him to eat cherries on wooden bridges. A few months later, a picture and a letter would arrive from Kyrgyzstan—he was resting next to the black tent of Turkomans with sheep and goats around him, the mouthpiece of the coiled pipe of a hookah in the corner of his lips and his half-open, mesmerized eyes darting around under a black sheep-skin hat. When he returned, he would claim that he had me before his eyes at every moment. He would place a book of poetry on my lap, kiss my hands and feet, cry, and say, 'Everyone is a fool, except for you. I am forlorn in the entire world. I have no one I can talk with who can understand my boundless imagination and humor. I wish to die under the green shade of your skirt.' The next day, he would once again become jovial in a gathering of friends, drink vodka, smoke cigars, and with his heart and soul, accept the praise of people of low substance. In all those moments, I was like a doll people put on their shelves and look at so much that it loses its identity—it becomes a part of the doors and walls. Deep inside, I would rebel. I also knew that I was smarter than Marenko. Nevertheless, under his false dominance, my color would fade. Then it was my turn. On a cold snowy day, I decided to go to Tbilisi. The bathroom sink faucet was leaking, his unwashed coffee cup on the table, his empty bed a mess as usual, violet curtains closed, lights on, a few half-open books scattered around the couch. I picked up my suitcase and got out. On the way, I was shivering from loneliness and cold, but I needed to cut it short. I thought, when he came back home, the dust-covered doll would no longer be on the shelf. Of course, he would not believe that anyone could leave Yuri Marenko—he considered abandoning someone an exclusive privilege of his own. He would sit waiting until nighttime, yank a few hairs from his blond mustache, open the curtains, and stare at the snow-covered street. A poem would come to his mind, in which he would split the clouds in half; he would hand clusters of grapes to the policemen; from the darkness of the city, he would dig a tunnel to the pomegranate garden; he would take merry-making and pleasures to the end of Baalbek. He would then call his friends and they would drink wine until morning. All was for naught. A hole would have been opened in his heart.

"I stayed six whole months in the Caucasus. I went back to the house in Tbilisi. They had sold it. In place of the old building, they had built an inn. In the corner of the courtyard, they had piled up several broken doors. I stroked the doors. I closed my eyes and felt the warmth of my mother's body under the pale sunlight, the commotion of the travelers, and the scent of ice flowers. In wintertime, I used to crawl under the velvet quilt, eat saffron-flavored pudding, and make up dreams. The future was the color of honey, sweet and warm. I would pull a feather out of the pillow, blow on it, and, as it was spinning, I would sit on the purple carpet. Peacocks opened their feathers like umbrellas in the snow. The inn was six stories. The tall building cast its shadow on the flowerbed. Then where had my Tbilisi gone? I ran out, got into a carriage, and went to the central square. I got one floor of the Ritz Hotel to myself. In the late afternoon, I would sit on the balcony, watch the people, and sigh. I did not recognize anyone. I wished to awaken the old city with my hands. I would come down and walk around various squares. One day, I went to the French woman's inn. Its gate with iron bars was locked and sealed. In its damp courtyard, plantain and crowfoot bushes had grown between the cracks of the brick pavement. I asked about the French woman. She had died five years earlier. The little fifteen-year-old girl who wore white had also gone with the wind."

She became silent and put her hands on her upper arms.

Vahab looked at the window and whispered: "Roxana!"

He jumped down from the platform and walked away under the rain.

Chapter 4

Around five o'clock, the Heroes would return from work and assemble in the parlor. They would eat legumes for supper. Waiting for the food, they would entertain themselves in some manner: sing, spin around in the middle of the room, and sometimes ask Leqa to play something light. Leqa would immediately consent and accompany their singing. The little girls would clap their hands and jump up and down, their chintz skirts bouncing in the air. The men would wash their hands and faces and change their shirts. They smelled of tallow soap. The women would brew the tea, and Kaveh and Yavar would serve it.

Early in the evening, Rashid placed a chair near the window, gazed at the canna lily flowers, and pounded his knee. "In the alms-house, my grandmother once asked me for red canna lilies, because she had dreamed about them. I searched the entire city, but I couldn't find any. I took her a bouquet of chrysanthemums. My grandmother picked them up one by one, pulled off all the petals, and said, 'I wanted red canna lilies for my hair. I had dreamed that my husband and I were becoming betrothed in the Azhdar Garden.' I picked up the chrysanthemums, and, on my way, I dumped them in a stream of water. I became concerned, thinking she might die soon." He looked at Leqa with bright, sad eyes. "I wish you had met that old woman!"

Leqa nodded. "What a pity!"

Mrs. Edrisi sat on the sofa. Her clear eyeglasses flamed up under the red light of the wall lamp. On the other end of the sofa, Hero Showkat leaned her back and arms against the colorful small pillows: "I feel depressed! I'm not in a good mood and don't have the patience for anything!"

Since the previous week, she had occasionally sunk into thought and kept silent. She would suddenly become enraged, grab someone by the collar for no reason and throw him or her to the middle of the parlor. Borzu would sit beside her. She would engage in whispering with Borzu, become angry, kick the leg of the table, run her fingers through her hair, claw and pull the entangled hair, and her quarrelsome eyes would shine like those of a ferocious beast. She no longer bothered Vahab. At the peak of her kindness, she would toss a small ball of kneaded bread, crumbled up paper, or a cigarette butt at the young man. Vahab would calmly pick out her donations from his hair, off the back of his neck, and inside his collar and arrange them on the table. Kaveh usually sat in the middle of the sofa between Mrs. Edrisi and Showkat and smoked a cigarette, with the permission of both ladies. Teymur would lean against the wall, put his unlit clay pipe in the corner of his lips, and, as his eyelids became heavy, doze off.

Hero Qadir's body was surrounded by waves of the smell of kerosene and linseed oil. He would scrape the paint off his fingernails with his teeth. He would hold his pocket mirror in front of his face and comb his hair. Occasionally, he talked about girls. He liked the blonde ones with good figures and rosy cheeks. He said: "When I raise my hat to them, they laugh hysterically and pinch each other's arms."

Hero Rashid asked: "Are you planning to get married?"

Hero Qadir burst out laughing and his cheeks turned red. The zest for life exploded under his young firm skin. "There is one who works in the spinning mill. When she laughs, her cheeks form dimples. She is such a steed! On holiday evenings, she comes out of the factory with a basket of red apples." He looked at the darkness of the night. "I'm afraid she might have a fiancé."

Hero Rashid put a matchstick between his teeth, chewed it, and spat out the broken pieces. "I'll take care of that for you."

Qadir scratched his wide chin. "Such a gentleman! You're the best!"

Rashid shot the head of the matchstick on the glass with a flick of his finger. Leqa dropped her head and stared at her hands. She moved the tips of her fingers and thought about why she was afraid of men, when they did not even see her at all. She got up and went to the entrance hall. She looked into the oval mirror. She stroked her swollen goiter. She pinched her wide loose cheeks between two fingers. Red blotches were left behind. Her eyes lusterless, her eyelids puffy, her eyebrows thick, and her skin white and withered, like, as her cousins said, "rice pudding without salt!" She remembered that a few years earlier, when young men passed by her on the street, she would turn around and run toward the house. She chuckled and bit her lower lip. Such futile fleeing! She lowered her headscarf and stepped into the parlor with her back bent like old people. She sat on a chair near the piano. Her spine shivered from the autumn chill.

Rokhsareh entered quietly, crouched up near Teymur, and hugged her legs. Her face contracted from pain.

Yavar prepared a cup of hot water and sugar for her. "Why don't you think about getting some real treatment?" He pointed at Borzu. "Then what is that quack good for?"

The woman's dry lips moved. "No, it's useless."

Hero Yunos arrived after dinner in his moth-eaten black jacket and rolled up his worn-out shirtsleeves. Leqa stared at him. She liked Yunos. But, really, why? The tattered clothes did not match the half-mad man's arrogant behavior. Despite his deteriorated appearance, impaired vision, and hunched stature, he had godly strength and firmness. A pale light followed him. He would sit in the middle of the room, displaying his sunken cheeks and the mismatched crooked patches of his clothes, a sneer in the corner of his lips. As though he were distanced from everyone. He would exit his frame and stand observing from afar. Occasionally, he was in the middle of the ruckus. Leqa could not figure out this jugglery. On a thin thread, the man maintained perfect balance. He would take Borzu's eyeglasses, toss them up in the air, and catch them. Borzu would curse and Yunos would laugh. He would run his fingers over the piano keys, and, with sleight of hand, he would pinch a medal from Hero Showkat's chest and hold it up in the air. The crossed erect crowbar, six-pointed star, and eagle with open wings shone as the medal swayed. He would attach the glittery insignia to his pant leg. Showkat would chase him, rip off his shirt sleeve, spit, and begin to punch and kick him. The ribbon of the medal would rip. Showkat would wet the ribbon with her tongue, pin it crookedly on her chest, and sit on the sofa, angry and panting. She would throw the small pillows, and Kukan would take a needle and thread out of his pocket and sew the ribbon.

One night, Haddadiyan entered the parlor with his mustache shaved and stroked his chest. "With greetings and veneration! Seeking pardon for procrastination!"

Hero Showkat clenched her teeth and asked Qadir: "What is this man trying to say?"

Hero Qadir shrugged his shoulders.

Borzu explained: "He apologized for being late."

Showkat shouted: "He's an idiot." She got up and pulled on the sleeve of Haddadiyan's jacket and ripped it from the shoulder. "Talk in a way that the workers can understand!"

Haddadiyan clawed the air and flared his meaty nostrils. "Last night when I was sleeping, some bastard had come and cut half of my mustache with scissors." He punched the wall. "There is no security in this house. In what words do I need to explain that I am ashamed of and hate the previous conditions? They coaxed me and duped me, and, since I had no willpower, I would become weak and give in to their filthy demands, until gradually I fell into the depths of disrepute and became the mayor." He burst into tears and covered his face with his hands. "I liked my mustache."

Hero Showkat toppled a chair upside down with a kick. "Get up and pack up the show! Don't talk about the past so much!"

The man leaned his bottom against the table and examined his ripped sleeve.

Showkat circled the table and stared into Borzu's eyes. "Was this your doing?"

The young man sat up and threw a napkin. "Was it that much of a precious mustache for someone to weed it?"

The vein on Haddadiyan's neck began to palpitate. "No! Precious is your mangy mustache! When I combed it, it would puff up.

It had one or two white hairs, the rest, as black as black agate!" He clapped his hands. "You were too jealous to look at it, so you mutilated it. I wish I had at least taken a photo of it. In the middle of the night, an incubus fell upon me, and, before I was conscious enough, he had done his deed. When he closed the door, I jumped up like a spring, flicked the light switch and looked in the mirror. I realized that he had not left me with any reputation."

Hero Showkat pounded his back with her hand. "Haddadiyan! Zip it up! It isn't your first time."

The man cried loudly: "I swear on the honor of the House of Fire that this was my first time."

Hero Showkat yanked off the golden eagle medal from her chest and threw it. "See how easily I throw away my symbols of honor? Why are you putting so much value on half a mustache?"

Haddadiyan raised his head. His eyes flashed. "Hero Showkat! Why did you do that? As simply as that, you throw to the ground the sacred symbols for which we have shed so much of our blood?"

Showkat shook a leg of the table. "Jackass! You spilled blood? While you're at it, go ahead and claim that you were the commander of the Battalion of Fire! Muck, that's what you might have spilled. In the House of Fire, some people regard blood to be the same as muck. I am not one of them." She went and stomped on the medal. "Gawk! See how I stomp on their cheap medals!" She shook her head and tossed her frizzy hair over her shoulder. "Hero Showkat is not afraid. Her past is like a mirror."

Haddadiyan chuckled. "How about the future? It might not be like a mirror."

Showkat spat on the floor. "The future is in our hands. Hang on till you hatch and the chaos subsides. They'll take the likes of you to the Gulag, you boot-licking bastard!"

Haddadiyan went toward the window and his full-length reflection appeared on the glass. His belly under his belt rose and fell in time with his breathing. He pushed his chest forward and parted his feet. "Hero Showkat! Not so fast! Show me someone who does not have a mask. You believe in your masks, I am aware of them." He slowly brought up his index finger and pointed it toward the ceiling. "You are the prisoners of the cocoon of your insignificant ideals—life, politics, and government. The people's demands are different from your dreams. Social conditions change moment by moment. So, woe to the person who is not riding the wave. Hero Showkat, you are a despotic and obstinate person. You might advance, you might have an impact on the masses, because you treat them like a herd. Who says this is bad? Everyone enjoys power—they worship despotism. Human minds need idols. Look at the statues of the MKCK bosses and the person of the Supreme Hero in the middle of every square! Their huge pictures above the golden domes of churches are a source of consolation for the people. I have no doubt that a limited group of people will grumble." He shrugged his shoulders. "These noises will disappear."

Pacing back and forth, Showkat was shaking her whip. She was foaming at the mouth. "You've learned to chirp quite well. Pity, you're facing a ferocious adversary."

Without paying attention, Haddadiyan continued: "The Central House of Fire used to count on you. They have not made a final decision yet. Why are you being defiant? You need to go along with the hierarchy!" Borzu rolled a glass marble toward his shoes. Haddadiyan scowled. "Watch what you're doing!" He kicked the leg of the table. "Are you dying to wash floors?" He turned to Showkat. "There is no problem with any order that comes from above. Accept it without any hows and whys! Only fools think." He picked up a small pillow from the sofa, tossed it up, and caught it with his toes. "I was a soccer champion in school. When I entered the field, there was a commotion. My fans would shout out 'Haddadiyan' so much that their voices would get hoarse." He frowned. "Alas, you understand nothing about politics! You do not know the problems involved in ruling the masses. The harness must be pulled tight, so that any likely desire for kicking is suppressed. You sit with these individuals and talk nonsense, and a few brainless supporters agree with what you say." He exhaled through his nose, which also emitted a few black hairs. "No, Hero! Governing is not child's play. One must be as fearless as a lion and as sly as a fox. We agents of power"—he put his index finger on his chest—"must adhere to one principle: absolute obedience!" The corner of Showkat's lips quivered. She turned her back to him in disgust. Haddadiyan began to cough. He covered his mouth. "Everyone has a weak point. Mine is related to my lungs. My grandfather had problems with his chest. Heredity is occasionally important."

Borzu chuckled. "New genetic science has refuted such balderdash."

Haddadiyan stood in front of Showkat. "Don't be evasive! Turning your back on me will do you no good. Hero! Did you not sign the bylaws of the House of Fire with absolute conviction? Your present actions are contrary to that decision. Do you now want to betray yourself? To turn away from the past? To say that you were a fool? One hundred percent, you will not be able to do so." He was fond of numbers and statistics. In most discussions, he sought the help of averages. "Do not be shuffled together with these people! It is shaky under their feet. Get off your high horse! Become reasonable! Think of the day when they put your picture as well on the walls, when the people shout slogans in your honor. They had considered you for a position of responsibility—now they have changed their minds." He opened his arms. "Why, Hero? Indeed, why? At what price? This is painful for me."

Hero Showkat brought her left foot up. The spur of the boot shone. "Haddadiyan! What trick do you have up your sleeve again? I see that you have gotten involved in the secrets and the dice games of the House of Fire. Little by little, you are cozying up to the central councils. You bring stink to every place. So, now I have reached a point that those little reptiles sing battle cries against me? When we came to the city hall, your butt print on the chair was still warm and you had the ring of the tsarist regime around your ugly fat finger. Out of fear, you were wagging your tail. You wanted to lick the soles of the shoes of each and every one of us with your big red tongue, hoping to save your ass. Your sweat of abomination hasn't yet dried on your body and, like some pretentious charlatan, you put your hands in your pocket and put on airs?" She punched him in the chest. "Don't flare your eyes in my face! That makes my blood boil. You think I am illiterate? I have read so many theories that if one percent of it would reach you, your brain would short circuit!" She burst out laughing and looked at the ceiling. "Look at what kind of stinkbug is talking about government and society!" She went to the window and blew on it. She then drew lines on the steamy glass with the tip of her finger. "So, people need harnesses? You're despicable! The things you say are as ugly as your own loathsome face and snout. Tomorrow, I will go to the House of Fire and pull the plug on you. I will expose your evil character!"

The man looked haughtily at the Heroes. "Save your yelling and pomposity for these simpleminded riffraff. Would anyone in the House of Fire pay attention to your buzzing noises? They have had it with your mouth, which has no locks and latches."

Hero Showkat leapt at Haddadiyan, completely pulled off his torn sleeve, and pounded it against the wall. The upside-down portrait of Grandfather fell down, and its frame smashed. "Get lost, you chicken shit!" She punched her own chest. "From the time when I was a kid, I worked hard to buy a piece of bread to eat. I was kicked around in the alleys and back alleys. Along with my brother, we used to sleep in abandoned ruins, under tattered rags. The foods that the likes of you poured into your bottomless pit of a stomach, we could only smell them." She wiped her damp forehead with the sleeve. "Once I fainted in front of a kabob shop. You de-mustached pig! Unlike you, we haven't gained wealth and riches by means of flattery. We've been just what you see, inside and out. We started the Fire Movement. Now here comes someone—the end-all and be-all of shamelessness!—to teach the precious gold in the depth of the city how to talk! Oh, the calamitous fate that you would face if the House of Fire would learn about what you hide inside you! I have no doubt that you have destroyed your file, but beware that renowned Hero Showkat has not forgotten anything. The drawstring of your pants would break in front of the heads of the military government and you would stay bent over!" She turned to Kukan and Borzu. "Such a serpent we raised in our sleeve!"

Haddadiyan walked away from Showkat with resolute steps, grabbed the door handle, and, before exiting, turned around, with a frightening glint in his eyes.

Showkat sat on the corner of the sofa, threw a small cushion at the door, and stared into the dark garden.

Chapter 5

That night, Roxana slept in the stable, on top of the hay on the platform. Vahab checked on her early in the morning. He brought bread for her. She said: "I would like to be alone."

He left the stable. The shoulders of his jacket and his hair were soaking wet from the rain. He saw the yellow silhouette of Showkat near the boxwood trees. With her hands on her hips, she was pacing, looking at the ground, and occasionally driving away an imaginary mosquito from before her eyes. She walked toward the stable, stood in front of Vahab, and punched him in his chest. Vahab fell in the middle of the flowerbed. Showkat kicked the stable door open. Vahab ran after her. Roxana was gazing at the falling rain from behind the window.

Hero Showkat went close to the platform and shook the wet whip. "What kind of ruse did you use to get out?" With tired eyes, Roxana looked at the woman from head to toe. Showkat clapped her hands. "You really have thick skin! You don't give in!" She pounded the wall with the tip of the whip. Several pieces of hay fell down. She walked the length of the stable. The soles of her boots were smeared with mud. She flicked her finger on the forehead of the white cow. The animal opened its eyes halfway. A string of saliva was hanging from its hairy snout. "I like cows." She paused. "I was raised with cows. They remind me of my mother." She walked closer to Roxana. "Now, spit it out." She picked up a handful of hay and slowly dropped it through her fingers. "I have never seen the basement of the House of Fire."

"Have patience! You shall see it."

Showkat pounded her fist on the platform. "Showkat is not a torturer!"

"Not in that capacity. Perhaps the reverse of that."

Showkat stared at her hesitantly from under her eyebrows. "Don't make predictions!"

Roxana sighed. "The basement is occasionally necessary for a bit of rest and relaxation."

"Don't talk nonsense! The people have erected that place."

"Then do not underestimate it!"

Showkat turned her back to her. "Did you have a secret relationship with the military government?"

"Having a secret relationship with governments is not my mission."

"So, something must be going on under all this."

Roxana started to get up. "Renowned Hero Showkat, pay careful attention! If you associate me with that government once more, you will end up really regretting it."

Showkat burst out laughing. "Everybody sings battle cries these days. People say that they have seen your picture in the newspapers with that wannabe good-for-nothing poet. They have started the rumor that the Supreme Hero has given a prize to that little fellow—I have forgotten his creepy name."

Vahab immediately said, "Marenko."

"Whatever that jackass's name is! Then why is it that the page has suddenly turned?"

Roxana held her head high. "Look, Hero! Marenko and I are two independent people. We go our separate ways. Also add this to the people's rumors! One year ago, I organized a show in the largest square in Moscow. I made the crowd laugh. I even danced Georgian folk dances. People's cheerfulness consoled me. But they gifted me with rotten apples and tomatoes. Given my excitement and enthusiasm, I preferred the smashed fruit to baskets of flowers. They sang along with me, they clapped, they yawned. They were themselves, straight arrows and honest. Once again, I had set my heart on something that deceived me."

Hero Showkat spat on the ground. "Shut your trap! The people are not deceptive."

"Of course they are not. The people are just people."

"Don't twist the words in a way that no one can figure it out!"

"I mean, they have been deceived. Do you know what the old women in Moscow do nowadays? They sit behind the windows, spy on their neighbors, and report what they see to the secret centers of the councils. The same tender-hearted old women, loving grandmothers, have so far sent thousands of people to the firing squads."

Showkat stomped on the knot of the whip. "We also write reports as dictated by our duty and conscience."

"Bravo, Hero! Do your duty! But the links of the chain, demonic circles, connect with one another somewhere. As soon as you open your eyes, you will see that the largest number of reports have been about you. Your file in the House of Fire is getting thicker every day."

Showkat looked at the ceiling. "Don't make up poppycock stories! I don't have the patience for it."

"I have seen it with my own eyes."

Showkat pounded the whip on the ground. "I am one of them, one of the fifteen main members."

Roxana laughed. "Graveyards are full of main members. Such titles are like writing on water."

Showkat knotted the whip. "Don't evade the question. I asked you, what ruse did you use to get out?"

"You should know better than I do. Aren't you one of the fifteen?"

Showkat kicked a piece of dried cow dung at the wall. Then she bit her thumb. "I have not received a report yet."

"Don't they trust you?"

Showkat ran her fingers through her hair, walked around the troughs, broke off blades of alfalfa, and with her hands on her hips, stopped in front of the platform. "The situation in the House of Fire is not the same as in the early days." Out of the corner of her eye, she watched Vahab angrily. "Are you eavesdropping?"

Vahab picked up a piece of alfalfa from a trough, held it toward the light, and shook it. "The issues of the House of Fire are as important to me as the incoherent writings in the so-called newspapers."

Showkat turned her back to Vahab. "Put it in neutral, wretch! Play with your alfalfa!" She walked closer to Roxana. "Lately, they close the doors and whisper, as if they're conspiring. Their appearances have changed. Their clothes are made of the most expensive fabrics. They get together one night a week and have caviar and vodka." She stared at the light of the window. "When I was a kid, I shared my portion of bread with the kids in the alleyway. I am not like them. I don't give in to the ways of the government offices." She lowered her voice. "Occasionally, I heard screaming and yelling from the basement of the House of Fire. When I asked what has happened, they would hold one hand in front of their pants and the other in the back and run away. They've brought several bosses from Moscow. Those shameless pack mules who all of a sudden sprouted out of the ground create files for all the people, each and every person. More than half of the House of Fire is occupied by the division of records. They all wear black suits. They shine their gold buttons. Worse than monkeys, they walk on their tiptoes. Wherever you go, someone with eyeglasses checks out your footprints. No matter which pit you go into, they sniff you. Everybody is suspicious of everybody else. On celebration days, they plant secret agents between every two people. Lack of trust in the masses is the new thing. Well, if the basis is friendship, what is the meaning of all these things they do? Every hour on the hour, they take a herd of people on trucks to somewhere around Sakhalin. Villages are in ruins." She went and hugged the cow's neck. Her eyes became tearful. "It wrenches my guts. I know they're pulling the rug out from under me. They're unhappy about my mouth, which has no locks and latches. They say that cursing like a mule driver is beneath the status of the councils. If I'm not like I am, I'm no longer myself. Like that, I would have to bury Showkat and sit beside her grave. Every nobody who just arrives tells me to be wise. In my opinion, what I do is wise. Fooling the people is not wise. There is some sort of new ethics in the society. They had instilled in us that Hero Qobad has lost some of his marbles. Well, we went along with that. We said, to hell with it, old age causes a thousand types of problems. Who can say that they won't stick that label on Showkat tomorrow? So, is everybody crazy, except for the boot-licking Haddadiyan?"

Roxana sat near the window. "Come up here!"

Showkat climbed onto the platform. "Hay sticks to my dress. In the House of Fire, they said this color is too gaudy, that I need to wear black." She touched the shiny yellow fabric. "But I like this color. It's like the sun." She picked up a stalk of hay and tickled the tip of her nose. She sneezed several times in a row and took a deep breath. "Something seems to be stuck in my brain. Last night, every time I was just about to doze off, I would wake up. I have two options before me. The first one is to wear all black, to walk in cork shoes and check every hole in the wall, to bend down like a flail tool in front of every known and unknown person who has stepped on the shoulders of the people to climb. They expect me to stuff my mouth with turnips and, whatever nonsense I hear, to keep my mouth shut and say it is fine. They say I'm not making any progress, the highest reward for which is for Showkat's picture to be published in the newspapers." She punched her own knee. "But I am not a fool. I've seen what people do with newspapers. They wrap baby diapers and any filth they find in newspapers. They even wipe their own butts with them. And now, let me talk about administration positions. Suppose I become the head of the social reforms department. How am I supposed to stuff myself behind a desk? Am I supposed to bundle up my arms and legs? I need an open space, like a factory." She poked Roxana's arm with her finger. "Occasionally, I feel depressed. I feel like going to the alleyways, deep into the city, to the ramshackle houses, the people who have nothing. I am one of them. I breathe better in that atmosphere." She swallowed. "The second option is to give up and get out of the House of Fire, to kick everything upside down, to air their dirty laundry. This is not wishful thinking. I know they won't leave me alone, that they'll yank my guts out and hang them on a spear. Even right now that I haven't said anything, Haddadiyan barks and Moayyad sticks cogs in my wheels. To hell with both of them! Hero Showkat is not someone who would be afraid of barking dogs. An honest person fights with those who match him in strength. Qobad and I are enemies, everyone knows—but being an enemy of such a man raises one's status. One hair of his is worth more than that jerk with the dog-tail mustache from head to toe. The House of Fire must realize that I am Hero Showkat. I was not one of the hooligan louts of the former government. I would never eat from the same trough as Haddadiyan. Who can I tell what's eating me? How do we know what these thugs from Moscow did before? They might be enemy spies. They all carried a card in their pockets with writing in weird letters. They say it is in codes. We are on the same team, why use secret codes? When they show up, my blood begins to boil. I want to grab their neckties and tear their ironed suits to shreds. I scratch my cheeks from anger. I say to myself, Hero Showkat, miserable Showkat, be calm! Everything will be fine. Just be patient! You aren't that educated. Wait till those who have read books, those who have full brains, clarify the future."

Roxana picked off a piece of hay from Showkat's skirt. "I was also feeling like you. Now, for me, that was the last straw." She bit her lower lip. "No! There is no light. We are walking in the fog. We have become instruments for the advancement of bullies."

Showkat bit her own forearm. "I don't like caviar. I just want agriculture to make progress." She poked her chest with the tip of her finger. "Well, that's me. You get it?"

Roxana wiped the steam from the window. She turned to Vahab. "Be kind and leave us alone!"

Vahab leaned on the creaky door and looked at the ground. A cow mooed.

Showkat began to get up. "Didn't you understand what she said? Get out!"

The man left the stable. The rain was slowing down, and the drizzling drops of rain were moving at a slant toward the west.

Chapter 6

When Leqa would close her eyes at night, with the revolving of the rings of unconsciousness, she would sink into the depths of nightmares, and end up in the twists and turns of images, the ruins of a forgotten city. In the twilight, she would pass through unfamiliar alleyways, windows would open, heads would move behind cloud-colored curtains, and curious eyes would gleam. She would go in the same direction as the wind, seeking shelter under stone arch ceilings. She was wearing her mother's overcoat. She would stick her hands in its pockets. The bottoms had holes and her fingers would stick out. A group of people dressed in black would climb the walls, their metal helmets shining under the moonlight. Whispering, they would laugh. They would jump down noiselessly, enter the entrance hall, the chain of the chandelier would break, and the red tulip-shaped lamps and cut crystal prisms would fall on the ground and shatter to smithereens. A white curtain would spin in the whirlwind, changing shapes, until finally it would take the shape of the piano keys, suspended near the ceiling.

They were pounding on the gable roof with hammers. Leqa jumped out of bed, dressed rapidly, braided her tangled hair, knelt before the picture of the female saint, stood up, opened the door, and went down the stairs.

Hero Kowkab was washing the balustrades with soap and water. She had a bucket next to her. She turned to Leqa. "Good morning. Go have some bread and tea and come to work!"

Leqa blinked. "I had disturbing dreams."

Kowkab dried off the soapsuds from the balustrade with a rag. "At night, don't go to sleep on a full stomach!"

Leqa leaned against the column. "Soon, they might kick us out of the house."

Kowkab pulled out a dirty looking towel from the bucket of water and wrung it out. "We're cleaning the house. Don't jinx it!"

There was a tone of taunting sarcasm in what she said. It was as though, with the help of some favorable luck, she had entered this house together with Leqa. With her head down, Leqa went to the courtyard. She had become accustomed to washing her hands and face at the reflecting pool. She splashed a handful of cool water on her face, which rid her of her drowsiness.

The sky was cloudless. Hero Rashid was standing on a stool, cleaning the windowpanes of the parlor. His strong muscles under the sleeves of his shirt flexed.

Leqa dried her face and shouted: "Hero Rashid! Don't work too hard! When did you start?"

Rashid pushed up the visor of his kepi hat. "After sunup. I have to clean the windowpanes by sundown."

"It's hard to clean so much dust."

With a crumpled-up piece of newspaper, Hero Rashid made a windowpane shine and stared at it. "I think I'll be able to handle it. No one has taken care of the house for years." He pointed at the clean windowpanes. "But they'll get cleaned."

Leqa took a few steps forward and shaded her eyes with her hand. "They shine in the sunlight."

Rashid smiled.

Leqa went into the entrance hall. Hero Showkat was walking around, issuing orders. Her cheeks were rosy and the seams of her skirt were split. As soon as she saw Leqa, she yelled: "You lazy-bones! Go stuff your face with your breakfast and rush back as fast as lightning! I need to talk to you." She opened her arms. Frizzed-up rolls of hair stood erect on top of her head. "Hero Qadir has brought three people to help him. They are jumping up and down under that rickety gable roof. What a surprise! You finally woke up. Don't you have any other duty but to eat, sleep, and pee?" She bit her lip and spat on the floor. "This individual makes me forget all about polite manners."

Leqa took a step back. "I have been awake since early in the morning. I saw Hero Rashid."

"Well, congratulations! What does breaking wind have to do with eyesight? I talked about Qadir, and you dragged Rashid's leg into the conversation? I have set aside a tall ladder for you. Wash the outside of the building!"

Color drained from Leqa's face and her eyes became blurry. She pressed her hand on her forehead. "I am afraid of heights. In my entire life, I have never climbed on a ladder."

Hero Showkat grabbed her by the arms and shook her. Leqa's head and neck jolted back and forth. "Shame on you, with that hefty body of yours! Is a ladder something that should scare you? I climb up to the top of walnut trees and swing on them as easily as one can drink water."

Leqa rubbed her arms. "Hero Showkat! Why do you always use yourself as an example? You do many things that the likes of me are incapable of doing."

Showkat grabbed the single braid of Leqa's hair and pulled it up and down. "You can learn it, too!" A strip of light was reflected sideways on the carpet from the seam of the ceiling window panes. She pointed at it. "Go and walk on that—let me see how you can keep your balance!"

Leqa opened her arms and walked toward the strip of light. The shadow of her body eliminated the rays of the sun. "But light has no corporal existence."

Showkat pushed Leqa aside. "You can walk on everything." She hopped on the shining strip of light and hopped back. Under her firm steps, the strip of light turned dark and light.

Leqa's knees were shaking from hunger. She leaned her hand on the column. "Will you allow me to have something to eat?"

Hero Showkat kicked the air with her left foot. "Yes, I know what a glutton you are. The tea is still warm. Stuff yourself till you burst!"

Leqa went to the kitchen. The water in the samovar was boiling with the diminishing heat of the charcoals turning to ashes. She picked up a glass from the dishes of the Heroes and poured tea into it. They had put away her special dishes. They washed the dishes and glasses sloppily. Blurry stains were evident on the fine crystal. She went to the parlor and sat at the table. She sweetened her tea. She picked up a piece of stale bread and began eating greedily. She heard a sound from the library. She raised her head, and saw the silhouette of Yusef in the dim light. He was picking up the books and dusting them off with a handkerchief. Leqa swallowed her food. "Hero Yusef!"

The young man came toward the table and shook the handkerchief. Dust scattered in the air. Leqa began coughing and put her hand over the glass of tea. "Right now, I wish I were in your place."

"I repaired the burned books. About fifty of them were destroyed."

Leqa took a sip of tea. "Do you read books a lot?"

"I had never seen so many books in one place before."

"I have read a few novels. What do you read?"

Yusef looked at the garden. The quaking aspen leaves glittered, trembling in the breeze. "I love books of poetry. Have you seen Roxana Yashvili?"

"Has she come back from the House of Fire?"

"Even if a deluge destroyed the world, you wouldn't know about it. Roxana came back the day before yesterday."

"She must have been genuinely scared."

"She is not scared."

Leqa sighed. "Roxana is like Rahila."

Yusef tossed the handkerchief on the table. "I know. I have heard that a hundred times." He stroked his chin. "No woman in the world possesses the charm of her words and eyes. It is not for no reason that our beloved Marenko set his goals in line with her. In debates, she defeats everyone. I was not fond of her photographs, but in person, she is something else. I have spoken in praise of Roxana so much that the members of our Komsomol wish to see her. I can't help it, I admire Yashvili, because she has been a beloved companion of Marenko." He wiped the moisture from his forehead with the back of his hand and took a deep breath. "Yes, there is no doubt, my wretched heart palpitates for Marenko."

He picked up the handkerchief and went toward the library.

Leqa swallowed a large bite with the help of some tea. "Aren't you going to turn on the light in the library?"

"I feel more comfortable in the dark. I find an opportunity to sketch a poem. I would like Roxana Yashvili to see my notebook of poems someday. She alone would understand my poems."

"Then what about Hero Yunos?"

Yusef hit the leather spines of the books with the handkerchief. "I wish he would give up on writing poems and concentrate on magic and witchcraft."

"Witchcraft has no buyers under the new conditions."

"Let him go back to where he was before, to the savages."

Golrokh entered the room. She had covered her hair with a blue headscarf. She turned to Leqa. "Hero Showkat needs to see you right away."

Leqa got up from the table apprehensively. "She told me to climb to the top of the ladder. She thinks I am a stork."

The girl blinked her eyes. "Which ladder?"

"The one that has no end, that reaches up to the sky!"

Golrokh scratched her cheek out of concern. "I am afraid you will fall down and break your hands."

Leqa forced a smile. "My hands are one thing, my bones will be crushed."

Golrokh looked at the piano. She drew in her chest and brought her thin shoulders forward. "Have you forgotten what songs you played? I go to sleep thinking about them."

Stunned, Leqa stared at her own rough red fingers.

Hero Showkat came into the parlor on her tiptoes and grabbed Leqa's arm. "You woke up too late, I said to hell with it. I didn't twist your ears. While everybody is working so hard that they are soaking with sweat, are you goofing off and having a good time?"

She dragged Leqa toward the door. Golrokh looked at Showkat's broad back in disgust. She ran forward and said: "Let me do Hero Leqa's work!"

Showkat pushed the little girl aside. "What? Leqa, a Hero? How dare you call her a Hero! Do you think you're now so important that you give her a title?" She took the middle-aged woman down the stairs. The tall ladder was leaning against the wall. "Hurry up, don't dillydally. Get up there like a hawk!"

Hero Rashid took off his hat and scratched his head. "I lost my concentration. Couldn't you find someone more agile than Leqa? Why don't you send Kaveh up there? He claims he used to be a look-out man on a ship."

Showkat frowned, and her eyes flashed with anger. "Kaveh says that and you buy it? When he sees a few gullible jackasses, he lies left and right. I tested him earlier. He hadn't climbed four steps when he looked like he was about to give birth and collapsed on the ground. I sent him to the kitchen to help Golrokh and Rokhsareh to scrub the backs of the cooking pots. This one has more oomph in her. I'm not a blind peddler—I know my customers. I believe that anyone in the world who is able to do one job well is better than others in any job you give him. This pickled eggplant is a skillful piano player. So she also must be capable of climbing a ladder." She pushed Leqa. "Don't dawdle!"

Dolefully, the middle-aged girl remembered her ill-fated dreams. She put her foot on the first step. The decayed wood groaned and the rusted nails shifted in place. She looked at the sky and climbed cautiously. She passed by the windows of two floors and reached close to the gable roof. She took a breath and looked below her feet. Hero Showkat had become small. The reflecting pool, the flowerbeds full of flowers, and the pavement of the courtyard seemed far away. The wind shook the ladder rungs. A pigeon was drinking water from the edge of the downpipe. The rays of the sun were sprinkling golden dust on the granite stone cornice.

Showkat shouted: "Did you just grab your big belly and go up like a spike? Where is your bucket of soapy water? Are you going to wash the wall with your spit?"

Leqa looked at the yellow-clad body jumping and running around. "My place is fine."

Showkat kicked the foot of the ladder. "Your place is beside my butt. You're no different from a crow! I didn't send you up to show off."

Leqa said: "Why didn't you tell me that when I started?"

"You didn't give me a chance. As soon as you saw this erected mast, you lost all control and jumped on it. The people in this family know no middle ground. They go from one extreme to another in everything."

"I was so afraid that I forgot."

"Don't wiggle and dance so much with those wooden arms and legs! Once Showkat decides, don't talk about fear anymore!"

"Hero Showkat! You can just go on with your pearly words of wisdom, but from up here, everybody looks small to me."

"Then come down!"

"I won't."

Hero Showkat shook the ladder. With her arms and legs, Leqa grabbed the highest steps and screamed. Heads stuck out of the windows of the building, and a group of people rushed into the garden. The bucket full of water was let go from Rashid's hand, hit the stone pavement, making a loud noise. The neighboring old man stood by the threshold of the window, showing off his tight woolen pajama pants, then disappearing immediately behind the curtain.

The women along with Teymur gathered around the ladder. Showkat dispersed them with punches and kicks: "Who do you think you are? Go away. Get to your work!"

Hero Pari stroked her skirt. "Our work today is not mandatory. We decided on our own to clean the house, but with your giving orders right and left and shouting and yelling, you discourage everybody. If that's the way it is, I, for one, am going to hit the sack. You think I'm fed up with my life?"

Others lent her their voices. Teymur sat in a corner by the wall and fixed his clay pipe to smoke. Hero Qadir crawled up to the top of the gable roof, and when he saw Leqa, he became frightened and grabbed hold of the chimney with both hands.

Kaveh came closer, dragging his feet. He spread his feet apart, put his hands on his hips, lifted his head, and looked at the top of the ladder. Leqa was hugging the ladder rails like a lobster. Her headscarf had slid to her shoulders, her single braid of hair swaying in the wind. Kaveh spat on the ground. "First, you pestered me, because I was a lookout man on a ship thirty years ago. Why aren't you paying attention? People change! I am not the Kaveh of yesterday. That fearless handsome young man is gone." He pushed his jacket aside. "My spine was damaged in an accident. What in the world would I do if I had been left there with my hands and feet trying to grab onto something to save my life?"

Hero Showkat put her hand into her pocket and took out a few gilded medals with their crumpled ribbons and stuck them on her chest. The crossed erect crowbar and chisel glittered in the sunlight. She stomped the ground with her boot. "Get out of my sight!" She walked toward the elm tree at the corner of the flowerbed and stood with her back to others.

Leqa yelled: "Make up your mind about what I am supposed to do!"

Hero Showkat turned around and waved her hand as if to shoo off an imaginary mosquito. "Don't fret and frizzle! Enjoy the landscape of the city!"

Leqa slowly straightened her back, turned around cautiously, pressed her back to the ladder steps, and opened her arms, as though she was crucified on the ladder. She gazed at the distant landscape. People were passing through the alleyways. Upon seeing the Fire Stokers, they slowed their steps. The seven white domes of the Saint George Church shone in the clear air. The picture of the Supreme Hero waved on the flags. A deacon was coming down the granite stone steps. The water in the ponds was evaporating, and the vapors were tenting under the arches. Behind the windows of a yellowish building, women were hanging curtains and cleaning the window-panes. On the platform of the fruit-seller's shop, pyramid-shaped arrangements of apples and pomegranates turned dark and light from the sunlight. The owner of the shop was polishing the fruit with a handkerchief. A tall girl in a purple dress stopped in front of the platform, picked up a pomegranate, tossed it in the air, caught it, smelled it, and, after a pause, put it back, and went on. A chestnut peddler was passing by the bend of an alleyway. He pulled down his pea-green woven cap and scratched his nose. The capable essence of life in the heart of the city was different from the dark alleyways of her dreams. She thought about working, about going out of the house and teaching piano.

Borzu came on the stairs. He was holding a carboy by its neck, shaking it. "Hero Showkat! What are your instructions regarding these?"

Hero Showkat turned on her heels toward the building. "Wash all of them! You must make the house shine like a cluster of ruby grapes!"

Borzu snapped his fingers and left.

Yavar stuck his head out of the window of the elderly lady's room. He saw the ankles of Leqa's legs on the ladder. He rubbed his eyes and inquired hesitantly: "Miss Leqa! Is that you?"

Leqa shook her feet. Yavar began to cough and called out to the elderly lady. With a handkerchief on her head and dusty eyelashes, the elderly lady came to the window. Yavar pointed to the ladder. "May God have mercy!"

Mrs. Edrisi scratched her cheek in distress. "Why is she on that thing?"

Leqa turned around and came down one step. "I like looking at the city."

Vahab joined the other two. He grabbed his grandmother's arm. "Aunt Leqa! Have pity on us! This scene is like a nightmare."

Leqa bent her head and chuckled. "Vahab! Stop it! You have always looked at me with demeaning eyes. Your eyes would ask why this one did not die instead of Rahila. My mother also regretted it. I understood everything, but I kept silent. My only refuge in the house was the picture of the female saint and the old piano. When I was a child, the only person who loved me was my nanny. After she left, it was Yavar. At sunset, I would sit by the window and bite my hands. I would whisper to myself, why did you not die, why did you not die?"

The elderly lady sat on the windowsill. Her thin shoulders were shaking. Leqa yelled: "Mother! Go inside! You're going to fall."

Mrs. Edrisi's pale face contracted. "Leqa! I am proud of you, because you are more real than Rahila. She was cold and arrogant, bewildered and indecisive, just like myself. She did not belong here. She had not grown in her own soil. But with your silence, you carried the burden of the tribulations of the family. You would come down as weightless as the light of day and play the piano. We were merely pretentious. Without talent and tenacity, we would talk about art. You alone achieved it."

From the top of the wooden steps, Leqa looked at her mother's face. "In all my life, I yearned for you to admire me, if only for once. What a pity that it is now too late. It is as though you are speaking about someone else. The voices that I loved have faded. Those days, when I spoke a few sentences with Vahab, I could not go to sleep because I was so happy. He was always looking for perfection—he would not consider me worthy of conversing with."

Vahab pulled Mrs. Edrisi inside the room and took her place. "Aunt Leqa! I have admired you from the time when I was a child. When you played the 'Song of Mary,' I trembled to my darkest core."

"No, in my absence, you made fun of me. It does not matter, those memories have faded, like dreams."

Mrs. Edrisi reached out with her hand toward the ladder. "Forgive us, my child! Get off that devil's contraption!"

Showkat's voice was loud: "Stop spoiling that pampered pile of dung even more! I'll be there myself."

Vahab and Mrs. Edrisi looked at each other, stunned. A few moments later, Showkat kicked the door open and rushed toward the window. Borzu brought a bucket of water and handed it to her. Showkat yelled: "Don't waste time, take it, quick!"

Leqa came down a few steps, took the bucket, and placed it between two steps of the ladder. "Thank you, Hero Showkat! Because of your kindness, I have learned of my capabilities."

Showkat flicked her fingers on the bucket. "What capabilities? Being a chatterbox? Cawing like a crow on the top of a ladder?" A teardrop rolled down Leqa's cheek, and she smiled. Showkat burst out laughing. "Hey, buddy! You're really funny. I like that."

Vahab grabbed Showkat's sleeve. "You seriously act like the devil."

Showkat pulled her sleeve back. The print of the dusty fingers remained on the fabric. She took a handkerchief out of her pocket and cleaned the spots with her spit. "Idiot! Don't touch me! You'll get my dress dirty. I don't like riffraff, especially when they want to rub themselves against me. I am Hero Showkat, not some slut in some house of ill repute, like the women you hung around all day and night, and got money from them."

Astounded, Vahab looked at her. "Hero Showkat! I am Vahab!"

"Be whatever shit you want to be!"

"Why are you toying with Leqa's life?"

"Since you insist, I'll pull her down by shouting at her."

She walked toward the window and held her hands around her mouth. Vahab and Mrs. Edrisi grabbed her arms.

Leqa bent her knees. "Why are you making so much noise? I need a duster. There are a lot of cobwebs under the overhang."

The elderly lady handed her own dusting cloth to Leqa. Her fingers were trembling. "The ladder is wobbly, be careful!"

Leqa got busy cleaning the building façade. She was rubbing the wet, coarse rag on the slippery stones, cleaning off the dust and dirt of the lost years.

While repairing the gable roof, Hero Qadir occasionally lifted his head and encouraged Leqa. Hero Rashid was singing. The breeze broadcast his deep voice.

Hearing the old song that he was singing took Leqa to the past. One day when she was coming home, a young scribe had run after her and handed her a letter. She had dropped it into a stream. After arriving home, she had looked at her red eyes and rosy cheeks in the mirror. A few days later, the scribe handed her another letter. Fearfully, Leqa took the envelope and opened it in the private courtyard. The letter was addressed to Rahila.

The water in the bucket had turned black. She climbed down the ladder, attached the hose to the spigot, and called to the twins: "On my command, turn on the spigot!"

She held the end of the hose, climbed up, reached under the cornice of the roof, and shouted: "Turn it on!"

She held her thumb on the end of the hose. Water ascended in the form of a transparent umbrella. The rays of the sun created a faint rainbow over the sprays of water. The soot and dust were washed away. She asked Rashid for help, and together they moved the ladder farther away. By noon, she finished cleaning the northern side of the building. When her work was completed, she sat on the green bench and leaned her head on her shoulder. The house was sparkling. Hero Rashid came off the stool, took off his damp shirt, and tossed it on the clothesline. His dirty undershirt was stuck to his athletic back and arms. He walked closer to the bench and gazed at the building. "It shines like pearls, Hero. I'm sure you are tired."

Leqa blushed at being called Hero. "You worked much harder. The weather has become warm."

She got up, went toward the building, and stepped into the entrance hall. Whistling, Vahab was cleaning the picture frames. His cheeks were glowing. He stopped working and looked at Leqa. "Wow! Hardened steel! You put the Heroes to shame."

Proudly, Leqa walked toward the stairs. "I am also a Hero, in a gray garb!"

Vahab grabbed her arm and burst out laughing. "Tell me the truth, how many lovesick suitors have you gained among the Heroes?"

Leqa flicked her fingers on his forehead. "Stop talking nonsense! They will hear you."

"Let them hear me! The truth takes precedence over everything else."

He pulled down the corner of her headscarf. Leqa picked up a vase. "I am going to hit you on the head with this." Vahab stepped back. Leqa spat on the floor. "You deserve such stains on your reputation. Tell me! How many girls have you caught in your net?"

Vahab put his dusty hand in front of his mouth and laughed noiselessly. "Oh, as many as you wish. Half the girls in the youth house shed tears upon being separated from me."

Leqa chuckled. "Wishful thinking. Who would pay attention to you? I think Hero Showkat has her eyes on you. The two of you are a good match. It just makes you feel all gooey, right?"

Vahab tossed the damp rag on Leqa's shoulder.

Carrying a broom, Hero Showkat was coming alongside the balustrade. "I heard my name mentioned, Vahab, you lazy bum. Get to work!"

Leqa smiled. "And there is my evidence."

Vahab held his head high. "Hero! It's not my fault. My aunt has become excited and is imagining things."

Showkat held the boom suspended in the air. "Imagining what? Has he become a rebel?"

"In one sense, yes. He wants to get married."

The sound of Showkat's laughter resonated under the ceiling. She became limp from laughing and buckled over the balustrade. The broom swung. "You must be pulling my leg!" She clawed her own belly. "Get married? Who has he fallen for?"

"He has not made a selection yet."

Borzu's head stuck out from between the double doors. Showkat jumped, brought him close to the balustrade, and pushed his head and neck down. "Do you like him?"

Borzu struggled and stood up straight. Blood rushed to his face. "What is going on? Who is the fool who should like me?"

Hero Showkat grabbed his collar and shook his scrawny body. "Don't you intend to get married?"

The student yanked himself away, freeing himself from Showkat's grip, and said in a husky voice: "Hero Showkat! Escalating reactionary foundations is beneath your status. Let worms feed on the decayed shells. Our duty is to build tomorrow's world."

Hero Showkat roared and stroked her forehead with her finger. "Tomorrow's victorious world!" Her tone lacked enthusiasm.

Borzu grabbed the balustrade. "You have found a good excuse to shirk from working."

With his mouth half open, Vahab looked at Borzu's face. "You are the one who is doing the tempting. Why do you show off your body to Leqa so much? She is not as beautiful as Berenice. Moreover, Hero Showkat cascades her rays like the sun goddess. And you are no less than Orpheus."

In the corner of the entrance hall, Haddadiyan was scrubbing the floor with a piece of burlap, panting. A thin cobweb was stuck to his spiky mustache, which moved up and down with each breath.

Hero Showkat shouted: "Scrub it well, Haddadiyan! I want it to be so shiny that I can see my reflection in the wood floor."

Haddadiyan threw the soaking wet burlap, stood under the chandelier, and shook his fist at the ceiling. "Go to the House of Fire! With an alert conscience, see how the organization has changed! The repentant fugitives are coming back group by group. The day before yesterday, I saw the supervisor of the theater of the province—such an educated person with a particularly interesting worldview"— he cast a look of disgust at Vahab—"a man who has read a lot of books—was bending down and cleaning the shoes of the third deputy director of the House of Fire." He opened his fist. "News has arrived from Moscow that the repentant beloved Alexi has also returned most proudly, and is busy writing as fast as a whirligig and portraying ninety percent of the suffering of the laborers. The Supreme Hero has pinned a medal of honor on his chest with his own hands. Elements such as musicians, theater directors, and journalists of the past era have expressed regret about their disgraceful past. Such humility! Such glorious brotherhood! Yesterday in the House of Fire, a first-rate actor was mimicking priests. The great Hero Captain Aqayev nearly fainted from laughter. The beloved Hero Ryakhovski began to cough. I ran and brought water for him.

Such glorious scenes will be engraved in the subconscious of the spectators forever, the reconciliation of culture and power!" He took a deep breath. The cobweb leaped into his nose. "Under such circumstances, it would be a pity to have them dominated by foul-mouthed people."

Hero Showkat ran the length of the interior balcony and came down the stairs, swinging her arms. She stood in front of Haddadi-yan and glared into his eyes. She raised her hand and, after some hesitation, dropped it and spat on the floor. "Are there any customers for you in the House of Fire, you serpent? You are precisely what they deserve. To the black hole of hell with them, when a bunch of clowns have picked up silk handkerchiefs and are massaging and cleaning the tops and the bottoms of the members of the House of Fire. If that's true, I, for one, will hand in my resignation tomorrow. Let the likes of you wiggle their tails for them."

Borzu grabbed Showkat's hand. "Don't squabble with this worthless fellow. I swear on your life he is a liar. He has not even stepped into the House of Fire. There is no place for a traitor in our organization that is made of steel."

Showkat threw the broom aside, went out of the entrance hall, and entered the garden. Leqa ran after her. Showkat sat on the green bench, held her head between her hands, and with the toe of her boot drew some lines on the ground. Her massive frizzy hair shone like gun metal.

Roxana appeared at the top of the stairs and held a lapis lazuli crystal vase up to the light. "Hero Showkat! Is this clean?"

Showkat did not respond. Roxana returned to the entrance hall. Leqa went up the stairs, following her. Clad in white, Roxana approached Haddadiyan. "Why did you throw the burlap? We are not cleaning everything so that you can return them to muck and stink!"

Haddadiyan scratched his nose. "You are also here?"

"Where did you expect me to be?"

"In my opinion, the graveyard."

Roxana laughed. "Such a cute man! You are an idiot in the fullest sense of the word."

Haddadiyan gazed into her eyes. "The life of your intellect is short, but my idiocy . . ."—he wrung out the burlap—". . . is, fortunately, eternal."

Roxana took a card with the red emblem of the erect crowbar out of the pocket of her jacket, then she immediately hid it. The man's knees began to shake, and he went close to the staircase. He held on to the balustrade firmly. Roxana turned her back to him, entered the parlor, and slammed the door shut. In the darkness under the stairs, a pair of blue eyes shone. Haddadiyan tiptoed to the outer courtyard. Leqa turned around and looked at the garden. Showkat was not there. Kowkab, Pari, and Torkan were spreading the white voile curtains on the clothesline. She went toward the kitchen and stood on the threshold. Brass samovars shone with a silvery light. The walnut wood shelves had been polished. Several rows of glasses were arranged on the counter on a gray piece of cloth. The silverware was shining light and dark, like fish scales, in a purple box.

With her hands on her hips, Rokhsareh came into the room and smiled. "This is what you call a kitchen!"

Golrokh turned off the faucet over the kitchen sink and turned to Leqa. "Hero Yavar says that you like cleanliness."

Leqa shrugged her shoulders. "Yesterday, I heard you singing. You sang the entire song without any mistakes. Who taught you?"

Golrokh jumped up. Her braided hair made a curved line in the air and fell back. "When I was a kid, I went with Yusef behind the Pink Rose Café. A woman used to sing there, and my brother loved her voice. We would stand in the dark garden. The smell of food would come through the crack of the window. The woman would sing and my brother would get teary eyes. When I would go to bed, my head was filled with songs. The café shut down, and the woman singer left."

Leqa leaned against the wall. The inside of her nose began to burn. Some summer evenings, she used to go with her maternal aunt and her children to the Pink Rose Café. They would sit at a long table. The male cousins dressed in fine suits and winked at provincial girls who were attracted to them. The table would be covered with food and wine. The female cousins paid attention to no one else. They mostly whispered together and observed the faces of the people around them. Their delicate faces flushed from laughing. They would press silk handkerchiefs to their mouths and criticize the trout sauce; they thought that the kebob meat was not tender enough; they did not like the desserts; and they would laugh at the checkered taffeta dress of the woman singer. The aunt would shake her threatening index finger at them. "Eat, or you will become feeble!" Under their guipure sleeves, the female cousins would shrug their shoulders and whimper through pinched lips. Rahila sat by herself. She shone brilliantly, like pearls under the light of a wall lamp. Among the gathering, only Leqa and her father ate food with an appetite. Around midnight, they would ride a droshky back home. They would pass by Warshawskaya Street. Everyone was happy, satiated, and joyful. They would let the wind blow through their hair, and, through the branches and leaves, they would look at the moon. The female cousins would close their eyes and tell their good and bad fortunes. From Leqa's perspective, what they did was magnificent, but Rahila would turn her face away, dismount in front of the door before everyone else, and run through the courtyard.

Leqa hid her eyes from Golrokh, went to the garden quietly, and busied herself with washing the rest of the building. Before sunset, the house was put in order. Leqa went back to her room, changed her wet clothes, combed her hair, put on a blue headscarf, came out, and checked on the rooms. With clean windowpanes, the window frames looked empty, the blue sky and the green leaves of the trees entered the rooms, and the colors of the dome-shaped ceiling, the clusters of the vine, the fairies, and the blue edgings had become bright. The tulip-shaped lamps and the prisms sparkled in the ruby and amber rays of light. The arabesques and the sea-blue medallion had blossomed in the middle of the carpet in the entrance hall. She entered the parlor. It was clean and shining, like the mornings before parties and banquets. The thin rays of light of the dove-egg chandelier sparkled in the stem of a Miskolc goblet, the bridge of the nose of the Vishnu statue from Benares, the corrugated ridges of the castle of the jasper and coral chess set, and the thin spout of a rosewater dispenser. Leqa looked at the garden through the window. Everyone was in the garden. Hero Showkat was talking and moving her hands. When she saw Leqa's silhouette, she yelled: "Come! Why are you hanging around in there?"

Leqa went down the stairs. Showkat touched her shawl. "Did you knit this yourself?" Leqa smiled. Showkat turned toward the group. "I would like to have our picture taken." Hero Qobad walked toward the lawn. Showkat put her hand on his shoulder. "Where are you going, Hero? You're going to sit in the middle."

Qobad looked at the horizon. "The middle is your place. Of what use am I to you?"

Showkat stomped the ground. "Hero! Why don't you get it? Everyone must be in the picture, even the children, even Rokhsareh, even stupid Vahab."

"But not me!"

Showkat rubbed her hands together. "Hero Qobad! Maybe the people who are going to be born later will want to see our picture, to see what we looked like. Don't expect us to come into their dreams with imagined faces!"

Carrying an old camera, Vahab came down the stairs.

Hero Qobad nodded and chuckled. Hero Showkat took the old man near the stairs. All the Heroes had cleaned up their faces and combed their hair. Showkat assigned their places. Hero Rashid, Kukan, Qadir, Yavar, and Teymur stood on the platform at the top of the stairs. Rokhsareh, Kowkab, Torkan, Pari, and Leqa sat below them on the top step. Showkat seated Qobad on the third step from the top, with Mrs. Edrisi on the left, herself on the right, and Yunos and Borzu on either side. She clapped her hands. "Roxana!"

Torkan bent her head. "She was taking Haddadiyan to the door, delivering him to the Fire Stokers."

Showkat took off the gilded insignia from the bodice of her dress. "Bravo! I couldn't make myself have my picture taken with that lazy bum."

Roxana came, running, and sat in front of Qobad's feet on the fourth step from the top. Yusef and Kaveh took their places on either side of her. Golrokh sat next to Kaveh, shoulder to shoulder with Yusef and Shirin. The children sat tightly on the fifth step. Gowhar hugged the doll, and Aslan, Sakhi, Bakhshi, and Saber sat near her in that order.

Vahab put his eye on the viewfinder and shouted: "Leqa! Come here for a moment!"

Showkat asked: "Why? Isn't it working?"

"You are all wet, Hero! It is working."

Leqa stood next to Vahab, took the camera, and looked through the viewfinder. The white building, the purple gable roof, and the arched window shone brightly. The windowpanes under the last rays of sunlight were aflame. She raised her head, and a faint smile brightened her face. "The house has become new, like the time before we were born."

Vahab dropped his eyelids. "Look at the staircase!"

Leqa nodded. "It is very familiar."

He put his hand on her back. "Go and sit in your place."

Chapter 7

Vahab was rolling around in bed, trying to read a book, but the words would flee, become empty of meaning. He pulled the heavy purple quilt over his head. Thoughts ran through his mind as fast as the wind, and in which direction they would blow he could not imagine. The current conditions were agreeable. Hero Showkat did not bother him. After dinner, he would sit in the corner of the sofa, quietly gaze out the window, occasionally doze off, and, a moment later, jump up startled and terrified.

Inadvertently, Vahab had learned that Showkat, Roxana, his grandmother, and Qobad met secretly in the room behind the library, and Borzu would pace back and forth in front of the door. The student was not sticking to studying and reading, as he had before.

In the late afternoons, Kaveh, Teymur, and Yavar would sit next to the flowerbed and take turns smoking the clay pipe. Kaveh had finally come to accept that he should keep company with old men like himself. He no longer talked about women, but he did talk about dangerous journeys: bloody wars in Crete, Ain Saleh, and Morocco, and braveries in fighting for freedom. He considered himself to be the Lord Byron of the new era. Teymur would nod in agreement, and, as soon as he had the chance, he would talk about his son. Just to console him, in telling his adventure stories, Kaveh would consider Teymur's son to be equivalent to himself. Following this ruse, Teymur would gaze at him and listen to him with his mouth open. Yavar would occasionally sigh. A few times, he got excited and told stories about his own brave acts. They both believed without any doubt that Kaveh's recollections were based on truth. The friendship between Kukan and Yavar had cooled. The combative old man no longer showed any interest in stories about scissors, needles, patchwork curtains and quilts, and the whispering of women. The smell of ironing and soap repulsed him. Hero Kukan would sit on the lawn alone, repairing the torn bedspreads, curtains, and sheets. Often a few short threads were hanging from his dried lips.

Borzu would talk to no one. He would sit in the window frame with his black hat on his head, and, drowned in thought, he would pound his heels on the wall. One day, he brought home the skull of a horse and drew some lines on it. Vahab watched the movement of his shaking hand. "Why didn't you bring a jackass head?"

The student turned his face away from him. "Because we already had one."

After work, Leqa and the women would sit under the shade of the maple tree and talk incessantly. Their eyes looked worried.

One day Vahab pulled Leqa aside and asked: "What do you talk about?"

"The news of the city. We analyze the situation."

"What news?"

"Six members of the Supreme House of Fire have been dismissed. The situation is topsy-turvy." Vahab shrugged his shoulders. Leqa frowned. "You are indeed in neutral gear."

"Apparently, you make up for it."

Leqa was incensed. "Kowkab, Pari, and Torkan know a lot. They understand the ups and downs of life, and they have a good understanding of politics."

Yunos would sit until morning under the grapevine arbor, write on the front and back of sheets of paper, and throw away some of them.

Tired, Rashid and Qadir would come back from work, eat dinner, and go to sleep early.

Showkat had said that she had found jobs for Leqa and Vahab. They were both waiting with anticipation.

Vahab got out of bed and opened the window. Roxana was sitting under the arbor. The light of the alleyway lamp through the branches and leaves shone on her white dress. Years earlier, occasionally, when Rahila could not go to sleep, she would sit under the arbor and look at the horizon until the break of dawn.

He put on a jacket and descended the staircase. He looked for the gleam in Qobad's eyes next to the column, but he saw no sign of it. He approached the arbor. Roxana turned around. "I got scared!"

"Of what?"

Roxana laughed. "The enemies."

"Do you not like them?"

"They give spirit to life."

"So, they take care of you more than your friends."

"Other than that traveling actor, I know of no friends."

"What about lovers?"

"They were expensively free of charge. No one sees you as you are. Every effort is futile, one must admit. When I look back, I have no regrets."

She put her hand on her knee. The moonlight illuminated her long fingers. Vahab sat next to her. "A curse on the destructive shadows of the past! In the early days, I would lie to myself. I would take refuge in the seeming similarity between you and Rahila. A very dangerous game awaited me. I had realized that you did not resemble Rahila at all. You were the opposite image, the kind of woman who would terrify me, passionate like my mother, fleeing creatures about whom we are worried every time we see them, lest that would be the last meeting."

Roxana stood up and looked at him with half-closed eyes. "Have you seen many women with such character?"

"They are everywhere. There is one waiting behind every door!"

Roxana put her palms together and knelt down. Her forehead shone in the moonlight. "How marvelous!"

Vahab shook his head regretfully. "One every one hundred years."

The woman held her delicate profile toward the sky.

The man stared at the shadows of the trees on the lit-up stone pavement. "In the old times, if I were told that I would be attracted to a woman, I would laugh from the bottom of my heart. I could not see any creature outside myself, until you came inside me, little by little. You pulsate in keeping with every beat of my heart. There is no escaping it. It is as though I have nurtured you. Like a fool, I speak to my imagined you."

Roxana leaned her shoulder against the wooden post and asked in a whisper: "What do you speak about?"

Vahab dropped his head. He was afraid of the woman's eyes. They were both warm and cold, penetrating, as though nothing would remain concealed from her gaze. He took a deep breath. "I cannot remember."

Roxana sat down. "Tell me the truth. Do I or do I not resemble that Indian woman in Kashmir?"

Offended, the man struck his forehead with the palm of his hand. "You make light of everything."

Roxana rubbed the toe of her shoe on the ground. "Just one sentence. I would like to know."

Vahab looked at the moon. "What is the use of repeating it? I babble. Wherever you are passing by, I follow the scent of your body to become one with the lines, with the silhouette of your form in the air."

Roxana locked her fingers. "You are more of a poet than Marenko!"

Vahab was incensed. "Marenko is not a poet at all. He wasted your magnificence for many years in small, tight rooms. You were his victim, not his inspirational goddess. I regret the days that he has stolen from you. He plundered both of us."

Roxana frowned. "I came here on Marenko's suggestion."

Vahab shrugged his shoulders. "You were brought here by destiny, in the same way that, many years ago, it took my mother to Tbilisi."

"He is willing and able to die for me."

"That man is only willing and able to die for himself, but I will stay alive for you."

Roxana put her hand on the man's shoulder. "The scent of jasmine flowers. I wish you did not understand anything."

"Alas, I do."

"Understanding will break us apart."

"We do not have much time. Look to your right! Death is standing there." He took Roxana's hand. "Come!" He took her toward the lawn. "I wish to pick the yarrow thorn off your skirt, to have the thorns penetrate my fingers, a memento of your wounds."

The clip of Roxana's hair opened, disheveled locks of hair cascading over Vahab's shoulder. The man inhaled their scent. He was becoming light, and the shadow of the clouds and branches and the rays of the moon spun around him.

In a whisper, Roxana said: "What a pity! Why do our dreams end in degradation?"

"Tonight is short. Do not waste it on experiences of the past!"

Roxana looked at the damp grass. "What should I waste it on?"

"A bit on me, since I am the grass of days."

"The dry grass on the top of the roof?"

"No, I have remained fresh for you. From here on, I would like to live within you."

Roxana stepped away from him. "No, I cannot bear it. I must lighten my load."

"We will become light, step by step, together."

"To the extent that the threads of our world break?"

"Since they are tied together, what fear do you have?"

"The fear of abandonment. I would like to be connected to the roots of the depths of the earth, even if they are decayed."

"What roots? Marenko?"

Roxana turned her back to him. "Oh, you are such an idiot!"

Vahab ran forward and stood in front of her. "Roxana! These people laugh at you. None of them is in love. They have a goal they want to achieve. The motivation in their efforts is a memento of the time of dwelling in caves, a howling that has remained incomplete in a cowardly ego, but it will wake up with a flick of the finger—it will come up bubbling, and reach the point of tunneling upward. I am certain that you have seen an origami Chinese paper lantern. As long as it is closed, it is just one, cut into a balanced shape. When the folds open, there are shapes, one after another, which are exactly alike. Be daring, look at the cover of your lamp. Is so much similarity not boring? Do you want to once again imprison your light between the folded papers?"

"Putting up with me will be difficult for you as well."

"I am not supposed to be putting up with you. What is different about me is that I do not want anything for myself."

The woman sat on a slab of stone. Dewdrops were shining on her shoes. "Your voice is warm, like your mother's. What a coincidence! I began my life with her—I might end it with you."

Vahab sat next to her. "Roxana! Do not frighten me!"

"It is already too late, Vahab!"

"We will begin anew. We will be born again."

Roxana chuckled. "You think you can?"

"I have no past. You are all there is."

Roxana tousled the locks of Vahab's hair. "Then where were you?"

"I looked at your pictures every day."

Roxana pulled her hand away. "Because of Rahila?"

The man stared into the woman's eyes. "Now I understand. Your own eyes attracted me. In some pictures, you smiled without joy and suffering, complicated yet simple, old yet a child. You were very young, but you could not contain yourself in your own body. Other than a forced smile, you had no path to liberation. I have looked so much at those pictures that the newspapers have worn out. By the way, where are your hats?"

"Oh, those hats! I gave them away. They are disintegrating in the houses of acquaintances."

"No, they will not disintegrate. They have touched you."

Roxana pressed her hand on her lips and laughed. "Oh, you little boy! I myself shall disintegrate sooner or later."

Vahab sank his fingers into the grass. "You prefer the nightmare. You have set your heart on being mortal."

Roxana's head bent over her chest. "I love the short life. What is appealing about immortality?"

"Your ancient magic is not short. The women of past ages are repeated in your being. The sound of your voice reminds me of Santa Sofia Church. Your eyes, shade by shade, extend to the depths of history. You are present everywhere. You are standing under the arch of the Red Rose Palace looking at the roaring Guadalquivir River. In the alleyways and back alleys of Jerusalem, your white headscarf blows in the wind. The scent of your body wafts in the olive groves of Baalbek. The jingling of your anklets resonates in the temples of Ajanta. Athena takes her light from you. You have taken the rustling of your dress among the porticos of Chartres Cathedral. In the Palace of Ali Qapu, you are leaning against a red-clay colored pillar, looking at the jetting fountain of the reflecting pool in the Naqsh-e Jahan Square. In the red sunset of Agra, you have fallen asleep under the white dome. The slab of stone on the edge of the Nile still retains the warmth of your body, and the wind carries the sound of your lamentation to the sugarcane fields. I see your footprints in all my dreams of ancient eras. I also know that I have been everywhere at your side, that I have gone to sleep with the caressing of your fingertips. Even if I sprout from the earth like grass one thousand years hence, you will flow in my veins. I call this immortality."

Roxana raised her head. "Oh, how far are you going?" Her eyes shone in the moonlight with the sparkling of tears. "Your warmth melts my ice. I am waking from a deep sleep." Suddenly, she shook her head. "Leave me alone! I can no longer bear any warmth. I will disintegrate. It is quite strange! Something came before my eyes, a faint light in the middle of a silver sconce. But how vibrant it was! Without your presence, this memory will remain in darkness to the end of my life."

The sky was slowly losing its color. In the lapis lazuli air, pine trees had raised their heads. Dewdrops shone brilliantly like stars on the tips of their needles.

Roxana stood up, opened her arms, and held her face toward the light. "It is morning. I would like to give you something."

She went toward the flowerbed and stopped near a rosebush. She held the brittle stem of a bud between two fingers. The petals were opening. Water dripped from the tips of the thorns. The bush cast its reflection over the lawn. Roxana turned around and looked at the man from head to toe. From the depth of the blue and golden rings of the eyes, a gentle ray began to shine. Vahab blinked, as though he were dreaming. Foggy colors were blossoming before his eyes. With a bright smile, he reached the age of thirty.

A thin steam was moving from the lawn toward the reflecting pool. In turn, the woman looked back and forth between the rosebud and Vahab. After a long pause, she walked away from the flowerbed. Vahab laughed and pressed his hand on his lips. That was precisely what was elegant about Roxana. Even Rahila would pick the buds of the white rose and put them on her head.

The woman walked toward Vahab and put the palms of her hands together. "I could not!"

Vahab took a deep breath. "Had you picked the bud, you would have hated me."

The woman's eyes sparkled. "You understand these things?"

Vahab smiled.

Roxana sat on her feet on the soaking wet grass. "When I was running away from Tbilisi, I could hear the sound of a lute and reed flute being played in the alleyways. I was frightened. I feel the same right now."

The man held the woman's hands. Her fingertips were cold. "Such unfounded fear!"

Roxana stared into the distance. "Everyone's share of life is as much as he deserves."

The man squeezed his head between his hands. "Do you like this commonplace cliché?"

Roxana bit her lip. "I am also commonplace."

"Extremely!"

"Then I am a sinner."

"Lucifer, indeed!"

The woman covered her face with both hands. "If only you understood." She lifted her head and pressed her chest with the palm of her hand. "Such a heavy weight right here!"

Vahab shrugged his shoulders. "You have invented this illusion yourself."

The woman raised her knees. "I have tasted the forbidden fruit."

"Well, that's nothing new."

"The same is true of compensating for it. I left my father and mother and went after what my heart desired. I would hear news from Tbilisi that the situation in our house had become chaotic. My mother would sit all day long behind the window and stare at the alleyway. I heard about the next incident from my nanny. After three months of waiting, she closed the curtains of the windows toward the alleyway and took refuge in the canaries. She opened the door to their cage, but they did not fly away. They were more loyal than I was. They would sit on her shoulders and her hands. She could not eat. She was wasting away more with each day. My father, who could not take it out on anyone else, would go after her with his fists. He would say, 'This disgrace to the family is your handiwork.' He concealed from my mother all the letters I wrote for three years. In the end, he gave up his hotheadedness and handed her the envelopes every week. What a pity that it was already too late. She could not recognize my handwriting anymore. There was a vast valley between her and the world. My father would just leave the house. He took refuge in alcohol. He was fired from his position. He brought home a young Circassian girl. Together, they resided in the outer courtyard building. The girl set up his drinking paraphernalia every night. He would drink so much that he would pass out on the floor. They sold the vineyard property, and the money was cast to the wind. Then they went after the remainder of his property. The spatula hit the bottom of the pot, the horses and carriages were gone. They let go of the servants. The girl took off. My mother did not bother them. She did not see their comings and goings. Her hair had turned white. From sunset on, she would sit in some corner by the wall and stare at the jetting fountain. Late at night, she would drag her feet going to the room with five sashed windows and collapse on the red carpet. She would not roll out her bedding."

Roxana burst into tears. Vahab stroked her hair. "You had no other choice. An eagle chick can be imprisoned. But once its wings become strong and its eyes see the mountain peak, it cannot be held in chains and shackles. You were not a domesticated pigeon. You acted according to your nature."

Roxana bit the palm of her hand. "But isn't this nature merciless? When I went back to Tbilisi, my mother had died. My father had completely turned upside down. He slurped pottage and soup out of the bowl, afraid that someone might snatch the bowl out of his hand. The wealthy had cast him aside. He now associated with servants, minstrels, smugglers, and horse groomers. The tip of his nose was red, and his eyes were damp. Because of him, I took an entire floor at the Ritz Hotel. I would receive money, but it was spent as fast as the wind. Waiters would as quickly as lightning fill the table with caviar, grilled sturgeon, grilled liver, and piroshki. We would sit across from each other. He constantly would get up, put his hand on his chest, and bow. When I was leaving Tbilisi, I put three thousand manats in the pocket of his jacket. He was so happy that he started to cry, and he kissed my hand. He had mistaken me for a charitable lady. He was standing at the city gate and shivering inside his old overcoat. In the dust of the carriage, he bowed many times. I cried all the way back. I wished he had died, like my mother, who received me alone with her gravestone in the shade and a yellow wildflower. His confusion and humility were worse than death. He did not have one iota of resemblance to the corpulent man who whipped the backs of the horses and drew out his revolver. This woefully wretched old man was of my own making. After the trip to Tbilisi, the image of his bent back and alien eyes reappeared in my nightmares. His revenge was even more powerful."

Vahab bent down and picked off the yarrow thorns from her skirt.

Chapter 8

Mrs. Edrisi went to the library, unlocked the abandoned room, and entered. The clock struck three. Dust had settled on the leather spines of the books on the interpretation of dreams, the astrolabe, astrology, geomancy, and alchemy. She wiped them with a handkerchief and sat in an easy chair. Roxana stepped into the room. "Hello, Mrs. Edrisi. Does anyone else in the house know of the existence of this room?"

"Hero Yunos."

Roxana picked up a pencil from the table and rolled it around in the light. Golden stars shone on the cylinder. "A few years ago, he was looking for Marenko in Yalta. We thought he was one of his followers, but his intention was to prove to Marenko that Marenko's poems would die before he does. Marenko waved a rake at him and drove him out of the house. All night long he couldn't sleep. He paced back and forth. Before sunrise, he sat at his desk and forced himself to compose a poem. Yunos's existence is nothing but art, but Marenko has some things you can grab onto, that attract the people, that make him a national hero, playing the role of the savior. Yunos does not belong to this age, but I admire him."

The elderly lady nodded absent-mindedly. "Showkat and Qobad are late."

"They will show up. Are you going to drop out?"

"I don't know. This is the final test. One is born only once."

"Vahab was of another opinion. Last night, he was claiming that I have been born thousands of times, and he, as well."

The elderly lady waved aside a thin spiderweb from before her eyes. "His ludicrous ideas have nothing to do with me. Vahab rubs that fish-smelling ambergris on himself"—she paused for a moment—"but was there a reason for all this imparting of pearly wisdom to you?"

Roxana drew a faint line on the table. "He said he was in love with me, from the dawn of creation."

The elderly lady raised her head. "One-sided?"

Roxana dropped the pencil. "Thus far, yes."

"When will it become two-sided?"

"I have no idea. I just wanted you to know."

"Of what benefit is it to me?"

"It is beneficial for me. Throughout your life, with the efforts of others, certain things have remained concealed from you. I do not wish to be their accomplice."

"Truthfulness is also some sort of ruse, isn't it?"

Roxana shrugged her shoulders. "The game is over, but I have not won a pittance. Alas! I always arrive too late."

"Then appreciate him! Regarding his feelings, he is sincere."

"But humans change. You have also changed."

"That which runs deep has not changed."

"Then let us forget Vahab."

"You forget him! I love my grandson. Why are you lying to yourself? Vahab has had an effect on you."

"I will eliminate that effect."

"At what price?"

"At any price."

"You have made everyone a partner in the final game. It is not that bad for an old woman like me, but you have started too soon for yourself. With Vahab, go across the border. I have a few coins at the bottom of my coffer. You can have them."

Roxana laughed. "Only a few coins? We have countless amounts of them."

The elderly lady held on tightly to the arms of the easy chair. "Is your treasure not an illusion?"

"You will find out later."

Hero Showkat appeared at the threshold. She took a look around. "Then where is Qobad?"

Roxana walked closer to her. "Be cautious!"

Showkat pushed Roxana aside, walked toward the window, and rubbed the sole of her boot on the carpet. "I lived in hiding for five whole years. I know about your kind of hide-and-seek game quite well. What's going on in your head?"

"Hero Showkat, the House of Fire intends to get rid of you."

Showkat slapped her knee. "I am a part of the House of Fire."

"Not since last month."

"To hell with that. The renowned Hero Showkat is like the cow with a white patch on its forehead that everyone in the entire city knows. Who would dare cast a sideways glance at her?"

"The Central House of Fire. They are masters of complicating simple tasks. They will first discredit you before the people. They will push you down to your neck in labels and accusations."

Showkat spat on the floor. "Not even one person would believe them. Showkat is pure."

"Spying for foreigners and taking money from the enemies is not a pleasant accusation." Showkat toppled a chair by kicking it. Roxana put her finger to her lips. "Hero Showkat! What are you doing?"

"I want to smash anything I can get my hands on. Did I take money? I spit on their graves! So why don't I own zilch? The House of Fire, as generous as it claims to be, has given me a pair of boots and a few trinkets. When it snows, my hands turn blue from the cold. If they are claiming what they claim, they should tell me in what hole I have stuck the money."

"The capital city is like Armageddon. They have jailed the most honest members of the Supreme House of Fire. Due to all sorts of torture, before anyone else, they have come to believe in the baseless accusations."

Showkat pressed her hands on her ears. "Shut up, you raven of ill omen!"

"Would naming a few people suffice for you?"

Hero Showkat growled. Roxana named six people. Upon hearing each name, Showkat would jump and punch the library bookshelves. When she heard the last name, she ran her fingers through her hair, leaned forward, and widened her eyes. "Commander Rezmanov? I heard his voice on the radio with my own ears."

Roxana smiled. "I did, too. Well, how was he?"

Showkat stared at the ceiling. "He had a cold. Borzu said he was suffering from pneumonia."

"Bravo Borzu! Good diagnosis. Alas, this illness has become a pandemic. Aren't you trying to prevent it?"

"Who is going to strike me?"

"The MKCK Agency! The eggshells have broken in the heat of the Central House of Fire and a bunch of monsters have emerged. What they do is easy and ancient—whoever is not with us is against us. Whoever is not with us is condemned to death!"

Showkat put her hands on her hips. "Do you think you've found a gullible jackass? Stop making up lies!"

"Me, Hero? Don't you see the phantom of the MKCK behind your head? How long should we continue to say that other people's fate has nothing to do with us? No, my dear. This crazed camel of calamity will raid everyone's house."

Showkat walked the length of the room. "I spit on my sense of honor! Where is last year's Showkat? You are the winner in this game. My lovely hair is turning white. Borzu says that every strand of white hair is a telegram from death."

"Don't take it so seriously! Take what Borzu tells you with a grain of salt!"

Showkat gazed at the floor. "I wish to die at the peak. That student, Borzu, is still fabricating dreams and delusions." She looked at the deep red lines on the palms of her hands. "I heard from a train porter that they lash the workers with whips in Moscow. I spit on their graves! I worked in the Sun Vegetable Oil factory for ten whole years. The banging of the machines shook my brain all night long and caused me to have disturbing dreams. I was given chicken feed for my wages. I had become a windup doll. Whether I was awake or asleep, I was always moving a frightening handle up and down. Up to the time I was twenty-nine years old, I didn't know at all whether it was spring or winter." She punched her own chest. "I know about the workers and what they go through. The House of Fire people have relieved themselves on the ground and stuck a flag on the top."

Roxana stood up from the table. "Yes, indeed!"

Showkat wrapped a strand of her hair around her finger and yanked it out. "Miss Spoiled Brat, have you ever made anything with your hands?"

Roxana bent down and picked up the pencil. "No, I only have imagination. Why were you sympathetic to Shirin? Were you a little girl, or ill? Neither! But you placed yourself in her shoes. This is what I am capable of. If I thought about myself, I would have fled. But I am worthless. I would be in tumult and restless even on the other side of the world. I would take the pains and illnesses of each and every one of you with me—the awful tumor of Rokhsareh, Teymur's cataract of the eyes, the chronic constant leg pain of Hero Kowkab, Pari's feigning smile in her misfortune, Torkan's frightened eyes when she stealthily stuffs Shirin into the stable, and, more than anything else, your obnoxious language, which you have made into a protective shield. I would constantly be worried about what has happened to Showkat. In the corner of which dump are her whip and boots decaying?"

Showkat rose in a fury. "As if Hero Showkat's whip and boots are discarded shovel handles to be tossed in some corner?"

"Where do they usually toss objects that have no owners?"

Showkat slapped her own upper arm and held her fist and forearm straight up.

The elderly lady perked up her ears. "Hero Qobad?"

They could hear the creaking of the crutch from behind the wall. Qobad stepped into the room, closed the door quietly, sat at the desk, and gazed at Roxana. His eyes were gleaming. "Well, I am here, my dear girl. Of what use is this tired, lame old man to you?"

Roxana put her hand on her chest and bowed. "The only thing is that, wherever he steps, he raises his surroundings to the level of the domain of mythology. He is the soul of a people, the ideal of a great nation!"

Qobad's lips moved beneath the strands of his white mustache. "Oh, so many slogans! All hollow, like the wind. I am neither a myth nor the soul of the people. Throw away the memory of fifty years of madness!"

"Throw it away? It is not in my hands. Others will preserve it. One night, I was walking near the Moscow Theater. A group of vagrants were standing around a bonfire. On the other side of the river, stone buildings were immersed in silence and darkness. I walked close to the bonfire to get warm. They were singing a song under their breath. Upon seeing me, they became silent. They made room for me. Their overcoats were in tatters. I held my hand over the flame and sang a stanza of the ballad. They accompanied me. The voices peaked in the empty space and reached the other side of the river. Lights came on in dozens of windows. The residents of houses stuck their heads out of the windows and waved their hands. Do you know what the song was? 'The Ballad of the Battle of the Mountain.'"

Hero Qobad ran his finger through the dust settled on the desk. "They were courageous. Why were they singing it? Have they set their hopes on me again? They are treading on the wrong path." He put his hand on his chest. "From the fire in here and the mountain, a fistful of ashes remain. I have nothing to do with the people. I wasted a lifetime with my love for them. I would sit awake until dawn, wishing to see the faint city lights." The furrows in the corners of his lips disappeared in a sorrowful smile. "I played the role of their physician, negligent of the fact that they did not need a healer. They wanted an executioner, someone of whom they were afraid. I hear that millions of people assemble on Red Square and march in front of the Supreme Hero, and that women go into rapture, scream, and faint. The leaders of the right factions prostrate themselves on the ground before him. Well, they all deserve each other. We were the only unwanted ones. Listen, my dear girl! I have turned my back on the world. I am tired. I beg you to leave me alone. Do you expect me to stand on one leg and once again be the scarecrow in other people's melon patch?"

Roxana crossed her arms over her chest. "They have metamorphosed the majority of the people. They dupe the laborers of the world. All sorts of photos of the Supreme Hero are stuck on the tops of sticks everywhere, in Greece, in France, in Germany and Italy, even in the most remote cities in Central America. His mustache looks like it has been fertilized, and his eyes under his thick goat-trotter eyebrows gaze at you like a wolf. This grand idol of the workers is merciless and a demagogue. He is quite cognizant of the soft spots of the riffraff—creating an atmosphere of intimidation and spreading lies. Every kind of assembly is prohibited in the capital city. His MKCK has become terrifying. It has run its roots everywhere. Everyone is afraid of his own shadow. There is no love among the people. Conversations are recorded in public assemblies, in hotels, in restaurants, and even in people's homes. Hundreds of new prison cells have been built in Vladimir Central Prison. They have raised the windows close to the ceilings. They stuff six or seven people in every solitary confinement cell. Among the common tortures is starving the prisoners to death. They employ Pavlov's theories. Last week, a group of poets and writers arrived in Moscow on his invitation. In the infamous banquet party of the Supreme Hero, indigenous artists, including Isaac, were present. They did not invite Marenko. Pastrovich did not breathe a word, but Isaac whispered something. They say he has gotten himself into hot water. He is in a dangerous situation."

The sky was becoming covered with clouds. It was drizzling. Hero Qobad looked at the garden. In the faint light, the wrinkles on his face deepened. "I know Isaac personally. Several years ago, he stayed with us for one day and night. Such a mischief-maker! Such enthusiasm! His biting satire spared no one, from the plebeian to the elite. He talked all night until morning about his recollections regarding the capital city. He described the scenes so skillfully that we could see them vividly before our eyes. The following night, he took off through the winding remote mountain paths. No one found out about it."

Roxana dropped her head and whispered: "Do you not have any recollection of me?"

Hero Qobad smiled. "You have not changed much—you still make a lot of noise. Let me be straight with you. I have never figured out what your motives are."

Roxana swallowed. "Would you permit me to sit down?"

"Yes, of course. I am not too keen on formalities. I resemble a wild beast. Be natural, like you were on that moonlit night! For a while, you were yourself, then you began playacting."

Roxana sat down and bit her lip. "I was frightened. You are the only person in the world who intimidates me. There is no playacting."

Hero Qobad nodded. "I know. The more you try to be yourself, the less you succeed. That ideal 'I' always dominates you. You submerse yourself in the character of the person whom you desire to be."

Roxana chewed on the nail of her baby finger. "You are also not immune to that 'ideal I.'"

Hero Qobad knit his brow. "In the end, every person is placed fixedly in some role. You also have no other choice. What a pity that you are not steadfast. Do you remember the letter? You put it in your purse. You were supposed to deliver it to its recipient as soon as you got back. But it was not delivered. What happened?"

Roxana jumped up from her seat. Her cheeks flushed. "Believe me, as soon as I arrived in Moscow, I went to the appointed place and delivered the letter to his own hands. He repeated the code sentence— 'It is raining, gather the clothes from the clothesline'!"

Hero Qobad stroked his forehead and clenched his jaws. "So, he was playing a double role. You know him by his fictitious name. You would find it amusing if you were to learn that he has become a member of the Supreme House of Fire. Our contact had alerted us that that person had secret dealings with the military government. We did not believe it, given that he had been in prison in Siberia for five years." He rubbed his cheek. "Humans are simple, yet complicated creatures. They are capable of everything. The list of traitors exceeds a long scroll. Even those close to us have stabbed us in the back. In that great battle in which we lost our most sincere self-sacrificing forces and I lost my leg, we discovered that the commander of the middle flank had given the enemy the map of each and every one of our positions. Yes, I gradually learned that that was the rule—I am not talking about the exceptions."

Roxana sat down and took a deep breath. "The world does not change with the rules—exceptions create the direction."

"Are you sloganeering again, my dear girl? If you had lived like me for a few weeks, you would have taken refuge in a convent. I do not intend to make you despair, but the same beloved villagers would deliver our wounded officers to the military government. In that situation, I would become outraged, but upon reviewing my recollections, I have learned that every condition has several aspects. So, I consider them to be in the right. War and violence are a vicious circle that expands exponentially. When the wheel begins to turn, more blood is shed every day. We were imposing the light of the fire on them. We were fighting the government, not ignorance. They despised freedom, because they did not understand it. Like a bubble, this word was suspended in the air, and discredited. They gathered around it from every clan and group and blew on it until it burst and was gone."

Roxana pressed her toes on the ground and restlessly shook her calves. "I am also in despair. No matter in which direction I have gone, it has been either too tight or full of abjectness. I am not without sin—I am one of these same people. I have told lies here and there. I have stepped on other people's shoulders to advance. I have whirlpools in my soul. Now is the moment to choose. One choice is to compromise with life, a gradual metamorphosis, moving away from the principles. Exactly tomorrow, I can go back to the capital city and sign dozens of pledges, and by becoming a devotee, acquire privileges such as the possibility of acting in the theater, receiving Yalta and Crimea grants, membership in the Association of Forefront Galloping Artists, commendations and prizes, and coerced friendships. I would get accustomed to it after a while. Getting accustomed to it would replace everything, even the truth. The passion that I have in my heart would be extinguished. Ashes would settle on me. Prospects would appear dark before my eyes. I would walk in smoke and fog as long as I live. I would sell my human warmth for the coldness of exile. I would continue like that until old age and death. They would stuff my corpse in a wooden box and bury me under the flakes of snow. And, in the end, they would place a plaque of honor with the erect crowbar on my grave." She held her palm up. "No, thank you very much!"

Mrs. Edrisi coughed and pulled her shawl up over her shoulder. "Does your future prospect not have more than one window?"

Roxana pushed her hair back. "Every path reaches a dead end, or it is incompatible with my state." She turned to Qobad. "How much time do you have left? How long do you intend to stand under the staircase, stare at the hands of the clock, and beg them for a place to sleep and a piece of bread to eat? Those around you might see you in a faint light, but the lives of three generations have become meaningful with the fame of Hero Qobad! During the nights when they closed their eyes in bed in despair and humiliation, an undiminishing flame quivered behind their eyelids. When we duped each other, when failed love affairs came to an end, and when the phantom of the military government breathed down our necks, a distant warmth melted the ice in our hearts. At the height of restlessness, we turned our heads toward the east. The flickering of every lamp had something of the fire on the mountain. That bright spot saved us from downfall. In the most calamitous of situations, we did not contemplate suicide. The chaos of existence turned into unity around the circuit of the thorn bushes of the mountain. We composed poems and songs. We went on the stage with passion. But now what?" She covered her eyes with her hands. "Cold and dark mountain peaks."

Hero Qobad stood up, tightly held the crutch under his arm, walked to the window, sat on the windowsill, and pressed his cheek on the window frame. "During this season of the year, sparrows build their nests. Snakes climb up the trees and eat their eggs. When we were there, we would not let them. Thunder and lightning wreak havoc. There are thousands of species of mountain flowers."

Roxana turned her chair toward the window. "A few months ago, I set out on the road on a bicycle. I rode on the remote narrow mountain paths and stopped at a precipice. I stared at the valley below. I wanted to jump down. There are many people like me. Suicide has become commonplace. I happened to look at the slope of the mountain before me. I saw a faint flame. I stepped back and sat on a rock. My heart was pounding. I tasted blood under my tongue. I remembered your sharp eyes. They have spread the rumor everywhere that you have lost your mind, that you lack intelligence and memory. From behind me, I heard a faint sound. I turned around and saw an eagle sitting on a rock. Its eyes were aflame. My legs trembled. I put my head on the grass and burst into tears."

Hero Showkat held onto the back of Roxana's chair and shook it. "You unfortunate little orphan!"

Hero Qobad walked toward the desk. "Well, go on!"

Roxana wiped the moistness from her eyes. "I jumped on the bicycle and peddled until I reached the city. The night patrolmen were dozing off. Through the alleys and back alleys, I went to a friend's house. His light was still on. I tapped on the windowpane with my fingers. He rushed to open the door. I took the bicycle inside and stepped into the room. He whispered, 'Has anything happened?' I said, 'I am returning from the edge of nonexistence.' He chuckled. 'We are all at that edge.' He pulled out his desk drawer and took out a revolver. 'The singular hope!' We made the first arrangement. I then went to Marenko. We contacted the dissidents. As of three months ago until now, we have formed a large group. We have influence everywhere, even among the disfavored members of the Supreme House of Fire, who every day are awaiting arrest and execution. Hero Qobad, all have their hopeful eyes on you! They have created secret nuclei groups to join the forces on the mountain. We do not have much time. Move! Today or tomorrow will be your turn. We have dug into your case. We have found a way to see the secret documents. Your name is at the top of the list, of course, with a red X. They have a plan. Eliminating Hero Qobad is not a simple matter. They have made plans to shatter the legend. All they need to do is to broadcast your voice on the radio while you are speaking nonsense. A few sentences uttered in a trembling voice will destroy the memory of fifty years of resistance. The limited collective mind-set remembers the final words in the same way that in the courts, the final statement of the convicted is the document of their existence." It was late in the afternoon. Qobad's face was moving into the shade. His eyes were clouded. "Read the newspapers. Three well-known founders of the Supreme House of Fire, Kinoviv, Zamnov, and a few days ago, Arkadin, all have been arrested on the charge of spying for foreigners. They were despotic, but you cannot stick espionage to this group with any kind of glue." She blinked at the sky. "In the trials, they supposedly confessed unequivocally."

Showkat grabbed Roxana's collar and shook her. "Shut up, you slut! Why do you mention those great names with your sinister mouth?"

Roxana released her collar from Showkat's grip. "It is going to rip. Don't get all huffy! Doesn't the news reach here? Or are you sticking your head under snow? What is that student doing? Is his only mission to knead dough?"

Hero Showkat shook her head and messed up her hair. "You bastard!"

Roxana took a folded newspaper out of her pocket. "If you are literate, read it!"

Showkat twisted her hand. "Watch what comes out of your mouth! In theory and in practice, I will put your behind-the-scenes instructor in my back pocket."

Showkat snatched the newspaper and walked to the window. As she was reading, her lips moved slowly and her eyes gradually widened. She raised her head, squeezed the paper in her fist, and pounded it against the wall.

Roxana bent down, picked up the newspaper, and unfolded it. "What are you doing, Hero? This issue is now difficult to find."

Showkat sat on the windowsill, gathered up her legs, pressed her chin to her knee, and grumbled under her breath: "Blight! Pest!" She stared at Roxana. "Spill it out! What trick do you have up your sleeve? Are you feeding from the trough of the regressives?"

Roxana held up her head. "I have spoken my final words. All now rests on Hero Qobad's decision."

The old man stood up, leaned against the corner of the wall, knit his brow, and, with his head dropped, gazed at the designs on the carpet. After a long silence, in a husky voice, he said: "Tune your instrument!"

Roxana walked to him. "The mountain has not moved from its place. The same is true of you, Hero. We will go up there again and start anew. We will send a message to the large group of people who are counting the moments to join us."

Qobad shifted the crutch and held up his head. There was fire in his eyes. "Have you done all your thinking? Under these conditions, any action means suicide. Do you have the guts and the courage for it?" He stared into Roxana's eyes. She lowered her eyelids. "I am old, but not so old that I would sacrifice other people's lives based on hollow promises. You nag and moan, because you are despairing, but when the actions peak, you stick to life more than anyone else. Disillusioned intellectuals can never be trusted. They are weak in their self-confidence. They are enamored of fame and glory. They consider themselves the center of existence. They cannot stand the sight of one another. They start a ruckus and chaos. My experience and awareness would make me prefer one person like Showkat over an army of them."

Roxana leaned on the desk. "Hero Qobad! We have nothing to do with them. Do not underestimate your devotees to this extent! We are also not emptyhanded. We have an absolute treasure."

Qobad smiled. "Talking about treasures is outmoded. Let that remain in legends."

"We are also among the legends."

"I have no argument, but a ridiculous legend!"

"Seeking freedom?"

"Why should it not be ridiculous when it is a commodity without buyers?"

"It will find buyers."

"As they say, without yeast, the bread would not rise. Let us talk about resources. How much money do you have?"

Roxana laughed. "Unlimited! Depending on what Showkat thinks."

Showkat grabbed her arm. "When I yanked off the cheap trinkets and stomped on them, it meant that I would have nothing to do with the House of Fire anymore." She extended her hand toward Qobad. "If I make a pledge to you, the ground under my feet will become firm. I will walk head and shoulders above everybody else. I would say, what does it have to do with me? Let the owners of shoddy merchandise take the blame!" She shrugged her shoulders. "Well, this is what I am. The renowned Hero Showkat!"

Qobad stared at Showkat. "Hero, think first, and then make a decision! On the path to the mountain, there is no membership in the House of Fire, whips, boots, and power. Everyone would turn his back on you. You will be rejected like a leper."

Hero Showkat clicked her heels. "What are you waiting for? When my mother was alive, she would tell me, 'Showkat, you vagrant! You'll finally have your head chopped off.' Now I want to prove what she said, because she was right, because I really liked what she said."

Hero Qobad nodded. "It is clearer than poetry and slogans."

Showkat held up her head. "When I was a little kid, my mother gave shelter to a man who was from your group. We had an old unused clay bread oven in the corner of the baker's shop. All day long, he hid in the oven. At night, he would come out, his head and clothes covered in dust. He would stand near the stairs to the courtyard and stare at the mountain. He said that if he did not get up there in time, the flames would die. When my mother died, he took care of us and sent us money from far away. All I remember of his face is a pair of piercing blue eyes. I just remembered him and my mother. All this time, I was not in my own skin. It was as though I walked around in borrowed clothes. I threw them away." She stroked her arm. "I have found my body."

Hero Qobad stared at the tree branches submersed in darkness. "We were talking about treasures. Where is your treasure, Roxana?"

Roxana walked closer to Mrs. Edrisi. "Do you have any suggestion?"

The elderly lady placed her hands on her knees. "My suggestion is not important."

Roxana looked at Qobad. "What do you think? It is destiny-making!" She asked the old man: "Don't you agree?"

"We took off for the mountain in the dead of winter and did not come down anymore, other than a couple of times."

Roxana knelt by the elderly lady's feet. "You have been with him from the beginning—why not be with him to the end?"

Mrs. Edrisi pressed the velvet arms of the chair. "Of what use am I to you? He separated his way from me fifty years ago."

Roxana whispered: "Close your eyes! Look deeply! Find your answer in what you see. The truth is undoubtedly there." Mrs. Edrisi looked at her, stunned. Roxana continued. "What are you waiting for?"

The elderly lady dropped her head and closed her eyes. The shadows of night were descending on the room. The hanging white strands of her hair shone in the twilight. Hero Showkat was pacing back and forth. Hero Qobad put his finger to his lips. Showkat immediately sat on the windowsill and held her breath. The elderly lady opened her eyes. Her shoulders were shaking. Quietly, she said: "The red ruby ring."

Roxana stood up and took a deep breath. "The treasure is in this very house!"

Chapter 9

Vahab had become accustomed to waking up at dawn. Around six o'clock, he dressed and went to the reflecting pool. Like the others, he washed his hands and face under the spigot and dried his face with a handkerchief. A gentle hand descended on his shoulder. He turned around. It was Yusef, sparkling clean, in a white shirt and blue trousers with his hair combed back.

Vahab looked the young man up and down. "Very attractive! Believe me, you have no match. Where did you get those distinctive eyes?"

Yusef's cheeks turned crimson. "You are pulling my leg!" He asked quietly: "Would women also like me?"

Vahab narrowed his eyes, pulled his head back, and smiled. "What kind of women do you mean? I am not a woman. Ask the women themselves!"

Yusef kicked a pebble into the flowerbed with the toe of his shoe. "There are no women."

"In any case, the time has come." Vahab rubbed the palms of his hands together. "One must fall in love."

Yusef kicked the runoff ledge of the pool. "Who has the patience for such things? Such weird things belong to the likes of you. In our harsh life, there is no room for pastimes."

Vahab's eyes clouded. "Say whatever you want!"

Yusef grabbed his arm, and they walked slowly toward the gravel path. Fog tented on the branches and leaves, scattered with the breeze, and, waving, would wrap around itself. Yusef picked a branch off the boxwood and squished its brittle leaves between his fingers. "What do you think of Marenko's poems?"

Vahab stopped abruptly and creased his brow. "What kind of question is that?"

"I would like to know your opinion about what he has done so far."

"He has done a great deal of all sorts of things. What do you have in mind?"

"For example?"

"He has smoked a hashish hookah in Kyrgyzstan, he has worn a papakha hat, he has danced six-four with the Turkomans, he has taken photographs on every other occasion, but, most significantly, he has destroyed a valuable life with his egotism."

Yusef stroked his forehead. "Whose life?"

Vahab picked up a pebble off the ground and threw it into the alfalfa field. "Can't you guess?"

Yusef stuck his hands in his pockets and in a trembling voice said: "Roxana Yashvili? She was not happy with Marenko?"

"If being squashed is happiness, she had no shortage of it."

Yusef grabbed Vahab's arms and shook them. "Have you talked with Roxana?"

"There is no need for talking. Look at her attitude! Does she resemble a happy person? Roxana is walking toward death with the same eagerness that people seek love."

Yusef stared into his eyes, stunned. "Is there anything we can do?"

Vahab leaned against the wall and crossed his arms on his chest. "I wish I knew."

Yusef grabbed Vahab's sleeve. "I am sure she has told you some things. Tell me, it's important to me."

"Ask her yourself!"

The young man punched the wall. "I am afraid of her. I cannot approach her sanctuary—she is unattainable."

"She is unattainable, you can be sure of that. Even for Marenko. He has spun around a great deal, trying to understand Roxana, but

he had been barking up the wrong tree. He thought that he was dealing with an egotistical, simpleminded person like himself."

"Then Marenko has not been the one to enlighten Roxana?"

"Yes, he has. You are right. Roxana has become enlightened by
understanding his darkness."

"You really dislike Marenko!"

"I consider a criminal to be nobler than he is."

"I don't understand."

Vahab stuck his clenched fists into the pockets of his jacket.
"One day in the heart of the Central American jungle, a parrot
was born. Each of its feathers was a thousand colors. Its eyes were
golden, and its beak purple. It ate the sap of flowers. It flew under
the bluest sky in the world, until it fell into a trap and into the hands
of a ship's captain. A professor of linguistics was a companion of the
captain. He spent his time on the parrot and taught it ten languages.
For years, the bird would sit on the high mast of the ship and look
out at the sea, until, as misfortune would have it, the ship happened
to pass by the Port of Marseille. In the middle of the night, it is not
clear with what sinister intent, the parrot left the ship and flew all
night long until the next morning, when it arrived at a remote village. It landed on a tree branch in a small courtyard. The owner of
the house came out and as soon as he saw the parrot, he blinked
and turned to his son, 'Fetch me a knife, quickly. What a pretty
sparrow!'"

Yusef gazed at the branches engulfed in fog. "I would like Yashvili to read my poems." He took out a notebook from his pocket and
handed it to Vahab with a shaking hand. "It is not a bad collection.
They have been composed with honesty."

Vahab rolled up the notebook and put it in his pocket. "Wait
here! I will be back."

The house was quiet. He went up the stairs and entered the
parlor. The breakfast table was full of breadcrumbs and empty tea
glasses. He heard Roxana's voice: "They have lost all their vim and
vigor. They just eat and leave."

Vahab walked a few steps forward. "Where are you?"

Roxana came out of the dark space of the library and sat in the corner of the sofa. "Don't address me with the formal 'you'! I am not your grandmother. In this downcast weather, you look like a ghost."

The young man approached the woman. "Were you plotting a conspiracy again?"

"Are you a detective?"

"I have a message."

"I hope it is not from yourself."

Vahab sat in the corner of the sofa. "I am a message from head to toe—I do not need to utter it."

"Then why don't you go and find a job?"

"You are my job! I wish you would become mine for only forty days. After that, I would be prepared to die. But, apparently, that is impossible."

Roxana picked up a small cushion, put it on her knees, and leaned her elbows on it. "You have understood it correctly. That is impossible."

The man pressed his temples. "Do you dislike me?"

Roxana shook her head. "I dislike myself. I have said it many times. Isn't that enough?"

"Why don't you cut yourself off from the past?"

"What am I supposed to say?" She put her hand on her chest. "It is frozen here."

"I am sure you have read the story of the Snow Queen. If she has taken you to her palace, like Gerda, I will melt the ice in your heart with my warm tears."

Roxana put her forehead on the small cushion. Her hair cascaded to the floor. In a faint voice, she said: "There is no time left anymore." She raised her head and looked into the man's eyes. "Vahab, why did you go to Kashmir? If only, instead of your mother, you had come to Tbilisi! In that case, everything would be left in its own place. The house would not have been destroyed. The city would not have changed. You and I would have lived happily ever after, like the heroes of stories. We would not understand the world. Knowledge is the beginning of decay and destruction. For every bit of new understanding, you must sacrifice a part of yourself." She pushed her hair back. "Indeed, why do we think about these things?"

"Well, don't think about them. No sage concerns himself with the hows and whys of phenomena. He passes through them. Do flowers and birds contemplate their lives?"

Roxana threw the little cushion. "Am I a flower or a bird? According to that philosopher, I think, therefore I am!"

"But I am not what I think."

The woman ran her fingers through her hair. "Oh, I am tired of all this! You, too, in a way, talk slogans. If it is that easy, stop yourself from thinking! As far as I know, in your entire life, you have either been thinking or fabricating far-fetched dreams. Look at Yunos! From morning, he goes and shovels the hard black soil. He is the one who fights his inner self. He gains calm through humility. If there is one person who has escaped with his life through the storms and whirlpools, it is he. Are you able to not look at yourself at all? Are you able to step on your pride? Look at him up and down. Other than the occasional sparkle in his left eye, what is the difference between him and a vagrant in tattered clothes? Victory over the ego is not the business of slogans and philosophy. It is a silent current in the depths. None of us has reached simplicity and contentment. In a week, a superior game will begin, and burn everything other than hatred and regret."

"Who has taught you these things? Marenko?"

Roxana leaned forward. "Life! Can your brain handle that?"

"How could life have done this? Look at the women in this house. Each has suffered many times more than you have—of course, your egotism rejects this comparison—why has life not taught them such nonsense? So, is hatred the only thing that can continue? Be kind and count me out! Speak with your own tongue!"

The woman bit her lip. "If only you could see yourself in the mirror. It began earlier than expected. Only out of anger and hatred do you hold up the women to me. You never paid any attention to them before."

"You know well that there is no hatred in what I say. But you wish to see it that way. Because you breathe and say: Do you see that

I was not mistaken—he is also like others? Do you enjoy humiliating yourself?"

Roxana stood up, stuck her hands into her pockets, walked the length of the room and back, and stood in front of Vahab. "Well, suppose I do enjoy it!" She sat on the floor and hid her face in the pleats of her skirt. Her shoulders were shaking under the material of her jacket. "I am inferior to all of them."

Vahab went to the window and gazed at the garden. He was biting the palm of his hand. He thought her weeping was an auspicious sign. After a pause, restlessly, he walked back to the woman and put his hand on her shoulder. "Don't promise a great deal to yourself! No one considers you to be inferior."

Roxana raised her head. "Tell me the truth. I can take it."

"I know you can. More than that, you are even prepared to ally yourself with everyone in order to torment yourself."

Roxana turned toward the garden. "It is raining. You are such a good man!"

Vahab knelt. "For you, I am as good as you wish."

The woman took a deep breath and pressed her palms on her cheeks. "I know."

Vahab stroked her hair. "What tumult is going on in this beautiful head?"

"It will calm down. Will it not?"

The man put the tips of his fingers on his lips. "I wish I could steal you away."

"Well, what are you waiting for? Coward! You can't."

Vahab was irritated. "I am not a coward. It is you who pulls back."

The sound of the woman's laughter resonated under the ceiling. "I pull back? This is not my first time."

The man sat on the sofa and frowned. "How many people have stolen you away?"

"Only one person."

"Who?"

"Myself!"

"What kind of pleasure do you get out of being a liar?"

Roxana shrugged her shoulders. "The same old story! My ears are full of being called a liar."

"Let everyone go to hell. Material stealing is not important. They have stolen from your life."

"You are wasting my time speaking about others. Such a dead end! Look at the other side of the issue as well. How do you know that I have not stolen from their lives?"

"You are really funny. They would not even dream of being under the same roof with you. When this dream became a reality, they lost themselves."

The woman smiled. "Marenko?"

Vahab messed up his hair with the tips of his fingers. "What sin have I committed that I must constantly hear the name of that little man? Every time I hear it, I get dizzy and get a rash. Think of me once in a while!"

Roxana got off the floor and sat on the sofa. "When I turn my back to anything, there is no going back. You have cocooned yourself in the past. Enough already!"

The man leaned his head against the back of the sofa and stared at the ceiling. "I will take you to Kashmir, to a boathouse. With every breeze, the flower petals pour in through the door and windows. It is always springtime."

Roxana looked at him out of the corner of her eye. "Eternal spring?"

Vahab's eyes sparkled. "From the bottom of the valley, we can hear the sound of trumpets and drums."

"But that sound is from Tibet."

The man stared at the floral designs of the carpet. "We must find the house under the veranda of which I was standing until morning. It had pink curtains."

Roxana frowned. "Was that girl very beautiful? Like Rahila?"

Vahab looked at the woman's profile. "While you exist? I do not think so."

"My time is past."

"You are a little girl at the end of the line."

Roxana gathered her legs and put her hands on her knees. "Another instability? I wish I were my own age."

"Then you would not be Roxana. You would be like others."

The woman smiled. "Much better!"

"From the moment a person becomes a possessor of dates and a calendar, he or she moves toward senility."

Roxana grabbed Vahab's arm. "Then when will my senility begin?"

"From your birth."

The woman laughed out loud. "I believe you. I am not very intelligent."

"Great! Otherwise, you would set the world on fire."

"It is not too late yet."

"Yes, you are capable of it."

"The people have reached a dead end."

"What is it to you? Are you their guardian?"

"They transmigrate into me."

"Don't make a big deal of it! It is not new at all. History is full of such things."

"You are so regressive!"

"I have no objection. But those who are regressive occasionally see more clearly."

"Because they are cowards and egotistical?"

"How about the progressives? Aren't they egotistical?"

"Between you and me, which one is more egotistical?"

"First, let us decide which one of us is more progressive."

The woman raised the corners of her lips in contempt. "You, of course! With your ambergris perfume, Regent suits, and medieval history."

Vahab bent his head. "You don't say, Your Excellency! Just because you wear cotton shoes and talk with Showkat in the stable?"

"So, should I talk with you instead?"

"Yes, at least that would be closer to civilization."

"Do you mean not understanding the people's pain?"

"Then is it when you invent fake pain for the people? Showkat was so happy she was cracking walnuts with her tail. You led her astray."

"Why do you express any opinion when you have no idea about what is going on? Have you seen the documents of the House of Fire? Do you know what a witches' brew they have concocted for her and Hero Qobad?"

"Hero Showkat does not need you. On her own, she can stand up to anyone. You jump into the ring to save two weathered wolves. Hero Qobad had a violent government spinning around his finger for fifty years. He needs no savior."

"What does that have to do with me? It is he who must play the role of the savior."

Vahab put his head on his hands. "How long must this futile sequence of violence and the roaring of guns and machine guns continue?"

Roxana stood up. Her foot caught on the table and toppled a vase. Before it fell to the ground, she caught it. "You do not understand freedom. It has no impact on your soul."

"Love has more impact."

Roxana put the vase back. "Love and freedom are made of the same material."

"Yes, love liberates, but it is unclear what calamity freedom causes for love."

Roxana turned her back to him. "You talk like those in the House of Fire. Have you been reading the newspapers a great deal lately?"

"Since when has the House of Fire become the messenger of love? Unlike you, I have not gotten on the train hissing and fizzing with pages of newspapers in my pocket. I have not looked at any of such scraps of paper, but I shall read them from now on."

"Oh, Vahab, oh, Vahab! Watch what comes out of your mouth! I am not the scarecrow of your melon patch."

"Ah! How good it would be if you were! Then I would not move an inch away from the melon patch. I would sit under your shadow and pull a woolen hat over your eyes."

"No one can pull a woolen hat over my eyes."

"Of course, other than the operators of the theaters, sham intellectuals, and masquerading artists, such as Marenko." Roxana punched the little cushion. Vahab put his finger to his lips. "Don't raise a lot of dust! Did you see that you got angry? Then you see some truth behind what I say—otherwise, you would have laughed."

Roxana lowered her eyelids and through the slits of half-open eyes stared at the corner of the wall. Her nostrils flared. "We were not good for each other. Marenko was not happy, either."

"I am not responsible for other people's happiness. He had to be stuck with you for a lifetime. Do you know why? Because he got inspiration from you to write poetry, to move beyond his capabilities. What does he do now? With a bunch of women, political party hooks and crooks, who emit political arguments like a soaking sponge, he goes here and there. But what has he accomplished? And as for poetry, that has been shut down as well."

The woman's eyes clouded. "Not as bad as that! Under the pressure of the environment, he has lost hope and metamorphosed."

"He gets pocket money from the Association of Forefront Galloping Poets and Writers—what a name! He spends his days like an ordinary middle-aged senile person."

Roxana nodded. "It must be very painful."

"What pain? He has reached where he deserves to be. Behind the glittery image of the Marenko of previous years was your breath."

"You are really going overboard! Just get it out and say that I had created him!"

"Something like that."

"He composed poetry from childhood."

Vahab tossed Yusef's notebook on the table. "Most people do such things in the tumult of their youth. Take it and read it! But what about those who continue?"

Roxana picked up the notebook and thumbed through it. "Read what?"

"Yusef's poetry of his youth!"

The woman closed the notebook. "That good-looking boy? Has he composed poetry? He doesn't look the sort. He is very hard and stubborn."

"He is asking for your opinion. Apparently, it is vital for him. I don't think he is hard and stubborn."

"Is he under the influence of Marenko?"

"In his circumstances, who isn't? Neutralize this influence!"

"That is not my mission. Time is a good teacher."

"He is awaiting an answer."

"Tell him they are excellent."

"You do not like people. You pursue danger on the basis of some broad assumption."

"Quit that, Vahab! Every moment has value."

The man put his hand on her head. "Roxana! Live! Nothing equals that."

Roxana looked into his eyes lovingly and grabbed his wrist. "How good is the shadow of your hands!" She leaned her head on the cushion. "Go outside, the darling of my heart!"

Vahab perked up his ears. He heard the sound of Hero Qobad's crutch. The old man stepped into the parlor. Roxana stood up in a hurry. Vahab said hello, went out, and returned to the courtyard. He stood by the flowerbed of tuberoses. In between the wet stems, he saw the torn pieces of a photograph. He squatted down and arranged the scattered pieces side by side. Marenko's lusterless eyes were disintegrating under the drizzling rain. Yusef was walking away on the gravel path.

Chapter 10

They had had potatoes for dinner. They did not have the appetite they used to have. Hero Rashid, Yavar, and Kowkab cleared the table. Hero Torkan shook the decorative lace tablecloth out the window. In the moonlight, bread crumbs fell to the ground, twirling. Hero Showkat sat in the corner of the sofa, facing the window. She leaned her back and arms on the small cushions. Borzu whispered something into her ear. Without looking away from the landscape through the window, Showkat said: "The same issue. Go!"

Borzu yanked off the glass bead of the cushion, put it on his palm, and blew on it. The shiny glass bead rolled under the easy chair. "I can't figure it out. Have you turned a hundred and eighty degrees?"

"Have you measured it? Showkat listens to the sound of her heart."

"What about the plans for the future?"

"Sing its swan song."

"I wanted to finish my education and become a doctor."

"Well, become one! Who's stopping you?"

"Do you expect me to stand up to you? Impossible! The ground under my feet has softened. I see what I could not see up to yesterday. There is wheeling and dealing going on in the hospital. They take the government drugs to the black market and sell them for several times the original price."

"Well, there you go! What did I tell you?"

"Maybe the House of Fire does not know about it."

"With all these snitches? That would be strange."

"The people have developed a bad habit. They should be taught the new culture little by little. It should be injected into their blood like drops out of a syringe. Why has your power of analysis diminished? Do you expect our sick society to be cured overnight?"

Hero Showkat grabbed his arms and slid him away from herself on the soft velvet of the sofa. "Don't talk so much! You are boring me to death! Your snout is constantly moving, and your spiky blond beard going up and down annoys me. You are blocking the moon."

"The moon is always there, but the average lifespan in underdeveloped societies is between sixty and seventy years."

"You can have it. We don't want a natural lifespan. Just this artificial lifespan is more than enough for us."

"But you aren't a rebel, are you?"

"Don't label me, you son-of-a-bitch. If you are offended, report me!"

"Others report it."

Showkat half rose and threw a small cushion at the cupboard of dishes. The Heroes ducked their heads.

Borzu whispered: "Even if they torture me by separating all my joints, I would not speak out against you."

Showkat shrugged her shoulders. "When water passes over one's head, it doesn't matter how high it is."

"That is precisely the point. It has not passed over your head. You can make up for it."

"So, I should make up for it? You mean I should go to the House of Fire and lick boots, like others do? Haddadiyan, who has dozens of faces, is now in charge of everything and makes threats against Hero Showkat. Should I go and kiss his hand?"

Borzu's hazel eyes widened behind his eyeglasses. "You are mistaken. He isn't even regarded as worth chickenshit."

"You must have been sleeping, my dear boy. Now he has become the special head chickenshit, because he is such a good flatterer. Now they shower him with perfume and candy."

"Where the hell has he gone now?"

"He'll show up. Don't worry your little head!"

The student removed his hat, put it on his knee, and crouched up. "I was the one who cut his mustache."

Showkat burst out laughing. "You rascal!" Her face suddenly became serious. "Borzu, look! I have a request of you. Forget about me! Go and get to your studies! Become a doctor. Serve the poor and hungry sick people to make me happy with you. It is not unlikely that you won't see me again. People are together one day, and they separate from one another the next day."

Borzu dropped his hat on the ground. His hands were shaking. "Hero Showkat! Without you, I am nothing."

"Stop that poppycock, or I'll punch you in the mouth, you moron! You are educated. Your existence is important for the society. What do you have to do with the vagrant rootless Showkat?"

"Hero Showkat! In any case, without you, I am nothing."

Showkat put his hat back on his head. "You are just beginning to not look like a scrawny stick. You've gotten some meat on your bones. How are the grades from your trimester? You must advance and take care of the people close to you!"

Borzu flushed up to his ears. "What people are close to me? You, at least, know that."

Hero Kaveh had crossed his legs and was whistling quietly.

Hero Showkat yelled: "Quiet, Kaveh! You have also become a calamity in our lives. Good for nothing! You either smoke like a chimney, stink up the air with your cologne, or show the six-by-four pictures of some sluts and say that they killed themselves because of your ugly little mug, mustache, and hair. And now you make noises like cockroaches in a public bath."

Hero Kaveh sat up straight. "It is an old song. They used to sing it for Qobad."

"What does Qobad have to do with you, you dandified sleazeball?"

Kaveh twirled his thumbs. "Don't underestimate me! I have been a fighter for freedom my whole life."

"But, of course, with women like that, you were smeared in muck."

"Hero Showkat, you are really steamed up tonight!"

Kowkab came close to the sofa. "What are we going to do? Are they going to make us homeless or not?"

"Put your tail between your legs, drop by the House of Fire, and ask them."

"What difference does it make? You are also a member of the House of Fire."

"Go, get off my back! You're all just sitting here in comfort and breaking all the pots and jugs over the head of wretched Showkat because you blame her. And you have nothing to worry about whatsoever. The members of the House of Fire are the implementers of the law. They aren't the lawmakers. By the end of the month, it will be decided in a meeting what everyone is supposed to do. They will either put the house up for auction, replace you with another group, or, the least likely, you are going to stay here for now."

Mrs. Edrisi leaned forward. "Put it up for auction?"

"Then, no, they'll pickle it. This was the plan from the beginning."

Vahab punched the wall. "You have piled up in this place, and we have learned to get along with you. Is that not enough? So now you talk about auctioning? Are you going to throw us out into the alleyway stark naked? Why don't you put something of your own up for auction?"

"I will put everything I have up for auction. Wait and see whether Hero Showkat is more of a self-sacrificer or you, fart-breath, who are clinging like a lobster so tightly to worldly possessions and walking backward!"

Vahab glanced out of the corner of his eye at Roxana, who was sitting by the piano, smiling.

"To hell with it! Auction it off. I will have a lighter burden."

"Get off it! Showkat knows you. When the time comes, you will be flapping your wings like a bloody fighting cock."

Hero Qadir flicked his finger on the wall. "The plaster has swelled up. The price of the house in this condition will go down."

Hero Showkat scowled at him. "In the middle of all this hullabaloo, all we needed was a real estate agent. Let it go down! What is it to you? Are you a buyer, or a seller?"

"If this house is painted, it will look like a pretty bride."

"The oaf of a bridegroom is shuffling his feet and coming. For now, stick with the bride. You are a real idiot!"

"I know my own work."

"A nobody like you, you stupid fool, should just think bread and cheese, before you drop dead in drool."

"Don't say something that would force me to answer you back!"

Hero Showkat, making smooching sounds and imitating someone sending chickens to their coop, began shoo-shooing.

Hero Pari turned to Torkan. "Some of her screws have come loose tonight."

The corners of Torkan's meaty lips dropped. "When were they not loose?"

Hero Rashid objected. "Enough already! Now everyone has become a big mouth. Why wouldn't you say a peep in front of her? Have you become bold now that you've found out her feet are not on solid ground? I spit on this world!"

Torkan began braiding her hair. Yusef was sitting quietly on the staircase to the library, looking at Roxana. In that dimly lit corner, his pale face was not visible. Roxana got bored and asked him: "You are always hanging around the library. Do you like to read?"

Yusef turned red and coughed. "I live with books. Do you know of a better friend than books?"

The cliché made him embarrassed and he bit his lip.

"Do you have a job?"

"I am a member of the Association of Forefront Galloping Artists."

"What do you do there?"

"We undermine one another."

Roxana laughed. "Nothing new."

"They want to shut it down."

"I read a few of your poems."

Yusef walked closer and sat on the stair. "What did you think?"

"Do you like Marenko's poems?" Yusef kept silent. "In any case, you are not exempt from his influence."

Sweat beaded on the young man's upper lip. "I know that I have not yet achieved anything. My work is unrefined; but from here on, I intend to be independent."

"Universal human issues are always the same. Only points of view and manners of expression change."

"For me, literature has to be tangible. Do you not believe in human salvation?"

The woman leaned her head against the wall. "I have not found the answer yet. There might be human salvation, but not in this lifetime."

"Salvation comes with kindness."

Roxana smiled faintly. "Who has been kind to you so far?"

Yusef whispered: "You!" Roxana laughed out loud. Vahab looked at them. "No, don't be surprised at all. The tone of your voice is absolute kindness. Despite all your worthy attributes, you display no arrogance. You make one feel secure, like an old friend."

The woman stared at the flushed face of the young man. "You are not old enough to have seen me onstage. How do you know about my worthy attributes?"

"If you had come here, I would have seen you onstage. I am old enough."

"I was not lucky enough, despite the fact that I have dreamed about this city since my youth."

"So, we lost an unparalleled opportunity."

"But if Marenko had come rather than me, it would have been more unparalleled, right?"

The young man held his chin up. "No!" He sank his fingernail into the palm of his hand. "You are different from everyone else."

Roxana looked at the ceiling. "You are wrong. Deep down, we are all alike."

Vahab had approached the piano. Disinterestedly, Yusef looked at him intently. "I am certain that you made this statement out of humility."

"For now, be content with that. But, years later, you shall laugh at such things."

"Hero Roxana. My character has been formed. I am no longer a youth. But if the day comes when I laugh at my beliefs, I will know that I have grown old. Like Hero Qobad, I will not grow old. Old age equals senility."

Showkat approached them and grabbed Yusef's hair. "Speak out loud. I despise buzzing. Vahab doesn't like it either. He has been eavesdropping for a while. Hero Showkat grabs whispers in the air, but this sneaky fellow here can't hear even one word."

Vahab was infuriated. He pounded on the piano with his fist. "Unlike you, I am not an eavesdropper. I have my principles."

"Yeah, sure! I know. If you get the chance, you even look through the keyhole."

Vahab kicked over a chair. "You are the spy, who even watches people's houses from above the jetting fountain to prepare reports for the House of Fire."

"I do what I do to achieve my goal, but you are a spy by nature."

"Keep your rotten beliefs to yourself. I'll blow the whistle on all your goals and moles. Unethical actions are not permissible under any condition."

Showkat assumed a posture of attack. "I will dislocate your jaws. I'd be worse than a rabid dog if I didn't throw everything you have to the wind."

"You have already thrown everything to the wind. Do you think you are scaring a kid? Call me a cuckold if I were to let people like you bully me. Go ahead, step into the ring if you want to wrestle!"

Mrs. Edrisi stood up. "This is not a wrestling ring. Go outside to settle your accounts!"

Roxana approached them and grabbed Showkat's arm. "At least have respect for Hero Qobad!" She glared at Vahab. "You, of course, do not understand these things."

Showkat spat on the floor. "In his skull, instead of a brain, he has cow manure. A mule understands better than he does."

Vahab spat at the wall. "Then, you who understands, please be quiet!"

Rashid joined the group. "Hero Vahab, I did not expect you to be like that! Please let it go."

Showkat brought her head forward and shook it uncontrollably. The tips of her rough hair touched Vahab's face. The man pulled back and scratched his cheek. Showkat bellowed: "Since when has this good-for-nothing become a Hero?"

Vahab clenched his fists. "I spit on all the Heroes! Do you think you are something special? Every horsefly nowadays is tying the title of 'Hero' to its tail. I do not want the title of those who work for the House of Fire."

Showkat puffed up her cheeks. "Go ahead and ask for it! Like they are offering it to you on a silver platter?"

Vahab threw up his hands, and the underarms of his jacket ripped.

In the distance, Qadir said: "He's become rabid."

With an air of haughtiness, Vahab said: "I have learned it from you Heroes."

Leqa circled the group and walked to her nephew. "Shame on you! You are worse than the riffraff. You show no respect for several ladies who are here."

Vahab pushed Leqa aside. "Several Heroes, not ladies!"

Showkat laughed boisterously. "Now I understand what irks the fellow. Obviously, he wishes he was wiggling among a bunch of pretty spiffed-up females and for us to make sultry eyes at him and wiggle our butts."

Vahab held his hands before his eyes. "Heaven forbid! I prefer the Angel of Death."

Showkat turned her back to him and walked away with her hands on her hips. "Let him go, man! Isn't it a waste of my time to make my blood boil for this sewage rat?"

Rashid ran and bowed to her. "Hero, I salute you!"

Mrs. Edrisi held her hand before her mouth and laughed inaudibly.

Leqa walked to her mother. "Why are you laughing? One had to cry seeing what he does. He makes that student, Borzu, look respectable."

The veins on Borzu's neck swelled. He stood up. "I do not at all want you to compare this good-for-nothing thug with me. I am a scholar and educated. I am dignified and have self-respect. He is a thug who puts one foot on this side of the gutter and the other foot on the other side and utters obscene insults."

Mrs. Edrisi nodded. "His mouth has no latches and locks."

Borzu picked his hat up from the floor, dusted it with his sleeve, and put it on his head. Frowning, he sat down and crossed his legs. He stroked his mustache with the tips of his fingers and turned to Showkat. "Hero! I must convey that speaking to such individuals is seriously beneath your status."

Showkat raised the corners of her lips. "I know that already."

Rokhsareh entered through the half-open door and sat in the corner of the wall. She raised her knees and pressed them to her belly. The color of her face was grayish. She was panting, and her throat was emitting moaning sounds.

Yavar bent down toward her and asked: "Would you like a cup of sweetened hot water?"

The woman shook her head in the negative. "What is going on? There was noise and commotion again. We have a reputation to protect before the neighbors. What my master, God rest his soul, said rings in my ears, 'Even if there is blood and blood shedding in the house, don't let the neighbors get a whiff of it, because later on, they will spread the news with bugles and drums.'"

Yavar hit his forehead in exasperation. "My dear friend! Those days are past and gone. Nowadays, disgracefulness is a source of pride."

Rokhsareh sighed. "Do you really mean that?"

With the gestures of his eyes and head, the old man pointed at Showkat. "Have you forgotten her disgraceful behavior? Rope jumping, knife throwing, whistling like a nightingale, and a thousand other shameful things. I have been in this house for nearly fifty years. I swear on all that I hold sacred that I had never seen any woman to do such things."

From the bottom of her throat, Rokhsareh said: "It is really shameful."

Teymur approached them and leaned against the wall. "The house is done for. They have put it up for auction."

Rokhsareh held her hands by her ears. "Did you say auction? But we aren't bankrupt."

"Then, with no clothes on our backs, do you think we are top merchants? If not, what would you say we are?"

"But the lady mistress is well-to-do."

Teymur took his empty clay pipe out of his pocket, placed it between his lips, and looked at the ceiling. "Like this house has a lady mistress?"

With her finger, Rokhsareh pointed to the elderly lady, Mrs. Edrisi. "Then what is she?"

"An unfortunate person, like us."

"Have they taken her wealth and property from her?"

"Everyone's property belongs to the government."

The woman scratched her face in distress. "Then where are they going to take us?"

"Your situation is clear. You'll go to the hospital."

"I'm afraid of hospitals. They stick brain-numbing needles into your veins there. God only knows if you'll get out of there. I wish I had a kennel, like dogs and cats, where I would put my head down in the dark and die."

Teymur puffed on his empty pipe. "If my son comes back, we will help you." He put the clay pipe on the floor and sat on his feet. He rubbed his rough hands on the coarse material of his trousers. "Last night, I dreamed that he had come back. He had become a total gentleman. He had a private carriage. He hugged me, and we got into the carriage and started going. We reached a bright place with a lot of jetting fountains."

Rokhsareh dropped her head. "Has he sent you a letter lately?"

The old man's chin quivered. "Well, he is young and busy with a thousand things. Hero Kaveh said that he had become a ship's captain who goes to the middle of the sea and catches tons of fish."

"So he sends you money."

Teymur shook his head regretfully. "No, the government does not allow it."

"Didn't he send money before?"

Teymur slapped his knee. "My pride would not let me. But a person changes. Old age brings humility."

Rokhsareh looked at her own crooked fingers. "I was humble from the beginning of my life. Pride belongs to the well-off. I tied the shoestrings of the children myself. I would not throw away leftover food. I would eat it. In front of other servants, my mistress would say, 'I appreciate Rokhsareh's frugality.'"

Hero Kukan joined them. Everyone became quiet and dropped their heads. The smell of leather mingled with sweaty feet from his old brown shoes assaulted Yavar's nose. The old man scratched his nose. "Kukan, don't you bathe? Your head and hair are greasy."

The man stroked his hair. He was wearing a long, narrow-waisted checkered jacket with four silver buttons. His short pants had cuffs, and the style of his clothing belonged to at least twenty years earlier. "I bathe twice a month. If you wash your hair too often, you lose your hair. Back then, the wife of a doctor was the customer of our tailor shop. She was cute, spent a lot of money, and she had taste." He locked the little fingers of both hands together like rings. "She and I were like this. Don't have bad thoughts, we were like brother and sister. She always said, 'Kukan, you make me calm.' While she waited for me to finish the hidden stitches on her new dress and sew the buttons, she would open her heart to me, shed tears, and drink coffee. One day she told me, 'Kukan, don't wash your hair so often!'" He smiled and his caked-up teeth became visible. His eyes sparkled. "At that time, I really took care of my looks. I wore fashionable clothes. I had my hair curled. Don't look at the way I am now! I was a sight to behold. When I shaved and freshened up, I would go for a walk around sunset on Warshawskaya Street. High school girls followed me step by step. I remember that I was incidentally wearing this same jacket." He turned around and showed the bow on the waist and the vent in the back. "It is a perfect style; it is becoming to my figure. A girl passed me by and made a cute humorous come-on. 'I wish there was a priest right now, right here who would marry the two of us.' When she walked away, I laughed so much that my knees buckled and I leaned my head on a tree. They were so naughty. I was telling you about the doctor's wife. She said, 'Dear Kukan, believe me, I love you like a brother. Don't wash your hair so much! Wouldn't it be a pity to lose that hair? If you wash it too much, it will fall out.' She had learned that from her husband." He stroked his greasy hair. "My hair isn't too bad. It hasn't turned white and it has not fallen out. May the doctor's wife always be fondly remembered."

Wearing a black cloak over his shoulders, Hero Yunos spun in the middle of the room.

Kaveh made a drawn-out whistle. "You are in a really good mood tonight."

Yunos clapped his hands.

"Drink wine in the moonlight,
Oh beauty that is moonlike
Since the moon shines a lot,
Although not on our lot."

Kaveh sang the song and Yunos danced, stomping his feet and swaying his head and shoulders.

Mrs. Edrisi turned to Leqa. "Accompany him!"

Leqa immediately sat at the piano and struck her experienced fingers on the keys. Kaveh, Rashid, and Qadir were clapping their hands. Under the light of the chandelier on the purple carpet, Hero Yunos jumped up and down. His black cloak flapped in the air like the wings of a bird, lifting him off the ground. His thin hair would land on his high forehead. His left eye shone like a red ruby.

Kaveh walked to Showkat. "Stop frowning, Hero! It is an interesting dance."

In disgust, Showkat held her nose. "This is the dance of sorcerers. He has learned it from the Blacks."

Kaveh lowered his head and snapped his fingers. "Yes, the Blacks are masters of dancing. Unfortunately, I have not seen the heart of Africa, the depths of the Sahara, and the jungles. But I did live for a while in Benghazi and Tangier. They say that they cure illnesses and depression with dancing and singing."

Showkat chuckled. "Such cheekiness!"

Borzu pushed up his eyeglasses. "Every child knows that the only cause of an illness is a microbe and contamination that can be cured by drugs or abstinence. I do not know when we backward people will be free from being enslaved to superstitions. A few days ago, I was passing through Seven Springs Square. I saw two old women who were tossing coins into a small pool. I went and picked up the coins in order to chastise them."

Teymur, Qadir, Yavar, and Kukan sat on chairs in a circle. Hero Qobad stroked his mustache, smiling. The foggy screen that covered his eyes had moved aside. It was as though from the strange dance of Yunos he had become ecstatic. Without the help of the crutch, he stood up, and, before falling down, he remembered the lack of one leg. He fell into the easy chair and slapped his knee.

Teymur put his clay pipe on the table, shook the dust off his trousers, and stood in the middle of the room. From the bottom of his throat, in a husky voice, he roared, and in the manner of desert dwellers, he spun on the medallion of the carpet, clapping his hands. He bent his knees, and, in harmony with the movement of his feet, he emitted a beast-like sound. His dance resembled the jumping up and down and attacks by demons. The rays of the full moon were making Qobad, Yunos, and Teymur ecstatic. They had slept for long periods of time on the mountains, in forests, and in deserts, and moonlight had been their blanket. The domestic Heroes did not have that experience.

Borzu removed his hat and bent down in front of Showkat. "Hero, won't you enter the dancing arena?"

The woman immediately jumped up, moved her head and shoulders, opened her arms, and punched her chest. "Yunos! Take away your tattered cloak! I would like to dance. If you get close to me, I'll smash your mouth and chin."

Yunos spun, and his cloak rubbed against Showkat's arm. Showkat tripped him, and Yunos stumbled, flashing the red rays of his left eye on Showkat's face. The woman pounded his side with her elbow. "Blind idiot! What eyes! They're horrifying."

Yunos closed his right eye, and the fiery sparks of the left eye lit up his face. "Is this better?"

Showkat shrugged her shoulders. "If only you were just a cyclops. What kind of sinister face is that? It reminds me of an incubus. If you come to anybody's dream at night, he'd jump off the ground a couple of yards. Heaven forbid! The kind of shitty creatures wiggling around on this earth!"

Hero Yunos opened his right eye and dropped the cloak on the floor. Showkat turned her back to him. "I don't know how to dance like monkeys, and I don't look like a monkey. Now, I'll show you."

Teymur came closer, clapping his hands. "Hero, instead of quarreling, dance and be happy! Our lives are like a dream."

Showkat clapped her hands and, jumping, stopped under the chandelier. She ordered Leqa: "Lezgi!"

She kicked the chairs away from around her.

Leqa bent down and moved her fingers on the keys. An exciting Lezgi tune resonated under the high ceiling. Hero Showkat sat on her feet and threw her right- and left-booted feet into the air alternately. She was spinning like a pinwheel, and her sweat-covered face would become concealed behind her hair. Kowkab, Pari, and Torkan watched with their mouths open. Leaping several times, Hero Showkat reached the table, picked up a chair by its back legs, and raised it slowly. The oval back cushion collided with the cut crystal prisms of the chandelier. Several teardrop-shaped crystal prisms broke. She went away from under the chandelier, cursed under her breath, and placed the two legs on her shoulders. The seat of the chair concealed her flushed face. She opened her arms, crossed her feet, and, in time with the music, she jumped up and down, clicking her boots every time before she descended. At the peak of rising, she would maintain the balance of the chair perfectly. From afar, she resembled a person with a big pot on her head, jumping up and spinning. Vahab was standing near the piano, leaning against the wall and laughing boisterously. Leqa lifted her head and frowned at Vahab. Roxana was clapping her hands enthusiastically. Hero Showkat bent her knees, held her head toward the ceiling, and placed a chair leg on her forehead. The muscles of her arms and back were contracted and quivering, her veins swollen, and her cheeks flushed. Leqa stopped playing. The onlookers held their breath. Only the sound of Showkat's intermittent breathing could be heard in the silence. She was pressing her lips together, and bubbles would ooze out of her mouth. The onlookers applauded spontaneously. In honor of Hero Showkat, by leaning on the back of the easy chair, Qobad began to stand up, held the crutch like a Brno rifle, pressed it on his shoulder, and shook it. Showkat's waist arched. She put her head on the ground, slipped the legs of the chair on the carpet, leaped up, and, with her hand on her chest, took a bow. For the first time, she looked embarrassed. Kaveh took the half-burned cigarette from the corner of his lips and squished it on the plate. Qobad's eyes sparkled. "Now, all of you, dance together!"

Rashid, Qadir, and Kaveh removed the chairs. With the exception of Mrs. Edrisi, Rokhsareh, and Hero Qobad, everyone stood up. They brought Vahab by force and formed a circle. The sound of the piano peaked with the music of the "Ballad of the Battle of the Mountain." Roxana sang the first stanza. Kaveh and Yunos continued it. Yusef, Rashid, and the women accompanied them. They sang the refrains in the wrong order. Qobad raised his hand. Everyone became silent. The old man sang the ballad from the beginning in a husky voice. On the other side of the parlor, Rokhsareh was clapping joyfully, as though she had come to watch a wedding celebration. The door opened.

Startled, Rokhsareh got up and took refuge in the library. A band of Fire Stokers stormed into the parlor and aimed the barrels of the revolvers at the inhabitants of the house. The broad-shouldered one and the scrawny one were standing in front of the group. The order was issued for them to fire. They shot toward the ceiling, which caused pieces of plaster to fall down. The smell of gunpowder filled the air. Moayyad and Haddadiyan stood shoulder to shoulder at the threshold of the door. Haddadiyan was wearing the uniform of the House of Fire. He was pounding the shiny leather of his boots with the tip of his whip. The chest of Moayyad's black uniform shone with stars and insignias. He walked toward the sofa and struck the table with his whip. The piano lid fell on Leqa's fingers.

In the corner of the wall, Mrs. Edrisi shifted from her place, held her head high, and smiled with dry lips. "In which direction did the sun rise that you remembered us after twenty years?"

The muscles under Moayyad's eyes quivered. He raised his thick eyebrows. "I do not recognize you."

The elderly lady nodded. "Yes, I had forgotten. You recognize people in accordance with the circumstances."

Moayyad drew an X in the air with the tip of his whip. "Be careful! We are armed."

"Be careful about what?"

"Every improper word will make the charges against you more substantial."

"What will happen then?"

"Naturally, you shall be punished."

"You have personally punished us already. You had a good memory, although you disappeared immediately."

"Advanced age has made you absent-minded."

The elderly lady bit her lip. "By the way, do you still own the properties in Afanasi, Gharajedagh, and Bahar? You and I know well the manner in which you came to take possession of them."

Moayyad raised his hands and looked at the ceiling. "My past is as clear as day. Everyone knows that I have given all I possessed to the people."

"To the government of the House of Fire?"

Moayyad turned to Haddadiyan. "Write it down. The meaning of what she said is to separate the people from the House of Fire."

Haddadiyan sat at the table, took out a notebook from his pocket, and stroked his newly grown mustache. "You can be sure, nothing will be left out."

Mrs. Edrisi pulled her shawl over her shoulders. "It is you who interpret what I said in that way. Obviously, you yourself have doubts."

Moayyad held his hands behind his back. "There is no doubt in my being. I am the embodiment of belief."

Mrs. Edrisi took a deep breath. "Seriously, has the House of Fire accepted you, despite all your past deeds?"

The man touched the stars and insignias on his chest. "You are shortsighted."

"It was rumored throughout the city that you had killed several farmers." She turned to Yavar. "Isn't that so?"

In the dark corner of the parlor, Yavar shifted on his feet and remained silent.

Moayyad sat down. His moist forehead shone. "Rumors belong to old women."

"If they belong to old women, should I pour all of them on the tambourine and reveal them all?"

Moayyad turned red and, in a milder tone, said: "Take a note of this! We have not come here to spend our time talking about the decadent past. The life of no human being is free from errors and transgressions. We were all victims of an unhealthy society. In the claws of repression, we did not have the opportunity for discussions. They stifled the voices of truth and justice in our throats. We had no lamp lighting our path to understand the lofty concepts of humanity. Finally, with the dawn of victory, the bats and flittermice disappeared. The sun of the dictatorship of the proletariat began to shine brightly."

Mrs. Edrisi took a handkerchief out of her pocket and rubbed her cheek. "How tender-hearted you are! Even though the situation and conditions were not as dire as you say. People distributed underground newspapers close by you; they were sent to prisons and exile, and at night one could hear the sound of gunfire from the top of the mountain. Perhaps it was not expedient for you to hear those sounds."

"Do you know about what goes on in other people's minds? Do you know this Moayyad? Do you know the things he has done? He has given up everything for the stability of the government. The servants of the masses, however, are aware of it. My constructive ideas, without the slightest changes, are at the service of the Central House of Fire. The new order requires decisiveness. Experience has taught me that nothing remains stable in the world. The efforts of the mountain movement during the rule of the military government were, of course, valuable, but in the rule of the masses, absolute faith and obedience is the requirement for victory."

Roxana came down the stairs of the library and stood in front of Moayyad. The man wiped the sweat off his brow with the back of his hand, stood up, walked to the window, and rubbed the windowpane with his finger. "What cold weather!" He turned around and looked at Roxana from head to toe. "So, you're the actress?"

"Don't be too sure!"

Moayyad swallowed. "Why have you come to this city? Do you have written permission?"

Roxana gazed in the man's eyes. "There is a thick file in my name in the House of Fire. Have you not seen it?"

The man walked toward the piano and opened its lid. Leqa turned her back to him in disgust. Moayyad flicked his fingers on the keys. "Are you a rebel?"

"Making accusations before the crime is proven is illegal. Did you know that?"

The man waved the whip. "Investigation is not necessary. You have committed a crime. The sound of your singing a song could be heard at the end of the alleyway. You have deprived the people of their sleep. The House of Fire considers such rebellious acts, absolutely and without a doubt, the commission of riots."

"What song did we sing? Are such things as condemning the military regime and honoring the movement of the mountain considered opposition to the House of Fire? Why do you, who constantly talk about the government of the people, not respect their wishes?"

"The House of Fire is the manifestation of the people. On whose order were you singing?"

Roxana turned to the Fire Stokers. "Do you know the song?"

The scrawny one lowered the barrel of the gun, held his head high, and sang the first stanza under his breath. Haddadiyan yelled: "Silence! Otherwise, you shall be put on trial on the charge of being an accomplice of the rioters!"

The scrawny one stood at attention.

Moayyad walked closer to the table and put his hand on Haddadiyan's shoulder. "Along with the Fire Stokers, keep watch on every individual in the house! I will go to the House of Fire to obtain the order of the central authorities."

Stomping her feet, Hero Showkat approached Moayyad and placed her hands on her hips. "Hey, you lazy moron! Have you forgotten that Showkat is here? You leech, are you trying to make her scared of the Fire Stokers? These kids grew up under my care. May you go blind from jealousy, I am still one of the main members of the House of Fire. Pack up your junk and get the hell out!"

Moayyad caressed the fleshy mole on his cheek and widened his eyes. "Not so fast! You are being dismissed."

Showkat picked up her whip from the ledge of the wall and drew an X in the air. "Have they announced the ruling for my dismissal? Then give it to me!"

"They will announce it one of these days. Don't be in a hurry!"

Showkat mussed her hair. "You are lying, you son of a bitch!" She walked toward the Fire Stokers. "Get out! Why are you looking so confused? Hero Showkat is ordering you."

The scrawny one and the broad-shouldered one clicked their heels, stood at attention before Showkat, and in orderly steps marched toward the door.

Moayyad shouted: "Wait! Where are you going?"

The scrawny one turned around. "Our commander is Hero Showkat!" He took a piece of paper out of his pocket and held it out to Moayyad. "It is a written order. Read it!"

Moayyad became enraged, pushed back the Fire Stoker's hand, and left the entrance hall.

Showkat stood on the stairs and shouted: "Come back again and I will break both your shins."

Moayyad opened the courtyard door and stood between the double doors. "The future shall reveal all."

Hero Showkat ran toward the man, picked up a rock off the ground, and hit the man on his leg, hard. Moayyad left and slammed the door shut.

The broad-shouldered one burst out laughing. Hero Showkat punched his arm. "That little coward of a squirt! He took off like a rat."

The broad-shouldered one asked: "Did you get upset, Hero?"

Showkat knit her brow. "Did you expect me to take pleasure in your gunshots and fire and the insolence of these two dogs with mustaches?"

The scrawny one sniffed a cluster of jasmine. "We are also baffled and confused. Wait, and everything will be fine."

Hero Showkat looked at the sky. The moon disappeared behind the clouds.

Chapter 11

Hero Rashid and the women took the fallen plaster to the courtyard and swept the floor of the parlor. Yawning, Haddadiyan climbed the staircase in the entrance hall. Showkat yelled: "Hey, jackass! Where are you going?"

Haddadiyan touched the buttons of his uniform. "From now on, you must obey me!"

Hero Showkat jumped, yanked off a button from his jacket, and smashed it under the heel of her boot. "You are showing off to Showkat with a handful of gilded pieces of tin? Didn't you learn anything? Go ahead."

Hero Showkat called out to Borzu, Rashid, Yusef, and Kowkab: "Come here right now. Let's tie the hands and feet of this bully of a thug and toss him in some corner."

They all assembled and grabbed the man. Haddadiyan yelled from the depths of his belly, threatening and cursing. Showkat took off Pari's headscarf, wrapped it around her hand, and walked to Haddadiyan. "I'm going to tie up your mouth and snout!"

Roxana joined the others. "Silence him! His yelling can be heard from outside."

Showkat punched him on the head.

Haddadiyan pleaded: "Don't kill me!"

Roxana went up the stairs. "Idiot! They have really duped you. They are testing you. How would it be possible for the House of Fire to prefer you to Showkat?"

Hero Showkat tied up the man's mouth with the headscarf. "Don't bother with him. Let him shut his trap!"

The Heroes took Haddadiyan up the staircase to the interior balcony. Showkat caught her breath. "Kukan's room has only one window."

Roxana suggested: "Close it!"

Showkat kicked open the door to the room. They tossed the man on the bed and bound him with rope.

Borzu and Rashid brought several boards from the basement and nailed them on the window.

Hero Showkat jumped up and touched the ceiling with her finger. "Good thing we got rid of him."

Yusef smiled and went down the stairs lightheartedly. His soft black hair swayed every time he jumped and changed color in the light of the wall lamps. His leaping resembled that of a fawn.

Roxana leaned on the banister and stroked the protruded designs. Mrs. Edrisi was standing beside the willow-leaf vase, looking at Roxana. "What are you thinking about?"

"I was thinking about youth."

"Are you distanced from your youth?"

"Several times more than others, I have expended love and excitement on life. Now I am worn out, to the marrow of my bones." She raised her head and came down the stairs. "Where is Hero Qobad? We only have until midnight."

A shiver ran through the elderly lady's body. "He is in the parlor."

Hero Showkat was standing in the corner of the entrance hall, leaning against the wall. Roxana approached and whispered something to her. Showkat walked to the middle of the entrance hall and clapped her hands. "Everyone, go to bed! Turn off the lights. I would like the house to look normal, as though nothing has happened."

Heroes Pari, Torkan, and Kowkab went upstairs, yawning. Rokhsareh went to the door of the kitchen. "This is my place. I will doze off on the chair. When the pain increases, I will make hot water and drink it with sugar cubes."

Hero Rashid went to his own room.

With a ladder on his shoulder, Hero Qadir entered the entrance hall. "I'm afraid it's going to rain." Holding onto the banister and, creasing his brow, he went to the second floor.

Yusef came into the entrance hall from the courtyard. Tiny drops of dew were shining on his hair. He sat in front of Showkat's feet. "Hero, you are extraordinary!"

Showkat kicked him. "Get lost! Get your butt to bed!"

"I am so happy that I have become sleepless."

"Who's worried about you sleeping? Go to your room and shut up. Pull the quilt over your head and roll around till morning."

"How cruel!"

"Have you met me?"

Yusef got up, and, before disappearing in the dark, he looked at Roxana from afar. The woman waved at him. The young man went up the stairs on his tiptoes.

Kukan came out of the parlor and turned to Showkat. "Where should I sleep tonight?"

Roxana came closer. "Hero Showkat, your room!"

Showkat frowned. "He smells."

Roxana called out to Vahab. He immediately appeared between the double doors. She said: "Spray some perfume on Kukan!"

Vahab frowned and shook his head in regret. "The rarest perfume in the world!"

Hero Showkat flapped her arms. "Oh, no! Don't even mention its name! The smell of rotten fish is far better than that concoction."

Vahab closed the door. "This essence has been prepared in the dark depths of the ocean, among coral branches, sea fairies, and sunken ships, and you don't like it?"

"Keep it all to yourself!"

Mrs. Edrisi laughed and turned to Vahab. "Aren't you planning to go to bed tonight?"

"Do you think I am a sheep?"

"Even if you are, I hadn't thought about it."

"I have had a sleeping problem for a lifetime. Now, are these the conditions you suggest for solving it?"

"In my opinion, the situation isn't that bad."

"Then go to sleep yourself!"

Showkat sent Kukan upstairs. "Take the sheet with you! Don't cover yourself with mine!"

Hero Kukan went upstairs smiling, proud of being able to go to sleep in Showkat's bed.

Showkat called out to Yunos. He came out of the parlor with the black cloak on his shoulders and his left eyelid closed. Showkat grabbed Vahab's arm and led him close to Yunos. "Take this unwanted nosy jackass with you!"

Vahab released his arm from her grasping fingers. "What you do has nothing to do with me. I can guess what kind of a jam you are going to get yourselves into." He looked at Roxana angrily. "It is not appealing at all."

Showkat pulled on a lock of Vahab's hair. "Then take him to the stable! He's used to that."

Vahab accompanied Yunos.

Yavar and Teymur came out of the parlor. Yavar said: "I do not want to be alone. I am frightened."

Hero Teymur suggested: "I will go to his room."

Showkat shrugged her shoulders. "What are you going to do so he won't be scared?"

"We will smoke the clay pipe and talk about the past."

"Why don't you just go to sleep, like a corpse? Tonight, everybody is twirling around our heads like horseflies." She clapped her hands loudly. "Get out of my sight!"

The old men disappeared in the darkness of the entrance hall.

Showkat, Roxana, and Mrs. Edrisi stepped into the brightly lit parlor. Kaveh was leaning his shoulder against the window frame, smoking a cigarette. Hero Qobad was sitting on the edge of the easy chair. He leaned his chin on the crutch, raised his head, and, in a whisper, asked: "Did they all go to bed?"

Roxana sighed. "We stuffed each one in some corner." She asked Kaveh: "Are you sure you are ready?"

Kaveh blew the cigarette smoke toward the ceiling. "Danger is the spice of life. Every day of my life has been different from the day before. I have traveled from this city to that without money or a future. I have seen death with my own eyes in the storm in the middle of the ocean. I was trapped in the snow in Crete. I have smuggled weapons. From Ain Salah to Agadir, I have traveled through scorching deserts and mountains. I have hidden in caves, and eaten snake soup."

Showkat spat on the ground. "You are making my guts come up my throat. You filth-eating glutton!"

Qobad smiled. "It does not taste too bad. It is similar to fish."

Showkat scratched the tip of her nose. "So, we are going to eat snakes?"

Hero Qobad nodded. "If we can find any."

There was a knock on the parlor door. Leqa called out: "Mother!"

Mrs. Edrisi rushed to the door and opened it. Leqa knelt and hugged her mother's legs. She was trembling and shedding tears. The elderly lady put her hand on her daughter's head. "Get up, my dear!"

Leqa stood up and pulled up her headscarf, which had slipped down. "Why are you meeting with these people in private?"

Mrs. Edrisi took her to the staircase. "I may be making a mistake. Let's go to bed."

They went to Leqa's room and sat on her bed. The elderly lady wiped Leqa's tears. Her daughter grabbed her hands. "I feel that life is spinning like a whirlwind while I am standing still."

"You have made progress."

"Not as fast as the rest of you. What is going on in this house? Tell me! Believe me, I am not an idiot."

Mrs. Edrisi put her arms around her. "Who says you are an idiot? In my opinion, among the members of the family, you are the only one who can stand on your own two feet, work, and build your life with your own hands. You are composed by nature. Unlike the others, you are not riding the wave of passion. From the time I saw you at the top of the ladder, my mind was set at ease. You can see clearly the prospects that the rest of us cannot see."

"Because you were by my side, I was not afraid of anything."

"In the course of all these years, I have not been by anyone's side. I was dragging the shadow of my past this way and that."

"You are being evasive. You have always been kind. In the morning, when I was cold, you would cover me with a blanket. You emphasized to Yavar that he wash my dishes thoroughly. Once, you cooked rice pudding for me. I have not forgotten the taste."

From the corner of her eye, a teardrop rolled down the elderly lady's face. "Is that all?" She opened Leqa's headscarf and straightened out her hair. "Once it grows feathers and plumage, every bird flies away and builds a nest. But some people have no place to lay down their heads."

Leqa protested: "Who does not have a place?"

"Heroes Qobad, Showkat, Roxana, Kaveh, and Borzu." She dropped her head, and after a pause, gazed into her daughter's eyes. "Your mother."

"Why are they destroying our nest?"

"From the beginning, we did not have a proper nest."

"Hero Showkat took care of that."

"The shell is cracked. What Showkat did was a game."

Leqa bit her lip. "Poor thing! So, they will take her to the public housing?"

"A bit closer. Perhaps to the public graveyard."

Leqa scratched her cheek in dismay. The elderly lady pulled Leqa's quilt aside. "Go to sleep for now. We will think about it tomorrow."

Leqa stood in front of the picture of the female saint, knelt down, recited a prayer, took off her outer gown, slipped under the quilt, and untied her braided hair. "Aren't you sleepy?"

"Yes. I am going to bed." She stood up and walked to the door. "If you wake up in the middle of the night, call out to me!"

Leqa closed her eyes and, with a faint smile, fell asleep.

Mrs. Edrisi leaned against the door, contemplating with what energy she should go downstairs. She was unwanted among that group. The train had set out years earlier. She held her head between her hands. But where was she going to stay? She had been detached from everyone. Leqa and Vahab would be able to continue. But what about her? At the end of the road for the second time, did she have to stay where she was, watch Qobad go to the mountain, lose the final opportunity for flight, and stay in an even tighter cage up to the moment of death? She dropped her arms and shook her head vehemently. She tiptoed down to the lower floor. The door of the parlor was half open. She entered like a shadow. Qobad's eyes sparkled. He breathed a sigh of relief.

Borzu was pleading with Showkat. "Hero Showkat, I can't! I can't! Where am I supposed to go?"

"Go and find someone!"

"The earth without the sun will turn cold. It will die. Without you, my fate is the same."

Hero Showkat twisted his thin wrist. "Get lost! You keep drilling such nonsense into your own head. You think I am something special, because you saw no kindness from anyone. I don't like ticks. I can't even pull together my own lazy bones, and you have become an unwanted pest for me."

"Hero Showkat, before, I used to like the way hospitals smelled. Now that smell makes me sick. The things that the professors say have become meaningless; they have no substance. They spin between the ground and the sky, like cardboard letters."

Showkat stroked his rough hair. "Then where is your hat?"

"I tossed it behind the desk. It was a bad omen."

"You superstitious fool. Go pick it up. My paternal aunt's husband had a hat similar to that."

Borzu ran, picked up the hat, and put it on.

Showkat raised her left eyebrow. "That's much better."

Roxana asked: "Is he going to stay?"

Hero Qobad sat at the table. Others followed his example.

Roxana put her hands together, stared at the ashtray, and said in a low voice: "Let's go look at the treasure!" She turned to Showkat. "You will be responsible for Borzu."

Showkat pounded her fist on the table. "For this tick, there's no difference between treasures and garbage."

Roxana stood up and walked toward the door. "Come, without making a sound."

They entered the hallway. Kaveh was lending his shoulder to Hero Qobad to lean on. They entered Rahila's former room. Roxana locked the door from inside, closed the thick curtains, and turned on the ceiling lamp. The bed, the mirror, and the vanity table floated in a silvery light. She rubbed her fingers on a spot on the wall to the right. The corner of the room made a noise, a gap opened, a door the color of the wall moved back, a stale smell filled the air, and the backroom closet became visible. The slanting light of the ceiling light fixture shone in the darkness, and particles of dust spun in the faint light. On a silver-studded trunk, in three barbotine porcelain vases, white flowers had dried. Roxana put the vases on the wall shelf. Dust had settled on the petals of the white hyacinth, azalea, narcissus, and tuberose flowers. Roxana knelt beside the trunk and lined up the numbers on the coded lock. A noise emitted from the rusted metal. Thin layers of paint turned into powder as her fingers touched them. She pulled up the silver latches and opened the lid of the trunk half-way. A reddish ray began to shine. In a tired voice, she said: "Hero Showkat, come and open it!"

Roxana sat in the corner of the backroom closet and leaned her head against the wall, her face drained of color, like the dead.

Showkat went forward hesitantly and opened the lid of the trunk fully. A shimmering vapor intertwined above the mass of gold and rose toward the ceiling. Continuous torches like meteorites began to shine. The red ruby ring in a gold-colored pool was dissolving in a fiery brilliant light and emitting sparks.

Mrs. Edrisi came forward, like a sleepwalker, picked up the ring, and turned it in the golden vapors. "It belonged to Luba." She put it back.

Hero Qobad leaned against the doorframe. "There isn't a hair's difference between this one and its pair." He rubbed his chin. "We must make arrangements for carrying it to the mountain." He asked Showkat: "Is it safe outside in the vicinity of the house?"

Hero Showkat put her hand under the coins. A roaring sound rose up from their jingling. "The Fire Stokers have definitely left. There is no danger, at least until tomorrow morning."

She came out of the backroom closet. Borzu grabbed her hand. "Tonight seems like a dream."

Kaveh twisted the tip of his mustache. "More than a dream, the stories of The *One Thousand and One Nights*. I swear the governor himself did not have this much gold. I had gone to his palace. Such daughters!" He rubbed his eyes. "But I have come to believe that wealth does not bring happiness. The poor man seemed to have died before his death."

Showkat sat on the bed and caught her breath. "That is exactly the fate of an oppressor."

Roxana got up, walked into the room off balance, went to the window, opened it, pressed her inflamed forehead against the windowpane, and quietly said: "The scent of the flowers is stifling." She closed the window, drew the curtains, stood in front of the mirror, and pushed back her disheveled hair. "Oh, my! I am scared of myself." She looked at those around her. "I have no idea who I am." She sat beside Showkat. "Your presence gives me calm. I had seen this in a dream, in Ashkhabad, in all its detail."

Hero Kaveh nodded. "I know this condition. It happened in Bukhara. A girl was looking at me from behind a curtain with glass-bead tassels. I felt my heart move, not because of her beauty, since I had seen more beautiful girls before, but she seemed familiar, as though she had created me. It was as though I did not exist, that I was a fabrication of her dream. I became frightened and ran all the way to the city square and held my face under the water of the jetting fountains."

Showkat pulled on his ear. "Talking about women again? You aren't going to give it up till you go to your grave, are you?"

Kaveh put his elbow on the wall shelf, bent down, and stared at the floor of the room. "Why don't you understand what I am saying? The story has nothing to do with women. Memories of the distant past flash in the mind like a dream one remembers in an instant."

"Don't make up phony stories! Any woman that you see, you immediately claim that she has come from some distant past."

"Of course, you are the exception."

Showkat put her hands on her hips and raised her left eyebrow. "The first night when your menacing feet brought you here, to endear yourself to me, you said that I reminded you of the captain of some stupid ship."

Kaveh raised his head. "I remember that. Such a resemblance!" He looked at the woman's arms and muscles. "He was the sultan of the seas."

Hero Showkat puffed up her cheeks, pushed her chest forward, and turned to Qobad. "This man talks too much. Not much time left till morning. Decide on the plan!"

Hero Qobad positioned the crutch under his arm. "We need several cloth bags."

Showkat grabbed Borzu's arm and pulled him. "Let's go to the basement!"

Roxana stood up. From the gold dust, her cheeks had taken on a purple ray. She opened the door, and Showkat and Borzu went out.

Contemplating, Hero Qobad walked the length of the room and came back. His lips were moving as he was saying something silently.

The elderly lady smelled the dried flower petals. "From the beginning of her illness, they hid my paternal cousin, Luba, in this room. The windows were boarded up. The wooden blinds were closed all day. They lit candles in the dark, damp room. She would sit at the top of the bed, often shivering. She would wrap the quilt around herself. They had covered the mirror with a lace cover. She could not stand to look at herself. Every morning, my grandfather would open the door, and the servants would bring fresh bouquets of flowers and replace the wilted ones from the previous day. My grandfather and paternal uncles said that the doctor had told them that Luba's mysterious illness could be treated with the scent of white flowers. I would look at her through the crack of the door. She would wave at me with a lethargic smile on her lips. She was twenty years old, tall, with luminous eyes and arched eyebrows. Her mouth was red, like a half-opened rosebud. A blueish dust had settled on her black hair. The color of her eyes would change. Next to a blue vase, they resembled the depths of the sea. When she went to the window, the reflection of the light from the lawn made them shine like emeralds. At night, they shone like black agate. At dawn, they would lose their color, and near noon, they were as bright as jasper. The shadow of the pine trees would fall on her forehead. The vivacity of her body and fresh face were the boundless essence of youth. It was as though milk flowed in her veins. A mysterious scent rose from her bed. Occasionally, she walked around in her room, talking loudly, and giving herself strange names. When they were taking Luba's coffin away, the house was filled with the scent of flowers."

She stroked her cheek. The wrinkles smoothed out for a moment. She remembered her own face during those days. It was as white as barbotine porcelain. She was crying for Luba. Teardrops left red blotches on her clear youthful skin. She looked at the backroom closet. The mass of gold was aflame. How had the treasure been accumulated? Inheritance from ancestors? She did not think so. What Roxana did, however, resembled witchcraft. She even knew the secret code of the trunk. She gazed at the woman's face. She had luminous eyes and arched eyebrows, and her mouth was red, like a half-opened rosebud. Perhaps Luba's soul had transmigrated into her.

Showkat and Borzu entered the room. The young man counted the gunnysacks and put them on the bed. He took out a rope from his pocket.

Hero Qobad straightened his body. "Did you check the surrounding alleyways?"

Borzu moved the sharp tip of his chin. The spiky blond hair of his beard rubbed on his dirty-looking collar. "Not even a bird is flying through."

Hero Qobad drew his hands over the coins and picked up the ruby ring. Mrs. Edrisi went close to him. "They bought both of them at the same time, for Luba and me. On Wednesday, October 3, our confirmation day, the day we were named, the drinking day."

Hero Qobad gazed at it under the glow of the light fixture. Coral rays shimmered on the ceiling and the walls. He turned to the elderly lady. "It is worthy of your finger! Until the day that we sell it."

Mrs. Edrisi took the ring. "It might not fit me. My hands have become old."

The ring fit her finger perfectly. Her cheeks flushed, and she stuck her hands into her pockets.

Heroes Showkat, Kaveh, and Borzu were pouring the coins into the bags. Qobad's face became serious. "Don't make them heavy! You have a long way ahead of you."

Roxana was tying the tops of the bags with pieces of the rope. The trunk was emptied. There were twenty bags.

Qobad put his strong bony hands under a bag and lifted it off the floor. "It can be carried. Now, go for a droshky. In the Waterfall Coffee House, on the right, the third bed, wake up Mir Hazhir. Tell him Qobad has sent you!" He turned to Showkat. "You would obviously know the night's watchword."

Showkat put her elbow on the wall shelf. "If they haven't changed it in the past few hours."

The old man pushed up the hanging hairs of his eyebrow with his fingers. "No, they have not changed it, because their minds are at ease. Make sure the droshky driver sets out with the canopy closed, and stops at the end of the alleyway under the branches and leaves of the massive elm tree. If they become suspicious of you, tell them in no uncertain terms that you are on a secret mission for the House of Fire. Pin all your insignias on your chest! Have the whip in your hand!"

Hero Showkat stood at attention. "You can be sure of that."

Borzu rubbed his hands together. "Are we setting out for the mountain? Truly?"

Qobad's eyes clouded. "Get going, quickly!"

Showkat and Borzu went out.

Mrs. Edrisi sat at the edge of the bed, put one hand on top of the other, and looked at the withered profile of Hero Qobad. "In the end, we have become fellow travelers. All these years, I felt that I was going through my period of exile."

Roxana was walking around the room. By pressing an invisible spot, she closed the backroom closet. "An appropriate name. The exiles!"

Mrs. Edrisi continued: "A long sleep. When we wake up, calamity will begin. Deep within our darkness, an abandoned child wails."

Roxana stroked the octagonal bottle of the Kashmir perfume. "We are no good for this world."

Hero Qobad stood in the corner. "Those who would save the world are those who are no good for the world."

Through the slit of the curtain, Roxana looked at the sky. "And those who belong to the world unwind all that they have spun."

Hero Qobad nodded. "Their time will come to an end. Didn't you say that the majority of the people are weary of them?"

Roxana pressed her hands to her cheeks. "It does not matter. They can live with weariness for many years."

"How about liberation and love?"

"No, I don't think so. There is no liberation. Change must happen from within. Without that change, a revolution is but the changing of the shell. You know that better than I do."

Hero Qobad put his forehead on the crutch. After a long silence, he raised his head and stared at the light fixture. "We came down from the mountain for some purpose. I escaped after I was captured. My shoulder was shot. I went to the depths of the city, places I knew well. Of the captured individuals, the first one was a fugitive soldier. He had the guts of a lion. He was flawless from head to toe. These qualities had made him arrogant. The second was a gamekeeper. Because he was rebellious, after an argument with his boss, he had joined the mountain group. He wanted to take revenge. He was belligerent toward the agents of power. From his perspective, anyone who rode in a carriage or wore a fur hat belonged to the enemy camp and was condemned to death. We did not think otherwise, either. Youth is merciless and full of arrogance. The third one had worked everywhere. Because he was so blunt in what he said, he had been kicked out. He made friends with everyone. We had a fixed line that separated the good from the bad. We would go berserk thinking that anything would be relative. We only knew two colors, black and white. Our line of vision was straight; his was spiral. His line of vision would sometimes peak and sometimes was on the decline. In any case, he was content. He did the cooking, washed the dishes, and agreed to do hard and menial jobs without protest. He had no expectations, a miracle or a conquest. He did not expect to be commended. He thought of himself as nothing. He also was not a staunch supporter of our group. He neither flattered anyone nor liked flattery. He would wrap his puttees around his legs and at night, sleep under the tree. His dark-complexioned face was wrinkled from the wind and the sun. Obviously, all three were tortured. Our beloved soldier, who had an iron will, was broken within the first few hours. I would not criticize him. This was perhaps his level of endurance. The gamekeeper cursed and kicked—the fire of revenge is not extinguished rapidly. After struggling for a while, he obtained some concessions and went and replaced his boss. The only one who did not say a word was the unassuming middle-aged little man with a pair of bloodied puttees. He had learned many things in the high and low points of life. He could recognize evil. He knew the level at which it would spread. The storm of calamities had bent his back many times. In the same way, he bent down again. He was the manna bush of the desert, not the ornamental thorny cactus. I only understood these details thirty years later, when I had become similar to him. They hanged him on the gallows at dawn on Easter. Such people are the manifestation of revolution."

Roxana bit the palm of her hand. "Such an impossible dream!"

"Then what are you seeking?"

"The dream of revolution! We had better not get close to reality, not see the bottom of things. When I was a child, they bought me a doll. It had curly coiled blonde hair. Its turquoise eyes were as pretty as a dream. When you pressed its side, it laughed and cried. I would put it on the wall shelf and look at it from a distance. Finally, one day, the devil got under my skin and I ripped the belly of my doll with a knife. I wanted to know the secret of how it laughed and cried. In the middle of its belly, I saw nothing but a handful of straw and a windup box. My fabricated delusions all turned to smoke and went up in the air. Disappointed, I threw away the torn-apart doll. I destroyed the source of my happiness with my own hands. Alas! From this experience, I learned nothing. Throughout my life, primal curiosity followed me like an unpleasant odor. Whenever I saw something beautiful, magnificent, and even sacred, I could not be calm. I would move forward to the point of finding the rusted box, or building it. Looking and admiring was beneath my sense of pride. I was distanced from wisdom and close to savagery and egotism. The frequent failures and distresses were the result of this greedy desire. Later on, with a great deal of difficulty, I learned how to merely observe, not to count common vulgar sly cunning as intelligence. Alas, it was already too late. With every experience, I had left behind a part of my faith somewhere. Now I want one thing, to stand on distant mountain peaks and to observe. This kind of love alone is the savior."

Hero Qobad looked at her sharply. "For us, being close or far makes no difference. We love human beings with all their weaknesses. Because we are all victims, instead of hatred, we have compassion. The character of every human being is the product of the conditions. We are weary of those conditions, not of the people."

Roxana held both her upper arms with her hands. "What do you mean by 'we'?"

The old man frowned. "Perhaps the dream of the dead."

Showkat and Borzu came in, fuming. Showkat shook her whip. "Well, the droshky is waiting under the tree. Move! Why have you flopped down like watery yogurt?"

Hero Qobad looked at her with kindness. "Did anyone get a whiff of it?"

"Hero Showkat is an expert in her own work."

They carried the bags on their shoulders and placed them inside the droshky. Qobad dispatched Showkat, Roxana, and Kaveh on their mission and gave them the necessary instructions. Before leaving, Roxana said to Mrs. Edrisi: "Don't have outlandish thoughts. I had heard the secret code of the treasure with all the other details from your daughter-in-law."

Mrs. Edrisi leaned against the jasmine arbor. "How did Rana know it?"

"Wasn't Rahila in that room from childhood?"

Chapter 12

The entire sky was covered with dark clouds. Leaning against the column until noon, Vahab was watching the entrance hall. A number of people were coming and going. Their clothes spun in the fog, gray and black, but there was no sign of white. He went to Roxana's room. The bedspread was smooth. The room resembled a lifeless corpse. He opened the closet and pushed aside the mass of clothes. A thin dust covered his fingers. He stood in front of the mirror. He picked up the Kashmir perfume bottle and turned it. From the points where the corners of the triangular designs of the glass met, waves of color began to shine: ruby red, emerald, gold, green, purple, and amber. He opened the lid of the bottle and smelled it. A mysterious mixture of Oriental perfumes had become close and familiar to him, as familiar as the soil, bread, and vinegar. He put the cap back on and thought about why he had not perceived the spell of these domestic scents: intimate, sheltering, like grass under his feet, like the stars, galactic, and familiar. He looked at the courtyard through the window. A brittle flower that had sprouted in the gap of the brick cornice of the wall bent back and forth in the fog. He heard a sound, the sound of the lute and reed-flute. He ran toward the door and went outside. Following the sound, he entered a dark alleyway. He followed a stream with clear water. At the end, he reached a fork in the road. Before him was a house with a green wooden fence, covered with hanging morning-glory flowers the color of lapis lazuli. Above the board-covered veranda, under the plasterwork ceiling, dozens of cages were hanging, full of canaries. They chirped in unison. A woman appeared on the veranda, wearing a blue dress, the locks of her black hair reaching her waist. She looked at the man from head to toe. Vahab leaned on the railing. "Did you hear the music?"

The woman looked at the ceiling of the veranda. "They sing all day long."

"Not the canaries, the lute and reed-flute!"

The woman came to the banister. "What is a lute?"

Vahab turned his back to her and left.

The woman yelled: "Who is playing the piano in that white house?"

Vahab followed the aspen trees and reached the square with the retail shops. In the flowerbed in the middle of the square, canna lilies were bending under the rain. They sold all sorts of things in the shops: hammers to break the sugar cones, tongs, iron tripods, and even redingotes of a hundred years earlier. Under a canopy the color of sunflower petals, a group of people were sitting, drinking dark tea in slender-waist tea glasses. While conversing, they handed around prayer beads, glass beads, and rings that had no stones for inspection. He approached the canopy. "Where did the musicians go?"

The secondhand-merchandise dealers burst out laughing. An old man with almond-shaped eyes stared at him, drank his last sip of tea, and spat out the remaining sugar. "What city are you coming from?"

"From around here."

"Would you like some tea?" Vahab shook his head. "They used to play several years ago. Now they aren't permitted."

Vahab began to walk. He reached the gate of the National Park, entered, and walked beside the swimming pool. He stopped under the arcade of the old palace. Beside the stone columns, peddlers sold roasted potatoes, corn on the cob, and bread baked with sesame seeds on top. Around each tray gathered a group of children who looked at and sniffed the food. He took off his soaking-wet shoes and dumped the water out of them. He went near the windows, put his face on a windowpane, and gazed inside the palace. The parlor was empty and dark. Chandeliers hung from the ceiling on bronze chains. The rays of the fire of the venders quivered on the red crystal of the tulip-shaped lamps. He saw a shadow by the railing, swaying and white. He pressed his feverish forehead to the glass. His heart began to palpitate. From the stone balustrade, a sheet glided down and spun in a small whirlwind.

He walked toward the garden and stood by a pond. It was raining, and tiny bubbles split open on the surface of the water. Petite old women in old clothes were opening worn-out umbrellas, fleeing the torrential rain. Vahab pondered that perhaps those tattered clothes and the umbrellas the ribs of which were broken presented the highest level of showing off and that each one of the decrepit old women had dozens of men in love with them.

He circled the palace and walked along the boxwood shrubs. He reached the playing field. A hand descended on his shoulder, startling him, and he turned around. It was Rashid, his hair dripping wet, and he was wearing a soaked knit shirt. "What are you doing here, out in the rain, without permission?"

"Aren't you out in the rain yourself?"

"I'm used to it. I'm on my way back from the factory."

Vahab rubbed his hands together. "Did you see Roxana this morning?"

Rashid stared at a cluster of daisies, bent under the rain. "Roxana, Showkat, Kaveh, and Borzu have disappeared."

Vahab grabbed his arm. "Were they arrested?"

"I'm really worried."

Vahab moved his big toes under the wet leather of the tips of his shoes. "Are you scared?"

Water dripped from the tips of the man's blond mustache. "Scared of what?"

"Of dying!"

A vein began to palpitate on Rashid's smooth rosy forehead. "When I start something, I stick with it to the end."

Vahab looked at his eyelashes, which were sticking together. "Isn't the situation dangerous for my grandmother?"

"She knows the paths and the potholes better than you and me."

"I have been restless since this morning."

Rashid patted Vahab on the back. "I'm going home." He began to run.

Vahab continued his own way. In Peace Square, he looked around, stunned and confused. The eight domes of the Church of Saint Nicholas shone like fish scales. Above each steeple, a flag with the design of the erect crowbar twisted and turned. Four Fire Stokers were pacing back and forth on the porphyry stone veranda under the shadow of the arched ceilings. They passed one another, proud, arrogant, and firm. From behind the visors of their rain-soaked helmets, they watched the people, chuckled at their frightened fleeing, and caressed the sheaths of their *shashka*s, their Circassian sabers. They were tall and handsome.

Vahab went to the middle of the square, and, from the covered entrance, he looked at the nave of the church and the altar. The rays through the glass panes shone on the statues. Cylinders of light passed through one another. A barefooted monk was circling around the columns, holding an unlit candle on which he blew constantly. He came to the threshold of the door and opened his arms. "Welcome to the wedding celebration!"

The sound of the laughter of the Fire Stokers resonated in the square. One of them threw a pebble at the old monk. The old man's white beard began to move as he recited a prayer, and his ecstatic eyes sparkled with joy. Vahab turned his back to him and walked away.

Beside a stream, Vahab sat under the canopy of an elm tree. He closed his eyes and tried to forget the fear and bewilderment of the church, the smell of rusty nails on the boards of the coffin.

He started walking under the rain and entered the densely populated neighborhoods. At the corner of the intersection of a narrow alleyway, a large pot was boiling over a fire. A middle-aged man was stirring the white liquid inside the pot with a ladle, spreading the scent of cardamom, milk, and rosewater in the breeze. He had tied back his hair. Over the steam, his nose looked red. He would fill bowls and hand them to people. They ate and tossed coins on the counter.

Vahab made his way through the crowd and got close to the pot. He picked up a bowl. "What is the name of this?"

The man turned his back to him. "Hot rice porridge."

Vahab said under his breath: "Pour me some!"

The cook filled the bowl and handed it to him with a zinc spoon. Vahab stood by the wall and ate it with pleasure. A few Turkoman men and women gathered around the pot. Their colorful shawls waved in the wind and rain. Their jujube-colored pleated skirts were splattered with mud. Their rosy faces in the faint light shone with amber rays. The bells of their anklets jingled loudly with every step. The men formed a circle. They wore long rust-colored and purple coats, felt footwear, and wide pants. When they talked, the resonance of their voices traveled far. They were slurping up the hot rice porridge and wiping the thin strands of their mustaches with the backs of their hands.

The whooshing sound of the rain was diminishing. Masses of fog were scattering in the city. Vahab arrived at a wide street full of trees. He continued ahead and found himself in front of the Central House of Fire. The black building raised its head in the fog. He looked at the red windows washed by the rain. A huge flag was turning and twisting on a pole on the gable roof. Behind the windowpanes, those clad in black were walking back and forth.

The gold-studded door turned on its pivot hinge, and the garden became visible. Along the wide sides of the path, masses of salvia flowers flamed up brilliantly, like fire. As they walked, the Fire Stokers stomped on the flowers. One of them was cutting down a green pine tree with a saw. On the lawn, a number of people had locked their arms together in a chain-like form, and, as they turned, they kicked their legs in turn to the front and the back and jumped up about one or two feet and emitted some sad sound from the depths of their throats.

On the third floor of the building, a woman opened a window, stuck out her color-drained face, and, with her bent nose, inhaled the air. Stars and insignias glittered on the chest of her uniform, golden tassels hanging from her epaulets.

A man came out of a droshky. He had his overcoat collar up, and the edge of his hat touched his eyebrows. Vahab was startled. It was Moayyad, walking hastily and entering the huge building through the scallop-arched door.

Vahab looked around. Not even a bird was in sight in the entire street. He turned away from the House of Fire. Some hands grabbed him. He turned around, frightened. Several athletic Fire Stokers were surrounding him. They twisted his arm. Vahab cried out. They stuffed a handkerchief in his mouth, took him into the courtyard, and dragged him to the end of the building. They opened an arched door. The smell of disinfectants hit his nose. They went inside. A long hallway extended into darkness. They imprisoned him in a room on the left side. It was empty and large. Its walls were rose colored. A tall mirror doubled the length of the room. The black velvet curtains were closed. A five-pronged chandelier reflected the red rays of the tulip-shaped lamps on the mirrorwork surfaces and broke every beam of light. He wanted to pull the curtain open. The golden filigree of the edge of the curtain was nailed to the wall. The coral-color marble wood stove was cold and completely swept clean. He sat on the black bench. From behind the closed doors he could hear the sound of the lute and reed-flute. He recalled Kaveh's story about the three daughters of the governor. He might have seen them in the same room. Where were they now? Were they in the National Park in tattered clothes with umbrellas the ribs of which were broken, fleeing the rain? Were they residents of public housing, sleeping under damp blankets? Or had they died in their youth, with red rose bushes having sprouted from their graves? An opiate-scented perfume, such as the scent of poppy, was withering in the smell of disinfectants: the scent of their youth.

A woman and three men came in brashly. One of the men was Moayyad. The woman struck her boot with her whip. He had seen her face behind the window an hour earlier. The tip of her pointed nose shone like silver. Her stiff uniform seemed to have been ironed a few minutes earlier. She stood before Vahab as firm as a statue made of solid steel, puffed out her chest, and took out of the pocket of her jacket a black notebook with the gilded insignia of the erect crowbar. Her blue irises were so pale that they were indistinguishable from the whites of her eyes. Vahab stuck his knees together. The woman sat beside him. She smelled of camphor. Vahab's nose began to itch. The woman gazed at his face, although she seemed to be deprived of sight. "What do you think about us?"

"Do you use camphor perfume?"

The woman pressed the tip of her fountain pen on his hand. "We disinfect. Everything must be clean, especially the society. But you have made this place dirty with your muddy shoes and trousers."

Vahab pulled back. "The only thing that I did not intend to do was to dirty up your place of pomp and circumstance. When a person is taken somewhere by force, it would be far-fetched to expect him to observe the rules of etiquette."

The woman wrote something in the notebook, held her chin up. With the shiny line on her nose, her face was divided in half. "You have fallen into the trap."

She gestured to the Fire Stokers. Two strong men grabbed Vahab's shins, pulled him down from the bench, laid him on the cold floor, and kicked him with the tips of their boots. The woman sat beside Vahab, ran her fingers through his hair, then pulled his hair harshly. The skin of Vahab's head heated up. He bit his lower lip, and tears welled up in his eyes.

Moayyad smiled. "Hero Rakhov, don't be too harsh! This man is not involved in the main issue."

"Then why is he so insolent?"

"Insolence is a characteristic of his family."

The woman loosened her grip. "A crooked branch needs to be cut off. Come, take a closer look at him! You might be mistaken."

Moayyad took a few steps forward. His boots made a chirping sound. "Do you not trust me?"

"It is our custom not to trust anyone." She widened her eyes and looked at the ceiling. The ants had lined up along a crack. She pointed to the ceiling. "Repair it tomorrow!" She let go of Vahab's hair, walked around him, and struck the ground with the tip of her whip. Dust rose from the waxed floor. "Why did you approach the Central House of Fire? No one does that. The residents of the surrounding houses have all left."

"I do not know the city well. I was following the sound of the lute and reed-flute."

The woman shook the whip. "You were raised here!"

"But in our house—"

"That house is finished."

Astonished, Vahab realized that this was nothing to be sorry about. "You are in charge."

"What does Qobad do?"

"Like an old bird, he stands on one leg, if you could call that doing anything."

"Does he stir the pottage with that one leg?"

"I don't know anything about the pottage."

"Are you stupid, or stoned?"

"I suppose both."

Moayyad nodded in confirmation. "He is right on that account."

The woman rolled her glassy eyes in their sockets. "Don't interfere!" She bit the palm of her left hand. "How about that slut, Showkat?"

"She is belligerent toward me."

"Say something new!"

"Nothing is new under the sky!" The woman struck his arm with the whip. Vahab moaned. Pain shot through his bones. "Free me from Showkat's claws!"

"But now the claws have become caressing hands!"

"Then do you know how I feel better than I do?"

"Together, you have formed a dangerous nucleus."

"Showkat, your Hero, claimed that she has bile."

The woman screamed. The reverberations of her voice made Vahab's spine shiver. "Don't call her Hero!"

"I am not fond of that. You made me do it. All those signs and insignias are intimidating."

"We will take back her insignias."

"Your problems have nothing to do with me. Just be kind enough to tell me what to call her."

"You might not see Showkat again. If you happen to see her, call her traitor!"

"Call a high-ranking member of the House of Fire a traitor?"

Hero Rakhov pressed the palms of her hands to her ears and screamed. Her pale face turned blue. "She was, but you ruined her."

"I, for one, did not tempt her. I have had as much influence on Showkat as I could influence you."

"The substance of my heart is made of steel."

"The substance of her heart isn't bad, either."

"In fact, in the middle of all this, who do you think you are?"

"How many times do I need to say it? Absolutely no one."

"Will you cooperate with us?"

"I am a dreamer."

The woman turned to Moayyad. "A dreamer? What does he mean?"

Moayyad stood at attention. "Dreaming when awake! This disease is hereditary among them. He takes after his aunt."

Hero Rakhov nodded. "The woman you killed?"

"I didn't kill her, personally. She grieved to death from looking at my face."

The woman scratched her pointed chin. "I think she couldn't avoid it. Even I, who am by no means a dreamer, get tired of seeing your face."

Vahab's eyes sparkled.

Hero Rakhov kicked him hard. Pain shot through his internal organs, and beads of sweat sprouted from the roots of his hair. "Can your grandmother endure kicks?"

Vahab sighed. "She is an old woman."

"Why does she not behave like an old woman?"

"She is exactly like an old woman. She tells fortunes with playing cards."

"She does not need to do that. Her fortune is ominous. Tell her not to look for any power other than us on earth and in the sky."

She kicked him again. "Is Roxana Yashvili putting on shows again? Does she perform sleight of hand? Does she pull white pigeons out of her hat?"

Vahab breathed a sigh of relief. He thought, so the House of Fire did not know where she was. "She rehearses old plays."

"You charlatan! You know very well that she has invented a new play with the cooperation of new actors, who are more stupid than the previous ones, even though in the end, instead of receiving an applause, they will receive rotten eggs and tomatoes from the masses." She stomped the floor with the sole of her boot. Her image in the mirrorwork on the wall split into a thousand pieces. "What kind of relationship does Showkat have with Qobad?"

"They were fighting last night."

The woman turned to Moayyad and shook her finger. "The assessment of the House of Fire. The conflict between them will intensify. They are both after power." She turned to Vahab. "Are there any conflicts among others?"

"As far back as I remember, there has always been hostility in the house."

Hero Rakhov brought down the whip on Vahab's head. Several strands of hair wrapped around the whip and were yanked out from the root. "Why did you leave the house without a permit, go all around the city, walk around in the National Park, look inside the abandoned palace, and approach the church? What are you looking for?"

"I said that I am a dreamer. I was following the sound of the lute and the reed-flute."

The woman stepped on his hand. "Be thankful for this. Otherwise, we would not let you remain alive. For now, we will leave you alone. Society does not feed you to have dreams for it. We are capable of blocking ailing minds." She opened her thin lips. Her small teeth were blueish white. "The force of terror is constructive. An undeveloped mind does not understand this advantage."

"Does that also extend to you?"

The woman raised her thin blonde eyebrows. "We are the only ones asking the questions; but this time I will answer you, because I am interested in this issue. Proudly, I say, yes! I am afraid of the secretary of the House of Fire to the marrow of my bones." The corners of her lips quivered. "Fear deepens the sense of responsibility."

"Fear is also enjoyable, right?"

The woman's jaws locked. Her eyelids lowered, her eyes became ecstatic, and her bony chest went up and down under her jacket with her panting. Sticky saliva was dripping from the corners of her lips. A moan reverberated in her throat. Her arms dropped lethargically.

Vahab turned his face away from her. "Thank you! I got it."

Silence dominated the air. He could only hear the sound of rain falling on the cast iron gable roof and arches.

After a long tremor, Hero Rakhov stood up, walked to the alcove of the room, did some athletic movements, and on her return, struck the black bench with the whip and stood beside the fallen man. "What is their plan?"

"Why don't you ask Showkat?"

The woman stuck her hand into her pocket, took out a sunflower seed, dropped it on the ground, and smashed it with the heel of her boot. "This is Showkat's fate!"

With regret, the thought occurred to Vahab that he wished he had not hit the target on the night when they threw knives.

With firm steps, Rakhov walked toward the door and commanded: "Throw him out!"

Chapter 13

The people of the house were having supper. A flock of crows came flying from the west and sat on the high branches of the birch trees. The sky was overcast. Cold air was blowing inside from the seams of the windows and under the doors. They were chewing the bits of bread quietly, and, when doors slammed, they would half rise from their seats.

Hero Qobad coughed. "The weather is getting cold."

Roxana gazed into the garden. "I wish we would make the crows fly away."

"There was no sign of crows on the mountain. Migrating swallows came flock by flock and left a few hours later."

Kukan took a sip of water. "All around outside the house is full of Fire Stokers."

Vahab stood up from the table, limped toward the sofa, and lay down. Leqa covered him with a blanket. Mrs. Edrisi put her hand on his forehead. "You have a fever. Why did you go and walk in the rain? What did you have to do with the House of Fire?"

Vahab moaned: "My bones ache."

Hero Qobad asked Kukan: "How many are there?"

Kukan swallowed his bite of bread. "I would like to take off and get away. Pity my patchwork quilt is in Haddadiyan's room."

"Have you given him food?"

Showkat smashed the soft bread with her fingers and looked around. Seeing Vahab's face, which was drained of color, she was disappointed and placed the bread ball at the side of her plate. "He has stuffed himself to the throat with lentil and rice pilaf. He has stunk up the room with his breathing." She turned to Borzu. "That dead mouse, Vahab, got himself exposed to the death gas vapors." She gazed into Leqa's eyes. "You like that higgledy-piggledy room of the entrance hall? Why are matchstick, naked women reaching with their hands to the sky? What is the meaning of the cluster of the grapes? Who is that chubby little kid with wings shooting at with a bow and arrow? Tell me his story. I like him."

Leqa's cheeks flushed. Stammering, she explained: "That child's name is Cupid, the god of love."

From a distance, Vahab said: "He is the son of Aphrodite and Hermes."

Leqa continued: "He shoots with his eyes closed. Whosever's heart is struck by his arrow, he carries the pain of love with him up to his death."

A bite of food got caught in Showkat's throat and she coughed. She took a sip of water. Borzu half rose. Showkat shouted: "Put your butt down! You think I have the flu?" She asked Leqa. "Falls in love with what?"

"It depends. I, for instance, have devoted my heart to music."

Showkat knit her brow. "I'm in love with it, too."

Leqa paused. "What do you yourself think?"

Showkat pressed her wide thumb on the table. "If I am not mistaken, the arrow of that rascal has also hit my steel heart. I remember the time when I was restless and beside myself, but I can't figure out these lovey-dovey games of Kaveh and people like him."

Roxana asked Qobad: "Where were you born?"

The old man pointed to the snow landscape painting. "Somewhere like that."

Roxana turned to Yunos. "In art, what are you after? The truth?"

"Other than that pointing finger, or, as Showkat says, 'chubby little kid,' nothing is important to me."

"Do drinking from the fountain of youth and stepping into the domain of immortality not excite you?"

"I laugh at such things. The human body and name are mortal. The earth knows the way. It makes things grow, and it kills them."

"How about the survival of your ideas?"

Yunos chuckled. "I have no ideas. I am an intermediary, perhaps transparent."

"Do you think you have endured great suffering?"

"No. I am not that much of a fool. Besides, what is the worth of suffering if you do not achieve constant pleasure?"

"Does anything disrupt your tranquility?"

"Many things. That is why I am a poet. Otherwise, I would be a mystic, like Hero Qobad."

Roxana turned to Qobad. "Are you a mystic?"

The old man's hands trembled and a date pit fell on the plate from between his fingers. "No, I had not thought about that at all. I know of no mysticism in my being."

Roxana asked Yunos: "Did you hear what he said?"

"Of course! Thinking is evil."

"What did you learn from the Black people?"

"Sorcery!" The Heroes around the table laughed. "I am not joking."

Roxana asked: "What does sorcery mean? Would you, for instance, turn me into a frog?"

"I would not do anything to you. I would become a frog myself."

The woman's eyes sparkled. "Become one right now!"

"There is no frog here. I will assume your form. Why are you terrified of death, and at the same time, chase it barefooted?"

The woman pushed back the empty plate. A glass toppled and the water spilled onto the tablecloth. "I am not terrified."

"You shall see."

Roxana stood up, wadded up the white napkin and tossed it on the table. "You are teasing me."

"I want you to have the calmness of those five."

Roxana wiped her damp forehead with her sleeve and leaned on Hero Pari's chair. "Everyone has abandoned me."

"There is punishment for egotism, not from mysterious forces, only from within."

Roxana rubbed her hands together. "Do I seem egotistical?"

"How many months have you lived with these people? Do you know any of them?"

She glanced at Kaveh. "Perhaps him."

"What kind of a person is he?"

"A butterfly. He lands on any flower, but he is restless. He has not thought about anything seriously."

"Poor Kaveh!"

She held her head between her hands. The electricity went out, and the parlor became dark. Hero Kaveh lit a candle. Yunos picked up a bundle from under the table—the threadbare cloak—untied its knot, and took out a mass of paper. Both sides of every sheet were covered with his handwriting. The rustling of thin sheets of paper disturbed the silence. The flame of the candle reflected a trembling circle on the ceiling. After gazing at Roxana, he read in a low husky voice:

He was the one and only son of middle-aged parents. His father had a carpentry shop at the corner of the Molla Aref Bazaar. His customers were mostly rural people. The family lived at the end of Taldi Kurgan Alleyway in a small, neat house. The mother had raised her only son with love. She filled his pocket with raisins and almonds. She fed him milk and eggs. She would save from the expenditures of the household to buy nice clothes for Kaveh. He was the best dressed boy in the entire neighborhood. He grew into a tall handsome young man. In his youth, he wore ankle-high glossy shoes and a silk necktie. His collars were all starched white. He wore padded jackets, went to an equestrian club, and in winter wore gaiters over his shoes and a fur hat. He had shiny black eyes and a comely figure. He held his head and neck high, and in the eyes of the neighborhood girls, he was seen as a prince. When they sat down together, they talked about Kaveh and giggled coyly. They would push unsigned anonymous letters addressed to him through the crack of the door of his house. Kaveh would pass by them without paying any attention. He had a rebellious and hard-to-please nature. His hangouts were in the upper city neighborhoods. He would sit under the awning of cafés, drinking coffee. He would open a book on his lap and pretend to be reading it. His friends were university students and novice journalists and artists. They argued and wished to change the world. Occasionally, they gathered in some house. They would eat snack food for dinner, drink a glass of vodka, and play music and sing. Kaveh had a pretty good voice. He played the mandolin, sang songs, and did the Lezgi dance. He was not much for studying. He often went home late at night, seeing his mother behind the window waiting for him. Upon seeing his silhouette, his mother would rush downstairs, open the door, and put her finger on her lips. His father would wake up and begin to beat the young man by punching and kicking him. The young man would hold as still as a rock, his bright eyes gleaming with contempt. Helpless as to what to do, the father would kick the son's leg, and go back to bed. They could hear his snoring a few minutes later.

One day, passing through Warshawskaya Street, Kaveh saw a young woman clad in black. She was carrying a heavy basket full of fruit, fish, and cabbage. Occasionally, she put the basket on the ground to catch her breath and rubbed her hands together. She was wearing a nicely made dress, her curly black hair hanging over her shoulders, a velvet hat tilted on her head, tall, full-figured, and well proportioned, but as nimble as a mountain gazelle.

Kaveh rushed forward, tossed his book, bent down, and looked at the woman from head to toe. Her almond-shaped eyes shone like emeralds, her eyebrows were arched, her nose slightly bent, her lips like a blossom, her face oval and pale, her eyes frightened, melancholic, and impassioned, and her carefree demeanor different from provincial women. She could have come from the capital city.

He picked up his book and stuck it into his pocket. He approached the woman, bowed his head, and, pointing at the basket, he said, "May I?"

The lady put the basket down and a tentative smile opened her lips. Kaveh immediately picked up the basket and set out shoulder to shoulder with the woman. After a pause, the young lady asked, "Are you a university student?"

Kaveh's cheeks flushed. "Yes, what else is there to do?"

"The university is a good environment. What are you studying?"

"Can you guess? What subject would be becoming to the way I look?"

The woman stared into his eyes. "Perhaps banking."

Kaveh slowed his pace and pushed back his fur hat. "Don't be so unkind! I am an artist."

The lady's lips formed a bud. "In what field?"

"Whatever you like."

The young lady laughed and held up the voile of her hat. "But you have chosen it already!"

Kaveh stopped and punched his chest with his fist. "If you do not like it, I swear to God, I will change my field."

The lady bit the corner of her lip. "Would you not be offended if I say it has nothing to do with me?"

"No, I will only be sad."

"All joking aside, you did not answer my question."

Kaveh paused a bit. "Performing arts."

"Then do you also act on the stage?"

"Well, I have been on the stage a couple of times."

"Interesting. What play did you act in?"

Something out of the blue crossed his mind: "Molière's *Tartuffe*."

The lady laughed out loud.

Kaveh shook the basket and a red apple fell and rolled into the street gutter. The young man ran after it.

The lady shouted, "Let it go!" She stopped in front of a brown door. "Put the basket down! We have arrived." It was an old house with an arched entrance. She stepped on the stone stair and unlocked the door. "You have been so kind." Kaveh leaned his shoulder on the wall with salty scales. "Be careful! Your nice overcoat will get dirty."

Kaveh sighed. "So, I won't see you again?"

The lady put the basket in the hallway. "We might cross paths again. Ashkhabad is not a large city."

Kaveh was vexed. "Yes, in any case, it is big. Aren't you from here?"

"I come from Yalta."

"Do you live alone?"

"How curious you are! No! What woman lives alone?"

Kaveh's ears turned red. "So are you married?"

The woman shook her finger threateningly. "Stop being nosy!"

Kaveh pressed his shoulder more firmly on the wall. "Please!"

"What difference does it make to you?"

Kaveh frowned. "Why did you get married?"

The lady went in and stood between the double doors. Kaveh grabbed the door knocker. "I did not mean to be nosy."

"Yes, I can see that. Not even knowing who I am, you are trying to dig into my life."

"You are attractive."

"I know."

"Why are you wearing black?"

The lady closed the door. Kaveh walked around the house for hours.

He could not go to sleep until midnight. He kept rolling over in bed and sighing. He would get up and drink water, stare at the sky through the window, and see the image of the woman among the branches of the pine tree.

At dawn, he jumped out of bed, had a cup of black tea, combed his hair and shaved in front of the full-length mirror, put on his best clothes, and went to Warshawskaya Street in a droshky. He got out near the woman's house and began pacing, as he had done the previous day. The door of the house opened halfway. An old woman came out. She had the familiar basket in her hand.

Kaveh ran forward and said hello.

The old woman responded hesitantly: "Who are you?"

Kaveh dropped his head. "I am an architect. The lady asked me to come and examine the roof of the house. She said it was cracked. Tiny cracks are not dangerous, but when it is in the foundation, it is a calamity. Before you know it, the ceilings will cave in."

The old woman's green eyes widened. "We are renting this place. The ceiling of the kitchen has a few cracks. Is it dangerous?"

Kaveh stepped on the stair. "I cannot tell until I take a look at it."

The old woman opened the door and grumbled under her breath, "Such dishonest people!"

Kaveh entered the house. The scent of coffee wafted throughout the dimly lit hallway. They reached the vestibule. There were flowerpots in every corner. Near the wall, a daybed, and several mismatched easy chairs around a rectangular table. Women's dresses were wadded up and left on the backs of the easy chairs. There were threadbare slippers in front of the doors. Two greasy plates on the table. Old crystal dishes were on the wall shelves in no particular order. The house was a mess, but full of the scent and hue of life. The scent of a fine perfume wafted in the air.

The old woman took Kaveh into the kitchen and pointed to the ceiling. "Most of the cracks are here."

Kaveh took off his shoes, climbed on the table, stroked the cracks. jumped down, and frowned.

The old woman stared at the ceiling. "Is the owner of the house responsible for the repairs?"

"Legally, that should be the case."

The old woman breathed a sigh of relief. A hair sticking out of her nose quivered.

Kaveh looked at the stove. The coffeepot was simmering slowly. He sniffed. "Wow! Such an aroma!"

"Shall I pour you some?"

"You are so kind."

The old woman picked up a cup and poured coffee for Kaveh. "Then please have a seat!"

They went back to the vestibule.

The young man's stomach was growling. "Do you have any pastry? Coffee tastes great with pastry."

"Would you like a piece of cake?"

Kaveh clapped his hands. "That would be marvelous!"

The old woman picked up the plates and brought Kaveh a piece of homemade cake.

The young man drank the coffee sip by sip and enjoyed the cake. "You have a nice house. Have the lady and gentleman gone out?"

The old woman frowned. "Which gentleman?"

Kaveh began to hiccup. "Amazing! Amazing! Interesting!"

"What is interesting?"

"Nothing. I was thinking about life. Life is hard. Even at my age, I have suffered a great deal. Doesn't my face show it?"

The old woman gazed at Kaveh's face with her weak-sighted eyes. "Poor young man! What ails you?"

"You are a noble lady, of high status and very proper. I do not want to torment you by explaining my troubles."

The old woman sat down. "It does not matter. Tell me! We are also strangers in this city."

"Woe to being a lonely stranger! You need not tell me about that. I am a stranger in the world."

"Do you not have any relatives?"

"Alas, my parents passed away a few years ago."

"What do you do now?"

Kaveh sighed. "Nothing. I hang around here and there, looking for a barley-grain's worth of love."

"Well, come here more often."

"I am afraid I will be an inconvenience."

The old woman smiled. "Such a modest young man! It is obvious from your demeanor that you were raised properly."

"After work, I study at night. I want to make something of myself."

"I am sure you will."

The door to one of the rooms moaned on its hinges. The young lady clad in black came out. She yawned and blinked her eyes several times. "Mama, what is going on? Do we have a guest?"

Kaveh's face was drained of color. He jumped up and bowed.

The lady stepped back. "What are you doing here?"

The old woman put her hand on the table and bent over. "Katya! This is the architect. You had asked him yourself to come here."

Katya grabbed the back of the easy chair and laughed. "So, Your Excellency is an architect?"

"I am an expert in everything. Yesterday, when you went in, I examined the foundation of the house and became concerned. I thought it might cause a problem."

"Well, is your mind set at ease now?"

Kaveh smiled. "Would you like a cup of coffee?"

Katya frowned. "Is this your house, or mine?"

"It does not make any difference." He pulled the velvet-covered easy chair forward. "Please, have a seat!"

Katya turned on the table lamp, sat down, and leaned her head against the back. "I am so tired. It is a rainy day."

Kaveh looked at the sky through the window. "The clouds are coming from the east."

"What difference does that make?"

"The rain from the eastern clouds passes through quickly, like spring rain."

"Stop talking nonsense!"

Her mother went to the kitchen.

Kaveh dropped his head. "Believe me, if I did not see you, I would be on the verge of death."

Katya drummed on the table with her rosy nails. "You are such a charlatan! You lie left and right."

Kaveh bit his lip. "This one is true. Look at the color of my face! I am twenty-three years old." He added three years to his age on the spot. "But up to now, I have not looked at any creature, any woman."

"Not even looked?"

"Of course. I am a proud young man. I am not accepting of anyone. Save me from the girls! If only you knew how boring they are, hollow, superficial. All they know is to cast a net of marriage for men."

Katya nodded. "Sooner or later, you also will be caught in a golden net."

Kaveh shifted in his place on the easy chair. "Impossible! I am not one for the cage."

"Let us wait and see!"

Kaveh looked at Katya's eyes and immediately dropped his head. "Have you moved to this city recently?"

"Three months ago."

"Please stay!"

"For now, I am staying. I have no other choice."

"Are you married?"

"You should not ask a lady that."

"You did not answer me."

The woman sighed deeply and stared at the wall in front of her. "I loved him from the bottom of my heart. He was a perfect man, brave and kind. The trips we went on together, to Crimea, to Tbilisi, to all the cities of Greece."

The young man reiterated under his breath. "Oh, of course, Greece."

"It is the most beautiful country in the world. Such grapes, such sunlight! Pure turquoise seas. Warm, lively people."

Kaveh sighed. "I envy you!"

"Would you like to see the pictures?"

"The pictures of Greece?"

"No, of my husband."

The young man bit his lip. "That would make me happy. May I ask where he is now?"

"With God in heaven."

Kaveh smiled and his eyes and teeth sparkled. "Such bliss!"

"For whom?"

Relaxed, Kaveh took a deep breath. "Death with honor is bliss."

"Did you know that he died in war? Boris was a cavalry officer. We receive a good pension, but what is the use when life is gray? No matter where you look, you see ghosts."

Teardrops began to flow from the corners of her eyes down her pale cheeks.

Kaveh also began to shed tears. "I understand how you feel."

The woman took out a handkerchief from the pocket of her dress. "Do you seriously understand me?"

"One hundred percent! Oh, the gray world!"

Katya went and brought a photo album from her room and showed him various pictures of her husband. He was wearing a white uniform, shiny boots, a row of insignias on his chest, tasseled epaulettes, and a sword hanging from his waist.

Kaveh praised the man. "Such a profile! How magnificent! If only they would make a statue of him!"

The man's eyes were blue and he looked lethargic, like a sheep with its head cut off, his chin and lips feminine, but, altogether, he was not bad looking.

The woman closed the album, covered her face, and began to weep. Her round delicate shoulders were shaking.

Kaveh was panicky. "Is there anything I can do?"

Sobbing, Katya said, "There is nothing anyone can do. One must surrender to destiny."

Kaveh went to the kitchen, picked up a cup, and poured coffee. The old woman was washing the dishes. "Is she crying?"

"Yes, seriously. It makes your heart ache."

"That is what she does every day."

Kaveh went back and put the cup on the table. "Drink some coffee! How fragile you are!"

Katya wiped her tears. Her eyelashes, which were stuck together, cast a shadow on the bright green of her eyes. After crying for a long time, her face looked like that of a child. "Everyone says the same thing, but I cannot control it."

Her mother came and sat in an easy chair. Kaveh told a joke. While drinking her coffee, Katya began to laugh. The young man was encouraged. He sang a song and recited a riddle. He showed off every talent he possessed. The old woman clapped her hands, laughing, and said: "Charming!"

The pale sunlight reached halfway through the vestibule. Noon was approaching. The young man stood up, kissed the hands of the ladies, bowed, and went out.

At the door, the old woman said: "Come again! It is good for her mood."

Kaveh put his hand on his chest and nodded.

After a while, he became the friend and companion of the family. He repaired the chairs and pounded nails on the walls to hang the paintings. He shoveled the flowerbed and planted flowers. He would go shopping and come back with a full basket. He would not accept money for it. They set the house in order and took out the belongings that had remained in the trunks. Katya ironed her clothes and hung them in the closet. Kaveh decorated the living room with crystal vases, walnut shelves, and antique dishes. Even though he would not do any cleaning in his own house, he made the windowpanes shine crystal clear and hung the heavy velvet curtains.

Katya would sing, wash her feet in the reflecting pool, and dry them with a silk cloth. In every room, they put a framed picture of the cavalry officer on the wall. Everywhere, Kaveh could see the listless eyes of the man following him.

They would wind up the gramophone and listen to melancholic Turkish, Armenian, and Greek songs. In unison with the singers, Katya would hum. She would pick a flower from the flowerbed and pull off its petals one by one. A hint of pink was appearing on her pallid cheeks.

They washed their clothes once a week. Kaveh would wring out the water from the large sheets and hang them on the clothesline, and his suit would get soaking wet. They had given him the husband's slippers.

One day, he stood in front of the mirror and put on the officer's white jacket and military hat. They fit him perfectly. Excitedly, he came out of the room. Upon seeing him, Katya screamed and fainted. Her mother rushed to her. "Mr. Kaveh! This was not the proper thing to do."

The young man was disgusted with himself. He took off the jacket and hat and threw them on the bed. The hat's visor broke.

At sunset, they would sit on the veranda and have tea and pastries. The old woman baked pastries because of Kaveh. The young man preferred cake, but he was afraid to neutralize the impact of his flattering loose tongue on the first day when he had met her.

Spring was approaching. The weather was pleasant and the air, fresh. The sun would set later. Despite her mother's insistence, Katya always wore black. She said that she would not give up that color to the end of her life. She incessantly talked about her officer husband so much that his habits and mannerisms had been imprinted on Kaveh's brain. The officer and his wife used to have a small dog named Blanche. It would sit on the husband's knee and eat rice cookies from his hand. He would lean back next to the wood-burning stove and smoke a pipe. He would occasionally spit into the fire. When he was cheerful, he danced the waltz and the mazurka. In Officers Club parties, people pointed out the young couple to one another and whispered, "Charming!" The woman's dresses were made of blue, lavender, and pink lace and chiffon. She tied colorful ribbons in her hair, put feathers on her hats, and made up her face. They had a carriage and servants.

Kaveh would chew his nails. He knew that he could never return the comfort and luxury of the lost days of the past to Katya.

At night before he went to sleep, he would make plans about becoming rich. He would stay awake until dawn, bewildered in his tangled thoughts, and not get anywhere. His only wealth was his youthful good looks, beautiful black eyes that seemed as though they had collyrium applied to them, an attractive face, and several fashionable suits. He had told them that his father was a lumber merchant, but, since his lies had been exposed many times, Katya and her mother paid no attention to what he said. What effect would the social status of the young man have on them? They wanted his help, his endless youthful excitement, and his warm companionship. They felt they were exiles in that city. From the moment of the death of the cavalry officer, their lives had been in a state of suspension. Kaveh's presence in the house would not diminish the feeling of suspension. They looked upon him as some sort of pet. In Kaveh's being, however, the fire of love and passion was ablaze.

One day, he unlocked his mother's trunk, took out her wedding candelabra, sold it to a secondhand dealer, bought a bracelet with turquoise stones for Katya, and tried to give it to her for Easter. They were sitting on the veranda. Katya would not accept it. Kaveh's eyes teared up. "You consider me to be nothing."

Katya peeled an apple and handed it to him. "But you have paid so much money for it. How could I accept it?"

Kaveh was incensed. He took a bite of the apple and said: "This gift is worth nothing. I am prepared to drop the whole world at your feet." The lady stared at him with her green eyes. A shiver went through the young man's body. He whispered, "I wish I would die right now!"

Katya asked, "What did you say?"

"I wish I could die!"

The woman's mouth was left half open. Her small teeth shone. She bent toward him and asked in a whisper, "Why?"

"Because I am so happy." Involuntarily, he knelt, grabbed Katya's skirt, kissed it, and rubbed it on his eyes. "I love you."

The sun was setting and the breeze was pouring the scent of the cherry and quince blossoms on their heads and faces. Katya put her hand softly on Kaveh's shoulder. "Get up! My mother is coming."

"I want the whole world to know."

The lady looked at him with languid eyes. "I don't." She increased the pressure of her fingers, "Please get up!" Kaveh grabbed her hand and put his lips on her scented palm. The lady did not protest. The young man kissed the tips of her fingers one by one. He was breathing intermittently. His mouth was getting dry and his lips were burning. Katya drew her hand back and started to stand up. "You are troubling me."

Kaveh was gazing at her with his burning eyes. It was as though his body was melting and falling to the ground drop by drop. "I would die for you."

The lady went to the railing and entrusted her black locks of hair to the blossoms and the evening breeze. Kaveh sat in the easy chair and put the tips of his fingers, as though hers, on his lips.

Katya turned around. "Rid your mind of futile thoughts!"

"Yesterday, I grabbed the collar of the neighborhood street sweeper and told him, 'I love Katya.'"

Katya laughed. "You are really crazy."

"Crazy about one person."

"Wait! When the time comes, you will see a beautiful young girl the same age as you, fall for her, marry her, and live happily ever after."

Kaveh pounded on the table with his fist. "You are the beginning and the end of my life. If you leave, I swear"—he looked around him—"I swear by this sunset that I will not marry as long as I live."

The lady sat down, fastened the bracelet around her wrist, held it against the light, and shook it. "Such good taste! It does not matter. I accept it, provided this is the last time."

Kaveh walked the length of the veranda. He pushed aside the strands of his black hair from his soft, swarthy forehead. "How good you are! Indeed, how did you come to this earth? I am constantly thinking that you are not an ordinary woman. When I look at the sun and the blue sky, I say to myself that Katya belongs there."

The lady's shoulders shook. "I also see Boris in the sky."

Kaveh ran the length of the hallway and threw himself outside. He walked around in the streets until nearly morning. He passed by closed shops and silent houses many times. At dawn, he was by the gate of the National Park. The head gardener unlocked the door. The scent of flowers wafted toward them. Kaveh sat on a bench and crouched up from the cold.

The gardener came closer. "Are you upset?"

"I am in love, Teymur."

"Why don't you get married?"

"She pays no attention to me. She thinks about her husband, who is dead, twenty-four hours a day."

Teymur scratched his head. "Why have you set your heart on a widow? Is there a shortage of girls?"

Kaveh stood up and held his face toward the light of the horizon. "Oh, if only you could see her! She is peerless in the world. She does not resemble humans. I have dreamed about such a woman since childhood. When she appeared before my eyes, I could not believe she was real. I followed her like a sleepwalker. I have done everything that she has wanted. I lowered myself to the level of a houseboy. Could I say no, when she looks at me with those magical green eyes?"

"She won't become your wife?"

"She is not interested in marrying at all. She does not consider men to be human. She is so above it all that no one's fingertips can touch her."

Teymur got busy watering the flowers. "May God grant you patience!"

Kaveh went home and did not leave the house for a couple of weeks. He would not eat. He paced around the courtyard and mumbled things under his breath. At night, he pulled the quilt over his head and cried quietly. Befuddled, his mother hung around him. Kaveh would cover his ears with his hands. "Don't say one word to me, or I will kill myself!"

One day, he got dressed, shaved, and combed his hair. His eyes were dull and sunken, his cheekbones protruded, and his well-proportioned nose razor sharp. His face was pallid and his knees were shaking. He went to Katya's house.

The door was wide open. Porters were moving their furniture. Kaveh rushed into the hallway and shouted, "Katya!"

The lady came out of her room, wearing a pistachio-colored velvet jacket and skirt and a three-cornered hat adorned with pink flower buds. Her face was made up and her eyes were sparkling. She walked, sauntering toward the young man in her high-heeled snakeskin shoes. "Be quiet! Why are you shouting?"

An emerald necklace shone around her neck.

Kaveh's knees weakened. Once again, he said, "Katya!"

He collapsed on the threadbare carpet of the vestibule.

Katya shouted, "Vasily, come!"

A man came out of the room. He was wearing the uniform of an infantry officer. Dark-complexioned and broad-shouldered, his mustache was twisted upward. He had wide eyebrows and listless eyes. He picked up the young man, put him on the sofa, and slapped him.

Katya said, "Gentler! I feel sorry for him."

The man chewed on the tip of his mustache. "Give him back the bracelet and get rid of him."

Katya turned to the man. "Go! I want to talk with him alone."

The officer walked away with firm steps and halfway turned around and scowled at her. "Don't take too long. We are in a hurry."

Katya held Kaveh's hand. "My dear, I married this man the day before yesterday."

Kaveh pulled back his hand fearfully. His eyes, red from sleeplessness, widened. "Married him? Impossible! You are pulling my leg. How about the soul of your husband? The gray life?" He took a look at the walls. "What did you do with the pictures? This little fellow can't even hold a candle to your late husband."

Katya's eyes welled up with tears. "No, he can't. But what am I to do? I love him."

Kaveh bit the palm of his hand in dismay. "You must be joking! What kind of a show is this?"

The lady touched her emerald necklace with the tips of her fingers. "Vasily bought this for me. Don't you think it's pretty?"

Kaveh kept silent. The lady continued, "He is an infantry officer.

He serves in Yalta and comes from a good family. His grandmother is a princess."

Kaveh laughed nervously. "With that ugly mug of his, I swear, his dear grandmother must be a dishwasher in a café."

"Don't be a pest! I have investigated. My paternal cousin has dug into his background. You know me. I am not the kind to just jump into the water before I look. His wife died last year. He has a small son. His mother will raise his son."

Kaveh began to stand up. "Now, where are you going to go?"

The woman clapped her hands. "Well, obviously, we will go back to Yalta. I felt depressed in this city. See what fate has in store for a person! Everything just worked out by itself. He serves in the same barracks with my cousin. They are friends. That rascal, Yegorushka, had talked about me so much that it made Vasily restless. One night, when he was sleepless, without asking for a leave, he took the train and came here. When my mother opened the door, the poor man was so tired that he could hardly stand on his feet. He knelt before me, told me that he loved me, lay down on the daybed, and slept until noon the following day. He is very passionate."

"I love you, too."

Katya puckered her lips. "There is a difference, my dear. He will take me to Greece."

"I would take you there, too."

Katya laughed and put her hand on his shoulder, which made Kaveh shiver from head to toe. She whispered in his ear, "Oh, you liar!" The porters were carrying a trunk. The lady shouted, "Be careful! It is full of fragile things." In the living room, secondhand dealers were examining the paintings and the old easy chairs. Katya explained, "We are selling all of them. Vasily has a big house. I will only take my bed." She knit her brow. "Why should I sleep on his ex-wife's bed?"

Kaveh shook his head, dumbfounded. "Are you going straight to his house? Then what about your old mother?"

"Of course, Mama will come with us. She does not like Vasily, but she will get used to him after a couple of months. Look, I am still young. My mama is a selfish woman. She expected me to be hers alone. Be fair! Would a person spend her whole life dreaming about a dead man?" Katya's lips quivered. "Don't frown! You always understood me. Do you remember that you could not bear to see my tears, that you wanted me to be happy?"

"Are you happy now?"

Katya tied her lace gloves together. "Oh, not bad. For now, I have cast caution to the wind."

"Is he as kind as your first husband?"

"No one is as kind as you are."

Kaveh put his hands over his face. "No, don't say that. I know it myself. Even now, I could die for you. You are being wasted. The demon is taking the angel with him. That corpulent idiot would not even give up his sleep for one night. I have not slept for three months because of you."

Katya caressed Kaveh's cheek with the tips of her fingers. Her hands were as delicate as quince blossoms. "My darling! I will never forget you. I have not told you this before. I really like your eyes."

Kaveh went into the kitchen, picked up a knife, and came back. He knelt before the lady and put the blade on his eyelid. "If you like them, take them with you. I would like to gift you with a jewel that no man has ever given a woman."

The lady grabbed the young man's wrist, and burst out crying again. Her delicate round shoulders shook. She took the knife, tossed it on the floor, opened Kaveh's fingers, and kissed his palm. "Now leave! I will keep your bracelet."

Kaveh ran toward the door. On his way, he bumped against several people. The spring sun was shining on Warshawskaya Street.

Kaveh got up and went out. Roxana closed her eyes. Hero Torkan sighed. Vahab shifted in place where he was lying. Showkat went to the curtain and touched the bottom of the tassels. The vague shadow of her eyebrows covered up the shine in her eyes. She had a cloudy halo around her head, which lit up spot by spot under the rays of the candles. She had lost a little weight. She was looking at the floor and squeezing the whip in her hand. Vahab thought about the weak scaffolding under the woman's feet. Termites had gnawed the inside of the wood and made it hollow. She had ascended from the darkness of the alleyways in the depths of the city. She had shone brilliantly in her shiny yellow dress, for a moment. Once again, chaos was dragging her down. The colorful bubble of foam was moving from light to shade.

Roxana knelt on the ground. "When with the delusion of doing some good I was taking refuge in the impoverished, I was making myself believe in sham altruism. In church, under the vapors of frankincense, entangled in rapture, I thought that playing the role of a benevolent lady was worthy of me. The priests, however, were more cunning. They chuckled at that image. They had seen similar ones. Why was I getting angry? Had I been in their place, would I have behaved better?"

Yusef grabbed Yunos's arm. "You are troubling her." He walked closer to Roxana. "Do not kneel! No one here is more sinless than you."

Roxana continued: "The afflicted! In indigence, helplessness, hunger, and being cold, I would become worse than they. I did not have the right to be offended."

Vahab bent forward. "Do not surrender to this game! Have faith in yourself!"

Roxana said: "I am sitting behind a cloudy glass. All the sounds outside are nothing but a hubbub in my ears. My fingertips neither touch nor feel anything."

Showkat began drumming on the floor with the toe of her boot and grumbled under her breath: "Too much whining! What a mess I've gotten myself into!" She shouted: "Stop that puppet show! Yunos, spit it out!"

Hero Yunos read calmly:

The happiest days of her life were those when she lived in a village. She picked fruit and climbed the rocky mountain. She separated the pits and placed them under the July sun. The scent of ripe apricots mingled with the aroma of alfalfa flowers. Her spine shivered from some vague desire. She would glide her enflamed hands caressing her breasts. As simple as the springs, animals, and soil, she was becoming ready to be fruitful. She would lie on hot rocks with girls of the same age. They occasionally whispered. The smell of the body sweat was penetrating and frothy. From the depths of their tissues, silent bubbles rose like the foam on the tops of bottles of wine. They would open their bosoms toward the sky and the sun. But the honey of their bodies upon touching the first man would slowly turn to vinegar. They were whipped. They would decay in forgetfulness.

Once Kowkab's man firmly secured his place, he stepped on the path to the tavern. The blossoming crisp body became the recipient of the blows of the fist, and the dreams of maidenhood diminished and withered with the rubble of insults. The woman was becoming accustomed to it. She was becoming confused and crumbling, and she would acquiesce to the insults. With the entry of the man into the house, her blood, the bile of degradation, melted down her very fibers in a dark agitation. Disgusted with herself, she would examine the black and blue scars of her arms and legs. She thought she was deserving of any humiliation, a punching bag and a sponge of lust.

The sunshine of adolescence and the cycling honey of fruition, which had grown from her belly under the midday sun as delicate as the petals of morning glory, were ripped apart into a thousand pieces with cactus thorns. A voluminous womb replaced the bubbling of the spring. With her head lowered, she walked into the small room, wobbling. Silently and patiently, she endured the pain of giving birth many times, and moaned with her lips closed. The man became wretchedly desperate from the commotion and clamor of the children.

The axis of their relationship was the double-edged blade of hatred. The man fled and withered in the taverns. They would drive him out of one door, he would come in through another. He slept under filthy tables, snoring. Kowkab, however, dreamed of him in the dew between flower petals, the torrential rains of spring, the colors of the rainbow, the flames of fire, and the rays of moonlight. She would conceal her doomed expectation from everyone's eyes.

Kowkab took out a handkerchief from her pocket, wiped the sweat from her brow, and muttered: "I have a shooting pain in my head." Yunos picked up another sheet of paper:

She spent her youth surrounded by bedpans, pale embryos inside glass, the smell of anesthetic drugs, and the moaning of patients. She slept in the room at the end of the hallway, chewing pilfered sugar cubes, a sweet shelter in the face of disasters. The oil lamp emitted smoke, and her ears were filled with the sound of moaning. The sound of the bell would interrupt her light sleep. She would check on the patients' rooms. She would advance in the semidark hallway, supporting herself with her hand on the wall, and would feed a spoonful of medicine to a young man who suffered from scrofula, and lay down a foul-smelling, injured thigh infected by gangrene on the mattress. The blueish blisters of smallpox would burst before her eyes, and she would wash off the bloody vomit.

The rays of florescent lights were gradually sucking up the freshness of her skin, until her face became as white as liquid plaster. At the age of twenty-five, she left the hospital, got married, and her man one year later left for the mountains. Her sister's family burned in a house fire. From that tragedy, her share was a mute boy. The child would scream in his sleep, had nightmares, and clenched his teeth. His pillow would be soaking with his saliva. He was a stranger to Pari. In the chaotic cold world, he only showed his love for Gowhar.

With the establishment of the Regime of Fire, the woman's time was spent on waiting in long lines. In the middle of winter, she would pound the frozen ground with her numb feet. Bewildered among the pages of files, she would take dozens of signed and sealed papers from one department to another. All day long, she would entrust the children to the neighbors. Six months of searching hospitalized her. In her feverish delirium, the dead in the hospital passed before her in a long line.

Hero Pari put her head on Kowkab's shoulder and closed her eyes. Yunos paused momentarily. Torkan smiled. He continued:

With his watery eyes in sunlight, her father could not see. Like two blue pearls, they gleamed faintly. He would sit in front of the house and recite prayers for the restoration of his vision. He would talk about a tree that had been sawed down many years earlier, about the sky and patches of clouds, about black and white goats.

In the beginning, those around him refuted what he said. They would say that goats do not make a sound with their hooves and do not bleat. The old man would shake his knotty cane and say that he could see them with his own eyes, those who said no, who wanted to kill him, were bitches and cuckolds. Later on, they let him be. He would sit in the sun for hours, lean against the adobe wall, and his daydreams would peak. He would describe frightening scenes out loud: the riders of the Kyzylkum Desert with drawn swords in hand in red garb, on galloping horses. In the heat of battle, a fairy in blue garb was splitting the clouds and descending. She was twirling her starlike staff, driving them all away. Her white body shone under her cloudlike garment. The old man would describe it in detail. Torkan's mother would strike him on the head with the broom handle, "In front of the girls? Shame on you!"

No matter which way the old man turned, the fairy would appear before his eyes leaping and jumping. She jumped up and down on the branches of the mulberry trees, on the domes of houses, on the backs of fruit carts, or between the sky and the earth.

A sort of rivalry developed between the fairy and the mother. The woman hated the fairy as though she were her cowife. When the old man would get tired, he would sit by the flowerbed, smoke the hookah, and spit toward the stems of the marshmallow plant. Mother used obscene language to curse the fairy. She would make fun of her body. Father would become enraged. The veins on his thin neck would swell up, and he would shake the hollow cane.

A river of insults would begin to flow from his mouth and accuse his wife of prostitution. He considered the fairy to be pure. Mother would be foaming at the mouth. She would say that the fairy slept in someone else's bed chamber every night, but she herself had been faithful to a decrepit, crazy old man for fifty years. She would then grab a cluster of her hair, yank out some strands, and toss them to the wind. Now, after all those years, she would say, her reward was for a slutty fairy to grab her husband. The quarreling would continue until the neighbors came in and put an end to it. After a while, the people of the neighborhood would talk about the fairy as though she were a real human being. When mother cried, they would console her. The women would tell her that ignoring the fairy would be more effective than a hundred insults, and that she would leave on her own, but the fairy continued her presence, until Torkan got married.

The young man was from the same village. He had rescued Torkan when she was six years old from a stray dog that had attacked her. He would go to the city and back on the carts that carried fresh and dried fruit. He wore a colorful shirt with paisley and flower designs and a red scarf around his neck. His blond hair bent like stalks of wheat in the wind.

They got married during the harvest season and moved to the city. The mother came to visit her daughter every month and told her about what was going on in the village, events which were no longer of interest to Torkan. The village had disappeared behind the dust of the wagon that carried the new bride to the city and had been replaced with canned Black Sea herring, mercerized cotton stockings, and the Spanish circus. On Sundays, they went on outings. They would sit on a blanket in the meadow of the Three Boots Distillery and eat saltwater pickles, eggs, and pomegranates. The young man would climb the trees, pick fresh almonds, and shell them for Torkan.

In conversations with her mother, she would only ask about how the fairy was doing. Her mother would get angry and say that she was as unfaithful as her father and that she had forgotten about the family, and she would tell Torkan that she cursed herself for having nursed her as a baby. Finally, she arrived one autumn morning and reported that the fairy had disappeared. Since the beginning of that month, no matter where the old man looked, he could not see the fairy. He would rub his eyes and, stumbling and falling, he would go all over the wheat field. They would bring him back home when his feet were bleeding. He waited for a week, concealing what he knew from others until he got sick and was put to bed. In his feverish delirium, he said that the fairy had left him and that because she was so messy and slutty, she was not worthy of him. He thought that it was a pity that she had that golden staff, and he compared her rump to the tail-fat of a sheep. The fairy was toppled from her position, and the wife became the darling she had once been at the beginning. The neighbors celebrated and brought sugarplums and dried raisins for them. The old man ate them fistful by fistful and shed tears. He expected to receive condolences. As long as he lived, in front of him, no one talked about stars, the color blue, or wings.

Torkan gave birth to Shirin and Aslan one after another. Her old mother visited them in the city more often than in the past. She had become mesmerized by Torkan's sewing machine. She would sew sheets and pillowcases, and she would take care of her grandchildren.

After the fairy left, the old blind man had lost his appeal. He could no longer incite his wife's jealousy. Empty of dreams, he would sit on the veranda, lean his head against the railing, and doze off, snoring. Only bees and flies circled around his head. His eyelids oozed out excretion, like a squeezed pomegranate.

The fruit production of the village diminished, and the wheat fields became infested by pests.

The young man changed his job. With a shovel on his shoulder, he went to the city square and joined the day laborers waiting to work as construction workers. One day, they brought Torkan the news that he had fallen from the scaffolding and died on the spot.

All three women dropped their heads.

Heroes Rashid and Qadir went close to the piano. Qadir grabbed Rashid's arm. "Let's run away! I'm afraid. Why are all these Fire Stokers surrounding the house?"

Rashid pulled away. "You can do whatever you want. I'm not going to abandon my friends."

"Do you want to be taken to the firing squad as one of the rebels?"

"What rebels?"

"The doors and the walls of this house press on my heart. When I hear any sound, I say to myself, they have come. My father's advice to me was, 'Avoid wounded snakes, shrewish women, and cracked walls!' As luck would have it, we've got all three here. Why did you imprison that dog, Haddadiyan? The neighbors were sneakily smiling at me this morning, tipping their hats to me. But they would not come close to me, as though I was a gunpowder depot. When they laugh at you this way, you should sing your swan song."

Kaveh entered the parlor.

Chapter 14

Roxana was pacing the room. Hero Qobad was sitting at the table, his head down. The rays of the flame shimmered on his profile. Vahab wiped the sweat from his brow with his handkerchief. He thought that Qobad's narrow nose, sunken eyes, and wobbly crutch were a myth in the making, as big as the old man's clenched fists. His life had passed by as swiftly as the wind among rocky paths, mountain peaks, and labyrinthine caves. For many years, the passage of time was marked by the full moon becoming a crescent in the sky, and then the crescent becoming a full moon, again and again. Along with his fellow combatants, they had washed their wounds in the springs, survived on eating common yarrow, awaiting nothing. Reviving the memory of the mountains was a game. Hero Qobad knew that. He smiled, talked, and ate with a sense of surrender. In his entire life, it was perhaps only on this night that he thought of himself as the head of a family

Borzu was seriously kneading the dough for the bread. Vahab gazed at him. So many nights, he had walked in alleyways in massive fog, shivering from cold in a light summer jacket, warming up his red, numb fingers by breathing on them, and he had passed by lit windows on on light feet, looking timidly inside, and carrying the memory of the flames!

Rashid put a date pit on the side of the plate and licked his lips. He did not understand the sense of suspension that dominated the atmosphere of the house. He spun between the past and future, bewildered. The house was a precipice, the factory depressing. He would run around the National Park. Gaining physical strength was an ointment he was applying to the wound of sudden loss, the death of his grandmother. He was capable of defeating ten strong men, but when he walked, he was careful not to step on the ants. With unusual strength, under the taut skin of his body, his muscles were nearly exploding. Rashid thought about his future. Maybe he would soon set his life in order. He would leave his house at dawn, and a sleepy wife with a baby in her arms standing between the double doors would watch him walk away. At night, in the house, the smell of bread, tea, and urine left in the bedpan would circle among the waves of hot air. After a while, the eagerness to see the rosy cheeks of his wife would no longer hasten his steps. Life would continue monotonous and bare. No sequins would shine in any corner. The memory of Mrs. Edrisi, the scent of ambergris, and the tulip-shaped lamps of the chandelier would be concealed behind fog, becoming shapeless, mashed together. Faces would intermingle. Showkat, Qobad, Roxana, Yavar, and Leqa would turn into a mass of fragments, ghosts that would flap their wings in dreams and in the morning be forgotten beside the glass of tea.

A moth was circling around the shimmering flame of the candle. Roxana approached the table. "It is attracted by the light. It is not looking for its source. Yet, on the order of the monster, I push aside the curtains to see the cobwebs behind them."

Borzu said emphatically: "Much better. We also open up the veins of the dead, split the cells, and place them under the microscope to find the source of life."

Yunos rubbed his left eye. "Have you found it?"

"Not yet. Science is still in its infancy."

"The fate of your science is to remain an eternal infant."

Hero Qobad turned to Yunos. "Read some more!"

Yunos held a sheet of paper before his eye:

The mother was undisciplined and airheaded. Near sunset, she would sit on the stone seat next to the house door and watch the passersby. When she talked with other women, the sound of her laughter reverberated under the arched ceilings. She would crack roasted melon seeds between her teeth and eat dried mulberries. She would puff up her pleated skirt, exposing her wheat-colored calves. She was tall and corpulent. Male passersby, upon seeing the dimples on her cheeks, row of shiny teeth, and freckled face would slow their steps, look at the woman clad in red with buyers' eyes, and occasionally wink at her. She would eagerly acknowledge the admiring glances. To show off her gold choker necklace, she would lean her head against the wall. At nightfall, the neighborhood women would gradually go back into their houses. When the last one, a public-bath attendant, would leave the stone seat in front of her own house, Qadir's mother would get up, yawn, and enter her house.

The father was a shoemaker. He dropped by his shop every other day. He was not fond of work. He would lie down under a blanket and read books all the time. In the evenings, there was no supper. The woman would forget to prepare any food. They often ate snacks. It made no difference to the father. He would sink a piece of flatbread like a snow shovel into a bowl of yogurt and sing in a whisper under his breath:

This artless twisted belly of mine
Awaits being filled with nothing that's fine.

Upon taking his last bite, he would drink a sip of water and shake his finger threateningly toward his wife.

The chicken will go where there is seed
Not where there is nothing for feed.

Clueless and confused, the woman would giggle and clear the supper cloth, toss the leftover bread pieces into the reflecting pool, where a couple of red goldfish nibbled at them, and, on the following day, the stale softened bread would dissolve under sunlight and mingle with the green algae.

She would dump the soapy water from washing dirty clothes into the flowerbed. The apple tree and the petunias dried up, and the flowerbed was left with soil filled with nothing but cracks.

After supper, the mother would bring out her makeup box and decorate her face. She applied red lipstick to her lips, rouge to her cheeks, and collyrium to her squinty eyes. She placed sequins on her hair and asked the man, "Do I look pretty?"

He would rub his sleepy eyes, shake his head, and recite the verse from Hafez:

The beloved is not the one with lovely figure and hair
Be enslaved to that face alone with an attribute so rare.

The woman would pick up the mirror and stare at her own image. The man would warn her with a line from Sa'di: "God-given beauty needs no beautification."

When late-night drunkards passed through the alleyway, the mother would perk up her ears, her eyes sparkling, and bite her meaty red lips. The father would shake his head in regret.

When your beloved is not at your side, face to face
There is no other choice but yourself to embrace.

The woman would ask angrily, "What?"

The man would doze off over the book. They would roll out the bedding. The father would immediately fall asleep. The woman was not the kind to sleep. She put on delicate dainty clothes, and, under the light of the moon, wrapped her arms around the wooden column of the veranda and hummed popular songs. With every shooting star in the sky, she sighed and said that it was the sign of a human's death. On the night when the father was in the throes of death , she had seen a long shooting star in the sky as well. After the man's death, she cried continuously for three days. She would pull out a handkerchief from her brassiere to wipe her tears and runny nose. On the third night, she felt sleepy. She pushed the neighboring women who were there to console her out of the house, ate a bowl of cabbage pottage, and said under her breath, "The chicken will go where there is seed."

The mother and son sold the books and used the money to buy a bicycle for Qadir. They made a trip to Samarkand, walked around in the bazaars, ate sweetmeats, and when they returned, they had some meat on their bones.

Qadir brought home two quail chicks. Whistling, he would go out of the house for a stroll and come back at night.

The mother sewed maroon-colored curtains and hung them on the window. As had been her habit in the past, in the late afternoons she would sit on the stone seat by the house door, cracking and eating roasted melon seeds. She would laugh and make her eyes look sultry. She fell for the poultry seller in the neighborhood. He was a short young man, muscular, with a dark complexion. He was about seven years younger than she was. Habitually, he would twirl a pocket chain around his index finger and hit a melon seed shell with it. His eyes, according to Qadir's mother, had a special glow, like a snake's eyes that nailed you in your place. The mother was nailed in place. She got married. The man, with his broad shoulders and half-bare chest, would sit where Qadir's father used to sit and eat yogurt with cucumbers. The mother would laugh. Her gold jewelry glittered in the twilight. She had become industrious and nimble. She would make mutton stew. She had planted flowers in the flowerbed, which she watered in the afternoon with a watering can. The stepfather began bickering with Qadir. In his absence, he chopped the heads off the quails. When Qadir got home, he cried for hours, clawing at the damp soil of the flowerbed. His mother said, "Don't be so hard on yourself! Quails don't cost that much."

Right in front of their eyes, Qadir urinated on the newly sprouted flowerbed and left. He got on his bicycle and pedaled away. He rented a room in the center of the city and became a neighbor to a house painter. As long as he had money, he spent it, until he hit the bottom. He began accompanying the painter to work. He painted the dark hallway of an elementary school. His coworker painted the picture of a swallow on the wall. Qadir stood back, looked admiringly at the picture, and said, "Add a pomegranate aril to the bird's beak!" At that very moment, he chose his profession. They painted houses, and they ate and drank well. His teacher, the master painter, would tell him that life was worth nothing. Qadir would nod in agreement. He would quote an aphorism from his father: "We will think about tomorrow when tomorrow comes." He developed muscles and strength. He lost the habit of quoting poems and aphorisms. Ten years later, his teacher died after developing pneumonia and was buried in the graveyard of the Qareh Aghaj Church. Qadir did not go to work for six days. He walked around in snowy and rainy weather, until he happened to pass through his old neighborhood. He sat on the stone seat of their house. After a while, he knocked. No one opened the door. The glass globe lampshade over the house door was still broken. An old man with a cane was approaching. It was Yahya Beyg, the vinegar seller. Qadir said hello and stood up. The old man blinked his eyes. The young man held the old man's hands in his. "Don't you recognize me? I'm Qadir."

The old man scratched his belly. "Where have you been all this time, son? They sold the house and left."

A crow sat on the top of the downspout. Without thinking, the first thing that came out of Qadir's mouth was, "So soon?"

He thought the tin downspout was rusted and needed to be painted.

Hero Qadir gazed at the garden. A coin slid from between his fingers and fell on the floor. Rashid patted him on his back.

Yunos took a sip of water, and continued:

One day, from behind the arbor of the Judas-tree flowers, he heard someone crying. It was early in the morning and people were going to work. Teymur became curious. He looked through the branches and leaves inside the arbor. A girl was sitting on the corner of a bench. Her eyes were hazel and her shiny auburn hair was in a braid. She was covering her face and sobbing. Turtledoves were jumping around her. She was wearing patched shoes and short socks inappropriate for her age. A slanted ray of light colored her delicate earlobe pink. She would look at the sky, and staring at the clouds, she seemed to be separate from the impurities of earth.

Teymur had come from Samarkand the year before, and had been recently hired at the National Park. He had an athletic body, befitting his new dark blue uniform. The breeze tousled his soft black hair. His vibrant amber skin shone. Every teardrop of the girl set the young man's heart on edge. He wanted to go, grab the hem of her dress, and tell her, "Stay with me, so that no one can bother you." He stood cautiously next to the vine arbor. The girl wiped her tears. The man sat on the bench across from her, scratching the ground with the toe of his shoe. "I hope I am not intruding." The girl did not respond. "Is something big the cause of your sorrow?" The girl shook her head. "No problem is without a solution."

"Except for my problems."

"You are not from here, are you?"

The girl dropped her head, "We have come from Moscow."

"Who are you living with?"

"My father and brothers."

"Do you not have a mother?"

"She died last year. The responsibility for the boys is on my shoulders."

She stood up, shook her skirt, and left through the eastern gate in slow, weary steps.

Teymur waited for a week. On Thursday afternoon, the girl came back with two little boys. Teymur picked a rosebud and ran after her. The girl took the flower coyly. Her hesitant hand seemed to be looking for a shelter in the air. The boys went to play, and Teymur and the girl sat on a bench. The man coughed, "Are you feeling better?"

"My situation has not changed. We were happy in Moscow, until my mother died and my father took refuge in alcohol. He was dismissed from the military. He had insulted the tsar. When he gets drunk, he can't control his tongue."

Teymur said, "You are so young."

"I am nineteen. I think I have grown old. Managing the house is difficult. I miss my mother. My father does not love us, he only takes care of himself. He wears a white suit, a red necktie, and shines his boots every day. Every night, he goes to the Pink Rose Café, eats goulash, and drinks wine. He comes home late at night, drops down on his bed with his boots on, and sleeps until noon. He is not really a bad person, but, what a pity, his heart is broken and he is depressed."

The boys came back. Teymur rushed to get four cold lemonades from the café. After finishing their beverages, the boys licked their glasses. The girl blushed and explained, "They don't get out of the house much."

Teymur accompanied them home. It was a cottage in the middle of nowhere, a big room with a bathroom and a kitchen.

For three whole years, the whitewashed room with four walls, the half-burnt grass, and the surrounding mud holes were Teymur's promised land. The father did not give them permission to marry, because he needed Anna, but he agreed to his daughter visiting Teymur once a week. The lieutenant would lie down on his bed and sip booze slowly. His shirt would roll up, displaying the hollow of his navel. In the height of drunkenness, he would bestow upon the queen an obscene insult, and fall asleep.

Finally, they got married. In their new house, Anna sang while she did the housework. She was gradually forgetting her happy childhood memories. After five years, she gave birth to a boy. With her son there, her attention was diverted from her brothers. She watched the slightest reaction of the newborn, his sneezing, blinking, or turning on his stomach. While previously she had paid no attention to religious observances, she hung dozens of amulets, portraits of saints, crosses, and rosaries on the walls.

Anna's father had a heart attack in his sleep in early autumn. The teenage brothers went to Moscow.

Hero Teymur was displaying the energy of his good fortune in the National Park. He adorned the arbor of the Judas-tree flowers like a flaming pavilion. He constructed octagonal flowerbeds in the middle of the lawn and planted different flowers in each. Violet, pink, purple, blue, and saffron colors on an expanse of emerald green. The colors of dreams and wakefulness, waving in the breeze.

The people of the city would gather around the flowerbeds, pointing out the flowers to one another. It was rumored throughout the province that any plant cutting would grow by his hand. He planted boxwoods on both sides of the paths, and he trimmed the pine trees, shaping them into the forms of balls, domes, and prisms. The dark and light plant greens were harmonious and refreshing. The National Park became the meeting place of commissioned officers, young lovers, and even merchants. They increased his salary, and he received a golden plaque with the image of a duck's head from the mayor.

He bought an apartment on Ursha Street.

The son was raised in comfort. They would buy whatever he wanted right away, hazelnut, chocolate, ice cream, balls, clothes, and many toys. The boy was raised like an aristocrat. He would attend singing classes, do target practice, and go horseback riding. He wore short checkered trousers, socks that reached up to his knees, a black velvet jacket, and a red vest. At fifteen, he was a head and shoulder taller than Teymur. He was handsome and dignified, with a pleasant complexion. His father's additional salary had turned into a layer of fat, spread over the son's shoulders, thighs, and rear end. A light mustache had sprouted over his upper lip. He used cologne and went to cafés and theatres. He became friends with the children of the affluent. When he turned eighteen, the only daughter of a senior officer fell in love with him and wrote him a letter on which she had glued a strand of her perfumed blonde hair. He was unparalleled in dancing the Mazurka. His mother was proud of him. Fearful and depressed, his father would shake his head, "He is ashamed of us. In the National Park, he acted as though he did not know me, because he was with his friends."

"He will turn out fine. He is still young."

Teymur would hold his calloused hands toward the sky.

The young man would often come back home late at night. His father could smell wine on his breath. Finally, one night, he lost his patience and slapped the boy's cheek. The young man left and did not return for three days. Anna scratched her own face in distress, wailed, and paced back and forth all night until morning. Upon hearing any sound, she would open the window. He came back at noon on the third day. Trembling, his mother embraced him and brought him pudding and shelled almonds. The boy ate them silently and wiped his pink lips with a silk handkerchief. He sat by the window and had a cup of coffee with milk under the autumn sunlight.

Teymur grabbed his shoulders from behind and pressed them with his strong short fingers, "The fruit of my heart! My son, my life, where have you been?"

The young man pulled back, stood up facing his father, his eyes burning with anger, and his cheeks flushed. He picked up a porcelain vase, "If you take one step forward, I will smash it. Look at me! Do I look like the son of a gardener?"

Teymur took out the gold plaque from the cabinet and tossed it on the table, "You bastard." He grabbed him by the throat and pounded his head against the wall.

Anna fell to her knees before her husband. Teymur ignored her. The woman brought the bottle of plant pesticide and said, "I am going to drink it."

Teymur's hands loosened. The faces and the furniture in the room began to spin around his head. He fainted and collapsed on the floor. He heard a soft sound. The son was dragging a large suitcase. When he opened his eyes, there was no one else in the house. The reflection of the afternoon sunlight on the windowpane was shining straight into his eyes. He put the plaque back into the cabinet. He took the dishes from his son's lunch to the kitchen and washed them. Anna's overcoat was not hanging in the wardrobe. He sat at the table, covered his face with his hands, and moaned, "What if he never comes back?"

He remembered Anna's father, in a white suit and red necktie. Maybe his son had taken after him. He rubbed his rough hands together and hid them under the table. He felt sorry for Anna. He pondered whether he had wasted the woman's life. She was now middle aged. The color and freshness of youth were leaving her face like the last particles of evening light.

Anna came back in the middle of the night. She tossed her purse on the ground and pounded her head on the tile counter. Teymur tried to stroke her hair. The woman jumped and screamed, "Get lost! Don't come close to me!"

For a whole month, it was as though she had taken silence pills. She walked around the house like a fleeing shadow. Finally, one day, Teymur heard her conversing with a neighbor's wife on the staircase. "His letter arrived from Izmir. He wants to travel around the world."

Teymur took the letter from Anna. There was a photograph with it. The young man was standing under a tree full of blossoms in a sailor's cap and uniform, a cigarette in the corner of his lips, frowning. There was a deep valley between him and the little boy who used to cut the whiskers of the cat with a pair of scissors, raised silkworms, and sat on his father's knees, looking at the pictures of horses.

The middle-aged couple reconciled. Their common sorrow connected them. The woman brought home a small dog. She named it Snowball. She spoiled it like a baby, giving it milk and cookies. She would even bake cakes for it. Maybe the animal's white hair reminded her of her father's suit. She knitted a jacket. When she took the dog out for a walk in winter, she dressed it in handwoven clothes. She had taught it to raise its front paws when they saw acquaintances and close its right eye. Snowball's cute tricks would make her laugh. She looked at her hand-trained creature with pride.

The intervals between the son's letters were increasing from year to year. Anna was getting old. One winter, Snowball got sick. It had a cough, and after three days, it went to sleep by Anna's feet with its wet snout and died. The woman wore black for an entire year. Unless absolutely necessary, she would not leave the apartment. Seeing other dogs refreshed the pain of her loss. Teymur's enthusiasm diminished, and the National Park lost its appeal. He was replaced with a young gardener.

Midday one day, Anna walked out in the falling snow, recollecting her childhood memories, paying no attention to her physical condition, her thin overcoat and shoes that had holes in them. When she went back home, her hazel eyes were burning from fever. She lay down and Teymur pulled a thick quilt over her. She was still shivering. She was whispering the names of her son and Snowball. Her husband called three physicians to come at the same time. After their consultation, they received a hefty fee and left the ailing woman. The old man saw them off to the staircase and stared into their eyes. He was moving the door handle up and down, waiting for a hopeful statement or smile. They were just chatting and laughing, making arrangements for dinner and playing cards.

After the woman's death, he picked up his clay pipe and went to the garden. He sat under the arbor of the Judas-tree flowers until dawn.

Chapter 15

Roxana sat at the table, gazing at the flame of the candle. "I fled from Tbilisi with a theater director. He was fifty years old. He was talented in everything. He played the violin, sang, and painted the stage landscapes. He was unrivaled in acting. He was able to show the core of the characters with a few movements, from Mephistopheles to Jean Valjean, as skillfully as a trapeze artist. Unlike most actors, he would not become one with the character of the play. Between absorption and awareness, his being was the essence of acting, a reflection of the world. With his natural capabilities, he could be at the same level as great actors, but he preferred to tutor the likes of us. And we were not anything special. But he took us by the hand and pulled us up, sweating. Once we became independent, he entrusted us to the stage and left. You never saw him without a smile on his face. He paid no attention to his own sorrow. He never complained. He did not talk about his past. In a dilapidated wagon, he went from one city to the next. He put some color into the lives of dispirited people in the most remote and isolated regions.

"I was playing a role in *Chayka*. He was sitting in the first row, a bit drunk. He smiled, and his eyes shone in the dark. Because of my guru and mentor, I had the best performance of my life that night. The balconies were full of people. There were several ministers and an ambassador in the state box. But would I look at them? I was only looking to see the gleam in his eyes. When the play ended, the large auditorium roared with applause. We took bows, and they brought us baskets of flowers. In the dimly lit theater, he got up and walked toward the door, his hands in his pockets and his back bent. His

disheveled hair reached his shoulders, and his old suit looked awk-
ward on his body. He turned around and looked at me. My heart
throbbed in my temples. It dawned on me that that would be our last
meeting. I knew his astonishing power of acting. Our group of actors
were like grade school children compared to my guru.

"I changed my clothes, jumped into a carriage, and went to see
him. Whenever he came to Moscow, he stayed in an inn downtown.
An Armenian woman was its manager. Its hallways were dark, and
on the staircase, they had placed flowerpots of withered geraniums.
With my arrival, a commotion began in the neighborhood. Heads
stuck out of windows. The old Armenian woman bowed several
times and said, 'You're too late. He picked up his suitcase half an
hour ago and left.' I asked, 'Where?' She did not know. I said, 'Show
me his room.' I climbed the stairs. There was a bouquet of wild violets by the mirror. He occasionally called me 'Wild Violet.' He knew
I would go to see him. In his view, that meeting would not have been
beneficial. He had finished his work. The wild violet had now become
an orchid flower, expensive and decorative. By leaving those flowers
for me, he wanted to tell me not to forget the wild violet. From then
on, how would I be able to grow by the side of streams, simple and
unpretentious, under children's feet, for my color and scent to belong
to the poor? I picked up the violets and came downstairs. People
were peeking inside. The innkeeper had uncorked her most expensive wine. I took a sip and took refuge in the carriage. I smelled the
withered bouquet and wept all the way back. Later on, I heard that
he had died in Kazan. He had had a heart attack on stage."

Silence dominated the air. Kaveh lit a cigarette.

Qobad pulled back his chair and leaned his head against the back
cushion. "Such individuals are rare among the new generation."

Roxana walked to the window, looking at the shadows of the
trees, the moonlight, and the water. "I feel lighter. I wish I could
climb a thin ray of light and reach him." She asked Yunos: "Where
is he now?"

Yunos folded the black cloak and put it next to his sheets of writing. "In the memory of each and every one of us."

Roxana sighed. "I wish I could reach out with my hand, grab the sleeve of his smoke-colored jacket, and say, 'Speak to me. Don't leave me on my own.'"

Vahab sat up and in a pouty voice asked: "What would he answer?"

"He would say, fly. Don't be a domesticated pigeon. Go high, peak!"

"Had you not peaked?"

"Often I have fallen. The girl I knew and saw in the mirror was left behind in wooden dressing rooms."

"What did you do with the violets?"

"I lost them, like I did myself." She turned to Yunos. "Please, read some more."

Yunos read:

The woman was twenty-one years old. She had children of different sizes. They were walking in muddy alleyways, and the husband was the guide. With a bundle under her arm, Rokhsareh followed the man step by step. The children were shivering from the biting cold. It was getting dark. They reached the end of the alleyway, and the man paused. There was a house in front of them with brick walls. Behind the window on the east, they saw a silhouette, and they looked at it in astonishment. It was the statue of a woman in actual size. Light was shining on it from behind. Her wings were open, floating in azure blue light. Her hair was golden, her blue eyes devoid of sight; she had large breasts and a narrow waist. They had dressed her in a purple velvet dress.

Rokhsareh was scared, "Is this a ghost house?"

The husband took his shoehorn out of his pocket and pulled up the backs of his shoes. He coughed and knocked on the door with the lion-claw door knocker. On the arched ceiling over the door, there was a tile with the image of an eye on it, a line in the middle dividing the cornea. Perking up her ears, Rokhsareh heard the clicking of high heels. The sound was getting closer to the door. The owner of the shoes stopped behind the door, caught her breath, and asked, "Who is it?"

The husband answered, "Kuhzad."

Coughing, the woman opened the door. There was not a hair's difference between her and the statue. She had a wide chest, broad shoulders, blue eyes, and golden hair. All she missed were a pair of wings. Rokhsareh hid behind her husband's shoulder.

The woman smiled, "Please, come in."

The children ran into the courtyard. It was dry and devoid of any flowers and plants. The courtyard was paved with rectangular amber-color bricks. The walls were high, with cornices and six symmetrical wall shelves on each of which was placed a lantern. Three stairs down led to the courtyard.

Kuhzad went down and took a deep breath. A stale odor mingled with the smell of opium smoke spread in the air from the basement of the house and the seams of the brickwork. The man's eyes sparkled. He rubbed the palms of his hands together, "Where should we go?"

The lady opened the door to a room with a reflecting pool. It was semidark. A diamond-shaped reflecting pool reflected the light from the blue tiles. In the northern corner was a wooden platform covered with a kilim. The lady drew a line in the air with her index finger. "This is the place we have."

Kuhzad scratched his nose and sneezed. "We've brought our beddings with us. Just give us a lamp."

The lady stepped into the room and opened a door. A lizard fled by the side of her crystalline heel. There was a hallway behind the door, close to a backroom closet. She walked toward the backroom closet and pushed aside its dirty curtain. "Take whatever you need. Have you had dinner?" Kuhzad looked at the floor. "There are potatoes and eggs." She yawned and, holding on to the railing, went up the stairs. "I am going to bed."

Her white calves were shining below her skirt. She disappeared in the darkness of the landing.

They rolled out the bedding. The children went under the blanket. From the makeshift kitchen, Rokhsareh brought out a three-burner kerosene stove and made tea. They had potatoes for dinner. They did not touch the eggs. They thought that would be overreaching their welcome. The wooden platform was hard and unstable. The children fell asleep right away. Kuhzad lit a cigarette and walked around the pool smoking it. Rokhsareh tossed and turned in bed until midnight. The shadows on the walls moved before her eyes. She bit the flesh between her thumb and forefinger and mumbled something. Around midnight, there was a noise coming from the upper floor. The lady was pacing around the room, and the carpet muffled the sound of her high heels. Every step she took felt to Rokhsareh like a blow to her head. She covered her ears and groaned. She remembered the picture she had made of the city in her mind for many years, with transparent houses like glass, lit-up alleyways, and bright four-horse carriages. Kuhzad had fallen into a deep sleep. He knew all the nooks and crannies of the house. So he used to stay there whenever he came to the city. She went to wake him up several times, but she held back, fearing a commotion.

The lady walked around until dawn. Then the house sank into silence.

Rokhsareh came out of the basement and took a look around. Wagtails sat on the cornices of the high walls. The thick green curtains of the upper floor room were closed. She washed her hands and face under the spigot in the courtyard, brought the water in the samovar to a boil, and made tea.

The children woke up, and she served them bread and tea. Kuhzad was still sleeping.

When the sun rose, the lady drew the curtains aside, opened the window, and took a deep breath. "Rokhsareh! Leave the house door open."

A woman stepped into the courtyard. She was wearing a pea-green jacket. She had her pink headscarf tied behind her head. With a sad face, she climbed the stairs. Immediately, another woman came in. She was chubby, with wide pale cheeks and black collyrium-smeared eyes. She smiled at Rokhsareh. "Are you the new maid?"

Rokhsareh stared at the soot-covered lantern without responding. The newcomer turned her back to her and climbed the stairs. A third one came, tall, broad shouldered, with a light mustache over her lip. She asked Rokhsareh, "Have they started the work?"

Rokhsareh gazed at her, bemused. The newcomer joined the others.

Around noon, the lady from upstairs shouted: "Rokhsareh, bring tea!"

Rokhsareh poured tea into blue porcelain cups, placed them on a tray, and went upstairs, frightened and trembling. She was mumbling a prayer and blowing around her to ward off evil spirits. The double doors were wide open, and the slanted sunlight shone on the red medallion of the carpet. Colorful particles of dust from silk cloths spun in the light. All three women were sitting at treadle sewing machines, with their heads bent over. The lady was cutting a large piece of fabric on the square table and singing in a soft, sad voice. Her golden coiled hair had created a halo around her head. Her face was pale, her lips bud-red. Teardrops fell from the corner of her listless blue eyes. The open wings of the statue glittered. Prints of pictures of angels hung on the walls. The lady's beautiful, cold face resembled them. Rokhsareh entered the room and stood there, confused.

The lady said in a quiet voice, "Put the tray on the table."

Rokhsareh obeyed, and, after a pause, she walked toward the door. "Anything else I can do?" Right away, she had accepted her role as a maid.

The lady faintly smiled. "My name is Zhena."

She dropped her head, and in between the continuous sound of the treadle sewing machines, she sang the rest of the song.

Rokhsareh thought the teardrops were boiling out from a pocket behind her eyelids. She went to the room with the reflecting pool. Kuhzad was sitting on the daybed. He yawned and struck himself on the ribs. The woman squatted by the man's feet. "Would you like a glass of tea?"

Kuhzad wiped the caked-up excretion from his eyes. "In a big glass. Do you like the lady?"

"Are we going to stay here?"

The man did not answer. The children were playing in the courtyard. The woman had more or less shed her fears. "How long have you known her?"

"What difference does it make?"

"Then why didn't you tell me?"

Kuhzad frowned. "Every man has some secrets."

"Are you going to look for a job?"

The man took a sip of tea. "I'm going out."

"Is the lady going to pay for our expenditures?"

Kuhzad held his head up. "Shut your trap! I am not a paid crony of women."

He pulled up the backs of his shoes and left the house.

Rokhsareh washed the dishes. Near noon, made-up women came group by group and went to the upstairs room. Their skirts made a rustling sound. From the courtyard, she could see them through the window. They would put on the half-completed dresses and walk back and forth, frown, and laugh with pins on the waists of the dresses in front of the full-length mirror. The lady marked the edges of the dresses with a cake of soap and stitched them. A few of them brought her homemade cakes, flowers, and cocoa as gifts. They would rest in their lace undergarments on the easy chairs, and laugh loudly as they conversed.

Rokhsareh thought of them as airheads. The scent of various perfumes wafted throughout the room and the staircase, the scent of quince blossoms, wild plums, cyclamen, and Arabian jasmine. The most vivacious of the women smelled like fresh apples. She was vibrant, with a slim waist, black shiny eyes, and lips as red as cherries. When she laughed, the windowpanes vibrated and the tips of the wings of the statue moved slowly. The hollow wings were made of plaster, and colorful feathers, of peacocks, pheasants, and parrots, had been glued to them. The statue's eyes had stared at the alleyway for so long that their blue color had faded.

The corpulent woman stayed for lunch. She put on a jacket over her undergarments. They had kielbasa and cold cuts. The lady gave a plate of bread and kielbasa to Rokhsareh.

Close to evening, the workers left. The house became quiet and creepy.

Kuhzad came back at sunset. Rokhsareh and the children were sitting on the wooden platform. The lady was pacing in her room. After Kuhzad's arrival, she opened the window. "You came late. I waited quite a while."

The man climbed the stairs like a sleepwalker. His pupils were shining in the center of his agate-colored corneas. His soft sweaty hair covered the collar of his jacket. His face was drained of color. His Adam's apple went up and down. He disappeared in the darkness of the staircase landing. Rokhsareh followed her husband on her tiptoes. She peeked through the door crack. The lady was still pacing. Kuhzad took a hand-printed tablecloth from the closet and spread it on the floor. The lady placed a velvet pillow under her elbow, lay down on her side, and said, "Lamp!"

Kuhzad brought the opium lamp, placed it on the cloth, pulled up the wick with some sort of wire, and lit it. The flame was reflected on the ceiling. He put the cover of the lamp on. The widespread light began to shimmer. The lady was mumbling a song, looking at the flaming clouds behind the window, and drumming on the cloth with her long fingers. Her hands were as white as lilacs, her fingernails delicate and rosy. Kuhzad took a box decorated with peacock feather designs out of his pocket, opened it, took out the black opium ball, held it up to the flame, kneaded it with his thumb and index finger, and sniffed it. The lady whispered, "Pipe!"

Kuhzad brought the opium pipe, and laid on his side with his elbow on a small pillow. Their eyes were shining in the faint light. He put the kneaded ball on the pipe-bowl and warmed it up. It fizzed and swelled. They were both leaning on their sides facing each other. The lady was gazing at the ceiling and sobbing in harmony with the fluttering of the flame. A stream of tears fell on the cloth drop by drop, soaking it. Kuhzad stuck the metal fitting into the hole of the pipe-bowl. His thin fingers were kneading the puffed-up ball on the pipe-bowl. He made a cone of a black substance. He held the stem of the pipe toward the lady. He tapped the opium pipe-bowl. The lady sucked on the stem with her red lips. A light sparkled from the depth of her listless eyes. She exhaled the smoke. A cloudy mass tented under the high ceiling. A thick penetrating odor filled the air. Rokhsareh began to cough. Neither noticed. Their faces were moving behind the smoke, mingling with the air, and losing their material form. The lady lay on her back, her eyes intoxicated. "Go fetch my wings!"

The man went and took the wings from the shoulders of the statue. They seemed light. The golden and blue colors shone in the final rays of evening light. Kuhzad placed the wings under her shoulders and once again laid at the side of the cloth. The feathers had fallen off the wings in some spots, and what remained was covered with a layer of dust. The golden locks of the woman's hair cascaded behind her delicate ears and palpitating neck. She moved her hair aside with the tips of her fingers. Her turquoise eyes flamed up through the slits of her half-closed eyelids. She put her hand on her chest. Her fingers were so bright on the purple fabric, as though moonlight were shining from under her bright skin. Her cheeks were flushed, the color of quince blossoms. Rings of smoke twirled above her head, spread over her body, and rose in waves, and the woman twirled softly like a pink rose petal in a gentle whirlwind. She put her head on the pillow, closed her eyes, and rolled on her side. The left wing bent and the tip of the soft peacock feathers rubbed behind her ear. The silk strands quivered with her breathing and moved in the dimly lit space like a colorful bow. Kuhzad blew out the lamp. The tall shadows of objects fell on the carpet and the cloth. He got up with difficulty.

Rokhsareh ran down the stairs to the wooden platform and crawled under the children's blanket in the corner.

The man entered the basement, bent over and pale. The brightness of his eyes was diminishing.

Rokhsareh pushed the blanket aside. "Would you like some supper?"

Kuhzad did not respond. He knelt by the tiled reflecting pool and lit a cigarette. "What a pity it has no water."

"We will fill it tomorrow."

"It might have a crack."

The woman looked at the walls. Three deep cracks starting from the base reached the ceiling. Everything in the house was cracked—the teapot, the plates, the brick pavement of the courtyard, the mirrors, the ironing table, and the winged statue, which was the nest of ants.

Rokhsareh sat by her husband. "When are we going to leave this house?"

The man took a puff of his cigarette. "Leave, and go where?"

They became residents of the house. The lady smoked opium in the morning and evening. Kuhzad was melting like a candle. The women were constantly coming and going. They would leave the house smiling in their newly tailored clothes. One night, Kuhzad did not come back home. Rokhsareh could not sleep until the next morning. The lady paced back and forth ceaselessly. She drank black syrup and lay down on her bed. Before dawn on the third day, she called out to Rokhsareh. The sun was coming out, and her delicate, lilac-white cheeks seemed blue in the morning light. She whispered, "Sit!" She held Rokhsareh's hand and kissed it. She put her palms to her cheeks, and tears began to flow from her eyes. "I cannot sing anymore."

"What calamity has happened to Kuhzad?"

"It was his last flickering. It always ends like that."

Rokhsareh screamed, clawed her hair, scratched her cheeks with her fingernails, rolled on the ground, stuck Kuhzad's pillow to her chest, and sniffed it. She remembered his big, bright, tired eyes. In the recent couple of months, they resembled the eyes of a lamb, bewildered, unsheltered. Everyone was aging, but he was going back to his childhood. Rokhsareh's love for him had a motherly quality. She felt that she had lost a part of her heart.

The man had developed a fever the previous week. She went close to him and touched his forehead. She could smell the scent of wild grass on his breath. Kuhzad kissed her fingertips with his burning lips. The memory of six years of shared living had been erased from her mind. She could only remember that scene, a fixed picture, with the bleeding of a fresh wound.

The lady rose from her bed and embraced Rokhsareh. Her body was burning. The scent of wild grass was spreading in the air from her moist face and behind her ears. She had dissolved, like a piece of clay soaked in hot water. She put her hot lips on Rokhsareh's face. Rokhsareh pressed the lady's face to her chest and caressed her golden hair. She was reminded of the sunsets when the lady would lie down facing Kuhzad at the side of the tablecloth, flowers of smoke blossoming from her mouth, twirling softly in the air, and remaining suspended under the ceiling. Their eyes through their half-open eyelids flamed up and their cheeks flushed. They would close their eyes and smile at nothing.

Rokhsareh took the lady to the edge of her bed, lay her down, and pulled the blue satin quilt over her burning body. She picked a peacock feather from the wing of the statue and stealthily put it in her own pocket. She went back to the basement, rolled up the bedding, wrapped it in a bundling cloth, grabbed the children by the hand, and left the house.

They walked aimlessly around the city for a while. One day, in the course of their wandering, they got tired, and they sat down on the stone seat of a house with marble columns. A servant opened the door. A graceful middle-aged lady stepped into the street, pulling her gloves up until they fit her fingers.

Rokhsareh stood up and said hello. The lady answered her under her breath. A carriage came out of the large gate of the garden. The lady walked toward the carriage, buttoned her cape, and, after a pause, turned around, stood in front of Rokhsareh, and in a dry and decisive tone asked: "Are you able to work?"

Rokhsareh's lower lip quivered. "In the village, I worked as much as more than five people put together."

The lady pounded the tip of her closed umbrella on the stone pavement. "What will you do with the children?"

Rokhsareh did not respond.

The lady turned to the servant. "Take them inside."

Rokhsareh's long period of service in the house of the Azarbeygis began. She worked for three generations. All day long, she washed clothes, swept the leaves, and polished the stone pavement. The lady was unhappy about the presence of the children. She said that they picked the flowers and messed up the flowerbeds. Rokhsareh came up with a solution. She locked them up from morning to evening in the chicken coop. She would take the washtub behind the chicken wires, and, while soaking and washing them, she would whisper to the boys. Occasionally, she gave them a piece of fruit, some moistened sweet bread, or a leftover pastry from the night before through the slit of the cage. Their eyes sparkling, they reached out with their scrawny hands, sat shoulder to shoulder, and devoured the food. Early on, the chickens would attack them and peck at their heads.

After a while, they became accepting of those strange creatures as another species of mismatched animals in their cage.

The children got sick in early winter. The lady was alarmed and told Rokhsareh to take both of them to the hospital. She picked up the younger boy and, holding the other boy's hand, set out for Nikolayev Hospital. They hospitalized the boys in the children's ward. She visited them three times a week after she finished the housework. They were getting weaker by the day. When she went back home, she would dry the corners of her moist eyes with the corner of her headscarf. The lady disapproved of depressed servants. She said that everyone in the household must be happy and laughing. She had four daughters and three sons. The young ladies studied from morning to noon with a tutor, a red-faced restrictive man, and took a nap in the afternoon. They often had guests at night or went to a party. They played the piano, danced, and sang.

In the dark, Rokhsareh would sit by the chicken coop and gaze at the moon. She liked the warmth coming from the cage.

The master and the elder son traveled six or seven months every year. The younger son was going to school. When Rokhsareh saw him for the first time, she was amazed. He had shiny black hair, big blue eyes, and glowing pink cheeks. That night, she said to the cook, "There is a boy in the house who looks like an angel."

The cook laughed out loud. "His name is Yashar."

Rokhsareh's younger son died on the last day of winter. When she was washing clothes at the end of the garden, she would weep quietly. At night in the maids' room, she would sleep near the window to look at the moon. If the clouds covered the moon, she would become worried about her elder son, and she would sit up awake in her bed until morning. She considered seeing a black crow as a bad omen. She would not step on the gaps between the stones of the pavement. She would not step on ants. She would give away her meager wages to the pilgrims. She lit candles in three churches. She would kneel down and kiss the robe of the priest. It smelled like roses.

The elder son died in the spring. When they buried him, petals of cherry and peach blossoms covered his grave. Rokhsareh went back home and cried all night. The lady found out before noon and summoned Rokhsareh. She permitted her to enter her room for the first time. She was lying down on a wide bed in the soft daylight. She told Rokhsareh to sit. She obeyed. The lady leaned her head against the pillow. "So, both died?"

Rokhsareh burst into tears. She did not expect such kindness. The lady consoled her. "No one is perfectly happy." She took a rose from the vase, smelled it, and tossed it on the floor. "I am also unfortunate. My husband is never home, and my daughters are going to leave and get on with their own lives one of these days."

Rokhsareh's great sorrow would allow the lady to open her heart to a servant.

Rokhsareh wiped her tears with a handkerchief. "I'll pray for you."

The lady nodded emphatically. "Do that!" Touched with great sympathy, she said, "I entrust Yashar to you. Be his private servant."

From that very day, Rokhsareh became Yashar's servant. She would go to his room early in the morning and place his boots, which were lined with fur, by the fireplace. Yashar would open his eyes. The tips of his long lashes rubbed against her eyelids. Rokhsareh would go to the kitchen to get breakfast for him, hot milk and coffee, several kinds of marmalade in crystal bowls, butter, honey, and hot bread.

The boy would ask, "What time is it?"

Rokhsareh would smile. "You have plenty of time."

Yashar would jump out of bed and wash his hands and face. Rokhsareh would spread butter on pieces of bread. The boy would sit at the table, drink milk and coffee, and eat breakfast. He yawned and complained about his teachers, classmates, and difficult subjects. They gradually got used to each other and became close. The woman would pick up his schoolbag and carry it for him to the carriage. The boy would get in and pull up the collar of his overcoat. She could only see his eyes. The carriage would set out, and, until it disappeared at the turn of the road, she would stand there under the snow. She would then go to the boy's room, put everything in order in the closets, sweep the carpet, shine his shoes, and dust his jackets with a brush. She would open the door of the glass shelf and arrange the toys tightly side by side. Six small and large bears, a windup train, furniture, hunting binoculars, a zoo, theater masks. He had kept everything perfectly undamaged, but he would not play with them. He said that he was tired of them and he wanted new things, but he did not know what.

At noon, she would go by the door of the house and wait for Yashar. If he was late, she would worry. She would imagine a bad accident had happened. She had lost her belief in the tranquility and order of the world. She believed that she would lose anyone she set her heart on sooner or later.

The boy was growing up. Occasionally, he went to parties and came back late at night. He was becoming less dependent on Rokhsareh. He would not listen to her stories. He said they were boring. He dressed without her help. He would stand in front of the mirror and examine his new mustache. They took the toy shelf out of his room. They hung the head of a mountain deer and two crossed rifles on the bare wall.

One day, he went hunting with his paternal cousins, and when he came back at sunset, he tossed the carcass of a baby deer on the pavement of the courtyard and said that he had shot it himself. The animal's big eyes were open, its legs bent stiff in the final throes of death.

Rokhsareh looked at him scornfully. "Now its mother will be looking for it."

Yashar took the rifle off his shoulder. "Well, it can give birth to another one."

They roasted the game meat at night for the guests and congratulated him for joining the circle of real men.

A few days later, Yashar said that he did not want to have a private servant anymore. The woman stayed awake all night, shed tears, and looked at the moon.

She became responsible for cleaning the house. After dinner, she put the dishes on a large tray and took them out. She would look at Yashar out of the corner of her eye. The young man paid no attention.

Her hair was gradually turning white. The corners of her lips and eyes got wrinkles. She would tie back her salt-and-pepper hair when she washed the dishes. The four daughters of the family got married. The house became quiet. The lady would sit on the veranda, Rokhsareh would bring tea for her in a tea glass with a silver holder, and the lady would point to the big elm tree. "I used to have a white goat. I tied it under that tree."

Yashar and the middle brother went abroad. In the absence of the boy, the house lost its spirit. The master gave up traveling. With his hair white and back bent, he would sit by the fire of the wood stove. It was said that he had another wife in Kazan, and he sent money for her expenditures every month.

Whenever Rokhsareh bent down and stood up, she felt a pain in her abdomen. It would intensify, but she would put up with it. One day, she fainted from the pain. They brought her a doctor. The physician diagnosed her with a tumor in her abdomen. The attitude of the lady she worked for changed. She no longer wanted to see Rokhsareh in the residential rooms.

Rokhsareh returned to the back of the garden. She fed and gave water to the chickens. She raised a henna-colored chick. She would open the door of the cage, bring it out gently, and set it on her knee. The chick would peck at her fingers, and Rokhsareh would laugh boisterously. Her eyes had weakened. She would hear unfamiliar voices from inside the house. One day, she tiptoed in that direction and asked the cook, "What's going on?"

"They are leaving. They are bringing buyers for the house. They are selling everything."

The following month, they paid the wages of the gardener and the servants and left. The younger servants found jobs. Rokhsareh put the chick in a basket, and on the advice of the cook, went to the public housing. They took the chick away from her, killed it, and made pottage with it. In exchange, they gave her a bed. They had closed the doors of her much-loved church. The deacon, who had become homeless, said, "The priest died."

Fearfully, Rokhsareh lit the last candle, placed it behind the window, and fled.

Kukan was continuously going out and coming back into the room and leaving the door open. The breeze bent the flame. Showkat walked closer to him. "Kukan, what the hell is wrong with you? You go in and out like the water in an enema. Why can't you calm down and stay in one place?"

"The Fire Stokers!"

"A stink on the Fire Stokers! Who cares if there are a thousand of them?"

"You, Hero, aren't you afraid?"

Showkat hissed and twisted the flesh of his arm. "Hero Showkat is not exempt from death, but exempt from fear."

Kukan fell to his knees before Showkat's feet. "I am a tailor, not some legendary champion, like the famed Amir Arsalan in the legends."

"Get up! I've had it with you."

"Will the House of Fire have pity on me?"

Showkat kicked him with the tip of her toe. "They don't need another pot to piss in."

Kukan sat in the corner of the wall.

Yunos picked up another sheet of paper.

He was a tailor's apprentice in a town on the way to the capital city. From a month before the New Year, they would sew all night until morning. They would put firewood in a cast-iron heater. The light of the lamps with round wicks shone on the fabric until dawn. The air was filled with the odors of hot irons, padding adhesive, and dirty bodies. Just before New Year, they would deliver the clothes and go to the bathhouse.

He had been raised in an orphanage. He worked from the age of ten. He had a place to sleep, a bite to eat, and a new suit and shoes at the beginning of the year.

The first square of the patchwork quilt was from the dress of a sixteen-year-old girl. It was pink, with raised flower designs. The girl's hair shone like gold. One day, she brought a large red apple for Kukan. In her newly made dress, she ran down the narrow staircase of the tailor shop, as nimble as a fawn. Before going to sleep, Kukan would look at the fabric for a while. When his eyes became heavy, he would put it under his pillow.

The next piece of cloth was a cutting from the skirt of a schoolmistress, who would take the boy for a walk on holiday evenings. They would walk around the squares, sit in a café, and have cake and hot milk. One night, they went to a circus. Throughout the show, the boy would jump up and laugh so much at what the clowns were doing that he would fall off the seat. After a while, the schoolmistress became bored with the small town and returned to Moscow. Kukan placed the second piece of cloth on top of the first one. It was a light seersucker with golden stripes.

He received the third one from an old Turkoman, who had colorful fabrics hanging on a folding screen in the peddlers' bazaar of the town. It was an agate-colored strip that sparkled and waved in the breeze. The old man asked, "Do you like this?"

The boy looked at the ground. The peddler gave him the cloth for free. On cold mornings, he would get himself warm in the bright red color of the cloth. He cut a triangle from the end of it and added it to his collection.

One day, the owner of the tailor shop closed his workshop and said, "We are going to Ashkhabad, to my wife's relatives." The boy set out with the tailor's family, and the following month, they rented the upstairs floor of a building on Warshawskaya Street and opened the Fragrant Tailor Shop. Kukan gradually learned pattern cutting. After the slow business of the early years, the tailor shop began to thrive. The vibrancy of youth cast a ray of light on the gaunt cheeks of the young man. On holiday nights, the apprentices of the tailor shop went to a tavern. Kukan would accompany them. He would feel bold, drink, and become joyful. One night, a friend fell into a gutter full of muck. Kukan laughed so hard that he lost his balance and broke the branch of a tree.

The next piece of cloth was pistachio-green chiffon from the wedding gown of the new bride of an infantry officer. The lady's first husband had died. The reflection of the color of the gown enhanced the brilliance of the lady's emerald eyes.

He gradually became familiar with the wives of the affluent of the city. They had peculiar habits. One lady brought her dog with her. The animal would run under the table and sniff the fabrics.

From among the fabrics of the dog owner, Kukan took a piece of lavender velvet.

The Azarbeygi family would send their expensive fabrics to Yaqikian, a tailor in Moscow. House clothes and everyday dresses were given to the Fragrant Tailor Shop. Kukan took five pieces of the mother's fabrics, and four of the daughters'.

The women's habits gradually had an effect on him. He was a chatterbox, the source of the news of the households going from mouth to mouth. Before going to sleep, he would think about the betrothal of the daughter of the police chief, the suitors of Zinaid the golden-haired maiden, the chronic flatulence of corpulent Lady Milanovski, and the abortion of Hava, the young wife of Bahador Khan. Moving red lips spun around his head. He brought the cup of tea delicately to his lips and held up his pinky. He wore well-tailored overcoats, silk neckties, and long bell-shaped jackets with vents. He considered black velvet collars befitting of himself.

He became acquainted with a girl on Warshawskaya Street. She was tall and had red hair, blue eyes, and broad shoulders. When she passed by him, Kukan said under his breath, "Empress!" The girl smiled. Kukan walked alongside her and began to talk with her. Her name was Mina. Her father sold buckles in the Chaharsu Bazaar. Her mother had died. She had peculiar beliefs. She considered cat hair to be harmful. Among all the seasons, she would choose spring. She was sensitive to certain perfumes. She was studying at the art school. Kukan was astonished. He had never met a girl that fearless and honest. He suggested that they go on walks. The girl said, "I don't know."

Kukan asked, "But, why?"

He drew out the final "y," which made his voice effeminate. Every sound chirped in his throat. They went up to Oscar Square. It was late autumn. The fallen leaves made a crunching sound under their feet. The smell of burning hay moved in the air. The drizzling rain made the girl's freckled cheeks wet.

On the next day, they went to a café together. They sat by the window. On Kukan's suggestion, they had London rocket seed tea. The girl was licking her lips. Kukan thought, "How innocent! The poor thing doesn't have a mother. I also have no one." He rubbed the tip of his right shoe on the girl's skirt. Mina gathered her legs, her short upper lip quivered, her mouth remained open, and tears poured out of her eyes. She could not find her handkerchief. Kukan gave her a wheat-colored silk handkerchief. The girl blew her nose and opened the buttons of her jacket. Flummoxed, the man apologized and ordered almond cake. Mina ate it, sobbing. She got up and pushed the chair back with her wide bottom. They went out arm in arm. It was raining. They took shelter under the balcony of a house. A peddler's pushcart hit the wall and the girl laughed. Kukan became hopeful. "What a day!" The girl trembled all over. She said that it was the first time that she had gone to a café with a stranger. She nervously scratched her cheek with her fingernails. "If my father finds out"—she gave Kukan's handkerchief back to him—"he will come after me with a rope."

Kukan accompanied the girl up to the vicinity of her house. All the way, Mina was looking around, fearing the neighbors tattling.

Kukan went back to the workshop and changed his soaking-wet clothes. He sat behind the sewing machine, and while he was sewing the seams, he sang under his breath. He took the handkerchief out of his pocket. It was still damp. He folded it and put it on his eyes. A turtledove came behind the window. He picked up a piece of bread and crumbled it. He put the breadcrumbs on his palm, and making a smooching sound, he walked toward the window. The turtledove flew away. Kukan thought that Mina was different from everyone else. He did not like the customers of the tailor shop—or, rather, they viewed Kukan as a shadow bent over the sewing machine. The gender of tailors had become neutral. Kukan got along better with older ladies. They sometimes opened their hearts to him, and talked about their ailments. Kukan would nod and recommend remedies.

Lady Amirov, the wife of the railroad chief, was fond of him. He often took the lady's clothes to her house, and the lady would invite him to have a cup of coffee. He would sit on a sofa from which springs protruded and move his legs rapidly and shift in his place. While drinking hot coffee, he would talk about his childhood, thinking that the lady was someone with whom he could share his secrets. One day, he showed her the fabrics for the patchwork quilt. The lady examined them. She liked Kukan's idea. In one of their meetings, he talked about Mina. He said that she had peculiar ideas, and that he liked her for that reason. The lady read the coffee grounds to tell his fortune. She smiled mysteriously. She shook her index finger. "We will go and ask for her hand together. I know you have no relatives."

The following Sunday, they rode in the carriage to the Molla Aref Bazaar. The lady got out. Kukan stood at the end of the alleyway. He paced back and forth, looking at the windows of the girl's house. A faint light shone through the flower designs of the metal latticework. Under the incessant rain, the shoulders of his checkered jacket were getting wet, and his shoes were getting muddy. After an hour, the lady came out of the house. Frowning and pressing her lips together, she told Kukan, "Let's go!"

They got in the carriage, and all the way up to the exit of the little bazaar they just looked at the brick walls in silence. The lady opened her polished handbag, took out a handkerchief, and wiped the tears from the tips of her mascaraed eyelashes. She sighed deeply, her chest rising and falling. "I feel sorry for you."

Kukan concealed his muddy shoes from her. "I could guess the outcome. I am sorry for having troubled you."

The old Lady Amirov shook her head, making a "tch, tch" sound with her mouth. "Helping a fellow human being is the duty of every person. But those people are not humans. They look at one's appearance. Money is important to them."

Kukan's knees trembled. He put his sweaty palms together. "Mina was talking to a stranger for the first time. She had not been to a café in her entire life. Do you know what the last thing she said to me was?" He shook his head regretfully. "'You are a real man.'" He swallowed and, in a husky voice, asked, "What was their response?"

"They were very impudent. They did not understand with whom they were dealing. Merely out of respect for you, I did not slap her retarded father in the face."

"God forbid, did they insult you?"

The lady chewed on the tip of her black glove. "They consider you to be nobody."

Kukan turned red from ear to ear. "They are right. I am nobody."

The old lady burst out crying. Her eyes welled up with tears. The carriage stopped. The lady went into her house, and Kukan began walking in the rain. The city seemed dark to him. He did not go to work for an entire week. The owner of the tailor shop threatened to fire him. Kukan put the vent of the padded jacket of the man on his eyes and then kissed it. He apologized and placed the treadle sewing machine next to the window. On the roof across from him, they were hanging the fiery red, purple, and orange spools from the dye shop on the ropes to dry. Looking at the colors brought cheerfulness to Kukan's heart. He gave up worrying about his appearance. He would not sew new clothes for himself anymore. He saved his daily earnings parsimoniously. The hair on his temples was turning gray, and his face was becoming wrinkled. His thin shoulders began to bend forward and his back arched, due to constantly bending over the sewing machine and the ironing table. Once again, all he thought and talked about was the sewing of the patchwork quilt. He bought a box covered with inlaid work and kept the colorful pieces of fabric in it. Until the time when the tailor shop was shut down and the Fire Stokers nailed two parallel boards on its door, he entrusted the box to someone to keep for him. He showed his calloused hands to the Fire Stokers, and he led the rally of the tools.

Borzu whispered something in Showkat's ear. She yelled: "Go away, I don't have the patience. Why have you become the pest of the gathering? Hit the road!"

Borzu stomped on the floor. "I am going to be with you to the end."

"They will skewer you on hot rods."

The student looked at the garden. There was a light coming through the neighbor's window. The fuzzy shadow of the old man was reflected on the curtain, and an orange light shone like a flame on the branches and leaves. He sat in the easy chair and held his head in his hands.

Yunos continued:

At the end of Qezel Arvat Alleyway, a cloudy purple light through the half-open door lit the stone pavement. The upstairs and down-stairs floors were the domain of men and women who stayed awake all night. Borzu and his sister had a room at the end of the upstairs hallway. They always locked the door and latched it.

Sara was paralyzed. All day long, she lay on a mattress filled with hay, the blanket pulled up to her chin. Scrawny and frag-ile, she would catch a fever with the slightest breeze. Although no more than twelve years old, she already had blue rings under her eyes, and her cheeks were bony, anemic, and lusterless.

The window of the room opened to the courtyard of the neigh-bor's house, the landscape of which was an area paved with broken bricks, a dry flowerbed with an almond tree that had grown volun-tarily, two dark basements, and a few hens and roosters.

Borzu would come home from school near sundown. Sara would raise her head with difficulty, part her hair, and braid it. Borzu would lean on the wall, take off his shoes full of holes and his damp socks, put his books and notebooks on the short table, and light the samovar. They would eat bread and cheese with sweetened tea.

From early in the evening to dawn, the house was crowded and noisy. They could hear the sound of insults, laughter, com-mon people's music and singing, and moaning and snoring. The wind would slam the shutters of the window. The two children would pull their blankets over their heads. Occasionally, they were awakened by the sound of quarrels and scuffles. From dawn, there was silence. Women went to bed with their heavy makeup on in whitewashed rooms next to filthy walls covered with fingerprints, snot, and squirts of urine.

Borzu and Sara would wake up with the crowing of the neigh-bor's roosters. The boy would wash his sister's hands and face. After eating breakfast, he would put on his threadbare smoke-col-ored suit, lock the door, tuck his old schoolbag under his arm, and walk down the stairs. Drunken men were sleeping along his route, in the middle of the octagonal vestibule and on the stairs, with their hands on the railing, snoring. From the crack of half-open doors, in the light of dawn, he could see a flowered nightgown, mussed hair on a pillow, a man's underpants, and a shoe with the back folded down. He would pull up the collar of his jacket, stick his cracked hands in his pockets, drop his head down into his collar to warm up with his own breathing, and hastily walk to school. After entering the classroom, he would hold his aching numb feet beside the wood-burning heater and wiggle his toes. His calves felt like pins and needles. When he was going back home, he would circle the squares and alleyways and hide from others along his route, so that his classmates would not find out where he lived. He had invented an imaginary house in Makivka Alleyway. It had a yellow door and a marble staircase, its walls hidden under heaps of honeysuckle. Occasionally, he claimed that he had a father and would walk alongside a pedestrian. One foggy afternoon, in the course of his walking and turning back in circles, he stopped in front of a shop. A candle was burning on the counter. Thinking of getting warm, he went in. On wooden shelves in parallel rows, hundreds of books were covered with dust. An old man with salt-and-pepper hair hanging down to his shoulders was sitting on a stool, dozing off. Borzu pounded the floor with the soles of his shoes. The old man jolted and opened his eyes. "Which book do you want?"

Borzu stepped back and touched the leather spines. "Are these for sale?"

The shopkeeper yawned. "We also rent them out."

Borzu searched his pockets. He put the money for his next day's lunch on the counter. "I would like one."

"Fiction?" The boy's eyes sparkled. He nodded. "Which school do you attend?"

"Danesh."

"What kind of stories do you like?"

"I don't know."

A heap of old books was scattered on the floor. The man squatted down, and, after searching through them, he took a book the cover of which was torn, and shook it. "This one is good for you." The title of the book was *The Torch*. Borzu took the book and thumbed through it. The old man continued: "Read and enjoy it.

It is an old story." The boy put the book in his schoolbag and rushed toward the door. The old man shouted, "Till the day after tomorrow."

Borzu rushed home, and, after getting warm, he had several glasses of tea. He showed the book to Sara. The girl said, "Read it to me."

Borzu read until late at night, and Sara listened. When her eyelids became heavy, she rubbed them with her hand. It was the story of a girl imprisoned in a palace. She could not move, for a sorcerer had turned her legs to stone. She would sit beside the turret and sing. One day, she heard the sound of a horse's hooves. A handsome prince was coming on a trotting horse. He stopped when he heard the girl singing, looked up at the high fortification, and lost his heart to her beautiful face. With the help of an old holy man, he fought through seven calamitous feats and gained the Torch of Rescue.

He set the palace on fire, killed the sorcerer, removed the charm of turning people to stone, put the beautiful girl on the back of his saddle, and took her to a brilliant land.

The boy fell asleep beside the book, and Sara stayed awake.

Borzu rented the next book. Colorful fables became the magic lantern of their spiritless life and brightened their nights. He carried a mass of old books back and forth, and read them all to the end. The old man befriended him and sometimes did not ask for money. Step by step with his paralyzed sister, the boy went on an excursion through the world of legends and fables with snow-covered plains, savior saints, dark and frightful forests, fairies of water and wind and fire, commanders of the seasons, demonic beasts, and carrier pigeons on the shoulders of eager maidens.

Sara would sit by the window facing the courtyard, comb her hair, and sing. She would scoot herself toward the samovar and brew tea. When the boy came back, she poured tea for him. She would pick up a small mirror, gaze at her pale face, and say, "I wish I was pretty like the princess and had a crown on my head."

The boy would nod. "First, learn to read."

The little girl stroked her paralyzed legs and looked at her brother scornfully. "Where? How?"

The boy would clench his jaws. Finally, one night, he brought paper and a pen and taught Sara the alphabet. The girl would write and practice all day, and show her writing to her brother at night. She was willful and eager. Her middle finger had become calloused. She filled both sides of the inexpensive sheets of paper. A year later, she had learned how to read and write.

Borzu would occasionally sit beside the old man and stare at the flame of the candle. He would talk about his sister, and a house under the ceilings of which the monster of disgrace and shame breathed. The old man would blink several times and wipe the tears off his cheeks with a handkerchief. "No, that can't be. It is not right. Get an education. Find a job, and take your sister by the hand and get away from that place."

Seasons came and went. From the end of spring, they opened the windows. The hollowed boards of the veranda moaned under heavy steps. The railing to the left was suspended in the air, swinging on a few bent nails. Their mother would perspire under her mauve taffeta dress. She walked around, issuing orders. With her rough henna-colored hair around her tired face, she occasionally checked on the children. The boy and the girl crawled to the corner of the wall and watched her with frightened eyes. The woman slid the dish of warm food toward them in the middle of the room. She sat cautiously near the door and lit a cheap cigarette. Borzu and Sara held their hands before their mouths and started coughing. The mother tossed the half-smoked cigarette into a full glass of tea. The red sparks crackled and went out. She put her hand on her back, complaining about aching bones. The children gazed at a fixed spot. The woman cracked her knuckles. "What a pity I have no money to rent a room for you." A vein swelled up under her left eye, her eyelids closed, and she whispered, "Sparrows! They still sing."

She was delusional and confused. Fearful about the future, she put the coins inside a metal box and buried it in the middle of the flowerbed.

One night, Borzu shouted, "Don't lie so much! You have money. Get us a room."

The mother rolled around the remainder of the sugar cube in her mouth and spat it into the tea glass. She swallowed her sweet saliva. "Let's see what our fate brings."

The boy picked up the saucer and smashed it against the wall. It broke into several pieces and fell. "This house is no place for us."

Frightened, the mother pulled her head back. "Going to school has made you cheeky." She blew on the palm of her hand. "I have nothing."

The boy's rosy forehead broke out in a sweat. He put his hand on Sara's shoulder. "I myself will take her out of here. You will see."

The mother laughed nervously, and her four gold teeth shone. "And I'll be rid of you." She took out a cigarette from her pocket, wetted it with her saliva, and struck a match. Her hands were shaking. "You don't love me." She pounded her head on the doorframe.

Sara shifted in place on the bed. "Yes, we do love you."

The woman covered her face with her veiny hands and burst out crying. "No, don't tell me that. It makes me depressed. You shouldn't love me. Put poison in my food some day. Death for me would be like a wedding night, because I have poisoned your lives. I will destroy this house. I'll make it collapse on their heads, I swear."

The boy chuckled. "On what are you swearing?"

The mother sat up and looked at the moon through the window. "I have faith in purity, chastity."

Borzu burst out laughing. "Then go and gather up your underwear from the clothesline."

The mother was enraged. "Do you expect me to go panhandling? I have set aside a lot of stuff for Sara, a gold choker necklace, rings, and cash. I want her to be happy in her life."

"She is already happy, imprisoned in this dungeon, shaking from fear twenty-four hours a day."

The mother shouted, "Just let someone even look out of the corner of his eye at this room and I'll pull out his guts from his belly."

"You are always busy anyway."

"I would be able to smell it."

"You sleep until noon."

"I am a light sleeper."

"Like a hibernating bear?"

He got up in a posture of attacking his mother. The woman ran out and made a ruckus. She pulled the railing off its place, kicked, and cursed. Women and men poured out of their rooms. Laughing boisterously, they patted one another on their shoulders. Half an hour later, the commotion subsided. Only the sound of the wind and the moaning of the door hinges resonated under the ceiling of the dilapidated building.

Sara asked her brother, "Where should we go?"

Borzu rubbed his palms together and smiled. "I have figured everything out. A faraway city. Wait another four years." He folded his thumb and raised his hand. "Just four years."

The corners of the girl's lips quivered. "It is even more than a thousand days. It must be a good city." She bent her head over her shoulder. "I'm dying to know! Where is it?"

Borzu pointed to the faint light of the flames on the mountain.

He started the ninth grade. On holidays, he would open the window and toss down the dried bread crumbs for the chickens. An old man came once a week, opened the lock on the house door, walked around the courtyard, opened the door of the chicken coop, and put water and seeds in it. The almond tree blossomed in spring, and the wind brought the petals into the room. The unripe almonds took shape. Borzu pulled on a branch with a hook. They picked the unripe almonds, rubbed off the fuzz, and bit into them.

They read *The Torch* again. Borzu wrapped a rag around a stick, soaked it in kerosene, and lit it. Smoke filled the room. The boy held the torch outside the window, shook it, and put it out. Sara fell on her back laughing and covered her face with her hands.

The boy's grades in high school were high. He sat in the front row and squinted his eyes. He could not see the writing on the blackboard clearly. The owner of the bookstore took him to an optometrist and bought him eyeglasses. The wall-posted school newspaper was prepared with Borzu's efforts. At the end of the school year, they took the distinguished students to the city hall to receive plaques of honor from the director of education. Borzu was among that group. As he was going up to the platform, his knees were shaking and his cheeks were flushed. After he received the plaque, he rushed down. He fell, and his trousers were ripped at the knee.

They put the plaque on the wall. Sara mended the trousers. Borzu sat on the windowsill and rubbed his sore knee. "We will get our wish in three years."

Sara pointed to the markings on the wall. "I know. I calculate it every day."

One cold morning, Borzu picked up his schoolbag and got ready to leave. Sara pushed the blanket aside. "I had a good dream last night."

The boy stopped at the threshold. "What was it about? Tell me."

"We had gone to that faraway city." She put one hand on the other and looked at the ceiling. The vein on her thin neck was palpitating. Her eyes were shining. "Oh, how pretty it was! Instead of walls, the courtyards of the houses had white fences, and the flowerbeds were full of flowers. The pavements of the alleyways shone like glass. The sun was shining. The red gable roofs sparkled. You held my hand and said, 'Come inside! The house is ready.' There was a round reflecting pool in the middle of the flowerbed with two red goldfish. Mother says if anyone dreams of fish, she will reach high places."

Borzu kissed her forehead, went out, and locked the door.

All day long, he was worried. He could not concentrate on the lessons. During recess, he paced back and forth, looking at the wall clock in the hallway. Outside it was cloudy. After classes ended, he picked up his bag and rushed home, running. He cut through the back alleyways. When he entered Qezel Arvat Alleyway, panting, he saw that the house door was wide open. The women were walking around the octagonal vestibule like shadows. He went forward apprehensively. His mother was sitting on the stone seat by the door and had ripped her collar. The rays of the red lamps made her henna-colored hair look like flame. Borzu climbed the stairs. A woman yelled, "Stop him!"

Several women with messed-up hair came to block his way. He punched their chests with his clenched fist. They pulled back and grabbed his jacket from behind. It ripped and his sleeve tore. He ran into the hallway and opened the half-open door with his shoulder. His heart was pounding against his chest. He could taste blood on his tongue. The open window, the plaque of honor, and the samovar were spinning around his head. His sister's bed was empty. He yelled, "Sara!"

The glass panes vibrated. Confounded and frightened, he rushed outside. He grabbed the rickety railing and bent over at the waist. "Where is my sister? I will kill all of you."

The women stared at the ground. His mother was yanking her rough red hair from the roots. Borzu bellowed, "I know how to make you talk."

A young scrawny woman with a gaunt face looked up. "She threw herself down."

Borzu shook the railing. The weak hollowed wood cracked. "Shut up, you whore! Where did you take her?"

A corpulent middle-aged woman sniffed and yelled, "Look into the little courtyard."

Borzu rushed to the window and bent over. The hens and roosters were clucking and fluttering their wings. The branches of the almond tree were bending in the wind. A motionless body was floating in the dark fog on the brick pavement. He stood on the windowsill intending to jump down. They grabbed him by his shoulders. He felt the slippery blue tile under his feet turning. He fell on the floor of the room and kicked the women away. A voice groaned, "It wasn't our fault."

Borzu jumped to his feet. "Don't touch me with your filthy hands!" He kicked the samovar away and grabbed a woman by the throat. "Tell me what happened!"

The woman struggled to open her mouth. Her eyes were bulging. "I'm telling you right now. She threw herself down, because she was raped."

The other women stepped back. Borzu threw her out. He closed the door from inside and knelt by Sara's bedding. Her homework notebooks, pencil, and *The Torch* were next to her bed. She had mended the torn cover of the book with glue. A few curly hairs were left on the indentation of her pillow. He lay down on his sister's bed. The warp and weft of the bedding were losing the fleeing particles of the warmth of her body. Stunned, he looked at the ceiling. On the edge of a long crack, a line of ants was moving forward slowly. He turned his head toward the corner of the room. On the swelled-up plaster were written numbers, the numbers of days and months. Borzu was shivering to his bones and his teeth chattered. He pushed the quilt aside. It was drizzling outside. He stuck his head out of the window. The small corpse was disappearing in the dark. He washed his burning cheeks under the raindrops. He went around the room, picked up and wrapped the blue plaid dress, the small mirror, the homework notebooks, and the book in a bundling cloth and put it under his arm. He picked up the half-burnt torch from the wall shelf and went downstairs. The octagonal vestibule was empty. The women had taken his mother to another room. The sound of ceaseless wailing resonated throughout the house. The wind was shaking the red light. The tall shadows of the columns were moving back and forth on the bare stone pavement. He shook the clothesline. Rosy lace undergarments spun and fell into the potholes and remained motionless, smeared with mud. He picked up the kerosene can from under the staircase. He splashed kerosene around the vestibule. He picked up the lantern by the door, broke it, and held the torch over the flame. He went around in the vestibule and touched the flaming cloth torch along the stream of kerosene. Red flames climbed the hollow wood of the railing. He ran out, stood at the end of the alleyway, and watched. Twisting tongues of fire were covering the door. Out of breath, he took off, disappearing in the darkness of the alleyways.

Chapter 16

Yunos gathered up the sheets of paper. Vahab stared at the man's nimble hands. "Hero Yunos, now I understand the meaning of sorcery. You shine a light on the dark corners. It is as though I have just awakened."

Yunos did not respond. He wrapped the stack of paper in his cloak and put it under the chair. The chandelier lights came on, and the Heroes dropped their heads. Hero Rashid turned off the chandelier. Yavar turned on the light switch for the wall lamps. A soft light filled the room. Borzu sat down and held his ankle. "It has gone to sleep. It's from nerves." He stood up and limped to the library. He stomped on the staircase and punched his leg muscles. "Damn it! Why did it get like that? Probably, my blood pressure dropped."

He walked to the middle of the parlor, turned around, and took off his faded shirt. His ribs protruded beneath his dirty undershirt. He unbuckled his belt.

Showkat grabbed Borzu's arm. "Are you getting all messed up in your head again?"

Roxana walked to Borzu and put her hand on his forehead. "He has a fever." She turned to Rashid. "Warm water!"

The student frowned. "It won't work. Scientifically, it has no effect."

Hero Showkat seated Borzu in an easy chair and took off his shoes, the soles of which had been repaired. The bottoms of his socks had holes. Rashid placed a pot of warm water and a cake of soap beside Roxana's hand. Borzu took off his hat and threw it on the table. "Ridiculous!"

Roxana pushed the pot forward, took off his socks, and splashed a fistful of water on his scrawny calves. His ankles and big toe had callouses. She soaped up the soles of his feet, rinsed them, and asked Leqa for a towel, which she wrapped around Borzu's feet.

Hero Showkat snatched away the towel and tossed it. She grabbed the young man's big toe and spat on the floor. She opened his toes and showed Roxana the caked up dirt between them. "Lazy good-for-nothing!" She rubbed between his toes and dunked them into the water. "This is how you wash feet."

Borzu burst out laughing. "Pardon me, Hero Showkat, but my feet are sensitive." He laughed hysterically and shook his calves. Foamy dirty water splashed on the women's faces.

Hero Showkat twisted his ankle and turned to Vahab. "Fetch your ambergris perfume! I want to fix his feet to be like jasmine flowers."

Leqa ran out of the parlor and a moment later brought the black bottle. Showkat opened the lid and poured it into the pot. Borzu pulled his feet back.

Vahab bent forward. "Slow down, Hero! It is not some worthless bear-claw perfume."

Showkat walked away from the pot and held her nose. "How many times do I need to say that in this country, no one is the owner of anything?"

"I have no argument, but a pinhole drop of that makes the whole place smell good. It is the purest perfume in the world."

Showkat began coughing. Tears welled up in her eyes. She put the bottle on the table. The steam from the pot circulated the dark mournful scent of the ambergris perfume in the air. Torkan made a dry vomiting sound.

Borzu gathered up his feet. "I prefer nitric acid to this filth."

Hero Showkat opened the windows noisily. "That postmortem Vahab, nothing he does resembles a human being. It smells like a dead dog that's been disinterred."

Vahab shrugged his shoulders. "The problem is with what your nose prefers."

Hero Showkat tapped the pot with her toe. "Take this mummy concoction outside!"

Qadir took the pot out.

Rashid put the lid back on the bottle. "I will bury it at the end of the garden."

In the kitchen, Heroes Pari, Rokhsareh, Kowkab, and Torkan were bringing pots of water to a boil.

Roxana leaned against the table. She rubbed her forehead with her fingertip. "Kashmir perfume!"

Vahab's eyes sparkled. Roxana brought the bottle of the perfume. Kowkab, Pari, and Torkan placed the pots of hot water in the middle of the parlor. Roxana poured a drop into each pot. The breath of wild flowers began to blow in the room.

Hero Showkat closed the windows and inhaled. "Oh, this scent takes me somewhere far away, beside the clay bread oven. That stupid Vahab always said that Rahila had gone to the middle of Kashmir flowers and rolled around on them like a donkey. I used to make fun of him. Now an idea has dawned on me. Maybe my mother is also there."

She seated Teymur on the floor and rolled up his smoke-colored pant legs. She put his wrinkled ankles in the pan. She put pressure on the arch of his foot. The old man moaned: "It hurts."

Showkat shouted: "Soap!"

Roxana tossed the cake of soap into the pan. The water swayed and spilled over the rim.

Showkat rubbed the old man's calloused heels. "A stink on you! They're cracked. Don't you use a pumice stone?"

Leqa sat down and covered her eyes with her hands. Her forehead was covered with sweat. She sighed. "Would you like me to bring a pumice stone?"

Yavar and Mrs. Edrisi looked at each other. Vahab smiled. "She is doing a really great job."

Leqa went out, came back with a pumice stone in her hand, put it on the carpet, and clenched her jaws. Her facial muscles were contracting, and a vein throbbed under her left eyelid. Hero Showkat scrubbed the soles of Teymur's feet with the stone. Through the steam, Leqa came forward like a shadow and held out a white towel to Showkat. With the help of his crutch, Qobad walked close to the wood-burning heater, sat down, struck a match, lit a piece of kindling, and held it under the firewood. A bright fire flamed up. Teymur crouched beside the heater and fixed up his clay pipe. Borzu was going around the room, whistling. Torkan took off her thick socks, placed her feet in the warm water, and pushed back a lock of her hair. Mrs. Edrisi walked to the pan and knelt down. "Dear girl! Let me help you."

Torkan's cheeks flushed. "I'll be embarrassed. You are like a mother to me." The exquisite designs of the carpet were soaking wet. Torkan shook her head regretfully. "It is such a waste. It'll fall apart."

"Then it will be just like me." The elderly lady gently poured water on the woman's feet and soaped her short chubby toes. Torkan dried her feet with her skirt. Mrs. Edrisi grabbed her wrist. "You are going to catch a cold."

The woman shrugged her shoulders. "Our hands and feet are in water from sunup to sundown."

Kaveh was sauntering around the room, smoking a cigarette.

Roxana shouted: "Put it out, Hero. It is your turn."

Kaveh put his hand on his chest and began coughing. "Please! I will wash them myself. I am waiting until there is less of a crowd."

"Hero Kaveh, I would like to wash them. What feet would be more worthy than your restless feet?"

Kaveh sat on the chair, tossed the half-finished cigarette into the pot, and covered the patch on the knee of his trousers with his hand. "In my youth, I dressed better than princes." Roxana took off the man's smoke-colored socks. Kaveh smiled. "What you said was nice. Yes, restless feet. As far as I remember, I went and went, looking for something that did not exist. Alas, I have grown old. Neither do I have the energy to go, nor can I bear to stay."

"Last night, I dreamed that I had killed a big snake, but an ant was chewing on my bones. Sometimes the power of an ant is greater than that of a snake."

Kaveh nodded. "I did not have much pride. From the beginning of my life, I was stepped on, and I went around idly and without purpose. I had set my heart on the land under my feet, on whatever came out of the soil, ripe fruits, purple grapes, women's colorful pleated skirts in farms. There was pure joy behind their laughter. They smelled of milk and bread."

Roxana dunked his foot in the water. "Yes, I understand. You have kept your pearls."

Kaveh held his chin between two fingers. "But you have tossed them to the wild boars, right?"

Roxana gazed at the darkness through the window. "The memories of those days now resemble a dream, the ghosts of which I have forgiven. Perhaps they were also dreaming." Kaveh bent down over the pot. Steam covered his face. Roxana continued: "How seriously we took our hatreds and loves, as though they would last forever."

"Are you now thinking about death?"

"No one thinks about things that are close."

She put her fingertips into the water. Kaveh's eyes filled with tears. "Your hands were like birds on the stage. I cannot bear to see them in dirty water."

Showkat perked up her ears. "You good for nothing! How about my hands?"

Kaveh lifted his head. The yellow dress turned dark and light behind the steam. "Hero Showkat, I cannot go along with that, either, because they are dear in a different way."

Showkat raised her fingers. "I have stuck these in any sort of muck you can think of. When my mother was alive, we used to smash whole pieces of cow dung on the wall. Yashvili also hasn't fallen from the sky. Well, suppose on the stage she flapped her wings like a brooding hen. Do you think she hasn't washed her own dirty clothes? Do you think she has not scrubbed her ugly scrawny feet with a pumice stone and soap? Don't butter her up so much. Let her do her duty."

Kaveh went in his bare feet and sat by the fire.

Showkat shouted at Qadir: "Come!" Hero Qadir shifted on his feet hesitantly. "Idiot! What are you waiting for? Get off your high horse!"

Qadir stared at the wet carpet. "My feet have warts."

Hero Showkat looked at him through squinting eyes. "So, you are proud of your warts! I knew someone who had warts on his face, but he didn't moan and groan like you. There's one thing you shouldn't forget. Feet go into shoes. Even if they are made of crystal, no one can see them."

Qadir smiled. "I got the warts because I splashed water on a cat."

"The dirt of both worlds on your head. It's all about a few warts the size of millets?"

"They aren't the size of millets. No smaller than lentils."

Hero Showkat walked closer to him and suddenly pulled his legs out from under him. The man fell on his bottom. "Let me see what treasure you're hiding." She took off his dirty socks and examined both of his feet. There were a few small and large warts on his toes. "Why didn't you wrap a thread around them to make them fall off?"

"I put the sap of figs on them."

"To make them bigger?"

"No. To make them fall off."

Hero Showkat turned to Yavar. "Get a pair of scissors! I'll get rid of them right now."

Hero Qadir threw his arms and legs every which way. "These are a memento from my childhood."

Showkat's fingers loosened. "I call such things 'flower of memories.' I have a scar, myself. When I look at it, memories bubble up from it like a volcano. It's above my elbow. My poor mother had bit it."

She scrubbed the tops and the bottoms of his feet with the pumice stone. Qadir complained: "You're scrubbing the skin off, Hero."

Showkat spat into the pot. "I scrub my elbows and knees. You think you've got something special?"

Every time the pumice stone moved over the warts, Qadir yelled. He punched his own head and pulled on his hair. "I wish I didn't have feet at all for you to go after them. How lucky Hero Qobad is!"

"Shut up! What a waste of bread that you eat! You compare yourself with him? If Qobad is missing a leg, it's because of the likes of you. Some people get shot without even saying ouch." She pointed at where Vahab was lying down. "Look at that feeble gangling thing. What does he have? A sound mind? Virtues? A good past? A good figure? They shortchanged him in everything when he was created. But he has been beaten like a dog and hasn't said ouch. I know the members of the House of Fire. They have no mercy, not even on their mothers." She shook the leg of the sofa. "You street drifter. Tell me!" Vahab started to get up and then put his head back on the pillow. "I didn't tell you to play hard to get. Since when have you become Berenice, that instead of yapping you make your eyes dreamy to pretend you are hard to get? Talk!"

"Hero Showkat! I confess that I did say 'Ouch.' And I have not been beaten a great deal."

"Dirt on your head! And no matter how much they beat you, it wasn't enough." She turned to Qadir. "He's crazy, a man who has no feelings, and he doesn't feel pain."

Vahab sat up with difficulty. "Wash his feet!"

"Of course I'll wash them. I only want to know who would wash your stinky feet."

"You, Hero! You yourself will wash them."

Showkat held her hand, full of soapsuds, before his eyes. "I wish they were buried in mud."

"They will be, Hero."

"May the hands of your grandma be buried in mud, you big mouth."

"Unfortunately, they also will be. They were talking about it in the House of Fire."

"Moron! Don't pester my ears with their gibberish!" She turned and yelled: "Kowkab! Stop all that splashing! Have you got something tickling you somewhere? This is supposedly a parlor for entertaining guests, not your village public bath."

"Didn't you tell us to wash our feet?"

"I opened my mouth and the wrong words came out, and now I am at a loss as to what to do. Now every big oaf who has just showed up takes off his stinking socks to show his wounds and warts and puts his calloused feet in our hands and says, wash them!"

Qadir put his suds-covered feet on the carpet. "Are you taunting me?"

"Who was talking to you? Come here. I think you have pretty feet."

"I know."

Showkat tossed a towel at him. "You're making me run out of patience. Even Caliph Abdolrahman was not as hard to get as you are, and he wasn't happy, either!" Showkat brought a pot and placed it by the sofa. "Put those matchsticks in here."

Vahab looked at the woman's broad shoulders. "I can't."

"Don't pretend to be hard to please. You're worse than Qadir."

"I am not. I feel sad."

"Why, you dead dog? When was it that you weren't sad?"

"I might not see those hitting hands of yours again after this."

"When did I ever hit anyone? The first time I saw you, I wanted to give you a real slap in the face, but that idiot, Kukan, didn't let me."

The man bent his head. "It is not too late yet."

"Such a sly fox you are! I can't anymore."

Vahab rolled up the muddy legs of his gabardine trousers. His pale legs swayed in the warm water like two dying fish. Showkat frowned at him. "You have no oomph in you. You don't eat right. You don't go on excursions and have fun. Yavar says you have bile. If I had the time, I would spend time on making you become a real human. Miserable wretch! You are still young. Your cheeks are supposed to be rosy. Look at Rashid and Qadir. When they walk, the ground shakes under their feet. Why have you stuck your head under your wings like a lice-infested chicken? Suppose your Aunt Rahila was still alive. What remedy would that be for what ails you?"

"We create everything with our imagination. While it is there, we cannot see it. When it is gone, we shower its memory with stars."

Hero Showkat soaped up his feet. "What will you do with your memory of me? Will you probably say, good thing I am rid of her?"

Vahab stared at the floor. Pain shot through his ribs on the left side. "We used to have a flowerbed full of sunflowers."

Hero Showkat grumbled: "I also turn toward the sun. Justice is light, is it not?"

Vahab blinked. "Tell me three words that you like more than all others."

Hero Showkat scratched her nose. Steam covered her face. "Mother, earth, sun. Tell me, what are your silly words?"

"To tell you the truth, I like all words."

Showkat flicked her fingers on his ankle. "Faithless good for nothing."

Vahab's eyes sparkled. "Hero Showkat! You are right. Faith is one of them."

"Don't snatch it out of my mouth! Think!"

"I have faith in one thing."

"Spit out the pearls of wisdom!"

"That, in its essence, life is not futile."

Hero Showkat pushed the pot of water back and forth. "How about this action? Was it not futile?"

Vahab paused. "No, I do not think so. It has some meaning that you and I do not comprehend."

"Then who does?"

"Maybe the pot."

Showkat shook her head. "Then you also have faith in the pot." She squeezed his left foot. "Where is your mind? Those three words."

"Faith, water, and sleep."

Showkat straightened her back. "You do the rest yourself. You make up such nonsense. All your power is in your chattering chin." She yelled: "Roxana! This locust asked me a riddle. I answered it right away. Choose three words from among all words."

Roxana stood up and rubbed her knees. She gazed at the vibrating pendants of the chandelier. A resonant voice reverberated in the midst of the steam: "Love, love, and love!"

Hero Kaveh covered his eyes with his sleeve.

Showkat stroked Rokhsareh's arm. "You're so feeble, a mouse could knock you down."

"I'm feeling poorly."

Showkat shouted: "Warm water!"

Hero Rashid brought a pitcher of hot water and poured it into the half-full pot.

Mrs. Edrisi grabbed Showkat's wrist. "Allow me to wash them."

Showkat looked at the elderly lady's moist, rosy face. "You look healthy and revived."

Mrs. Edrisi rolled up Rokhsareh's twill pant legs and placed her feet in the warm water. Rokhsareh sighed. "The night before last, I dreamed that a blue-eyed angel came by my bedside and said, 'I have brought you your recovery. Come with me!' I didn't consent. I pulled on her skirt from behind and asked, 'What happened to your cracks?' She said, 'That was how you saw them.'" She took a deep breath. "She wasn't a stranger."

"You have become weak."

Rokhsareh wiped her nose with the sleeve of her dress. "On the nights before holidays, I used to light candles in the church for her. I both hated her and loved her. Later, I could forgive people's evil ways. My mistress was just a little girl."

Mrs. Edrisi dried her feet and put her own green shawl over Rokhsareh's shoulders.

Kukan was walking barefooted in between the pots of water. He was shifting the measuring-tape case from hand to hand, occasionally taking out the end, measuring an invisible object in the air, and immediately letting go of the end of the tape to let it go back noisily into the case.

Showkat yelled: "Kukan! Enough marching. You're going to bump into the pots. If it's no trouble, you need to wash your own feet."

Kukan sat down and stuck the measuring tape into the pocket of his trousers and stared at his bent toes. "Hero Showkat! You don't like me. No, no one has ever liked me. Throughout my life, they only wanted me for my work. They would say, 'Kukan, dear, sew the bottom of this skirt. I need to have it for tonight's party. Fix the padding of the waist.' I would be dear to them close to the holidays and New Year. When business was slow, they would totally ignore me. All I had to keep me happy was the patchwork quilt, and then you stuffed that he-monster, Haddadiyan, in my room. You look at me like I don't exist, because to you I'm like a weed. All of you have had some relatives, dead or alive. Have I had anyone to think about? Am I the trunk of the tree of hell?"

Showkat's voice softened. "Why are you bawling like you lost your mother? Have you forgotten that I used to whisper secrets to you? That I listened to your cawing? That you were my hand-trained crow?"

Kukan rolled up his pant legs. "You needed me for snitching and stitching and sewing. But you like Borzu in your heart."

Showkat flexed her right arm over her chest with a clenched fist. "To hell with your mixed-up snitching. Don't get so upset. In the House of Fire, your reports were used to clean dishes. Tell me the truth, you filth! From what part of you did you pull out that soap and cloth? Not even a jinn could think of that. And now, about your stitching and sewing. Did you, with your butter fingers, do the sewing for this family? Whenever my skirt was ripped, what did I do? Don't you remember? I mended it myself! One time, it jumped out of my mouth and I asked you for durable thread. You pounded that shrew's bloating belly on my head, and I didn't see any sign of your mule tail spool of thread. I was chummy with you just for your own sake. I found a place for you. The House of Fire wouldn't consent, so I raised a ruckus and yelled at them, 'As for this Kukan, forget about his stupidity! He has been breathing the dust and debris of the tailor shop since he was a little kid.' You miserable wretch that looks like you've never seen water! Do you think washing your feet and legs is a sign of friendship? If that was the case, all the bath attendants would be lovesick guys like those famous Romeos, Farhad and Majnun."

Roxana turned to Kukan. "Why don't you learn from Rashid?"

"Well, Rashid's situation is different. He is sure of himself, because Mrs. Edrisi likes him as much as she does Vahab."

The old lady lifted her head from over the pot. "Kukan! Do you remember how much of my antique embroidered cloths with all the gold and silver threads woven into them that you cut with scissors? You tore them to shreds, like the heart of Potiphar's wife, and wasted them just to make a pair of spiffy trousers, each pant leg of which was big enough to stick a large watermelon in. And then you yellowed up the seat of the pants with a hot iron and had Yavar wear them. Several times, I wanted to ask you if you thought Yavar was an Ottoman sultan, or you were the royal court tailor who could not make himself touch any cloth that was not embroidered with gold thread. But I bit my tongue and said to myself, 'That's what he loves to do, let him be happy.' Is this not an indication of kindness?"

Kukan shrugged his shoulders. "What difference does it make? In the end, the antique cloths would have been sent to the storage house."

"Yes, but they would not have ripped apart the intricate cloth left to me from my ancestors before my very eyes to make pants for Yavar."

Kukan scratched the sparse stubble on his chin. "I also had love in my heart for you. I set aside a triangle of that embroidered cloth."

He rolled up his pant legs and suddenly jumped into the pot. Water splashed on Roxana's head and face. "Your feet thirst for water like a fish."

Kukan picked up the soap and handed it to Roxana. "In the orphanage, babies were left in wet cloth diapers for one whole day and night. You'd get blisters and sores on your crotch. They burned so bad that you would remember it for the rest of your life."

"But you were a baby."

"Even now, at night, I scratch my thighs remembering those nights."

Showkat came closer to Kukan. "Don't say I don't like you again. But I think it is wise for you to give up that habit."

"I dream they are blistered."

"Your dreams are also something else. Whatever it was, it's in the past."

After his feet were washed, Kukan, whistling, went and sat down in front of the fire.

Hero Showkat stood in the middle of the pots in the center of the steam, tousled her hair, and clapped her hands. "Whose feet have not been washed?"

She pulled on Leqa's sleeve, knocked her down, and took off her thick dark socks. Leqa looked at the water in the pot. Dark soapsuds were caked around the side. "Whose feet have been washed in this before?"

"How would I know? Drop your head!"

Leqa closed her eyes, sank her feet in the water, and moaned under her breath: "What difference does it make?"

Hero Showkat stroked the braid of her hair with her wet hand. "You're getting to be all right."

She scrubbed Leqa's feet with soap and a pumice stone. Leqa clenched her jaws. Tiny beads of sweat covered her face. After rinsing her feet, she put on her socks and ran out of the parlor.

Roxana was washing Kowkab's feet. She had corns on her toes. Roxana lightly squeezed one of them. "Does it hurt?"

"No, they're old."

Roxana turned to Showkat. "Hero Kowkab has worked a lifetime. Now it is time for her to rest. Why does the Central House of Fire not allow these people to retire?"

Showkat spat on the floor. "Don't even mention that pigsty in front of my face!"

Mrs. Edrisi poured water on Hero Pari's feet. Her scrawny shins were covered with protruded veins. The elderly lady's hand shook. Pari gazed into her eyes. "Aren't you tired?"

"I wish I had left home in my youth."

Pari chuckled. "In your imagination, you have thought that poverty is paradise. If you had been in our shoes for one week, you would not have this wish."

"The bosom of poverty is warmer than that of affluence."

"It doesn't make any difference. The bosoms of both are cold. From the time I came here, I found out that the wealthy are also not fortunate."

"You came to the wrong kind. The rest live it up happily."

"Because they have no backbone. They have left to live in exile. Won't they get bored?"

"They never think about death. They pile up money to their last breath."

"For their kinfolk?"

"In fact, they have no kinfolk, and they dislike one another."

Hero Pari pushed back her damp hair. "How were your relatives?"

"Scum, like the rest."

Showkat brought Rashid to Mrs. Edrisi and put her hand on the elderly lady's shoulder. "Since you look like his granny, you can take care of him."

Hero Rashid stepped back. "I'm not a baby. I can wash them myself."

Pari left her place for him.

Hero Showkat grabbed Yavar by the back of his collar and dragged him. The old man's feet slid on the carpet. "Leave me alone! Since when has the dirt of the feet become holy water? Such things were not done in the parlor of the house of the Edrisis. Hero Showkat! Don't claim to just have bile; I swear on my life you have black bile. Steam is rising from your body. Calm down for a moment!"

Showkat punched him on the back. "Do you want me to smash and rearrange your face? If need be, I'll throw your carcass into the tub."

Yavar fell down on the ground. Showkat took him by the waist and dragged him to the edge of the pot. Without warning, she grabbed his ankles and sank them into the water. The old man shouted: "Hero Showkat, I hope you suffer for this!" She shook his head so vehemently that she messed up his white hair. "Oh, God! Who is going to rescue me? They are all just staring like stunned goats."

Showkat grabbed the legs of the embroidered trousers. They ripped, and the old man's shins stuck out. The ripped embroidered cloth looked stiff, like deer hide. The golden threads sparkled.

Showkat was laughing. "See how wacky he looks!" She turned to Roxana. "He irritates me. I won't use soap. I'll wash them once-over-lightly, like cats do." She spat into the pot. "We have no towels. Get up! They'll dry by themselves."

Roxana called Yusef. The young man's face flushed. "How could I let clouds touch my feet? You will leave, I know. Weariness will begin from sunset until midnight, like dripping water. A few years ago, I had a nightmare. I felt I was sinking into a bottomless abyss. I was walking around the courtyard. Everyone was sleeping. The moon was going behind the clouds. The sky was getting close to the earth, like a damp canopy."

Showkat came near Yusef and asked Roxana: "Is he yapping again?"

She took the young man to the pot. Roxana poured water and Showkat washed his feet.

Heroes Rashid, Kowkab, and Pari took the pots out. Hero Showkat dried her hands with a towel. Yusef stood up and whispered in Roxana's ear: "I got my wish. You did not touch my feet. From early evening, I had built a talisman in my mind which remained intact." His fingers were shaking. "I might be the last person who touches you."

Chapter 17

Hero Rashid rushed nervously into the parlor. "They are surrounding the house like ants and locusts."

Showkat went upstairs and entered Vahab's room. She jumped on the windowsill and stood in the middle of the window frame. Her body against the light filled the length and width of the window. She whistled loudly. Sleeping birds swayed on the branches.

Vahab grabbed the bottom of her dress. "Hero! Come down. They are allowed to shoot."

Showkat spread her feet wide apart and put her hands on her hips. Her shouting resonated in the dark air. "Why are you silent, you sons of bitches?"

A shot split the air and struck the cornice. Showkat laughed boisterously. "Fire shots as long as you can breathe."

Hero Qobad came in. Roxana struck her own cheek nervously. "She is going to get herself killed."

Borzu jumped to the side of the window and grabbed Showkat's boot at the ankle. She kicked him.

Hero Qobad said in a decisive voice: "Autonomous actions are not acceptable. I prefer to step aside."

Hero Showkat jumped down from the windowsill. The bottom of her dress ripped. "You mean you want me to crawl into my shell?"

"Unfortunately, you do not have a shell. You have a sheath that is visible in the other end of the alleyway."

Hero Kaveh appeared at the door. "The Fire Stokers sent the old man neighbor away from the window."

Borzu sat down and held his head between his hands. The revolving spotlight was directed on the house. Vahab lay down, burning from fever. Roxana pulled the quilt over him. "You've gotten yourself beaten to a pulp."

"I have found the other side of the coin with you: my mother. I see her sitting under the milky light of the lampshade. All of life melts in her eyes." The spotlight fell on Roxana's face for a moment. "At one time, you were the angel of her rescue. Now come to my rescue. Without you, the world will be covered with a lead-colored dust."

The spotlight was sliding toward the western side of the building. Yusef leaned on the balustrade of the interior balcony. Kukan went to the courtyard and came back. He rubbed his wet hands on his trousers. Showkat and Borzu were going around the interior balcony. The young man whispered: "The day I first saw you, it was raining. Half an hour later, the sun came out. We were strolling in Perm Shrine Square. You had been fired from the textile factory, and you said, 'The employer hung around the female workers. Once he began to zoom in on me. I twisted his arms like a metal wire, tossed him on the ground, put my foot on his chest, and yelled, 'You cuckold! Now, I want you to chirp.' When I heard all this, I felt choked up. I said to myself, oh, goddess, your place is above the clouds."

Hero Showkat pounded her fist on the balustrade. "He was an ugly thick neck, that whoreson bastard. No one in the world has the right to get a watery mouth for Showkat."

Borzu covered his face with his hands. He bent his head over his chest. In the faint light of the wall lamps, he looked diminished and feeble, like a lost child.

Showkat pulled on his hair. "What are you remembering again?"

In a whiny, scratchy voice, Borzu said: "Hero! You are the symbol of purity and strength. You squash the evildoers. I am afraid of the color red. To be honest, I do not like the flag of the House of Fire."

From inside her boot, Showkat pulled out her half-burned whip and struck the floor. "When I was a child, we had a hen that laid eggs with double yolks." The blinding rays of the spotlight lit up her entire body. She shook her whip: "Dragon eye, go blind! I like milking cows more than any other animal. Once I got sick, and they fed me donkey milk."

Hero Rashid asked the elderly lady: "Would you like some canned cherries?"

Mrs. Edrisi shook her head.

Yusef leaned against the doorframe of Vahab's room.

Roxana said: "Come inside."

The young man stuck his hands into the pockets of his jacket. "In the evening, I used to go by the side of the Pink Rose Café and stand behind the window, looking at the Polish singer through the seam of the curtain. She wore a blue plaid dress, with her head dropped. The light shone on the part of her hair. When her voice rose, the nightingales of the National Park would come one by one and sit on the surrounding branches. The customers talked, laughed, and ate. The woman could not hear them. She sang with her eyes closed, as though they were not there. Late at night, she would come out and walk toward her house. I would stand under the shadow of the trees and watch the way her dress waved from afar. Many times, I wanted to walk up to her and say, 'You are extraordinary!' I never gathered up the courage, until the night when she was no longer there, and I painfully realized that as long as the earth rotates around the sun and the galaxy exists, I will never see my angel again. I punched myself in my sides, yanked up the grass in the garden, and lamented, 'Why, why didn't you at least say hello to her?' I do not want to regret once again. Roxana, the salt of the earth are the artists."

Vahab smiled at Yusef.

Roxana left the room. Hero Qobad was standing by the corner of the wall. His eyes were shining. Roxana knelt and grabbed the base of his crutch. "Help me! I am afraid. A piece of hot coal is burning in my chest, and, still, I am shivering. I am terrified of life and death equally." She burst out crying. Her broken voice resonated in the silence. "No, I do not want to die. I will be alone. How much darkness, how much?" She moved away from Qobad and tightly grabbed the balustrade. "I will throw myself down." She tossed her sweaty hair back by jolting her head. "Mother, come to my rescue! How fragile was the yellow wildflower!" Her tone became like that of a child. "Let me kiss your feet. Put out my fire!" She reached out toward the empty space. "Smile! The canaries flew away. I would count your white hairs one by one. When you were coming closer, your sandals clicked. Don't frown at me! Braid my long hair. Put a golden bow on it. Take my hand, and take me for a stroll around the square, behind Araz Hospital, alongside the stream, under the shade of the aspen trees. Don't walk fast. I get tired. Are you chuckling? I am not like I was before. I have become sane and amenable."

Showkat twisted Roxana's ear. Roxana closed her eyes and collapsed on the wooden floor. Showkat spat on the floor. "What kind of lamentation was she singing, this hussy?"

Qobad touched the designs of the wallpaper. "I have seen scenes like this a great deal. Not everyone has to be alike."

Borzu took off his hat. "Hero Showkat! I have no fears."

Showkat turned her back to him. "Borzu! The things you say! Like pottage left in the sun for a whole month."

Borzu yelled: "Roxana has no one."

Vahab grabbed the young man's scrawny arm. His head dropped to his chest.

Hero Showkat gave Vahab a sideways glance. "The only thing you're good for is filling in an adobe wall."

The elderly lady wiped Roxana's perspiring face with a handkerchief. Roxana's eyelids were quivering.

Vahab leaned against the wall. "They have come and gone. They have jumped up and down in her heart as though it was an elementary school. They have written obscenity on its walls. They have slammed its doors." He raised his head with difficulty. "When she looks back, she has no memories other than the cages of ownership with open doors, the begrudging eyes of hollow people. Borzu's little finger is worth more than all the admirers of Roxana Yashvili."

The irritating ray of the spotlight turned on the interior balcony. The elderly lady shielded her face with her hand.

Showkat's fist split the ray of light. "Pigheaded bastard! Keep turning; it's a good omen."

The spotlight turned toward the alleyway. Showkat's eyes followed its course. "I hate hunters. I like cows."

Vahab said out loud: "Then you are a Hindu."

Showkat assumed a posture of attack toward him. "Your daddy is a Hindu, you illegitimate seed. In this house, when a person makes a sound, some mule sticks a label on her, like she is from some dump like India. Let me set your mind at ease. I hate snakes; I have never had baklava, but you, rascal, have. Tell me, what does it taste like?"

Vahab leaned against the wall. "I have forgotten all the tastes."

Showkat turned to Qobad. "Hero! Have you ever tasted this filth that swarms of flies land on?"

Qobad smiled. The tips of his white mustache quivered in the faint light. "Hero Showkat! I have no fondness for sweets."

The door to Leqa's room opened. Showkat shouted: "Who's there?"

Leqa answered: "It is me, Hero."

Showkat approached her. "Are you peeking?"

"No, I was reciting prayers."

"So, did this hissing sound that was bothering my ears come from you?" After a pause, she continued: "Don't you light a candle under the picture of that female saint? My mother did, too. Wherever I go, a female saint turns into a horn and grows out of my forehead. Ask her if she has or she hasn't had baklava."

Leqa smiled. "Female saints don't have anything but milk."

"With or without a nipple?" After a pause, she added: "Recite whatever prayer you were reciting. But, Hero Leqa, you have an ugly female saint! Her eyes are crooked. The only thing I like about her is that she looks after the sheep."

Kaveh was walking on the other side of the interior balcony, whistling some tunes and occasionally tapping the floor with his feet.

Showkat shouted: "Why is it you're hanging around so far away?"

Kaveh came to the balustrade. "Hero Showkat! What a pity that you haven't seen the kind of people Greece has. They take advantage of every moment."

Vahab cleared his throat. "Similar to all the survivors of ancient civilizations."

Kaveh was coming forward slowly. "I miss the sunlight, pure wine, and tossing pebbles on the waves of the sea. Such songs! The voices had life in them."

Showkat laughed out loud. "What a surprise, you didn't tell us about the women!"

Kaveh thrust open his closed fist in the air. "Their story has hit the bottom. They have become narrow like a reed and sunken into darkness. I cannot even remember the face of one woman. Oh, the summertime women! Which roof did they fly to? Hero Showkat! I was not their roof. To tell you the truth, I was not a roof at all. When I went there, I took a ruins with me. My wall was broken, and my house was without a ceiling. Only their shadows appeared and disappeared on the curtain. Now, the shadows have vanished. The old men were better, the old musketeers, heartbroken people who would take the poison away from the world with buffoonery. Maybe I was made of the same material." He took his calendar out of his pocket, ripped the pink sheets to pieces, and tossed them down into the entrance hall. They descended, twirling, to the maroon background of the carpet. He showed the calendar to Showkat. "It is from forty years ago."

The woman spat on the floor. "Regressive!"

"When I bought it, it was wrapped in clear cellophane marked with stars. When I was walking right now, I could see those stars in my mind, light pink. Sometimes a very small thing flies away from one's memory, and it becomes so real that it encompasses one's entire life."

Showkat turned her back to him. "Kaveh, you're such a fool!"

Roxana stood up and held on to the balustrade. "It was such a lousy condition. Occasionally, something like a whirlwind spins in your head. It is nothing short of epilepsy."

The sky was fading. The crows were cawing. The spotlight was transfixed, shining a faint light on the wall of the alleyway.

Hero Qobad entered Leqa's room and opened the window. "It is twilight, neither daytime nor night. The birds hopping around. I like this hour. A white royal falcon would come, flying, and sit on my head. I would give it a piece of salted meat. The city was visible from up there. They would turn the lights off in the squares. It would occasionally disappear in the fog, as if it were an ant's nest going underwater. From that distant height, I wished to blow the clean breath of life on the depressing, sleeping, withered cities. But it turned out to be the reverse. The city swallowed me down its dark throat. The white royal falcon now flies on the empty mountain, pecking at old boots, squished and smashed zinc bowls, and spent bullet shells."

There was a ruckus in the alleyway. Vahab looked out the window. The lock on the house door broke and the door was opened. An army of black-clad Fire Stokers poured into the courtyard.

Chapter 18

A bullet broke the chain of the chandelier. The chandelier fell, and the red tulip-shaped lamps shattered and scattered over the floor of the entrance hall. Yavar pressed himself into a corner. The children ran into the garden. Kukan came out of Yavar's room and buttoned his trousers. The folded measuring tape was sticking out of the slit of his pocket, hanging down farther toward the floor with each step he took.

The staircase was shaking under the boots of the Fire Stokers, and the small pieces of the crystal were being smashed. Hero Rakhov stepped into the entrance hall. The chest of her black uniform appeared so ablaze from the glittering of the insignias and stars that it irritated the eyes. A Fire Stoker bent over the balustrade of the upper floor. "Hero Rakhov! The outlaws are here."

Hero Riyakhovski, the military commander of the House of Fire, and Moayyad entered. Moayyad shouted: "Find Haddadiyan!"

Rakhov nodded her approval.

Her hair disheveled and face flushed, Hero Showkat put her hand on the balustrade and tossed her whip near Hero Rakhov's feet. "Take it! It's yours. Have another one."

Rakhov clenched her jaws. Her pointed chin vibrated. She crushed the wooden handle of the whip with the heel of her boot.

The Fire Stokers brought Haddadiyan downstairs. His cheeks were covered with a spiky beard. A smile opened on his thick cracked lips, which revealed his shiny teeth. He raised his right hand. Rakhov came forward and clicked her heels. Moayyad's loud voice resonated under the ceiling. "The House of Fire salutes Haddadiyan, the Hero."

Rakhov shouted: "Bring the outlaws downstairs!"

A Fire Stoker pressed the barrel of his revolver on Showkat's shoulder. "Get moving, immediately!"

Hero Showkat put her hands on her hips. "Don't surround me! I have legs. I have learned how to go down. Your ugly faces aren't familiar. Which sewer do you come from?"

She came down the stairs, stepped on the glass shards, and stopped in the middle of the parlor. A blue ray of light lit up her entire body.

The elderly lady put her shawl over her shoulders and, with her head held high and a pale face, joined Showkat.

In Leqa's room, Kaveh stood in front of the mirror, took a comb out of his pocket, parted his graying hair, combed it back, and twisted his mustache. He held the yellowish bottle of cologne up to the light. It was empty. He picked up Leqa's glass, poured a few drops of water into the bottle, shook it, and sprinkled the diluted perfume onto the collar of his jacket. He tossed the triangular bottle. It slid to the corner of the room. He came out, took a deep breath, and went down the stairs.

Roxana took a black cardigan from Vahab's closet. Her teeth were chattering. She turned to Vahab. "It is a cold day."

Vahab leaned against the wall and closed his eyes. Roxana left the room. Yusef knelt beside Vahab. "She flew out of the cage."

Vahab smoothed the dirty collar of his flannel jacket. "We are going downstairs."

Yusef stood up, and they began walking shoulder to shoulder. Vahab's eyes were clouded.

Rashid was sitting in the corner of the interior balcony, chewing on his nails. Vahab touched him on the shoulder. Rashid gazed at him with his sad blue eyes. Vahab took Rashid's arm. Rashid stood up, and together they came down the stairs and stood in the corner of the entrance hall.

Borzu was leaning against the column. He put his hand in his pocket and took out a small ball of dried bread dough. He aimed at Haddadiyan's wide jaw and hit it on the target. Haddadiyan jolted. "Despicable!"

Borzu scratched his head. "Haddadiyan! I was the one who cut off that dog-hair mustache of yours."

Rokhsareh was peeking through the half-open door of the kitchen. Rakhov raised her whip. "Who is being nosy there?"

The woman came out, her back bent, pressing her hand to her belly. "Whatever God wills."

Hero Rakhov struck the floor with the whip. Rokhsareh sat down on the floor.

The door to the parlor opened quietly. With his hand on the wall, Hero Qadir stepped into the entrance hall. He rubbed his eyes. "Where are my shoes?"

Moayyad turned to Haddadiyan. "Did they beat you?"

Haddadiyan dropped his eyelids and rounded his big mouth to make his lips look like a rosebud. "Nearly to death. In mercilessness, they are cohorts of Satan."

Rakhov raised her whip. "Satan does not exist!"

Haddadiyan bowed. "I consent that such expressions are too commonplace. Please forgive me. A curse on Satan! He is not a relative of mine, so that I would beat my chest for him under his banner in front of you, my superior masters."

Rakhov nodded. "He has the potential for advancement."

Haddadiyan sighed. "At your command!"

Moayyad's double chin moved. "He is knowledgeable about the principles of polemics."

Haddadiyan put his hand on his chest. The wide tips of his fingers slid close to his navel. "The functionaries of the previous government were most oppressive. They created a climate of intimidation and terror. Brothers were afraid of their brothers, and fathers afraid of their sons. But now, a nobody like me is allowed to speak what is in his heart before you, my superior masters."

A Fire Stoker came in through the door toward the garden and clicked his heels. "A very odd person is sitting under the vine arbor, writing suspicious things on a sheet of paper."

Rakhov's mouth shifted to the left. "It is Yunos, the sorcerer. Bring him immediately!" She looked at her watch and commanded: "Qobad!"

Surrounded by Fire Stokers, Hero Qobad came down the staircase. A clamor began among the residents of the house. He stood by the column. Hero Rakhov walked up to him and gazed into his eyes. She then placed her hand on her forehead and turned her head. "His eyes are like those of a serpent."

Moayyad stared at the ceiling and moved his toes under the shiny leather of his boots. "He is a mesmerizer. He has a talisman."

The military commander, Hero Riyakhovski, stepped forward. "Belief in the superstition of talismans is contrary to the principles." Moayyad's ears turned red. "Throw away decadent perceptions! He practices magnetism. This man was on the mountain for fifty years. Those who possess the power of practicing magnetism stare at the sun."

Qobad smiled.

With the tip of her whip, Rakhov drew an X in the air. "The firing squad is ready."

Hero Qobad pounded the floor with the tip of his crutch. "So, the train has set out."

Rakhov lowered her eyes. "Very rapidly. There are no obstacles on the way. Our movement is forward. It will not end."

"High speed makes control difficult."

"We are good at what we do. Without our mandate, not a leaf on the branches will move."

Yunos entered the parlor and stood by the stairs. Hero Rakhov looked at him from head to toe, laughed with a piercing sound, and pulled Yunos's cloak down. His glassy eyes in the ruby rays turned the color of coagulated blood. Rakhov said: "Your elimination has not been included in this plan, but you shall not have any share of public property, not even at the level of something to eat and a place to sleep." She struck Rashid on the back with her whip. "We will send you to the camp. You need treatment. Your association with the sorcerers has short-circuited the wiring in your brain. It emits unpleasant sparks."

She walked toward Kukan, pulled out the end of the folded measuring tape from the slip of his pocket, and handed it to Haddadi-yan. "Neo-Hero! Deliver the tailor's patchwork quilt to the storage house."

Haddadiyan bowed at the waist.

Rakhov stood in front of Borzu, narrowed her eyes, and struck his temple with the handle of the whip. "Your impudence is despicable." She ordered the Fire Stokers: "Discipline him!"

Several strong men approached the young man. Pari screamed. They threw Borzu on the floor and kicked him in his sides and back. His eyeglasses broke and blood began to ooze out of his nose, dripping on his threadbare jacket. Haddadiyan let go of the measuring tape and smiled. Hero Rashid took a handkerchief out of his pocket and held it under the young man's nose. Showkat lifted Borzu up. He moaned: "My glasses."

Showkat grabbed Rakhov's arm and twisted it. "I will turn the Central House of Killing into a mound of dirt."

Borzu rubbed his eyes and leaned against the balustrade. "Hero Showkat, let go of them! There is no virtue in arguing with these people."

Rakhov ordered: "Take them next to Qobad. Tie their hands." She struck Pari on the shoulder with the whip. "You have a loud voice. It is suitable for the camp."

Kowkab scratched her cheeks in distress. "She is epileptic. She screams without meaning to."

With the tip of the whip, Rakhov twisted Kowkab's hair. "How about yourself?"

Torkan knelt. "We are innocent. From morning, we would go to the edge of the reflecting pool and wash clothes until sundown. We each have several children, without a bread-winning husband, a guardian."

Rakhov twisted Torkan's cheek. "In the New Society, no children without a guardian exist. The Central House of Fire is the guardian of children. The Supreme Hero is their beloved father."

"So do they not need mothers?"

"That has not been specified. We shall make a decision."

Torkan burst out crying. "Anything you say."

Hero Qobad pounded the tip of his crutch on the floor. "So, by the fire, we were warming the seeds of a bunch of monsters."

Leqa knelt and raised her hands to the sky. "Oh, God, let not humans become rulers!"

Commander Riyakhovski pounded the middle of Leqa's shoulders with the bottom of his Mauser. "What a den of leopards!"

Leqa ran toward the wall.

Rakhov yelled: "Where is Yashvili?"

Roxana came out of the darkness under the staircase.

Hero Rakhov shook her clenched fist at Roxana's face. "You have a scandalous file! Scandalous, and thick!"

Roxana held her five fingers in front of Rakhov's eyes. "How many are there? Can you see?"

Hero Rakhov shouted: "Where did you get the black card?"

"I stole it."

Rakhov's nostrils flared and she turned her back to Roxana. The Fire Stokers took Roxana to the side of the stairs and tied her hands behind her.

A light fog was drifting inside, gradually filling the parlor. Dawn birds sang in the garden.

Rakhov asked Moayyad: "How similar is Yashvili to that woman, Rahila?"

Moayyad contemplated. "Both, alien to reality. Fortunately, their species has been eliminated."

The woman shifted the weight of the revolver on her waist. "We will replace them. They will be firm, positive, and constructive. The future generation will have no deviant characteristics. The disease of love will be eradicated. Strong men and women will be at the service of reproduction. They will step into the arena for the advancement of industries, after doing their duty of reproduction. I am proud of the prospects of this generation."

She stood in front of Kaveh. "You delivered weapons to the Camp of Fire three times." She brought her head forward. Her narrow nose shone. She sniffed. "Why do you use cologne?"

Kaveh raised his left eyebrow. "I also used it during that period."

The woman messed up his hair with the tip of the whip. Kaveh took out the comb from his pocket and raised it toward his head. Hero Riyakhovski grabbed and squeezed his wrist. His fingers loosened and the comb fell.

Rakhov ordered: "By the stairs!"

Kaveh bent down and wiped the dust off his old shoes with his handkerchief. They took him by the staircase and tied his hands in back. He stood next to Showkat and whispered in her ear: "I would like women to dance on my grave." Showkat kicked him on the shin. Kaveh continued: "We shall not exist, but as long as the sun shines and flowers and grass grow on the earth, love will sprout in the human heart."

Showkat laughed hysterically. "Oh, love! Hidden dove!"

Rakhov stared at Vahab. "On what charge am I required to see you every day?"

"You have the option not to see me. You are the one who wants to, not me."

"Apparently, the beatings have made you more thick-skinned."

"I need kindness."

The woman grabbed his collar and pounded his head on the wall. "Here is a bit of kindness!"

"Complete it, with a bullet!"

"Unfortunately, your name is not on the list."

She laughed sideways, and her mouth remained crooked. She groaned through her locked teeth. Moayyad grabbed the woman's head and twisted it in one jolt. Rakhov's neck bones made a sound, her mouth straightened, and her lips moved. "In our business, such reactions are normal."

Moayyad nodded. "Quite rational! I remember that when I visited the capital city, I had the honor of attending the interrogation ceremonies. It was a special room, ten steps below ground level and equipped with very powerful spotlights. They would tie the criminal to a chair and adjust the blinding light precisely on his face. They had advanced methods. In the course of the interrogation, the interrogator general suddenly got the tremors. His eyes became droopy. He took off his suit and boots and began to run. He would lift his knees and pound them hard on his belly. He would bend down and adjust his thighs and buttocks in the four main directions. I took the liberty to say, 'Your Excellency! Please explain the wisdom behind these movements so that we can also benefit from them.' He said, 'Son! Interrogation is one of the most difficult skills. For balance, the soul and the body must be coordinated. Every detail of these movements is based on science. By this method, we transfer the unpleasant effects from the skull downward.'"

Vahab chuckled. "What about massacres? What scientific methods did they have for that?"

Rakhov took out a red handkerchief, wiped the sweat off her forehead, and stared into Vahab's eyes. "Don't talk about that. It gets my coccyx hot."

"Why does it start there?"

"Because the spinal cord reaches the brain."

"Do you kill with your spinal cord? So, the spinal cord of the Supreme Hero must have several additional vertebrae."

The woman closed her eyelids in respect. "Everything of him is more perfect than that of others."

"Even Triceratops? The dinosaur of His Excellency?"

The woman's pupils widened. The color of the iris mingled with the whiteness of the sclera: "I know you would like me to spend a bullet on you. But we still need you."

Fuming and restless, Rakhov walked toward Mrs. Edrisi and raised her whip. "According to the reports, you promised Neo-Hero Haddadiyan that you will cooperate."

"I did suggest to him that he wash his head and body. I did not know that was called cooperation."

Hero Rakhov stood in front of Haddadiyan. Blue veins palpitated under her thin skin. She held up the boar's head insignia and gazed at it. The gilded engraving glittered. "It is magnificent, right? Do you need camphor soap?"

The man looked at the crystal shards scattered on the carpet. They were emitting sparks here and there. "As you command."

Rakhov nodded. "Neo-Hero! I can forgive the way you reek, because of how you are so meek."

She grabbed Mrs. Edrisi's arm and took her to the stairs. The elderly lady's gray hair shone and swayed in the blue light. The large wrinkles of her face were fading behind the fog, her eyes ablaze. She gazed at Vahab. Blood was freezing in her veins. She leaned her head against the wall.

Whistling, Yusef went to the window and looked at the garden. Hero Riyakhovski walked toward him quietly. He put the cold barrel of the Mauser to his cheek. "Would you like to forget whistling forever?" He grabbed his collar from behind and dragged the young man to the middle of the parlor.

Rakhov raised her whip. "The Association of Forefront Galloping Artists has sent unpleasant reports about you."

"Do they believe I have been less forefront galloping than the quorum?"

"You have organized discussion and debate sessions. Judgment is the exclusive right of the organization."

"The natural mind, in any case, makes judgments. Do you expect ears not to hear and eyes not to see?"

"Limit your vision to the size of your worth."

"I have no idea about my worth. You measure it."

The woman stomped her heels. "The presence of Qobad in this house has been the cause of corruption. This infected abscess should have been lanced a long time ago. We had planned to take him to the sanatorium. That filthy Yashvili ruined our plans."

The sound of a heavy vehicle was heard from the alleyway, and Moayyad raised his hand. "The truck has arrived."

Rashid picked up Borzu's glasses from the floor, straightened their bent frame, removed the broken glass shards, and put them on the young man's face. Borzu opened his eyes. "It is better now."

Rakhov ordered Qobad: "Old man! Get going in front!"

Hero Qobad shifted the crutch under his arm. "Are we going in a truck? That will be interesting for me. I have never ridden in one before." He paused at the top of the stairs and took a deep breath. "This breeze is blowing from the mountain."

The elderly lady stood shoulder to shoulder with him. "The scent of common yarrow. Not everyone is so fortunate."

Yavar ran and sat on the floor at the elderly lady's feet. "You will catch cold on the mountain. Your lungs are weak."

The elderly lady smiled. "Yavar, the Jack of Hearts!"

The sun came up. Fog tented over the arbor. Qobad descended the stairs and looked at the branches and leaves of the plane tree in the alleyway. "I engraved your name on this tree with the tip of my knife. It has now gown so tall. Last night, it was lit for a moment when the spotlights turned. It will grow even taller."

Roxana came outside. Several of the buttons of her black cardigan were open. Vahab bent down and buttoned her cardigan. "You have arranged this scene for fun, right, Roxana? You will come back, I know."

The woman opened her dry lips. "We reached each other precisely at the border. Your mother had kept you in rooms with doors closed until I came. She gifted me with the fruit of her life. What a pity that I did not figure it out! I always figure out too late. Leave this place. Go to Kashmir."

"It is of no use. The whole world is cold, Roxana."

"The valleys are still warm. Wild violets grow by the river." She tapped the pavement of the courtyard with the toes of her cotton shoes. "I have it now. It does not shake under my feet."

"I wish I were your ground and earth, Roxana."

"You would be shaking, my darling."

The man leaned his head against the downspout. "My eyes are clouded, Roxana."

Showkat stood at the top of the stairs and opened her feet wide. "Fog has taken over everywhere."

Kaveh and Borzu joined her. Showkat raised her right foot and moved her toes under the dull leather of the boots. "They have really fallen apart. Did you see how that woman, Rakhov's, boots shone? She greases them with fat, I know. I know everything."

Borzu asked: "With what?"

"With pig fat, Borzu. The smoke from the truck goes above the wall. A while back, I saw a truck with five milk cows in it near the city gate. I wish I had asked which way they were coming from. It won't be possible for me to know anymore."

The student asked: "Was it under sunlight or rain?"

"A rainbow. How many primary colors do we have?"

Kaveh said: "Three. Blue, yellow, and red."

"It will rain; yes, it will rain. When I'm gone, stupid Vahab will go by the edge of the reflecting pool and cry. His heart is not made of steel."

The breeze disheveled Kaveh's hair. He gazed at the sky. "It reminds me of a rendezvous with a beautiful woman in my youth."

The crows were cawing on the branches of the aspen tree. In the alleyway, Rakhov was pacing and giving orders.

Hero Qobad stood on the threshold of the door and caught his breath. Yunos came to him. A bolt of lightning flashed in the sky. The poet pulled the cloak over his shoulders. "Bon voyage, Hero!"

The old man extended his closed fist to the sorcerer. "In trust to you!"

The red ruby ring was concealed in Yunos's palm. "Tuberose, white hyacinth, narcissus, and azalea flowers! Luba was divided. The gold went to the mountain. The quicksilver of fire is with you." He opened his hand, the ruby shone. "The ring of elixir, the magic ring! I am grateful."

Qobad stared at the ground. "We all will be divided after death."

"You will not be. You have only one manifestation."

"What manifestation?"

"Absolute goodness."

"If you wish to make a myth of me, be happy with that idea. But I do not accept it. It is enough, now." He went out of the house and disappeared behind the fog.

The elderly lady leaned against the arbor post. Leqa pulled up her green shawl and smoothed it. "Where should I put the album?"

"Throw it away."

Vahab grabbed his grandmother's arm. "To whom shall I go for shelter?"

"To love, my dear. The thought of Rahila was a delusion, but Roxana is real. She is so unsheltered and small that she can be the source of strength."

Hero Rashid was leaning on the wall, wiping his nose with a faded checkered handkerchief.

Yavar stuck a bag in the elderly lady's pocket. "Marshmallow and violet flowers. Borzu's medicines are only worthy of himself."

"Yavar! The things we saw, and how we grieved for nothing! No, it was not worth it."

The Fire Stokers took the elderly lady toward the door. She turned around and smiled.

Vahab and Leqa leaned against the wet wall. Kaveh came forward and paused near Leqa. "I am grateful for the celestial charm of your talent."

He stepped into the mud, raised his head, walked alone, and faded into the fog.

Roxana stood under the arbor, sneering, a lock of wet hair stuck to her cheek. Yusef pushed it aside with his index finger. "They never recognized you."

"They often do not recognize a guest who is a stranger." She looked at the sky. "The game is over." She left with nimble steps.

Yusef ran into the alleyway. A shot was fired. Rakhov yelled: "Catch him!"

In the midst of the sound of the boots of the Fire Stokers and the running truck engine, someone shouted: "He escaped."

Moayyad's yelling voice was heard: "The bullet hit his heart."

Vahab sat on the bench and stared at the wet ground.

Hero Showkat kicked the arbor. The decayed wood cracked. A Fire Stoker pressed the stock of his rifle between her shoulders. Showkat shook her shoulders. "Where did they take the other Fire Stokers?"

Hero Rakhov appeared at the threshold of the door. "Don't answer any questions!"

Showkat grumbled under her breath: "Shrew!"

Hero Rakhov drew an X in the air with the tip of her whip. "Moron! You are nothing anymore."

Hero Showkat burst out laughing and shook her elbow. "You are the moron. Killing us will cause a riot to break out, even in the House of Fire."

Rakhov screamed: "The people have already buried you before your death."

Leqa brought Borzu's hat. Borzu bent down. "Thank you, Hero. Put it on my head."

"I will pray for Showkat."

"You are very kind, but we have thrown away the superstitions."

Vahab picked a cluster of violet jasmines from the canopy arbor. He sprinkled the starlike flowers on Showkat's hair. Showkat gave him a look out of the corner of her eye. "Vahab, don't be a toady! What do I need flowers for?"

"On behalf of the people who love you but are silent."

She spat on the ground and walked away in firm steps. Borzu ran after her.

Slanted raindrops were falling on the helmets. The branches of aspen and maple trees bent and swayed in the wind. Lights in the windows across the way were turned on one by one.

Vahab ran into the entrance hall. The crystals of the chandelier were crushed under his feet. He climbed the staircase. He could not feel his own weight, he was walking above the ground. He stopped at the threshold of his own room. He leaned his shoulder against the doorframe. The mussed-up bed and the purple quilt seemed to move back and forth before his eyes. He walked to the window. He took a deep breath. The truck was passing through the alleyway, its headlights splitting the fog. A pale light slid across the cornices of the walls and the leaves of the Russian alder tree. Blurred shadows moved behind the closed curtains across from him. The sound of the lute and reed-flute mingled with the sound of rain. The roofs were getting soaked.

The scent of coffee and toasted bread wafted out of the windows.

PART 4

Chapter 1

The wind slammed the shutters of the window. Vahab opened his eyes and sat up in bed. A narrow streak of light lit the edge of the bed and the door of the closet. The house was immersed in silence. He tossed a jacket over his shoulders. Some sort of pain was shooting throughout his entire body from the marrow of his bones. Cylinders of light from the skylight crisscrossed each other. The broken chain of the chandelier swung in the breeze. They had swept up all the broken crystal shards. Only some particles of the pale red glass shone here and there on the carpet and the staircase. He checked Leqa's room. Below the picture of the female saint was a scalloped wooden shelf with a lit candle on it. The faint flame bent left and right. Leqa's bed was made up neatly, and a blue headscarf was waving on the headboard of the bed. He opened the doors of several rooms. They were all neat and clean, without any signs of children's shoes, jackets with torn linings, freshly washed dresses, and color-faded bundles. The purple bedspread of Showkat's bed enveloped the bed, and its silk tassels stirred against the floor. They had removed the boards over the windows of Kukan's room, with only a few loose nails left on the window frame. He looked under the bed. There was no sign of the patchwork quilt, the measuring tape, or the scissors. He went to the entrance hall and took a look behind the column. The midday sun was shining on the bay laurel shrubs. A spider climbed up a silvery web and came down spinning. The pendulum of the wall clock was swaying slowly and quietly. He bent down and picked up a piece of broken crystal from the floor. The light red color was frozen in the texture of the broken glass. It slipped from between his fingers. He went into Roxana's room. The perfume bottles were arranged in front of the vanity mirror, all empty. He pushed the bedspread aside. A few strands of hair were left on the pillow. He picked them up, wrapped them around his finger, and put them into his chest pocket. He pulled the alder-wood chair toward the window, opened the lace curtains, sat down, and put the soles of his feet on the wall. Tiny dewdrops were shining in between the grass blades. Butterflies and dragonflies flew hastily among the marigold flowers, tufts of spongy thistle, and peonies. The sap of pine trees was oozing out, shining from the tips of the needles. On the downslope of the stone slabs, the water in the potholes was evaporating. A rose mallow bush moved. He was startled. A turtledove flew off a branch. He rubbed his chin. The roughness of several days' growth of his beard bothered his fingers. He wondered how many days he had slept. What day of the week was it? In which month of the year? He opened Rahila's closet. Silvery glass beads, snowflake sequins, and pomegranate-aril pearls separated from deteriorating strings and fell to the ground. He remembered what Showkat had said: "When we opened the backroom closet, a bunch of dried flowers and mixed-up glass beads of all colors spilled out on the floor. Throw all of it out!" He scratched his forehead and thought: "The Fire Stokers will throw them away. By the end of one week, they will rot in the corner of the damp storage house."

He had no regrets. He had been so distraught that he had buttoned Roxana's cardigan with the buttons in the wrong buttonholes. A feeling of lightness, like a light from behind steamed glass, was shining on Vahab's soul. Roxana would not return; yet, in any case, she had walked on this earth for many years. She had migrated from one city to another. She had raised the dust of the curtains of dozens of theaters. Perhaps they had been together from the beginning. He saw himself as a white wall under the Crimean sun, beside which the woman passed before noon, stroked its puffed-up parts with her fingers, and touched its shells. A pink room in an inn in Yalta with a window toward the sea, where the woman stayed for a few days. In the crack of the beams of the ceiling, the scent of her body had remained and would come and go with the breath of the sea. The light of a carriage at midnight, her profile behind smoke-covered glass windows. Or the aspen trees in Tbilisi, when Roxana had passed by them, playing. The colorful lantern above the door of the house, an apricot that was slowly fermenting on the lawn, its pungent smell fading with the wind along with her youthful dreams.

He left the room and went to the entrance hall. He saw his face in the oval mirror. Blue rings had formed under his lusterless eyes. He blinked, and thirty years were added to his age.

He stepped into the garden. In the stagnant green water of the reflecting pool was the white reflection of the building. The breeze moved a yellow leaf along the stone pavement with a rustling sound. The ornamental orange trees had blossomed, and the scent of orange blossoms was disintegrating in the sunlight, spreading toward the shade and wrapping around the alfalfa. He sat on the green bench and rubbed his knees. The bare clotheslines were rubbing against each other, the safety pins clinking. Vahab picked a leaf, folded it, and put it between his teeth. He blew into the fold and made a whistling sound. For an instant, the silhouette of the figure of the neighboring old man appeared behind the window and immediately sank into darkness. He made a switch out of a willow branch and whipped the standing water. The sprays made his head and face wet. He opened the jetting fountain and stared at the spray. He saw a yellow shadow behind the window. His lips quivered. "Hero Showkat!"

He heard the sound of boots hitting the stone pavement of the outer courtyard. He leapt up and went around the building.

Next to the jasmine arbor, the broad-shouldered one and the scrawny one were walking around. The broad-shouldered one pointed at the stone landing of the stairs. "We brought back your canopy curtains."

The crushed velvet was on the stone landing. Vahab stroked it. He touched the blue bottle.

The broad-shouldered one came closer. "The sleeping pills."

"I know. At dawn on that day when they took them away, you were not there."

The broad-shouldered one was walking alongside the length of the arbor. "No, we weren't there."

"Were you punished?"

"We agreed to it. Are you going to hang this trashy curtain around your bed again?"

"What do you expect me to do with it?"

He put the bottle of pills into his pocket. The Fire Stokers took the heavy curtain upstairs and covered the bare canopy of the bed with the dark thick velvet.

The broad-shouldered one clapped his hands. "It looks exactly like a tomb again."

The scrawny one forced a smile. They passed by Mrs. Edrisi's room. The scrawny one turned to the broad-shouldered one. "You broke her chair."

The broad-shouldered one frowned. "We did it together."

They went downstairs and waved to Vahab. The sound of the door shutting was heard from the courtyard. Vahab sat by the balustrade, leaned his head against it, dozed off, and when he opened his eyes, he saw Leqa. It was dark. The wind was raising the dust on the floor through the gaps of the doors. A few steps away, Yavar was crouching. Leqa grabbed Vahab's shoulder. "You were sleeping for an entire day and night. They took the other Heroes on the order of the House of Fire."

"Where to?"

"To the public housing. From the time that Yusef got lost, Golrokh and Kowkab have had no calm and are restless. The Central House of Fire has searched all the nooks and crannies of the city. If he had died, his corpse would have shown up. The last traces of him were a few drops of blood on the stone pavement of the alleyway. Hero Rashid has managed to dodge exile, but he has been sentenced to one year of unpaid labor."

Vahab's pale lips moved. "In the same place as before?"

"Rashid and Qadir live in the same housing complex. Kukan goes to the workshop. He has to sew uniforms for the House of Fire for the rest of his life."

"Where is Yunos?"

Yavar spat on the floor. "Let him go to his black grave. Present company excepted, sorcerer-poets are all bastards."

Vahab shook his head. "How many of them have you seen?"

"Five or six. They were all bad omens. May God create a person as a dog, rather than as a poet-sorcerer. The ruby ring!" He suddenly burst into tears. "He stole it and put it on his crooked finger. All of them were straight and honest, except for that devil."

Vahab put on his overcoat and left the house. He went to the alleyway on the right. He walked alongside the stream. He stopped in front of the fence of the woman clad in blue. The mass of morning glory flowers quivered in the wind. Dozens of yellow canaries were singing simultaneously. He could hear the sound of a jetting fountain in an invisible small reflecting pool. The woman clad in blue peeked through the window. She seemed to whisper. Vahab put his hand behind his ear: "What did you say?"

The woman came downstairs. She put her elbow on the fence. "There were six of them."

Vahab picked a flower. "How do you know?" He crushed it between two fingers. "I am very depressed."

"Time is a good nurse. I used to do all sorts of geomancy. It is forbidden for everyone. Did you find the lute players?"

"Where is Roxana?"

The woman pointed to a spot between the ground and the sky. "I used to see Luba, occasionally."

Vahab felt a shooting pain through his spine. He looked at her intently. Her black eyes shone enchantingly. Her face was youthful and vibrant, her body vivacious, full, and tall. "They say no one could bear to look at her."

"Yunos still does."

"You have stayed young."

The woman put her hand on her chest and took a deep breath. "The scent of morning glory! It has removed this curse, death and old age, from my house."

"Kill the morning glories."

"Impossible. They have established roots. When you cut one stalk, another grows." She gazed at the horizon. "I will die one day, I know."

"Are you tired?"

"Flustered."

"Roxana was young."

"But worn out."

"More alive than all of us."

The woman closed her eyes. "Everyone is as alive as he or she is."

In the shadows of the sunset, the man saw the woman's face as a blur. The canaries became silent. "I need to leave."

He ran the length of the alleyway. Out of breath, he arrived home. The kitchen light was on. He stepped into the entrance hall. He mumbled under his breath: "I wish to read a book for my mother. Roxana! Where is my source? Your frenzy was wisdom. Do not smile. Do not smile at anyone in this way. I see your particles in every translucent ray."

Leqa came out of the kitchen carrying a tray. "Come, have dinner!"

Vahab followed his aunt into the parlor. Yavar was walking alongside the windows. All three sat down at the table. The old man picked up the teapot and poured tea into the glasses. Leqa divided the bread. Yavar put a piece in his mouth and took a sip of tea over it. "I make the bread moist with tea. The chandelier! What a waste!"

Vahab spread the playing cards on the table. "It is not a full set. It lacks six cards, the Jack of Hearts, the Queen of Spades, the Queen of Diamonds, the Queen of Hearts, the Ace of Diamonds, and the Ace of Hearts."

Yavar was dozing off. Vahab gripped his arm. "You are tired. Go to bed."

The old man stood up and, holding on to the wall, left the parlor. Leqa and Vahab sat facing each other. The screech owl was hooting.

The aunt sighed. "They are sorely missed."

"Who?"

"All of them. Hero Rashid was assigned to bring tea."

She picked up a tiny ball of dried bread dough from the table and rolled it between her fingers.

Vahab folded his napkin. "Do you need to have herbal tea?"

"No, I will go to my room."

She went up the staircase, her doughy face disappearing in the darkness of the staircase landing.

Vahab pulled out the drawer to the right in the library. His hands were shaking. He pushed the sheets of cardboard aside and took out the folded yellowed sheets of newspaper. He turned on the lamp, sat at the table, unfolded the paper, and stared at Roxana's pictures. At first glance, he saw her as before, unattainable, a well-known actor of the Moscow theater. The pictures had faded. The worn-out edges of the paper were turning to dust and falling on the table. The woman's picture in a black velvet dress attracted his attention. Two shiny bejeweled combs adorned her mass of hair. Her face was young and vibrant. A faint sneer in the corner of her lips, big slanted eyes, proud and bold, facing the camera. The date of the photograph was thirteen years earlier. She had been twenty-three years old, perhaps at the time when she had gone to the mountain. The twofold expression on her face was hiding some secret, and a fear at the bottom of the eyes from some unknown source. But her eyes sparkled; they were not downcast and dark, as in her final days.

The picture fell from between his fingers onto the table. "If only I had seen you at that time. When you came to me, you were incurable."

He gathered up the newspapers and put them in the drawer. He picked up *La vie de Gargantua* and sat in the corner of the sofa. He put his elbow on the small cushions. He opened the page where he had placed a marker and read a few sentences. He heard the rustling of the leaves. He got up, frightened, and looked into the courtyard through the window. In the moonlight, the shadow of the cat was reflected on the stone pavement. He pulled the handle and the window opened. The cat came in, growling. The backs of its legs were wet from the dew on the grass in the garden. It jumped on the sofa, between the small cushions.

The man smiled. "How are you, my old friend?"

The cat closed its eyes and put its snout on his knee.

Vahab leaned his head on his hand. The book slid and fell down. He could not read. The old habit seemed futile to him.

He got up and went into the kitchen. He turned on the stove, filled the teapot with water, and put it on the flame. The wind was scraping a willow branch against the windowpane. He approached the window. Hero Yunos was sitting under the arbor. He was scribbling on paper under the moonlight.

Vahab's eyes became moist. He opened the window and shouted: "Hero! Good evening."

Yunos raised his head. "Good evening, Vahab. I have a lot to do. Be quiet."

Vahab sat on the windowsill, gathered up his legs, and gazed at the man. "I wish to watch you until dawn."

Yunos folded the papers, put them in his pocket, and got up. "You make me lose my concentration."

"Where are you going?"

"To the end of the garden." He walked away, shuffling his feet.

Vahab turned off the stove, went upstairs, and leaned on the balustrade. He listened to Leqa breathing. The wind slammed shut the door of Hero Showkat's empty room. He went around the interior balcony and stopped in front of his grandmother's room. He caressed the handle. He looked through the keyhole. The room was submerged in darkness. Several tiny evenly distanced spots on the floor sparkled. He searched his memory. The buttons of Grandmother's smoke-colored gown were shining like a blue flame, like the eyes of Hero Qobad.

He went to his own room, pushed aside the dusty curtain, got into bed, shut the curtain gap, lay down, and closed his eyes. Yellow rings were spinning behind his eyelids and his breathing was becoming heavy. He got out of bed, pulled the curtain down, ripped it, and tossed it out the window.

Chapter 2

Leqa woke up early in the morning, opened the small door, and stepped into her mother's room. A faint hope pulled her toward the bed. The window was open and the silk dress was under the legs of the chair. A small whirlwind tossed dust and debris into the room. Dust settled on the mirror and the side tables. She straightened the bedspread. The embroidery work bundle and the spools of silk thread became visible. In the folds of the white cloth, waves of iris, green, blue, and vermilion colors slid and shone on the unfinished flowered needlework. Leqa sat on the floor at the foot of the bed and covered her face with the handiwork. A streak of the scent of violet flowers remained in the warp and weft of the fabric. She remembered her mother's youth. She had a beautiful oval face and black shiny hair that reached her waist. In front of the mirror, however, she would frown, and the corners of her lips would quiver. She wore dark, outmoded clothes. With annoyance, she would toss a shawl over her shoulders and, timidly, with her back bent like an old woman, go down the staircase. Leqa was twelve years old. She thought her mother was as beautiful as an angel, but she could not understand her sorrow and seclusion. In the late afternoons, she would sit on the eastern veranda and silently watch the descending of the night until darkness covered her face. Shading her eyes with her hand, she would gaze at the fire on the mountain. Often, she went to bed early. In the middle of the night, Leqa could hear the sound of the springs of her mother's mattress as she tossed and turned.

From the garden, Leqa heard the swishing of the broom. She got up and stood by the window. Yavar was sweeping the garden and dumping the leaves into the gutter. He threw a stone and made a crow fly off the maple tree.

Leqa shouted: "Yavar! What are you doing this early in the morning?"

"I am keeping myself busy with my work. I could not sleep a wink last night. The house has become like a graveyard. I remembered the nights when Mrs. Edrisi used to sit under the arbor. She liked to mingle with the Heroes. We would scold her. Now I am cursing myself. When my wife, Tuba, died, I used to pour my heart out to Miss Zoleykha, Mrs. Edrisi, as if she were my sister."

Leqa bent down through the window. "Let's go visit the Heroes."

Yavar leaned the broom handle against the corner of the wall. "The tea is ready. Come downstairs!"

Leqa closed the window, took an old overcoat from the closet and put it on, and tied the corners of her thick headscarf under her chin. She went to Vahab's room. He had fallen asleep curled up, with his knees bent, his lips pressed together, and his pale face covered with tiny beads of sweat. A fly was circling around his head. One of his hands was holding the bedpost tightly and the other was hanging down, his blue veins swollen from the rush of blood. Leqa thought that the only person who remained for her was that morose and distraught being. She bent down and kissed the tip of his middle finger. He opened his eyes, startled. "Aunt Leqa, is that you?"

"Yes, my dear. Why are you curled up? Are you cold?"

He looked at his aunt's face with astonishment. "I have never before heard you call anyone 'my dear.' I was having a pleasant dream." He sat up in bed. "The Caucasus and Delhi had become one. Grandmother, Roxana, and Showkat were standing in the covered bazaar." He suddenly laughed. "Hero Showkat was wearing a yellow sari. The tail of her thin silk headscarf was flapping. She was barefooted, with gold anklets on her ankles. A man was playing the reed flute, and a cobra was twisting and turning. Hero Showkat stepped forward and hit the snake hard on the head." He sighed. "Yes, it was the Caucasus. I had a dream."

Leqa's eyes welled up with tears. "Would you to go together with us to visit the public housing dormitory?"

Vahab jumped up. "I will get dressed right away."

Leqa and Yavar finished their tea and went into the courtyard and sat under the arbor, waiting for Vahab. The young man came out of the building. He was wearing a long overcoat and an old fedora hat.

They left the house. Alongside Qezel Urda Alleyway, they passed by the Monday Bazaar and reached the narrow, dark Charju Alleyway. The cement building of Dormitory No. Five, called Ordzhonikidze, cast its shadow on the walls. A foul-smelling gutter ran through the stone pavement of the alleyway. Several old men were sitting across from the dormitory, surrounded by flies. Patched overcoats, thick woolen shepherd vests, and short embroidered velvet jackets that were falling apart covered their scrawny bodies. Their bare feet were sunken into hand-woven cotton peasant footwear and wide slip-on shoes, and their shins had turned blue from the cold. As they conversed, they would doze off, their noses dripping to the tips of their mustaches. Their dirty heads were protected against the cold by faded turbans and moth-eaten fedora hats that had been handed down several times. The seats of their pants were wide and yellowed. Occasionally, they wiggled and broke wind noisily. A small bell was hanging above the door. They had tied colorful pieces of rags on the door's iron bars, similar to pilgrims who tie pieces of cloth to the sepulchers of the shrines of saints. The moisture from a crooked downspout on the concrete wall was spread in the shape of a huge wing. The guards, who were Fire Stokers, stepped aside. The three visitors entered the dormitory and descended a brick staircase. The flickering of a few wire cage lamps lit the narrow hallway. Leqa went ahead and opened a door. They entered a large, horseshoe-shaped, half-lit room. The smell of disinfectants, fermentation, and stale air wafted in the entire space. Metal beds were arranged tightly side by side along the walls, and the small windows were close to the ceiling.

A middle-aged woman was dragging a bucket full of dirty water behind her and cleaning the concrete brick floor with a piece of burlap. Leqa walked hastily toward a bed. Under a patched blanket, a hunched body moved. Leqa sat on the edge of the bed and pushed the blanket aside. Rokhsareh's watery eyes, blue lips, and sniffling nose became visible. She pressed Leqa's wrist with her bony fingers. They had cut her hair short, her graying strands of hair intertwined like matted camel hair. She tried to sit up. Leqa leaned the hay-filled pillow against the bed, held her arm, and helped her sit up.

Rokhsareh spotted Vahab and Yavar. She opened her lips with difficulty. "I'm so sorry." Her dry tongue clicked against the roof of her mouth. "They don't allow chairs."

Vahab took off his hat. "We are comfortable, Hero."

Yavar stepped closer to the bed. "We miss you in the kitchen."

"You're so kind." She hid her eyes with embarrassment, as though there was a valley between them.

Leqa adjusted Rokhsareh's headscarf. "You look better today."

"I was in pain till sunup."

"Don't they give you medicine?"

"Someone came and gave me an injection." She stared at the light reflected on the whitewashed ceiling. "The good old days! We had such a good time! If it isn't too much trouble, light a candle for me in the church."

Leqa whispered: "They won't allow it."

Vahab spun his hat around his finger. "I will make the arrangements and take care of it. I know a monk who has not left his place."

Rokhsareh wetted her lips with her tongue. "How is the lady?"

Leqa was taken aback. "Have you forgotten?"

Rokhsareh's eyelids drooped. A glossy fluid covered her corneas. "Wasn't she feeling well? Have you seen my sons? They're playing in the courtyard with the rest of the kids. Their daddy was in my dream. He was leaning on the clouds. His eyes were open, he wasn't dozing off. He said, 'Come!' Suddenly, there was thunder and lightning. The wind took the cotton cloud away." The slits of her eyelids closed. "They give me sleeping injections. They mix poison in them to get rid of me. They don't like patients."

Leqa held Rokhsareh's hand and caressed the protruded joints of her fingers. "Don't let bad thoughts into your head. You are going to get well."

Grumbling, the woman closed her eyes, pulled her hand back, and put it on her withered chest. Her lips moved. "The vegetable shop is so cool! Such good aromas. I wish I was a leaf of an herb." Her chin tilted toward her mouth. "Hero Yavar! Wrap a fistful of fresh grass around my head. It will ease my tiredness."

She sunk into a deep sleep.

Leqa heard Golrokh's voice on the other side of the dormitory. She got up quietly and circled the big room with light steps. The children were sitting on the stairs, leaning their chins on their hands. The faint midday light of the cloudy day was shining on their backs. As soon as Golrokh saw Leqa, she jumped up, ran toward her, and hid her face in the folds of her smoke-colored overcoat. Leqa knelt and hugged Golrokh. The little girl burst out crying. "I missed you and Mr. Vahab and Yusef a lot."

Vahab took a few steps forward. Leqa pointed to him. "Here is Vahab. Yusef is also going to show up."

"Won't they send him to the camp?"

"Why would anyone send a member of the Council of Forefront Galloping Young People to the camp?"

Golrokh wiped the tears off her cheeks. "Wasn't Hero Showkat a member of the Central House of Fire?"

Several old women moved under their blankets and stuck their heads out.

Leqa bit her lip and whispered: "Don't mention Showkat's name anywhere!"

Golrokh stood up, raised her head, and shouted "Hero Showkat" three times.

In the private courtyard, a Fire Stoker pulled the breechblock of his revolver. An old woman in a mussed-up bed began to get up. A few knuckle-lengths of her tangled hair were white, while the rest was a dark henna color. Her face was wrinkled, and there were blurry furrows around her lips. Her green eyes rolled in their sockets. She turned to Golrokh and opened her mouth, revealing a black hole. "I will tell the Fire Stokers what you said. Do you know what they will do to you? They will pull out your nails. They will gouge your shameless eyes out of their sockets." She giggled in a high-pitched voice.

Leqa hid Golrokh's face between the folds of her overcoat.

Vahab walked to the old woman's bed and put his hat on her face. The woman flailed her arms and legs, and her thin calves were uncovered.

Leqa shouted: "Leave her alone."

Vahab put his hat on his head, bowed, and said: "Mind your own business."

Yavar covered the woman's legs with her blanket and turned his back to her. Golrokh and Leqa sat on the stairs. The children surrounded them. Saber pulled on the sleeve of Leqa's overcoat. Gowhar put her doll on Leqa's lap. "She misses the house."

The twins rubbed their heads against her knee. Shirin stretched her thin, shaking arm toward Leqa. "See! I don't have a fever anymore."

Aslan swallowed. "Did you bring candy?"

Leqa dropped her head. "Next time."

Gowhar knelt. "When are we going back to the house?"

Leqa whispered: "Where is your mother?"

"She has gone to work. Last night, someone died here. She was from Sagiz."

Vahab leaned against the wall. The old woman asked: "What are you? A rebel?"

He remembered the games that Roxana played. "I am an agent of the House of Fire."

The old woman laughed. "You are lying. Why are you not wearing a uniform, and why don't you have medals and insignias?"

Vahab winked. "I am a secret agent. You are really out of it."

The old woman went under the blanket. "Be merciful, Hero. We are poor people; we can't think straight."

Golrokh explained: "Her name is Katya. She gives everybody a headache. Her husband was an infantry officer. He was killed fighting the Fire Stokers. They had taken her to the camp. They released her last month. She is afraid of everything."

The old woman cried out: "Have mercy on us."

Yavar approached her bed. "Where are you from?"

"Yalta, Hero."

He became quiet and stared at the ceiling. The sun went behind the clouds, and the atmosphere of the dormitory became dark.

Leqa put her hand on Golrokh's shoulder. "Do you know how Teymur is doing?"

"He is in the men's section. He has been given a dark damp place. Rokhsareh was moaning all last night till morning. They might take her to the hospital." She walked the length of the room. "She has not eaten anything." She reached Rokhsareh's bed. "She is breathing strangely."

Leqa and Yavar ran toward Rokhsareh's bed. She was pressing a bright peacock feather between her fingers. Her breathing was sporadic. Her bony chest rose and fell. Her face had yellowed. Leqa took her pulse. Distraught, she shook her head. "I don't understand."

Yavar pulled the woman's eyelids up. Her eyes turned slowly. "She is still alive. Call a doctor."

Leqa knelt by the bed and began praying. Rokhsareh shivered from head to toe, held the peacock feather toward the ceiling, and uttered an incomprehensible word. Her hand fell. The golden, blue, and rusty colors of the feather shone for a moment in the slanted light.

Leqa looked at those around her, stunned and confused. "Did anyone understand what she said?"

Golrokh lowered her eyelids. "I think she said, 'Lady.'"

Vahab took off his hat.

Chapter 3

Leqa put the sheet music of the song on the piano, pulled her stool toward her, and sat down to play. She played a few notes several times to warm up, striking the keys with her fingers. The strings roared. The rings of the curtains moved. The ceiling was flying.

The door opened and Vahab stepped into the parlor. He straightened his hair with his fingers and walked forward, terrified. His aunt was preoccupied with playing. Her back and shoulders shook. Her hands moved back and forth on the white keys, as her fingers bent and straightened.

He grabbed Leqa's arm. His aunt jumped up, startled. "What is it, Vahab? The Fire Stokers?"

"That is what I should ask you. What is this music?"

Leqa straightened her back and closed the piano. Her eyes sparkled. "They have officially invited me."

"Who has invited you?"

"The manager of the Municipality Theater."

"To do what?"

The aunt raised her left eyebrow. "Obviously, that which I am capable of doing."

Vahab sat in the easy chair and caressed the red bead of the parrot's eye on the small cushion. "To play the piano?"

Leqa rubbed her hands together. "Believe me, they want me. They have no one else."

"Of course I believe you. Why did you accept?"

Leqa scratched her forehead. "Vahab, I am not the kind of person who thinks. My head starts spinning. But I would like to live as

268

long as I am alive." She opened her arms. "Living means playing. When I sit behind this, it is as though a flock of birds is flying around my head, protecting me."

"Not so fast, Leqa. What does this music have to do with birds?"

"It is the anthem of the Regime of Fire."

Vahab ran his fingers through his hair. "That is what I surmised."

"A group of actors have come from Moscow."

He picked up the cushion and pressed it to his chest. "Somebody said that they scream. Screaming is all the rage now."

"From whom did you hear that?"

Vahab caught his breath. "An expert."

"Will you not come?"

He looked through the window at the reflecting pool and the bench. His eyes clouded. "Of course I will. I cannot bear staying in the house."

"That is strange, Vahab. I have also become like you. So why was it that we would not step out of the house all those years?"

"We were prisoners."

"Prisoners of what?"

"Habit and compulsion, laziness. Yesterday morning, I dropped by Rahila's room. The perfume bottles and the clothes were unfamiliar, like objects in an inn."

Leqa's mouth hung open. "Don't you love Rahila?"

He pounded his fist on the arm of the easy chair. "Yes, yes, I do, but in a different way. How can I explain? She has descended from the summit. Now neither does she breathe behind the bougainvillea flowers, nor is the shadow of her body cast on the Ganges River. Like other people, she lived in obedience and helplessness, and she died in the prime of her youth." He rubbed his eyes. "But her smile was beautiful, as beautiful as the glance of Roxana Yashvili."

Leqa sighed. "So, did your dreams go up in smoke?"

"They have been divided. Did you see how the chandelier of the entrance hall shattered in an instant, but every piece reflected a ray of light? One could also live devoid of dreams. What would be wrong with fierce reality?"

"You are not who you were before."

"No one is who he or she was before. We change. We grow old. One has to pass through this path."

"But my mother and Hero Qobad remained faithful to their dreams to the end."

Vahab scratched off a piece of dried bread dough from the velvet of the small cushion with the tip of his fingernail. "Kaveh, Showkat, and Borzu also remained faithful. Their temperament is different from ours. Maybe they were from a different generation."

"How about Roxana?"

Vahab looked at the garden. A shadow covered his eyes. "In one sense, Roxana also did not break her pledge."

"Vahab! Did she not want you?"

"I have thought about this a great deal. She did, and at the same time, she would flee. The suffering of an ancient sin weighed down on her shoulders, as heavy as the sins of humankind."

Leqa got up from the piano and stood facing him. "Tell me more clearly. To tell you the truth, I was not her enemy, but I had no love for her. I don't understand people like that."

Vahab walked toward the door. Before leaving, he turned to his aunt. "It is better that you never do."

Leqa's anxiety began at noon. She would feel blazing hot, go to the courtyard, and sink her head into the water.

She sat on the bench and stared at the window of her mother's room. "I wish you were here. You would take out your old dress from the bottom of the trunk, and we would go together. You would sit in the front row with your eternal smirking face. In the end, you would find out that Leqa was not that inept and incompetent. One always gets going late. Nothing happens when it should."

A hand touched her softly on her shoulder. She bit her thumb. "Is that you, Hero?"

Yunos sat beside her. "I am so tired. I have been writing without a pause for three days. I would like to entrust my book to you."

Leqa put her hand on her chest. Her eyes widened. "Entrust it to me? Someone who does not know anything about poetry?"

"That is an advantage."

"Yes, I know. You have been taken by the magic of the moon." She got up and turned on the jetting fountain. "I wish my mother were here."

"So that you would continue to remain at home?"

Leqa took offense. "She would encourage me."

"The problem was with you. You put your burden on her shoulders. Her strength kept you and Vahab in the shadows. Now, there is no one to put a sheet over you when you faint. People laugh at your fear. When you wake up, you have to tell your nightmares to the rain and the wind. Others find what you talk about tedious. Other than yourself, you have no one. Hence, all your energy is spent on staying alive."

Leqa bit her fingernails. "Yunos! You are so cruel. My mother was not like them. They joined hands and deceived her."

"Anyone who continues his or her own path to the end is liberated. The pledge breakers are bewildered."

Leqa picked a leaf off the tree. "Are we bewildered?"

"Play the piano to the end of your life."

"Yes, I will. For God, and my mother." The entrance hall clock struck four. "I have to be there at five thirty."

On her way, Leqa recited prayers under her breath. She pressed her sweaty hands to her cheeks, spat on the ground, and caught up with and then got ahead of Vahab and Yavar. They entered the municipality garden. The water in the swimming pool was low, the inside ledge was visible, and particles of muck bubbled up to the surface of the water. The late afternoon sun was ablaze on the window-panes of the building. Vahab and Yavar entered the uncrowded hall and sat in the third row. Leqa hesitantly stepped into the backstage hallway. The doors to the dressing rooms were open, and in front of the mirrors, the actors were putting on their makeup. The male actors were donning fake mustaches and beards; whistling, they hung the suspenders of their trousers over their shoulders and buttoned up their silk shirts. Wearing wigs, the female actors were sauntering around in satin dresses.

The manager of the hall came to welcome Leqa. He shook and squeezed her hand with restless hot fingers. "Hero! With your talent, I would like you to show these Muscovite chicklets that they are no big deal. Pompous peacocks! They just go around and issue orders, criticize everything, and stomp the ground. It is not just that we don't have the resources, they even grumble about the weather. That arrogant director smokes cigars. He is among the last group that received a degree from the 'New Theater.' He also plays the violin. Last night, they went to the garden, danced under the moonlight, and stomped our best flowers."

Leqa looked at the women. "Such dresses! Isn't wearing those a crime?"

The hall manager threw back his head, laughing boisterously. The tip of his blond goatee pointed at the ceiling. "It is a cute play. Pure criticism of the corruption of the military government." He shook his index finger. "To be fair, the actors are incomparable. I watched the rehearsal last night. I laughed so hard, I got a bellyache."

"Were they screaming?"

The man raised his eyebrows and stared at Leqa with his moist hazel eyes. "How do you know?"

"An expert said so."

The man rubbed his palms together. "They have been very supportive of us since two weeks ago. They pay attention to this remote city, economically, culturally, and socially. It is a source of pride. Hero Leqa, go on the stage, sit at the piano, and wait for the bell signal."

Leqa stepped onto the stage and sat at the piano in the dark corner. The curtain was drawn. She could hear the sound of footsteps and the hubbub from the audience hall. The hinges of the seats creaked. After a while, a bell was rung and the dark blue curtain was pulled to the sides, hissing and whizzing. The pulleys rolled one after another, grinding away. It was as though a weight was pulling Leqa's heart down. Below her blurred vision, the crowd was a waving mass.

After the program announcement, the anthem choir entered. Leqa immediately attacked the piano. The people in the audience hall stood up at attention, staring at the stage. With trembling fingers, Leqa hit the keys hard, as though she intended to yank them out. An uproar resonated under the ceiling: "Iron, iron, iron crowbar! Jump out of ambush where you are!"

The anthem choir hit the air with their clenched fists and, with resonant cries, challenged the echo of the piano to a battle. After the "Anthem of Fire" ended, the crowd applauded vehemently. They waved paper flags marked with the erect crowbar over their heads. The anthem choir repeated: "Iron, iron, iron crowbar! Jump out of ambush where you are!" The people lent their voices to them in unison. Beads of sweat poured down Leqa's face from the roots of her hair. She pounded on the piano keys with her exercised, pestle-like fingers. The people and the anthem choir pushed their voices to the peak in rapture. A woman screamed. A commotion broke out in the audience. When they took her out, she was thrashing her arms and legs in the air and her mouth was foaming. She fainted by the exit. Crows began to caw on the branches of the aspen tree, and, flying, they pecked at the gable roof. Leqa's swollen goiter was throbbing. She began to shake and cry. As she was playing, tears fell on the piano keys. The anthem ended. They closed the curtain and opened it again. Arm in arm, the singers jumped up and down, took a few steps back, and ran forward rapidly. The people were throwing the daisy flowers from the garden toward them. Leqa covered her face with her hands. The hall manager softly tapped her shoulder with the tip of his cane. "Hero Leqa! Bravo. You played magnificently. Our city will never forget such an exciting ceremony." Leqa raised her head and stared at him, bewildered. She was hearing his voice from a distance, as dry as gold foil wrap. The man lowered his cane. "Are you crying? A salute to sensitive hearts! A hundred salutes!"

Leqa ran the length of the hallway, stepped into the restroom, and locked the door hurriedly. She splashed water on her face and stared into the mirror. She saw a stranger in the glass and mercury. She shouted, "Mother!" In the tight space, her breathing was blocked. She turned the key in the lock. It was stuck and would not open. She pounded with her fist on the thick wood. She heard a delicate voice:

"Hero Leqa! Come out!"

"Golrokh! I can't."

The door handle turned, and Rashid yelled: "Would you like me to break the door?"

"Let me catch my breath and I will try again."

She closed her eyes and leaned her head against the wall. She remembered her mother looking at her when she was on the top of the ladder. "Leqa, you are more real than Rahila. Every morning, you came down and sat at the piano. No one paid attention, but you played the most beautiful tunes." She saw Showkat beside the flowerbed. With her hand on her hips, she was hitting the rim around it with the tip of her boot, saying, "Rashid, open up your ears. Anyone in the world who is able to do one job well is better than others in any job you give him. This pickled eggplant is a skillful piano player. So, why shouldn't she also be capable of climbing a ladder?"

Leqa opened her eyes and turned the key softly. The latch turned back in the lock with a clicking sound and the door opened. She walked out smiling. Hero Rashid held her arm. "I kept crying along with you."

Yavar rushed forward, bent down, and kissed Leqa's hand. The middle-aged girl became angry and pulled her hand back. The old man looked at her in astonishment. It seemed as though she had changed. He said: "Bravo! You have such talented fingers." Leqa shook her fingers. "The people were climbing over one another to see you. The hall manager announced that by hearing the thunderous roar of the masses of Heroes, you had become emotional. We were so worried that we came here to see whether that was true."

Vahab was leaning on a column in the faint light. Leqa ran to him. "I was bursting from grief."

He faintly smiled. "I saw that you were shedding tears."

Actors were running in the hallway, throwing up their arms. A young man approached their group. A cigar was emitting smoke from between his two fingers. His chubby cheeks looked red. Perhaps he had pilfered a bit of rouge from the actors' makeup. He stomped the ground and shouted: "Get out of here, hit the road! A curse on me if I ever again come to a provincial city. This place is like a stable, not a theater hall. No matter in which direction I look, I see a bunch of donkey glass beads wiggling around. Is this an almshouse or a dressing room?"

Rashid turned red from ear to ear. He raised his clenched fist. His biceps swelled up beneath the sleeves of his jacket. "Hero! The almshouse is not a bad place. It has nurses who take care of old women."

The young man puffed at his cigar. "That is also one way to look at it. So round up your gang and leave." He pointed at Leqa. "Only that woman is obliged to stay."

Leqa approached him. The man's height barely reached her shoulders. "No one is obliged to do anything."

Vahab stepped forward and pushed back a strand of hair from his forehead. "What is the name of your troupe?"

The young man raised his left eyebrow and blew cigar smoke toward him. "The Cricket Theater Workshop."

Vahab creased his brow. "I have not heard of it. It is unknown. With whom did you work previously?"

The young man held his head high. "Nikolay Alexandro."

Vahab stared at his shiny Circassian eyes. "You are bluffing. I have not heard the name of your theater troupe from him."

The young man's ears turned red. He dropped the cigar on the floor and crushed it with his heel. "Do you know him?"

Vahab leaned against the column. "Ah, the good old times! Such a company. All of them top-tier, not crickets of the eighth rank. The skillful Raisa Mulchanvaya, the humorist Nikolai Batalov, the lovely Khatchaturov, and the magnificent Yashvili."

The young man's chin quivered. He took another cigar out of his pocket and lit it. "Have you seriously met all of them?"

"Moron! We were friends. They consulted me. Unfortunate are the people of this city. Did they deserve nothing more than the Cricket Troupe?"

The young man bowed. "May I inquire with whom I am having the honor of speaking?"

Vahab shrugged his shoulders and walked toward the garden. Leqa smiled. The young man asked: "Did that gentleman know you?"

"He is a newcomer. He has come here with Roxana Yashvili."

The young man blinked. "Is Miss Yashvili here?" He spoke in a drawl, and his voice sounded like a child's. "Is there any chance that she might possibly see our show?"

Leqa put her shawl over her shoulders. "I do not know." She went and sat at the piano, like a shadow.

Ready and in glittery, eye-catching costumes and makeup, the actors who played the leading roles were coming and going, practicing their lines under their breath.

The young man clapped his hands and shouted: "Attention!" Everyone gathered around him. He took a long puff of the cigar. "In tonight's performance, you must give your best. Quite likely, the top-tier personalities of theater, the brilliant stars of this profession, will be watching your performance."

A woman dressed in red grabbed the young man's arm. "They call me Yelena Petrova, Purple Princess."

The young man laughed noisily. "My dear! You have invented this title yourself. It doesn't matter. But it is not unlikely that a princess as bright as a star will see our show."

The woman put her left hand on her hip and pounded the tip of her pink boot on the floor. "I do not know that person."

The young man turned his back to her. "Naturally, you don't know her." His eyes clouded.

The woman stood face to face with the young man. "Tell me the truth! Have you invited anyone of the officials of the House of Fire, ministers, and the commanders?"

The young man gazed into her eyes. "Purple Princess! In your opinion, is art only understood by such people?" He tossed away the cigar. "I am going to the garden."

A short fat man blocked his way. "Maestro! Wait!"

"I cannot. The play makes me sick. I recalled the great actors. They were the generation of sorcerers who were only alive on stage. Fire circulated in their veins."

Leqa chuckled.

The woman dressed in red was angered. "What are you laughing at?"

Leqa shrugged her shoulders. "I don't know. Many things. I mostly laugh at myself."

The bell was sounded. The hubbub in the audience hall subsided. Two women and three men sat at an oval table. Yelena Petrova held a fan in front of her face. Only her brilliant black eyes were visible. A lusterless moon—a round yellow board—emerged from behind the trees of the stage scenery.

The woman tossed the fan onto the empty table. "Why did the General not come?" She stared at the wall clock. "It is three past nine. He has always been punctual, for ten whole years. How quickly time passes!" She stood up and walked the length of the stage restlessly. Her starched skirt made a rustling sound, sweeping the dust off the wooden floor. An old woman in a black dress and white apron entered. "The messenger of His Excellency is at the door. Would you permit him to enter?"

Yelena Petrova stopped. "Oh, Holy Ivan! Highway robbers. Immediately!"

The old woman bowed and left. The short fat man sighed, stood up, and stroked his fake mustache. "Chaos and riots threaten our vast country. The storm roars. We have a dark future before us."

Yelena Petrova stomped with the heel of her boot. "Lezhnev! Please be quiet! You do nothing other than pamper yourself and lounge around at home. How could you know what awaits us?"

A rotten apple was thrown at the stage from the crowd, straight to Yelena's skirt. Screaming, the woman went behind the table. A tall, broad-shouldered young man appeared at the threshold and said, panting: "His Excellency was assassinated."

The audience in the hall applauded.

Yelena Petrova shouted: "Death to the General!"

The troupe of actors, even the old woman and the messenger, accompanied her in shouting. To encourage them, the audience threw persimmons. The short man, despite his corpulence, was jumping up, snatching the persimmons, biting into them, and tossing them on the ground. The crowd burst out laughing. Two people began fighting and grabbing each other's collars. Others got involved and tried to mediate. Several chairs were broken, and women screamed. Frightened children fled. The hall manager closed the curtain. Actors ran toward the dressing rooms. Leqa started to get up, held on to the side of the piano, and closed her eyes. The people left the audience hall clamoring. When Leqa opened her eyes, no one was on the stage. Smashed persimmons had stained the floor here and there. She walked through the dark hallway, entered the garden, and sat on a stone slab near the pond. The wind was twisting the branches of the elm tree, young cypresses were bending down, and darkness was descending.

She heard Yavar's voice. "Mr. Vahab! I found her." Leqa smiled. Yavar rushed to her. "Miss Leqa! Were you hurt?"

Leqa bent forward. "How about you? You weren't trampled on?"

"No, Miss Leqa. We pulled ourselves to the side. Such a disgrace and disaster! We went after you to the dressing room. Your colleagues have been offended and upset. They are leaving to go back to the capital city tomorrow."

Leqa shrugged her shoulders. "Have you seen Golrokh?"

Vahab tossed a pebble into the pond. "She left with Hero Rashid. Let us go back home."

Leqa pulled the shawl over her head. They walked slowly alongside the dark pool and pest-infested boxwood shrubs and stepped into the street.

Chapter 4

It was a cold, sunny day. Vahab left the house intending to visit Rashid. Rashid had given him his address on the night of the show. He buttoned up his overcoat and stuck his hands into his pockets. He was going through the streets absent-mindedly. It was as though he saw the carriages, the people, and the shops from behind a fog. He was distant, suspended, and without memories. He knew no one and he had no place to go. He lacked Leqa's ability to adapt. He occasionally saw the Heroes. There was ostensibly some friendship between him and them, but the relationship was superficial. He would get depressed in the house, but the city could not curb his sense of alienation. Roxana had asked whether he would go to Kashmir for her sake. Perhaps. But he could not lie to himself. That journey would not be for anyone's sake. No faded dream awaited him behind the houseboats and bougainvillea and common stock flowers. Kashmir had also become distant from him. Kaveh had taken refuge in Greece. Vahab preferred India. The clothes of the people of Benares were white. Perhaps he would lose himself in that whiteness. Behind the fleeting rays of light, he had seen the various faces of Roxana, and the faraway image of Rahila had also fallen apart. If only it had remained untouched! If only the boundaries of love, hatred, and fear had not mingled and become shapeless. Yusef had seen the bright aspect of the woman, Roxana: a luminous line, a brilliant meteor in darkness. Vahab also was cognizant of the whirlpool and the darkness in her soul. His oneness with Roxana had reached the extent that he was able to hate her, in the same way that he hated himself. He stroked his cheek. Under his fingers, he felt a twofold warmth. He stared at the tips of the toes of his shoes. He was walking with the woman's restless feet. Roxana had dissolved within him. He viewed power as nothing, was continuously at war with everyone, and saw a ruse behind every smile. His simple world had been mingled with the chaotic lines of that woman; he would go up to the end of the line and, in game within game, neutralize the ruses. His grandmother, Showkat, and Borzu had gone toward annihilation with a fragile hope. They had seen an eternal ray of light in their incomplete nonexistence; however, Qobad, Kaveh, and Roxana did not expect any echo after crossing the line. The motivation behind the efforts of that woman, Roxana, was perhaps to prove the futility of the ways and customs of the world. He could not figure her out, but now he thought she was right. He carried the threadbare lightness of Roxana with him. He wandered around weightlessly among the branches and leaves of the trees, the gable roofs, and the domes of the temples.

Alongside a stream, he went toward the outskirts of the city. Orange peels, pieces of wood, puffed up paper bags, and empty tin cans rolled on the ripples and proudly collided with the banks of the stream. The odor of muck and dead fish wafted in the air. He stopped in front of a ten-story cement building. The windows on each floor opened to a balcony that was one meter wide. On each of the balcony front walls, a few articles of clothing were turning and twisting in the breeze. These were the only signs of life in the tall gray building.

He pressed the bell for the fifth floor. Wearing a tank top, Hero Rashid bent down from the balcony. His straw-colored rough hair shone in the sunlight. He waved. "I'm coming down."

Vahab stepped into the pine grove. The grass was burned here and there and colorful pieces of tattered rags were caught between the blades of grass. The height of the newly erected buildings made him dizzy. The city was expanding, and from every spot a crowbar seemed ready to leap toward the sky. He leaned against a dead tree. Children were playing in a small area partially paved with bricks. The dust of construction lime settled on their hair. A few steps further, workers were laying mudbricks upon mudbricks, raising the walls rapidly.

Rashid came out through the iron door of the building. Vahab ran forward. Rashid was wearing his work overalls, and the strap of the left shoulder had slipped down. He shook hands with Vahab. Vahab opened his fingers. "You are so strong."

"Hero Vahab! It is you who has so little strength. Let's go to the National Park."

They went along a narrow stone-paved path and entered the alleyway. Vahab sneezed. Rashid stopped. "Have you caught a cold?"

"Not yet. How is everything?"

"One year of unpaid labor. But being sent to the camp is not an issue anymore. I'm not unhappy, Hero."

Vahab spat on the ground. "Are they forgiving and kind?"

Rashid bit his lip. "I wouldn't say that. But, if not for the factory, I have no shelter." He pressed his thick thumb between his eyebrows. "I'm not a thinking man, like you. I put up with what I have."

Vahab crossed to the other side of the alleyway. "Is your place okay?"

Rashid scratched the tip of his nose. "Well, it's a roof over my head. I have no furniture. I've spread newspapers on the floor of my room."

Through the large northern gate, they entered the National Park. A sheet of half-torn metal was hanging from the gable roof of the abandoned building, vibrating noisily in the wind. Old women were scratching their heads under the sunlight. Old men were dozing off with newspapers on their knees. They walked near the swimming pool. Vahab caught his breath. Rashid sat on the bench. "Look for a job!"

"It is not possible, Rashid." A sparrow flew away from the flowering broom shrub. "With my mixed-up record?" He grabbed Rashid's arm. "I need your help."

The man blinked. "What sort of help?"

"It will cause some headache."

"I'm not an ungrateful person."

"Make arrangements for me to cross the border. I have found traces of a few operators, but I am afraid there may be spies among them."

Rashid chewed on his mustache. "No! Hold on, Vahab. Where are you going to go? Like last time, to Kashmir?"

Vahab smiled. "Do you know of a better place?"

Rashid scratched the wood of the bench with his fingernails. "For you, no. I will keep what you're asking in mind. Here and there, I have some friends." He rubbed his thumb and index finger together. "How is your money situation?"

Vahab sat beside him, closed his eyes, and put his head on the back of the bench. "I will come up with something."

Rashid warned him: "Don't even think of letting Yavar know."

Vahab opened his eyes. "Do you think I am a little kid? Yavar will start making a commotion. Leqa should not know about it, either. You are the only one who knows."

"Crossing the border is dangerous. They kill the runaways."

Vahab leaned his chin on his hand. "It does not matter."

"Won't you stay with your aunt?"

"No, I cannot, Rashid. The old shell has broken. Reading books and sniffing Rahila's perfume bottles is no longer enough."

"Tell me! What do you want?"

"Some sort of human warmth."

Rashid shook his head regretfully. "Why didn't you keep her?"

"I tried, Rashid. If she had been a white royal falcon, I would have put her in a cage. But she was not. She was Roxana Yashvili, my certain fate."

Rashid stared at the sprays of water of the fountain in silence. "If I had been in your place, I would have protected her."

Vahab drew a star on the sand with the toe of his shoe. "I am certain of that, Rashid. You had the strength."

Rashid leaned toward him. "Did you see Teymur? He went to the arbor of the flowering Judas trees."

Vahab stood up and coughed. "Let's go and find him."

Rashid grabbed Vahab's arm. Alongside the wooden fence, they slowed their steps and saw Teymur from between the branches and leaves. He was sitting on a bench, looking at the clusters of flowering Judas trees in the sunlight. He was muttering to himself: "Anna, dear! Poor little Anna. Don't cry. I am here."

Rashid whispered: "He now walks with a cane."

They entered the space of the arbor. Hero Rashid patted Teymur's back. "How's it going, Uncle Teymur?"

Teymur lifted his head and looked at him with the eyes of a stranger. "Today, they gave me permission to get some fresh air." He took his clay pipe out of his pocket and stuck it into his tobacco pouch. He hit the back of his hand. "Oh, my! It's finished. They don't even give me hay to smoke."

"What do they give you to eat?"

"Some sort of gruel and slipslop. My legs have lost all their strength." His eyes moistened. "Hero Rashid! Do something to help me get out of the basement. They have an empty bed on the second floor. Remind them that when they were children, I had made a pleasant National Park for them. I am not an old pair of pants to be thrown away. Why did they take away my house? Had I stolen it?"

Rashid punched himself on the knee. "The former salary earners are all in a bad situation."

"But we weren't just anybody. We didn't have desk jobs." He held up his five fingers and shook them in front of Vahab's eyes. "This is the result of forty years of hard work. No one gave us anything for nothing. Come to the dormitory, and tell them everything."

He stood up and picked up his cane. The wind sprinkled the Judas-tree flower petals on his head and face. He grabbed Rashid's sleeve. "Come, now!"

"Hero Teymur! Who would listen to me? I am in a worse situation. I have been sentenced to one year of forced labor."

Vahab put a flower petal on the old man's hair. The lively red color shone against the white strands. "Hero Teymur! I will come and fix it for you."

Teymur turned around and looked at him from head to toe. "Mr. Vahab! Do you think they would give any weight to your words there?"

"Of course, Teymur. Did you not know?" He hooked his little fingers together. "The glass-eyed woman and I are like this."

"I'll be so grateful, son. The second floor gets light. If you only knew how great it is, like a real celebration. The old men are smiling like blossomed buds, sitting on their beds. There's all sorts of people among them, even university professors. They have sheets and blankets. They put a glass of water by your bed. There is no sign of bedbugs and lice. If my son comes back, I won't be embarrassed in front of him."

Vahab patted him on his back. "I will make the arrangements. You just take your time coming. We will go to the dormitory right away."

He began running. Rashid ran after him. "Wait! Don't make a laughingstock out of the old man! They will shoot your shadow if you show up there."

Vahab's eyes sparkled mischievously. "Don't worry about it. Come!"

In front of the dormitory, Vahab shouted at the head guard: "Where is your boss's room? I have a message from the House of Fire."

The man bowed in confusion. "Third floor, on the left."

They started going up the staircase. The blue paint on the rails was dirty and flaking off. On the backs of the dusty windowpanes of the landing, flies buzzed. In the corner of the ceiling, a spider was weaving its web. The smell of disinfectants made Vahab feel dizzy. He closed his eyes. Rashid grabbed his shoulders. "Come on, give it up. It isn't worth the trouble."

Vahab opened his eyes. "Do you like this smell?"

Rashid inhaled, and his short red nostrils flared. "It is for disinfecting."

There was a restroom in the hallway. Vahab washed his face, drank a few sips of water, and dried his face with Rashid's threadbare handkerchief.

They went to the third floor. A man in a guard's uniform was dozing off on a rickety wooden chair. Vahab shook the chair. "Are you sleeping on the job?" He told Rashid: "Write a report!"

The man jumped up, startled. "I wasn't sleeping. The light bothered my eyes, I just closed them."

"You ought to be ashamed of yourself. What light? This place is darker than a stable. Go tell your boss an agent from the House of Fire wants to see him."

The man entered the first room and came back. He opened the door and bowed.

Vahab and Rashid went into the office of the dormitory. Files were stacked up on the floor between the two walls. A slanted ray of light shone on the maroon felt of the desk. The metal penholder was faintly shining. A rectangular telephone was visible in the shadow. A small nimble man stood up from behind the desk, came to the middle of the room, and shook hands with Vahab and Rashid. His thin neck wobbled in the collar of his flannel shirt, swaying a bald head in one direction and another. He offered them chairs to sit on, sat in his own seat, and asked: "What can I do for you?"

Vahab crossed his legs and twisted the tip of his mustache. "Do you not have shelves for these files? Dust them! And clean up the dormitory. The condition of this place is cause for ruining our reputation."

The man looked at the files, as though he were seeing them for the first time. He blinked in astonishment and drew a line on a piece of paper. "Unfortunately, we do not have the funds. Of course, the House of Fire is not to blame in this case. We all know that the necessary expenditures have priority. Have you seen the eleven dormitories throughout the city? Be fair! The situation here is better. It has been no more than one month that I have had the honor of serving. If it is not taken as self-praise, we have accomplished a great deal. Did you notice the restroom in the hallway?"

Vahab nodded. "Yes, I did. It is a positive step. However, have the staircase swept. The condition in the basements is dire. Bedbugs and lice have tyrannized the place."

The man raised his eyebrows. "Previously, the Central House of Fire did not place that much importance on this matter."

"Now it does. Have you not been informed? Reconstruction has begun."

The man stared at the white sheet of paper. A narrow strip of light from the window moved back and forth on his bald head. "Yes, I am aware of that. In the country of the progressives, the remnants of poverty, disease, and pollution must be eradicated."

Vahab sat up. "That is sufficient for now. An old man by the name of Teymur resides in the basement. Have him transferred to the second floor."

The man looked at Vahab suspiciously out of the corner of his eye. "Do you have a written order?"

Vahab put his hands in the pockets of his overcoat. "Is that what you think? Issuing a written order for such a minor matter is beneath the status of the House of Fire." He pointed at the telephone. "Does that work?" The director of the dormitory nodded. "Call the House of Fire!"

The man picked up the receiver, turned the handle of the crank, and several times said, "Operator!" After the operator answered, he continued: "Connect me to the House of Fire."

Vahab snatched the receiver from him.

A muffled sound said: "Central House of Fire."

Vahab shouted: "I need to speak to Neo-Hero Haddadiyan."

The room went silent. Rashid's jaws were quivering. The director chewed the tip of his pen. Vahab whistled. On the other end of the line, a panting voice said: "Neo-Hero Haddadiyan speaking. And you are?"

Vahab responded harshly. "Neo-Hero! I have an important message for you. Come to Dormitory No. Five, Ordzhonikidze, immediately."

Haddadiyan hung up the receiver. Vahab sat beside Rashid. "Our friend will be here soon."

The director called the office worker and ordered tea.

Vahab ran his finger along the spines of the files. "The windows of the dormitories are too close to the ceiling. Microbes grow in insufficient light."

Stammering, the director said: "You are absolutely right."

The office worker came in holding a tray with cups of tea in front of them. They took the tea and took a sip. Rashid began to cough. Vahab patted his back. "He has developed a problem with his larynx, because they send him on dangerous assignments so often. Last week, he went to Krasnodar to investigate a shameful incident. The hand of a traitor had carved an arrow-crossed heart on the trees of the square. He dealt him the necessary punishment."

The director bent forward. "That is not believable."

Vahab frowned and put the cup on the table. "Lies have no place in my vocabulary!"

The director dropped his head. "I apologize most earnestly. When I heard what you said, I felt like someone struck by an electric shock."

"You need to know everything. Open your eyes and ears. Don't trust anyone!"

The director stroked his moist forehead. "You are absolutely right. I have learned a great deal from Your Excellency. No, one should not trust anyone. Caution is inherent in me. I do not say anything I shouldn't, not even in front of my wife and children."

The door opened and Haddadiyan entered, dressed in a completely black uniform. The insignia of the gilded erect crowbar sparkled on his chest. He was wearing high boots.

The director jumped up, ran forward, and, bowing, shook hands with the Neo-Hero.

Haddadiyan pushed him back and told Vahab: "Hero! Come outside, I have some private business to discuss with you."

Vahab smiled. "Of course!"

They walked to the end of the hallway and stood face to face in the dimly lit corner. Vahab touched the man's insignia. "Your pheasant sings really well, almost like a rooster. If someone did not know any better, he would think you had fallen out of the belly of the first Group of Fire."

Haddadiyan chewed on his spiky mustache. "You seem to have an itch. What kind of bamboozling is this? Spit it out!"

"I have a message for you. If the House of Fire gets a whiff of it, your place as well will be at the bottom of a ditch."

Haddadiyan whispered: "My file shines bright."

"It will turn dark from now on. Tell me the truth. What secret goings on did you have with Yashvili?"

Haddadiyan punched his own chest with his fist. "Me and Yashvili? Don't talk nonsense!"

"Didn't she entrust you with the insignia from the Supreme Hero?"

"Entrust it to me? Have you gone mad?"

Vahab spat on the ground. "Only in your evil eyes! There isn't any tree left on which you have not pooped. Last night, at about one o'clock, there was a knock on my door and I immediately opened it. Someone who had covered his face with a black scarf came in. Only his eyes sparkled in the dark. He held up an insignia from the Supreme Hero and said, 'Do you recognize this?' I said I did not. He said, 'Haddadiyan has one just like it. Roxana Yashvili had given it to him, along with a blacklist of our supporters.' I asked, 'Who are you?' He answered, 'The Group of the Hook.'"

Haddadiyan unbuttoned his jacket. Next, he unbuttoned his shirt. A mass of curly hair on his broad chest protruded. Vahab turned his face to the wall. Haddadiyan shook his jacket and shirt. "I swear by Saint George that that slut could not bear to look at me. And then you think that she would entrust me with the list of the hooksters?"

Vahab burst out laughing.

Haddadiyan put his palm on Vahab's mouth. "You won't be laughing when they wash you on the mortuary slab, Vahab. This place is full of spies."

Vahab pushed his hand aside. "Since when have you decided to believe in Saint George?"

"It just jumped out of my mouth, man! Enough of your nitpicking. When they put a label on you, removing it is like going to hell and back. Help me!"

"First, button up your clothes, and then have that bald guy move Teymur to the second floor. They have an empty bed there. Once you are finished doing that, we will have enough time to talk."

Haddadiyan buttoned up his clothes, touched his gilded insignia, and walked away in hesitant steps.

Vahab leaned against the wall and closed his eyes. The window opened partially and the cool breeze blew on his cheeks. Roxana was standing under the chandelier. Grandmother was coming down the staircase. Showkat was pacing the length of the entrance hall, shaking the tip of her whip. A hand touched his shoulder. He opened his eyes. Rashid was smiling in front of him. "Well done, Vahab. They brought Teymur upstairs. The message from Haddadiyan is for you to go to the laundry house."

"I don't know where it is."

"We'll go together. It's nearby."

They passed through several twisting stone-paved alleyways and arrived at an open door. Dozens of clotheslines were tied along the length of the courtyard on which large white bedsheets were spread. Haddadiyan was walking in the corner. A piece of swaying laundry occasionally hit his face. With a gesture of his finger, he called Vahab to come to him.

Vahab shrugged his shoulders, went down the three stairs, and approached him. A stream of dirty water from the laundered clothes was running down toward the sump and, after spinning, sank into the dark hole. Vahab leaned against the wall. "Say what you have to say! I am tired."

Haddadiyan widened his eyes. "To hell with your being tired! Does a human life have no value for you?"

Vahab's eyes clouded. "No, Haddadiyan! Nothing in this world has value."

"How about your own life?"

"Don't talk about that. Do you think any life is left for me?"

"Then who is having this conversation with me?"

"I have no idea, believe me!"

"I will send you to join those who are gone."

"You are so kind, Neo-Hero."

Haddadiyan stomped the ground. His hanging cheeks shook. "You bastard! I will report your cooperation with the Group of the Hook to the House of Fire."

Vahab burst out laughing. "I have no doubt about your stupidity. Send the report. But your own tail will be caught in the trap more than mine."

Haddadiyan crumpled up a sheet. "Then get rid of them and I will secure three rooms in the house for you, Leqa, and Yavar."

"Your relationship with Leqa and Yavar is your own business, but I need no room."

"Do you want to be homeless?"

Vahab chuckled. "It doesn't make any difference. The fellow sent you the message that if you do not return the documents, he will come after you."

"Nobody knows where I live."

"If they want to, they can find any place. Hand over the documents."

"You are despicable! What documents?"

Vahab twisted his ear. "Watch your mouth!"

Haddadiyan turned red. "I will crush you."

Imitating Showkat in the dream about the bazaar of the Caucasus, Vahab pounded the man's head with his palm. The man straightened his messed-up hair with his fingertips and kicked the wall with the toe of his boot. "I wish the House of Fire had removed the seed of your menacing family from the face of earth."

"To save yourself, you have no other choice but to surrender. Even if you are telling the truth, no problem will be solved."

Haddadiyan tugged on the sleeve of Vahab's overcoat. "Can you come up with a solution?"

"Make a fake list."

Haddadiyan widened his eyes. "Do you mean I should make myself a criminal by my own hand? With evidence?"

"It doesn't matter. That evidence is useless."

"How would I know?"

"The Group of the Hook is at war with the House of Fire. Also, knowing about your friendship with Roxana, they will leave you alone."

Haddadiyan slapped his red, sweaty forehead. "And then, I will become some sort of double agent. To put it more succinctly, a stick with both ends dipped in shit."

"That would be an interesting position. You will be able to play both sides at the same time. I don't think you would dislike such wheeling and dealing."

Haddadiyan turned his face toward the wall and pressed his thumb on several ants to kill them. "You are such a sly fox! Your head has started working. But there is a problem. Supposing I write down a bunch of fake names on paper. When they follow them up, they will realize that they have been duped."

"How simpleminded! How could they find the owners of fake names? Would they have a town crier shout them out under the eyes of hundreds of detectives in the capital city? Idiot! They will keep the names for a rainy day."

Haddadiyan frowned. "When will that rainy day come?"

"Don't worry! Maybe your grandchild will see it."

"How would I fabricate the names?"

"The telephone directory. Where is your head? Mix up the names and make new ones."

The man grabbed Vahab's arms and shook them. "I would like to kiss your noble forehead."

Vahab pulled back. "No! Exempt me from that gift."

"Such a begrudging person!" He blew on the palm of his hand. "Let's blow the past away smooth and clear, and let bygones be bygones."

"I will send that past to the barber, along with your mustache."

Neo-Hero winked. "So, till next week." He walked out of the laundry house with firm and nimble steps.

Vahab stood in the middle of the clotheslines and deeply inhaled the scent of the sheets. He closed his eyes and felt light. He flew around the courtyard with the flapping sound of the laundered clothes on the clotheslines. He reached out and grabbed a damp piece of cloth. Time had slipped from between his fingers. A hardhearted world was rising before him. The petals of narcissi, tuberoses, white hyacinths, and azaleas had been cast to the wind. He had no regrets. Alongside destruction, liberation was bringing a lightness of burdens. He was a spectator. He opened his eyes. He pressed the damp sheet to his cheeks. The brick walls and the flapping of the cloth were a faraway undulating landscape behind the tears in his eyes. In a whisper, he said: "Roxana tied the string of her balloon to the black foundation of the Central House of Fire. What should I tie mine to?"

He ran toward the street. Rashid, Pari, and Torkan were having a conversation under the shade of a tree. They were moving their hands. None of them saw him.

He hid among the crowd on Qezel Urda Street to walk home. A transport cart was standing at the end of the alleyway beside the wall. He walked in through the wide-open door. A group of Fire Stokers were taking the furniture out. Watching them with dazed eyes, Leqa and Yavar were walking back and forth alongside the length of the arbor. They put the seagulls and the snow landscape painting in the cart. Vahab chuckled.

Leqa said: "They are emptying the house."

"That's life, Leqa. They have to take them."

Yavar was weeping. "The parlor has become naked. I fear the day when its owner returns."

"Yavar! These things are called 'ownerless property.'"

"As God is my witness, I am confused. I don't know what is good and what is bad. I wish the lady, Mrs. Edrisi, were here and would teach us."

"She has taught us. What kind of person was Qobad?"

Yavar scratched the tip of his nose. "Well-wishing for the people."

"I do not know. I have lost my sense of judgement. If that is the case, what is the meaning of well-wishing for the people?"

"He wanted happiness for everyone."

"How can people achieve happiness?"

"With kindness and love."

"Bread dough will not rise without yeast, Yavar. Hero Qobad thought the people's happiness meant the distribution of wealth. My grandmother went along with him. She left the odds and ends junk and left."

Vahab turned his back to them and stood near the stairs. Soaked with sweat, the Fire Stokers carried the heavy easy chairs on their shoulders. They were dull, small, and tired, as though they had not experienced any deep joy their entire lives. He shouted: "Hello!"

No one responded. He crouched in a wicker easy chair under the arbor and closed his eyes. He could hear the singing of the canaries of the woman fortune teller from far away. As the Fire Stokers passed by, the darkness behind his eyelids became denser. He leaned his chin on his knee and opened his eyes. They were taking out Rahila's dresses. The colors of white, silver, fish-scale, gold, melted snow, and pearl glittered in the daylight, and satin, silk, and Kashmir embroidered linen fabrics swept the pavement of the courtyard. The sequin-embroidered bodice reminded him of the apple juice incident. The small faint stain spread and covered all the dresses. Had he behaved with more refinement, perhaps everything would have remained stable. He contemplated that there is a reaction to every action. Manipulating the order of existence is not without consequences. The circles of chaos expand. If only living were a creed and every body, a temple.

Chapter 5

Leqa was walking around in the courtyard. The warmth of the sun was evaporating the dewdrops between the flower petals. There was a knock on the wooden door. She ran and opened it halfway. Golrokh's face appeared between the double doors.

Leqa blinked. "Is that you? Come in!"

Golrokh stepped into the courtyard. Leqa bent down and kissed the girl's cheek. "Did you get permission to come?"

Golrokh breathed in deeply. "The scent of jasmine! Oh, how depressed I felt! I had gone to the National Park. On the way, I saw Kukan. He had a message for you. Vahab's suit is ready."

Leqa leaned against the doorframe. "What suit, Golrokh?"

"My brother was wounded. And he might be dead."

Leqa held on to the wall. "Do you know Kukan's address?" Golrokh dropped her head. "Will you come there with me?"

"I have permission until noon."

Leqa ran and put on her overcoat and covered her hair with a dark shawl. At the threshold of the kitchen, she saw Yavar.

The old man stepped forward. "Where are you going in such a hurry?"

"To Kukan's workshop."

Yavar shut the door to the kitchen. "I am coming with you."

They left the house. Golrokh was running ahead of them. Halfway through Warshawskaya Street, they arrived at Kukan's workshop. They climbed the poorly lit staircase. Leqa stopped on the landing. "Twenty years ago, I came here with my mother and Rahila, but I did not notice Kukan. Maybe I did not pay attention." She pointed to the oval skylight. "My mother stopped right here and said that she did not feel like coming. It was windy in the alleyway. The staircase was new and smelled of perfume. We forced her to come upstairs. Rahila ordered a white taffeta dress, and I ordered a coal-colored jacket and skirt. We did not come back anymore, because Rahila died the following month."

They arrived at the door of the workshop. Golrokh went in, and Leqa and Yavar followed her. The sound of treadle sewing machines resonated under the soot-covered ceiling. The tailors were sitting in four parallel rows, sewing black uniforms. The fuzzy sepals from the plane tree blew in through the open window and floated in the air. The tailors all resembled one another, pale, middle-aged, and bent down, with disheveled hair.

Kukan got up from the sewing machine and came to welcome them. He shook hands with Leqa. His fingers were cold and damp. He pulled two old stools forward, on which Leqa and Yavar sat down. Golrokh went to the window. The tailors raised their heads, looked at her with blurred eyes, and immediately bent down over what they were sewing.

Kukan whispered: "It is such a pleasure to see you." He pointed to the large hall. "And this is my house. I have become familiar with every handspan of it. It is a comfortable place." He looked at the ceiling. "It is an old place now." He brought his head closer to them. "Early on, it resembled a palace, with white walls and gold trims."

Leqa dropped her eyes. "I know, Kukan. We came here with Rahila and my mother."

Kukan rubbed his hands together: "It was really pretty, wasn't it?"

"Kukan! What are you sewing now?"

The man frowned. "On the order of the House of Fire, we sew black uniforms. Would you like a glass of water?"

Leqa shook her head. "Has Vahab ordered a suit?"

Kukan squatted in front of Leqa's feet and whispered: "At night, when the workers leave, I sew it. It is almost finished. All that is left to do are the buttons." He went to the window and called Leqa and Yavar. "Would you like to see my place?"

They both joined Kukan. On the roof across from them, spools of thread were hanging on parallel clotheslines. The dome-like adobe mounds of the roofs were blurred behind the fog, and the dripping branches of the mulberry trees cast shadows on them. Occasionally, a crow sat on the chimney of a flaky gable roof, cawed, and flew away.

Yavar put his hand on Kukan's shoulder. "It is a depressing place, son."

Kukan raised his eyebrows. "What? You should see it when it's sunny. It's amazing. The spools of thread shine brightly, and the colors, red, henna color, maroon, and purple." He scratched the old wood of the sewing machine with his fingernail. "I like it."

Yavar peeked out the window. "The mulberry trees are nice, but in spring, you get no rest because of mosquitos and sparrows. You've gotten used to it. That is all."

Leqa whispered: "Show us Vahab's suit."

Kukan's eyes sparkled. He took them to the end of the hall, stood in front of the dressing stall, and cautiously opened the door. It was nearly dark inside. The white suit on a hanger shone like pearls. He touched the fabric. "He brought the fabric himself. It is of high quality."

Leqa covered her face with her hands. "I don't want to see it."

Kukan closed the door and smiled. His sparse mustache quivered. "I have worked on it a lot." He held his hand in front of Leqa's face and opened his fingers. "When he puts it on, you will find out what Kukan's hands can do."

Yavar twisted his mustache. "You didn't do such a good job when you sewed my trousers. Mrs. Edrisi did not like them."

Kukan scratched the back of his ear. "I didn't have the right equipment, Yavar."

Yavar looked at the ceiling. "Don't make excuses, Kukan. You didn't put enough effort into it for me."

Kukan grabbed Yavar's wrist. "Don't get upset, Uncle Yavar. I'll make it up to you. Go check Mrs. Edrisi's trunks and bring good fabrics, so that when I sew it, you will say, well done, and girls will start coming after you."

Yavar cautiously looked at Leqa out of the corner of his eye and pushed Kukan's hand aside. "Don't joke with me about such things."

Leqa went to the window and stared at the roofs in a daze. Golrokh grabbed her forearm. "Let's go outside. The air in the workshop is too heavy for you."

They walked toward the door. Kukan saw them off. The tailors were ceaselessly moving their feet on the iron pedals and sewing the seams of the uniforms. Their heads were down, and they breathed sporadically.

Kukan rubbed his hands together. "Godspeed! With your permission, I'll go back to my sewing. Late afternoon every day, an agent comes to collect two complete uniforms from each worker."

He tiptoed back and sat at the sewing machine. He placed the thick fabric under the needle, took a look at the landscape, and smiled. His greasy, sweaty forehead shone. More hair had turned white on his temples.

Golrokh left the other two on Warshawskaya Street. They went home quietly. Leqa immediately went to her own room, closed the door, and took off her shoes. She took off her overcoat, tossed it over the back of a chair, went to bed, and fell into a deep sleep.

She woke up near sunset. She stumbled to the window and leaned her chin on her hand. The fountain was on. Yavar was watering the flowers, and Hero Yunos was sitting on his feet on the bench, staring at the horizon. He had a notebook by his side and was chewing on the end of a pencil and spitting the chips out. A blue light was turned on through the window across from hers. A shadow moved behind the voile curtain. Leqa closed the curtain, went to her mother's room, and turned on the bedside lamp. Halos of pink light waved on the velvet bedspread. She picked up the photo album and turned the pages. The transparent protective sheets between them moved as she breathed, revealing the discolored photographs of her grandfather and uncles, her maternal cousins, her paternal aunt and her confidante maid, and Mrs. Edrisi's sisters-in-law. She turned the pages rapidly until she reached the picture of her mother on the semicircular staircase. A starched white ribbon shone on her black locks of hair, like a butterfly. Leqa bent her head and kissed the puffy skirt of the little girl in the photograph. Her eyes clouded behind a thin curtain of tears, as though she were looking at the picture of her own lost child. She had exchanged places with Mrs. Edrisi. She wanted to put the girl on her lap, comb her hair, braid it, adorn it with hairpins and flowers, hold her little hand and take her for a stroll, watch her grow every day, and, when she was twenty years old, invite Hero Qobad to her house, and kick her paternal cousin out the door. Leqa was not fond of her father. On holidays, a tall man wearing a silk robe would walk along the flowerbed smoking a pipe. The children were not allowed to call him "Father." His older son called him "Khan Brother," and Leqa and Rahila called him "Atabak." He constantly fretted over his looks. He oiled and combed his curly hair in front of the mirror. He even touched up his eyebrows. He had a private barber and tailor. Early in the evening, he would go to the room at the end of the interior balcony and lock the door. The heavy smell of opium smoke would ooze out of the seams of the door, circle in the air, and rise to the ceiling. When he came out of that room, he was cheerful, and his black eyes sparkled. He would wear a tight redingote, varnished boots, and a silk scarf around his neck over his black velvet overcoat. He would pick up his silver-handled umbrella and fur hat from the closet rack and jovially leave the house. When Leqa caught typhus, he did not even know about it. During her long convalescence, one day when she was coming down the stairs on shaky feet, he saw her, burst out laughing, and whispered: "A dog with a burned paw!"

The smell of his sweat and perfume caused Leqa's insides to contract.

She put her finger on the picture of the little girl. "My little child! Such a fate!"

She wondered where the little girl was now. Was she wearing a wide ribbon on her hair again? Was the skin of her face radiant from exuberance? Was she sliding down the mountain slope, picking mallow flowers? Would the white royal falcon sit on her shoulder? Other than the child on the stairs, she had no image of her mother in her mind.

She unbraided her hair, stood in front of the mirror, combed her hair, frowned, and the corners of her lips quivered. She went to the closet, picked out one of her mother's dark dresses, put it on, and tossed a green shawl over her shoulders. Coyly, and with her back bent, she opened the door and walked to the eastern veranda as slowly as an elderly woman. With her hand on the railing, she gazed at the dark horizon for a long time. She held her pale face toward the mountain. She blinked.

The garden was submerged in darkness. The screech owl hooted. A bat flew above the lawn and the movement of its wings made the leaves vibrate.

Her nostrils flared. She pressed her fingernail into her palm and slapped her cheek. Behind the branches and leaves of the maple tree, a distant fire was aflame.

Chapter 6

Since the previous week, Vahab had slept in Rashid's former room. He would lie down on his bed. He had brought the small cushions scattered around on the floor of the parlor and placed them under his forearm and shoulder. Occasionally, he thumbed through a book and read a few lines. He would be bored by the abstract concepts, long sentences, and raw emotions. He would chuckle at the past, put his hand under his chin, and look at the white daisy flowers under the moonlight.

The clock struck three. He came out of the room and went into the kitchen. He had a bitter taste in his mouth and his lips were dry. He filled the kettle with water, put it on the stove, and stood by the window. Hero Yunos was dozing off under the arbor.

He opened the window and sat on the windowsill. "Hero! It is a moonlit night tonight." Yunos nodded. "Why aren't you writing?"

"My work is done, finished, son."

"Could it ever be finished?"

Yunos drew a circle in the air with his finger.

"Are you happy now?"

Yunos put his feet on the table and leaned on the back of the chair.

Vahab asked: "Do you still see Luba?"

"Neither the moon in the mirror, nor the mirror in the moon."

Vahab pressed his shoulder on the window frame, closed his eyes, and began to see blurred images: a loose button on the sleeve of a man's shirt, the moth-eaten parts inside Borzu's hat, the window of an abandoned house, a yellow cat with crossed eyes and cut-off whiskers behind the window bars staring at the alleyway, the ice cream shop on the corner of Clock Road, the descent of flies on the scalloped edges of crystal dishes.

Vahab opened his eyes. "My faith in goodness and beauty has weakened. With all that enthusiasm and passion, why did I set my heart on things that are subject to change?"

"In this workshop of creation, everything changes."

"My origin, Yunos, where is it?"

"I miss the pink dust on the grapes under sunlight. I will return to the place of my birth."

Vahab drew a circle in the air with his finger. "Happiness."

"I said, I like the color of the grapes. That is all."

The young man looked at the sky. "Its boundlessness is maddening." Yunos pounded the ground with his toes several times. Vahab smiled. "You are right. The sap of my body might someday run in the veins of a grapevine."

"Work wherever you arrive, like others."

"Would it be a problem if it is like myself?"

"Be more alive than yourself."

"I will go to a remote city and choose a trade, embroidery, lathe-work, manuscript gilding."

"Keep the moment like a fresh fruit between your hands." He held his middle finger under the moonlight. The red ruby stone shone. "A memento from your family! If you believe in family."

The chimneys of the gable roof across from him were turning violet. Yunos came closer to Vahab and slipped the ring into Vahab's pocket.

Vahab smiled. "Did you know that your left eye occasionally turns this color?"

"If it does, that is enough for me." He grabbed the young man's arm. "Bon voyage!"

His eyelids were half open, and a fragile smile as thin as morning fog and devoid of happiness and suffering and regret flickered across his lips. Vahab touched the moth-eaten cloak of the man with the tips of his fingers. Hero Yunos walked away, dragging his feet.

Vahab ran into the entrance hall, climbed the stairs, went to his own room, and pulled the curtain aside. The clouds in the east were expanding. The lead-colored light of dawn lit up the bedpost. He took a suitcase from the closet and opened it. Streaks of the amber-gris perfume had been absorbed by the felt lining. He filled it with a bunch of clothes. He placed the white suit on top of the other clothes. He put on a long smoke-colored raincoat, combed his hair, and set a black fedora hat on his head. The ends of his long hair had curled. He was reminded of Marenko's curly coiled hair. Where was he now? Was he smoking a hookah in a black tent? Was he taking pictures of Turkoman children? Or had he accepted guild membership in the Association of Forefront Galloping Artists? He turned his back to the mirror, closed the suitcase, and set out. He listened to Leqa's breathing. He stroked the door with his finger and came down the stairs. Pigeons were flying around the remaining chain of the chandelier. He passed in front of the arbor. Fog was tenting on the rooftops. He could hear the sound of the lute and reed flute from afar.

He opened the door and was taken aback. The fortune teller was standing before him in a blue dress. They started walking shoulder to shoulder. They stopped under the shelter of the branches and leaves of the old plane tree. Water dripped from the tips of the leaves. The woman opened her purse, took out the brass music box, and opened its lid. The tune of "Jesus Christ Is Risen Today" resonated under the umbrella of the leaves. Vahab put the suitcase down and took the box. The shadow of church steeples moved on his wrist. Seven coins were shining on the red velvet. He quickly opened the suitcase and concealed the box between the clothes. He gazed into the fortune teller's eyes. "Did Roxana visit you?"

The woman wrapped a lock of her hair around her index finger. "She was terrified and in a hurry. She gave me the box and told me to be on the watch, so that when you decide to leave, I could hand you the box."

Vahab scratched the wall with his fingernail, pulled out a straw, and put it between his lips. "I like the scent of adobe that has been rained on."

"Are you going to stay there? God is the companion of lonely strangers in a strange land."

Vahab picked up the suitcase, turned around, and looked at the building. Behind the glass panes of his window, two red tulip lamps were lit. He thought that it must be Yunos's doing.

In the twilight, he walked along the sidewalk of Warshawskaya Street and went southward up to the Shami Khalen Gate. Rashid came out from behind the gate through the yellow fog and began walking toward the plain. Vahab followed him. They passed by farms. The wind was entwining the clusters of wheat. The ruins of Tamerlane Palace, the Three Springs Arches, the porphyry stone verandas, and the horseshoe arches all seemed to sway behind the fog. They arrived in the middle of the desert.

Vahab turned to Rashid. "Is everything set, Hero?" Rashid nodded. Vahab sat on a rock by a farm. "On this road?"

Rashid picked a wheat stalk. "So, you will leave us on our own?"

Vahab pushed a pebble back and forth with his foot and stared at the palace. "What magnificent verandas!"

Rashid looked at the building. "We have all been uprooted and thrown around. What a pity!" He pointed to a spot in the middle of the wheat field. "They have brought tractors."

Vahab leaned forward. "Mechanized farming?"

Rashid picked a stalk of wheat and handed it to Vahab. Vahab put it in his pocket.

Rashid took a few steps, came back, and gazed into Vahab's eyes. He took out a newspaper clipping from his breast pocket. Anxiously, Vahab asked: "Has anything happened?" He snatched the newspaper and read: Yuri Marenko passed away of a heart attack. He handed it back with his shaking hands and grumbled under his breath, "Miserable son of a bitch!"

Rashid nodded. "The rumor is that he killed himself."

Vahab spat on the ground. "Undoubtedly, Rashid."

Rashid put the newspaper clipping into his pocket.

A white sedan came forward through the fog, carrying three men. Rashid ran to the edge of the road. The car stopped and the driver jumped out. He had puffy Tatar eyes and a sunburned face. He conversed with Rashid.

Vahab picked up the suitcase and advanced with shaky steps. The driver came out and put the suitcase in the trunk of the sedan. Vahab kissed Rashid's cheek goodbye. Rashid's coarse blond hair tousled in the breeze. A teardrop rolled down his cheek. "Have a safe trip, Hero!" He grabbed his arm. "I hope to see you again, Vahab."

Vahab pressed his hand. "Keep an eye on Leqa."

The driver asked: "Do you have any contraband?"

"No, just a couple of suits."

He got in the car, closed the door, and rolled down the window.

Hero Rashid wiped his eyes with his threadbare checkered handkerchief. The car began to move slowly. Vahab stuck his hand out and waved it under the drizzling rain. The tractor was coming closer, mowing the clusters of wheat.

Chapter 7

Yavar was sweeping the stone pavement of the garden. He was collecting the dry leaves and piling them up in a ditch. He was restless. He would say that his heart was telling him that the lady of the house would come back one of these days. Occasionally, he saw the shadow of Yunos under the arbor.

Leqa rarely left the building. Shedding tears, she walked around the house, checking the rooms, going through the familiar old objects. Holding Vahab's landscape View-Master viewer up to her eyes and with her mouth open, she would gaze at the rows of Jomna cypresses, the bazaars of Simla and Chandigarh, the excavated cities of Mohenjo-daro, and the statues of the demigods Agni and Indra. She would ask the old man: "Where is Kashmir, Yavar? Is it far or near? What is its weather like?"

In the evening, they sat on the eastern veranda of the building, and, upon seeing the faint fire, they prayed under their breath and took the flames with them in their hearts to bed.

On Tuesday morning, Yavar was washing dishes at the side of the reflecting pool when he heard a sound. He lifted his head. The window across from the building opened and the neighboring old man stood on the windowsill.

Yavar went close to the window. "What is it, Yaqub?"

The neighbor put his finger on his lips. His scrawny legs trembled in the sheath of his tight seersucker pants. In a husky voice, he said: "Come to my house! Take a good look around you to make sure nobody finds out." He shut the window and closed the yellow curtain.

Yavar went out of the house and took a look around. No one was in the alleyway. He walked forward along the wall to the left and stepped up on the stone stair. The amber-colored door was half open. He entered and shut the door quietly.

Yaqub appeared at the top of the stairs. He held on to the railing. His nostrils flared, and he sniffed. His dark pearly eyes were staring at some spot far away. "Take off your shoes. Watch out for the ants."

A gray cat came out of the room and stood by his feet. It yawned, and its shiny eyes sent waves of algae-colored spectra toward Yavar. He took off his shoes and, in threadbare woolen socks, climbed the stairs. At the corner of the landing, Yaqub let Yavar embrace his feeble figure. "Let me smell you!"

His disheveled white hair stood erect on the top of his head. He breathed irregularly and rubbed his foot on the carpet. He put his hand into his pocket, took out a piece of red candy, and put it in Yavar's mouth. "Come in! You are going to catch a cold."

They entered the room. Mussed-up bedding was spread on the maroon carpet, with three tasseled cushions leaning against the dirty wall. A round short samovar was boiling in the corner of the room.

The old man lay down on the bed. "Pour yourself a cup of tea."

Yavar sat on his feet. "What has happened?"

"It's rumored throughout the city that Hero Qobad has gone to the mountain. The people say that he will not die. Someone has seen him from a distance. He has become young again. He leaps over the valleys like a leopard. Half a million armed men are at his command." He scratched his belly. "Do you know Zoleykha?"

Yavar bent forward. "You must be kidding. I grew up with her. Where is your head? She is none other than Mrs. Edrisi."

Yaqub recited a verse from the Torah: "Why, O God, hast Thou cast us off for ever? Why doth Thine anger smoke against the flock of Thy pasture? Remember Thy congregation, which Thou hast gotten of old, which Thou hast redeemed to be the tribe of Thine inheritance." His eyes closed.

Yavar went down the steps, entered the alleyway, closed the door, and started to run. In the middle of the street, he stopped a droshky, got in, sat down, and shouted: "Go to the foot of the mountain!"

The droshky driver looked at him and scratched his neck. His greasy hair hanging from under his kepi hat became entangled. "How much are you willing to pay?"

"One whole suit, when we get back to the house."

"Are you from the house of the Edrisis?"

Taken aback, Yavar crawled under the canopy. "No, I am just visiting. My kinfolk live by the foot of Mount Shahbaz."

The driver burst out laughing. "You liar! I am Mir Hozhabr, brother. The Waterfall Coffee Shop. A friend of Heroes Qobad, Showkat, and Borzu." He punched the leather seat of the droshky. "We took the gold in this."

He took out a bottle from his breast pocket and took a sip. The smell of vodka wafted in the air. Yavar whispered: "The gold?"

Mir Hozhabr scratched his mustache. "The treasure of Hero Zoleykha."

Yavar looked at the sky. "Such strange times! I was the one who kept the treasure. When Hero Zoleykha ordered us to carry it to the mountain, I said, 'Certainly.' Tell me, how did you take it?"

The driver hiccupped. "In bags."

"How many were there? I can't remember."

Mir Hozhabr struck the horses with the whip. The droshky took off with a jolt. "Your humble servant will take a shortcut. I am the only one who knows this route. The spies don't know about it."

They passed through the anise plants and common yarrow bushes. When the moon rose, they were at the foot of Mount Shahbaz. The driver took off his kepi hat, opened his arms, removed his shoes, and walked barefooted toward the stream. He washed his face and watered the horses.

A group of people were sitting around the iris plants. Yavar walked to the middle of the plain and shaded his eyes with his hand. The slopes of the mountain peaks were dark. A faint fire was burning behind the branches and leaves of the birch trees. He knelt and held his hands toward the sky. His trousers and shoes became wet from the dew. He inhaled the scent of shade moss and irises. He walked rapidly toward the ruins of the house of the landlord of the village.

Someone approached Yavar and put a hand on his shoulder. The old man turned around fearfully and saw the profile of a young man in the moonlight. He was a stranger, so he stepped back.

The young man whispered: "I am not a spy."

"What do you want?"

The young man pointed to the mountain. "There were six of them, but their number is increasing day by day. When the agents of the House of Fire launch a surprise night attack, they go into the caves. Hero Qobad knows the nooks and crannies of the mountain like the palm of his hand." He pointed to the cypress forest on the slopes. "He planted the saplings with his own hands."

Yavar spread his feet apart wide and, with his hands on his hips, raised his left eyebrow. "What is Hero Zoleykha doing?"

The young man stared into the old man's eyes. "Who are you?"

Yavar stroked the front of his short jacket, as though touching insignias with his fingertips. "Bravo! I am Hero Yavar, one of the original members of . . ." He did not finish his sentence. "In fact, what business is that of yours?"

The young man smiled. "You should have said that earlier." He shook Yavar's hand firmly. "Welcome, Hero Yavar! I figured out right away that you were different from the others. You have the heart of a lion, like Hero Showkat. We used to work the same shift. She was the representative of the labor union from five years ago."

Yavar nodded. "We were close chums. She learned knife throwing from me. No one could match her strength." He looked at the sky. "Yes, poor Mr. Vahab lost to her."

The young man knit his brow. "Mr. Vahab?"

Yavar snapped his fingers and laughed: "We just called him 'Mister' for fun. We pulled his leg. He really hated this title. He would curse and glare at you. Those were the good old days. We were stuck together like grapes in a cluster. Alas, we have been scattered all around."

The young man sighed. "Why didn't you go up there?"

"Somebody needed to stay in the city. They chose me. Aren't you going up, yourself?"

The young man whispered in Yavar's ear: "I am thinking about it. Who knows? I might suddenly go."

A group of people gathered around them. The young man patted Yavar on the back. "This brave man was among the first group."

Yavar shook his head in regret. "Fifty years on the mountain."

A man from among the group said: "Yuri Marenko committed suicide."

Yavar raised his left eyebrow. "He was not worthy of Hero Roxana." The others agreed. Yavar twisted his mustache. "Only Mr. . . ." —he scratched his head—"Hero Vahab was worthy of her."

A middle-aged man objected. "Roxana was free. Only the mountain was worthy of her."

Yavar put his hands on his hips. "Hero Vahab was a marvel. All by himself, he could fight ten armed men. He was an athlete, and he could shoot a fly with a revolver. His aunt, Hero Rahila, grieved to death in the hands of the military regime."

The crowd yelled: "Keep the name of Hero Rahila alive forever! Salute to Hero Vahab!"

Yavar's eyes sparkled. Facing the moon, a man recited a poem in praise of Heroes Qobad, Zoleykha, Showkat, Roxana, Kaveh, and Borzu.

Yavar applauded him. "Bravo! Make more poems. All the poems we made for Hero Qobad for fifty years. The sorcerer, Yunos, me, and the rest. Yuri Marenko came late."

A voice resonated in the air: "Our legend, Hero Qobad, is immortal."

A second person clenched his fist. "He has become young again. His white royal falcon was once again flying in the sky yesterday."

Yavar shook his finger threateningly. "Hero Zoleykha became young first. When Qobad was twenty years old, he would come to our house. At night, he made battle plans with Hero Zoleykha under the shade of the willow tree."

Mir Hozhabr came to the middle of the crowd and raised his clenched fist. "I brought them myself. I was Qobad's right eye." He yawned and collapsed on the ground.

The sound of the rapid steps of the Fire Stokers resonated on the stone-paved road. The crowd fled and hid behind the cypress trees. Yavar ran into the forest and walked until dawn. He arrived at the house before sunup. He knocked at the door, and sat down on the stone seat.

Leqa immediately appeared between the double doors. She looked pale and her eyes were red from sleeplessness. She knelt and raised her hands toward the sky. "Oh, Lord! Thank God, he came back."

Yavar entered the courtyard and, limping, went up the stairs and sat in the corner of the entrance hall.

Leqa ran after him. "What happened? Where were you? Every footstep that I heard, I thought it was you."

Yavar pounded his knee with his fist. "What? Don't you know? I had gone to them. They have started such an uprising! Half of the people of the city have gathered at the foot of the mountain."

Leqa's eyes widened. "Are they alive? What were they doing?"

"It is all calm and quiet, not a leaf has fallen from any tree. I must tell you, Hero Qobad and your mother have gone back to their youth."

The corners of Leqa's lips quivered. "I do not believe it. It is all lies."

Yavar moaned: "Ouch, my leg. From far away, they were so glorious. Not to compare, but, like angels. They have made such poems about your mother. They call her the famous Hero Zoleykha."

The middle-aged girl laughed and covered her mouth with her hand. "Hero Zoleykha? Have you lost your mind?"

Yavar pounded on his chest with his fist. His ribs protruded. "Do you think Hero Yavar is lying? Thanks a million! Everybody fell to his knees before me and told me, 'Hero, go up there. You belong there.'" He slapped the back of one hand with the other in regret. "I didn't agree to it. For whose sake? You alone. I said to myself, I won't leave Leqa on her own. But in this house, the famous Hero Yavar is called a liar. That's my luck!"

Leqa went down on her knees. "All right, I apologize. Believe me, I cannot think straight. My tongue is tied. When you disappeared, I said to myself, 'Here you are. This one was the last one.' I wrapped several dresses in a bundle, and wanted to go to the Ordzhonikidze Dormitory."

Yavar's eyes teared up. He placed his heavy, tired hand on Leqa's head and hiccupped. "Don't think about such things, my girl! Do you see now that your Yavar is back?"

Leqa burst out crying and kissed the old man's hand. "Yavar! I consider you my father."

Yavar closed his eyes, stretched out his legs, and fell asleep. Leqa put a pillow under his head and covered him with a quilt. When he opened his eyes, the wall lights of the entrance hall were shining on the blue satin quilt. Leqa was sitting on the stairs, leaning her head against the banister and staring at the empty space where the carpet used to be on the wooden floor.

Yavar sat up and smiled. "Miss Leqa! I had good dreams."

Leqa walked to the kitchen, dragging her feet. The smell of cooked lentils wafted in the air. She spread a tablecloth in the corner of the entrance hallway and brought out dishes and glasses. She placed the bowl of lentil soup in the middle. They began eating. After supper, Yavar went to his room.

The door facing the garden turned on its hinges. Yunos entered the entrance hallway. He had a black bundle under his arm. He sat down and put it beside Leqa. "I need to be on my way while the road is lit by moonlight. I am going back to the village of my birth." He stroked the knot of the cloak. "I will not take this with me. My work is done. Completing it is yours."

Leqa bit her lip. Her cheeks were flushed. "Your handwritten manuscript? No, I am undeserving of it. I wish you had entrusted it to Vahab."

Hero Yunos frowned. "I am the one who decides."

"I am not that much of a reader. I have only read six novels."

Yunos moved the bundle up and down, as though weighing it. "Now, read the seventh! It is familiar to you."

Leqa's eyes sparkled.

Chapter 8

There was a knock on the door on Wednesday morning. Leqa jumped out of bed, put on a long robe over her flannel nightgown, ran to the interior balcony, and bent over the balustrade. "Yavar! Are you awake?"

The old man rushed out of his room and buttoned up his jacket. "Miss Leqa! They are here."

Leqa smiled.

Yavar ran to the door and came back with four Fire Stokers. Leqa came down the stairs. A tall, morose Fire Stoker took a piece of paper out of his pocket and handed it to her. "Official order of the Central House of Fire. You must vacate the house. A deadline has been set." He clicked his boots. "You have only one hour."

Leqa looked around herself. "Where are we supposed to go? The dormitory?"

The Fire Stoker stroked the leather holster of his revolver. "Hero. You are in luck. You will have a room. Also, tomorrow morning, you must go to the House of Forefront Galloping Young People to perform your duty. Freeloading is over."

Leqa frowned. "What duty?"

"Teaching music."

Leqa nodded. "That will be fine." She turned to Yavar. "Gather up your things!"

Yavar shook his head. "How could we just leave the house? What if its owner comes back?"

Leqa's eyes clouded and the corners of her lips drooped. "Yavar! Stop dreaming!"

The Fire Stoker jumped up toward the chain of the chandelier. "I was here when the chandelier was broken."

The old man's head bent over his chest. He walked away with shaky steps. Leqa went up the stairs. The tall Fire Stoker and his comrade joined her.

Leqa asked: "Is it necessary for you to be here?"

The man looked at the plasterwork of the four fairies. "Yes, during the entire process."

Leqa entered the room, pulled out her suitcase from under the bed, went to the closet, and put a few dresses in it.

The Fire Stoker pointed his index finger at her and shook it. "Only personal items!"

Leqa touched the oval mirror. "May I take this?"

The Fire Stoker said out loud: "That will be fine. Do you look into the mirror a lot?"

Leqa looked at him in disgust. "No! The way I look would not make me inclined to look in the mirror." She picked up her diary from the edge of the bed.

The Fire Stoker asked: "What is that?"

"My daily journal. If you are suspicious, you can read it."

The Fire Stokers sat shoulder to shoulder on her bed, opened the diary, and began to read. Occasionally, they burst out laughing and clapped their hands.

Leqa pushed the suitcase by the closet, picked up Yunos's bundle, and concealed it between her clothes.

The men continued to laugh. The tall one lay down, rested the thick heels of his boots on the headboard, took an engraved silver cigarette box out of his pocket, and said to his comrade: "Would you like one?"

The second one went to the window. "What the old man said wasn't too off. This place needs protection."

The tall one lit a cigarette. "Such particulars are not a part of our duties. The main fifteen members must decide. If you only knew some time ago what a ruckus a bunch of lunatics had raised under these ceilings. It was worse than a stampede of donkeys. They didn't believe in obedience. Everybody played his own tune. Their grating noises pestered and plagued the members of the House of Fire. They reported it to the Center till finally an order was issued and they were all swept up and dumped into a ditch." He made a smoke ring. "They got rid of them with no headache."

Leqa closed her suitcase and walked toward the picture of the female saint. She loosened the nail on the left.

The Fire Stoker got up. "Stop!"

"This copy has no value. It is old."

The Fire Stoker grabbed her wrist and twisted it. "Pick up your suitcase and go by the door without any argument."

Leqa began to tremble. "What harm does this picture cause you?"

The Fire Stoker pushed her toward the door. "None of your business."

Leqa picked up the suitcase. She paused for a moment in the entrance hall and stared at the blue and purple rays of the skylight glass panes. A few pigeons were sitting on the asymmetrical dimensions of the plasterwork of morning glories and grapevines. She looked at the garden, at the surface of the reflecting pool. Green foamy clots were spinning with the breeze. The cows mooed in the distance.

Leqa left the entrance hall, came to the top of the stairs to the courtyard, and filled her lungs with the air scented with jasmine flowers.

Yavar was standing at the door with his bundle on his back, surrounded by the Fire Stokers.

Leqa walked toward the old man and said: "Let's go, Yavar!"

They got into an old jeep that was parked under the shade of the wall and set out. They passed through Warshawskaya Street, Molla Aref Road, and Peram Mausoleum Square, and reached the outskirts of the city. The jeep stopped at the corner of a small square without flowers or greenery. A high dark building cast its shadow on the ground.

Hero Rashid came to the balcony of the fifth floor, gave them a smile of recognition, and immediately went inside.

One of the Fire Stokers jumped out, stretched his arms, and yawned. "In a couple of years, this will be a part of the city. You have no more than three quarters of an hour's walk to the street."

Leqa looked at the building. Two rows of balconies were visible from behind the fog. "It is stifling."

The Fire Stoker went close to the gutter full of muck and kicked the mudguard of the vehicle with his heel. "Your rooms are on the seventh floor."

Leqa gazed at the half-burnt grass of the cypress grove.

An old man with a stool in his hand stepped onto the balcony of the sixth floor. Upon seeing the Fire Stokers, he removed his hat and bowed.

After whispering to the doorman, the tall Fire Stoker called for Leqa and Yavar. They picked up the suitcase and the bundle and walked forward. They entered a semidark hallway, blinking their eyes, and climbed the narrow dusty staircase. Occasionally, they would stop to catch their breath. Two low-ranking Fire Stokers passed by them, talking and running up. At every landing, Leqa and Yavar came close to the round windows that looked like the mouths of wells, looked outside, and saw the tall Fire Stoker on the brick-paved square, leaning against the jeep, whistling.

The staircase was covered with cement and lime, which left a white dust on their shoes. Here and there, on the upper floors, a door would open and young women with babies in their arms would check them out from head to toe. Yavar would frown and sit on the ground. They reached the seventh floor. Two Fire Stokers were standing at the threshold of the doors across from each other. Yavar leaned against the concrete railing. "Is my place and Miss Leqa's place not the same?"

The Fire Stokers pushed the old man into the room to the left. The knot of the bundle got caught on the doorknob and ripped open.

With her head lowered, Leqa went to the room on the right.

The two young Fire Stokers tossed keys to both of them and went down the stairs noisily.

Leqa stood by the window, and yearning to see the house, she looked at scattered purple gable roofs. It was drizzling. She held her hand under the raindrops and rubbed her hand on her face.

~

The room was small and empty. Its ceiling was low and the walls were made of plaster. She went to the closet, opened the suitcase, took out the clothes, and arranged them on the shelves. She hid Yunos's bundle under a dark overcoat. She leaned the mirror against the wall of the wall shelf.

Someone knocked at the door, hard. Leqa jumped up and rushed to open the door. The short doorman was standing in the hallway, smiling with his mouth open, making his saw-like, jagged teeth visible. He extended a pair of folded smoke-colored blankets toward Leqa. He stuck his hands in his pockets. "I am Hero Ghazanfar, the doorman. I wanted to ask if you were brought here from the public housing." Leqa nodded. The man closed his reddened eyelids and touched the hair sprouting from his ear. "So, you must really have connections."

"Thank you for the blankets."

Ghazanfar's neck straightened like a lever. His elbow leapt up. "The residents of the buildings have their lunch and dinner at the mess hall. It is on the corner of the third alleyway. Which dormitory did you come from?"

"Ordzhonikidze."

"How many were you?"

"An army."

The doorman burst out laughing and turned his back to Leqa. As he was going down the stairs, the sound of his boisterous laughter resonated in the dark staircase.

Chapter 9

Since Thursday morning, Leqa would go to work and return near sunset. She had about fifty students. She was teaching them the musical alphabet, scrupulously. The residence of Hero Qadir was in the adjacent complex. He occasionally came to visit Yavar and Leqa. One day, when Leqa was not there, he painted the walls of her small room white and the window frame and the closet blue.

On her way back from work, Leqa would see Rashid. They would walk on out-of-the-way roads, conversing, until they reached home.

On sunny days, Yavar would go to the cypress grove and sit on the burnt grass. He would talk to the children and attribute the past history of Heroes Qobad, Kaveh, and Showkat to himself. The children would be transfixed, viewing him as a legendary champion. He had befriended the old man on the sixth floor. Occasionally, they went to the National Park, shoulder to shoulder. The man wore a brimmed hat and cleaned his shoes with a handkerchief, and sometimes people said hello to him in the park.

At sunset, Yavar would sit on the brick pavement of the little square. As soon as he heard Leqa's footsteps, he would jump to his feet and walk a few steps forward to welcome her. He would go into detail about the trivial incidents of the day, such as a child who had fallen, a new neighbor who had just moved in, and the virtues of the old man, his new friend, who had been a professor of history, had read a lot of books, and was respected by all the people in the city.

Precisely at seven-thirty in the evening, they would go to the mess hall to eat a bowl of watery soup, half-cooked beans, and dry barley bread. A swarm of lifeless flies and mosquitos were lined up on the dusty windowsills and the edges of the windowpanes. The final rays of the sun would shine on the metal tables and fade away. Fingerprints, graffiti, and splattered tea stains were left on the bare walls.

Leqa did not have time to think. She was gradually forgetting the memories of the past. Occasionally, the image of the reflecting pool and the jetting fountain, the blue window, and the spiral staircase appeared in her mind. She had gotten used to her room. Heroes Kowkab, Pari, and Torkan had brought her an old kilim. She could smell soap in the warp and weft of the rough wool. The faded colors of the designs gave the room an appearance of familiarity.

One day, she looked carefully at her face in the mirror. Deep solid lines furrowed her hard, sunburned skin. Her gray eyes shone from small daily joys. With a smile devoid of the past and future, she turned away from the mirror.

One day when they were off from work, they brought her piano to her room and placed it parallel to the wall. Early in the evening, enthusiastically, she would play Italian capriccios, Liszt's rhapsodies, Mendelson's romances, and, finally, the "Song of Mary." She would then close the piano and become young for a moment, but it would not last long.

When construction workers passed by, they would look up and, after a short pause, continue on their way until they became accustomed to the sound of the piano; and the tunes, the sound of hammers, the commotion of cranes, and the moaning of the windlasses became a part of the routine daily sounds. The light breeze would carry the low and high pitches of the songs far away, spin around the branch of a pine tree and vibrate a curtain and tent under the sky.

On clear nights, the fire on the mountain flickered with a small flame. Leqa and Yavar would sit on the balcony and watch it. The professor of history from downstairs would say: "It is caused by static electricity that is produced by the rubbing together of the branches of the pine trees."

Yavar would laugh nervously, and when the professor was not looking, he would stick his tongue out. Leqa would agree with the historian's opinion, which made Yavar feel alone. To honor the people on the mountain, he would whisper a passionate slogan in the ears of the neighbors. They would immediately walk away. No one, except for the children, believed what he said. He would point to Rashid as his witness, but Rashid would not utter one word. In private, Yavar would grab his collar and shake in anger: "You ungrateful young man! Would it kill you to praise their bravery?"

Hero Rashid would gently remove Yavar's hand from his collar: "Yavar! Stop clowning around! Why do you say things that smell of danger? Have you heard anything about the conditions in the camp? Barbed wires, forced labor, polar cold, hunger, and lashes. Nowhere throughout the snow-covered plains around the camp is there any sign of mountains and fire. Then how are you going to keep yourself warm?"

Yavar would turn his back to him in contempt. "All of you have lost your minds. Mr. Vahab had foresight and gave up and left this humdrum city."

Old age and hopelessness were gradually bringing him to his knees. He sat on the edge of the little square under the sun for hours. If a passerby asked him for the direction of an alleyway, he would point to it. His relationship with the history professor had been severed. Any evening when he could see the flickering of the fire on the mountain with eager eyes, he bent down over the railing and shouted: "Isn't that something? The pine tree branches won't let go. They keep rubbing against each other."

On cloudy days, he would lie down in his room under the coarse blankets and stare at the whitewashed ceiling.

Leqa would bring food for him from the mess hall, but the old man would not touch it. The pottage and the bean dish would congeal. Leqa would hold the mirror in front of his face. "Look at your gaunt head and face! You have become all skin and bones."

Yavar would smile. "It doesn't matter, Miss Leqa. The cup is overflowing."

Leqa would burst out crying and leave his room.

On a holiday, Golrokh came to see Leqa. She had brought her a bunch of wild violets. Leqa put the flowers in a vase. The girl sat on the kilim and spread her skirt. "I will be your student starting next Tuesday. The House of Forefront Galloping Young People has accepted my application."

Leqa smiled. "Do you remember the first thing that you said to me?"

Golrokh looked at the ground. "Is there music in that box?"

Leqa nodded. "I answered that everywhere is full of music."

Golrokh raised her head. "The Pink Rose Café!" She came closer to Leqa. "Yusef has gone to the mountain."

Leqa held her arm. "Is that really true?"

"A messenger brought the news yesterday. A group of people have gathered around him. They are keeping the fire lit."

Leqa looked at the sky through the open window. She took the girl's rosy cold hands in hers. "Don't tell Yavar. It will make him despair."

The girl squeezed Leqa's middle finger. "I know."

They went to Yavar's room. Golrokh sat beside the old man's bed. "I have brought good news. A messenger came from the mountain yesterday. They are fine. Hero Zoleykha sends her greetings to you. Yusef has also gone up there."

Yavar jolted and sat up. "Oh, how I wish to pound the bald head of the professor of history with this news!"

Leqa opened the door quietly and checked the landing. "Yavar! Talk quietly! You need to keep this secret close to your chest."

Yavar turned toward the wall. "You yourself are a witness that I have crawled into my shell. I won't say a word to anyone."

Leqa dropped her head.

Golrokh pulled Yavar's blanket over his chest. "Take him for a walk once in a while."

Yavar turned to them. "Have they said anything about coming back?"

The girl asked: "Who, Yavar?"

"Come on, girl! You are also confused. The famous Hero Zoleykha."

Leqa interrupted him. "She will come, Yavar. Very soon."

Yavar's eyes sparkled. "Of course she will. The dream I had that day is gradually coming true."

Golrokh squeezed his hand and got up. "I will come to visit you again."

"I hope you live a long life, sweet girl. You brightened my heart."

Leqa saw Golrokh off up to the landing.

Early in the evening, Yavar opened the window and spread a blanket on the balcony. "Miss Leqa! Come and sit down, the sky is clear."

He had combed his hair and was wearing cashmere trousers. He buttoned his smoke-colored jacket to his throat.

Leqa looked at the old man from head to toe. "Aren't you going to have dinner?"

Yavar's eyes sparkled mischievously. "Why wouldn't I?"

She took something wrapped in a handkerchief out of her pocket, opened it, and spread it on the raised edge of the balcony. "Here! It's cooked potatoes. Rashid brought it."

They sat side by side and ate the potatoes. Yavar took a sip of water, folded his handkerchief, and put it into his pocket: "It tasted really good." He bent over the railing and said to the history professor: "Hey, old man! Good day to you. We are sitting on the balcony to see the fire on the mountain. The fire that has been lit by human hands."

The old professor took his hat off and put his hand behind his ear. "Pardon me? I could not hear exactly what you said."

Yavar shook his head. The breeze tousled his white hair. "Doze off, old man. Your brain can't catch up with what I'm telling you. You read four and a half books seventy years ago. That was all. Our Hero Vahab was a thousand times more educated and had read more books than you, but he wasn't that big-headed. Boast in front of someone who hasn't seen actual smart people. I have spent most of my life in the library." He clawed his hair. "Do you think I made my hair white in the flour mill?"

The history professor waved his hand and shifted on his stool.

Yavar sat down and punched the raised edge. "What a bastard! He is pretending to be deaf."

Leqa laughed and held her hand in front of her mouth. "Yavar! I hope you live forever. Why do you pull his leg?"

"Huh! You don't know him. He likes it. He has suffered so much loneliness that he aches for someone in the world to talk to him, even if he hears curses and insults. He has heard a lot of insults, I am sure. But in response, he just waves his hand." Leqa picked up the potato skin, which was covered with dust. The old man gazed at some faraway spot. "Do you remember your special plate and glass, Miss Leqa?"

A mosquito bit Leqa's arm. She scratched the bite and licked it. "They throw so much trash and garbage around here that we can have no peace and quiet because of the mosquitoes."

Yavar gathered up his legs and rested his chin on his knees. "What do you think they have done with the house?"

"I do not want to know at all. I am sure the flag with the erect crowbar is twisting and turning on its gable roof."

Yavar sighed. "In this season of the year, red apples would ripen."

Leqa buttoned up her cardigan. "I will buy some apples for you tomorrow. Fruits help improve one's health."

The old man stretched out his arms. "As for me, I am fit and fine. Believe me, I didn't mean anything. Talk for humans is like chewing on the cud for cows."

A fire flickered behind the pine branches far away. Yavar stood at attention with his hands on his chest and bowed. He asked Leqa: "Do you see it? Such a fire! Why have you turned to stone? Say hello to your mother. Has the House of Forefront Galloping Young People taken away your feelings?"

Leqa did not answer.

Yavar stretched his neck to see the fire better. He grumbled under his breath: "I can't understand why the lady has sent the message there. Are Kowkab, Pari, and Torkan dearer to her than we are? To tell you the truth, I was offended."

"Yavar! Use your head! This place is full of spies. Minders and report writers wiggle here like worms. Why does the history professor always sit on the balcony? Have you been watching the women? When they hear any sound, they stick their heads out. Under these conditions, do you expect her to send the messenger to bring her greetings to you and me here?"

Yavar sat in the corner of the balcony, took out his clay pipe, and stuck it into the pouch. Hero Rashid and Leqa made sure he always had tobacco. Yavar filled the bowl, struck a match, took a hard puff, and sent the smoke with pleasure toward the stars and the sky.

The shadow of a man appeared on the balcony to the right. His dirty tank top was lit up in the moonlight. In a husky voice, he said: "We are trying to catch a wink. This place belongs to high-level individuals, not the hungry panhandlers of the dormitories who yap till midnight." He shot his spit toward the sky. "I can't figure out why they have brought feeble old men who shit in their pants here." He shook his clenched fist and strong arm. "Put that damned thing out. My job isn't writing reports, but when you put your foot on my tail, I will get you any way I can."

Yavar immediately pressed his palm on the clay pipe to put it out.

Leqa walked quietly to her room, folded her overcoat, put it under her head, wrapped herself in the blankets, closed her eyes, and fell asleep.

She got up at dawn and rubbed her eyes. Yavar was still on the balcony, leaning his head against the railing, staring at the rising of the sun, his frail body bent, his hands hanging, motionless.

Chapter 10

Fog had covered the entire city. It was drizzling. After passing through Molla Aref Road, Leqa stepped onto Warshawskaya Street. She tightened the knot of her thick headscarf under her chin, stuck her frostbitten hands into her pockets, crossed the street, entered the alleyway, walked toward the adobe wall, and stood in front of the house. The faded gable roof was shining under the rain. The stone platform seats by the door were wet, and the door was half-open. She took a peek inside. She saw no one. With the soft pressure of her hand, the door turned on its hinges. She went in and took a look around. Drops of water were washing the clusters of purple jasmine and falling down. Under the arbor, wicker chairs, the color of which had faded, were arranged around the table. She stepped on the stone pavement. The sound of her footsteps echoed in the silence. She peered into the kitchen through the glass windowpane. The doors of the cupboards were open. There were no frying pans, samovars, and porcelain dishes. Only Vahab's zinc kettle was left on the stove. She stepped back. The house was standing away from her, a fleeting vision, or a suspended memory. She touched the wall of the building. Her fingers glided over the furrows of the marble. It was warm and alive, like a rural clay oven after the baking of bread at dawn. She went around the building and entered the garden. As she crossed the lawn, lily thorns and strands of algae stuck to the bottom of her raincoat. She took off her headscarf. Her gray hair slid over her shoulders. She stood behind the boxwood trees. A few branches of the Russian alder and oak trees were burnt. Herds of sheep were grazing here and there in the alfalfa field. The door of the stable was open, and the black and white cows were lying on the dahlia flowers. She looked at the gray building through the fog. There were no curtains behind the windows. They had removed the orange flowerpots from the two sides of the wide, arched staircase. Water sparkled in potholes in the indentations of the marble. The wind was intertwining the branches of the willow tree. The area around the overflowing reflecting pool was full of sheep drinking water. The sweetbrier arbor bent over the flowerbed, and the drooping buds shivered under the rain. A lamb stepped on a decayed piece of wood and got caught between the branches. It began bleating loudly. Leqa ran forward and pushed away the thorny intertwining branches. Her hands were scratched in several places. She picked up the animal in her arms and let it go on the pavement of the courtyard. She walked toward the cows and clapped her hands. They raised their heads and shook their wet snouts. Small pieces of green leaves were caught in their drooling saliva. They slowly got up, approached Leqa, and sniffed her hands. Their black eyes shone. Dewdrops had landed on their long eyelashes. Their mouths were closed and their jaws moved slowly. Leqa petted them on their heads and snouts. She took a deep breath and walked toward the gravel path. She reached the grapevine arbor and leaned her shoulder against the post. She stroked the back of a broken bench. The space under the trellises was barely visible. Clusters of grapes were hanging under the low arbor, in every grape, as though a light was lit, and under their brittle skin the sap of life was twirling. A few pieces of crumbled paper were slowly disintegrating under the rain in the warm soil. She stepped into the alfalfa field, walked toward a wet stone slab, sat on it, put her hand under her chin, and looked at the burned oak branches. She turned in the direction of her mother's room. The window was open and rain was pouring inside. The downpour was washing off the dust on the clotheslines. The stalks of tuberoses were smashed under the hooves of the sheep. In the corner of the flowerbed, only a white cluster was quivering behind the vapors. She approached the window. She touched two gray spots on the wall, the places where the heels of Borzu's shoes had hit. The sun shone its rays through the mass of fog. A few newly sprouted sunflowers were lit up next to the stream. The yellow petals wrapped around the disk of the smoke-colored seeds in the breeze, smoldering within a red halo.

She climbed the stairs, stepped into the entrance hall, and looked at the dome ceiling. The faded blue, diminishing pink, dusty purple, and discolored green dresses of the fairies were turning to vapors in the blue flames under the transparent glass tent. The glass panes seemed to be smiling. The broken chain of the chandelier vibrated with their breaths. She entered the parlor. The cat had fallen asleep between the folds of the embroidered tablecloth next to the wood-burning fireplace. She walked toward the library. She stroked the wood of the empty shelves with her finger. A half-burnt book was on the floor. She sat down, picked up the book, caressed its swollen leather cover, placed it on her knees, and opened it. "Verily, verily, I say unto thee, Except a man be born again, he cannot see the kingdom of God." She closed the book and put it on the top shelf. She walked out of the parlor and went to Rahila's room. Rain was pouring on the windowsill, running down, becoming a narrow stream, and passing under the door. Leqa followed the stream and reached the staircase. She held on to the banister and walked up. The glass panes of the landing window were broken here and there. With every step, a soft dust surrounded her. The door to Vahab's room was open. The brown velvet curtain hanging on the bedpost, torn and in tatters, was swinging like a hollow cloak. There remained the blurred prints of muddy boots around the bed and near the window. In the rooms that were all empty, yellowed newspapers that had tossed themselves to the wind made a monotonous rustling sound. On a dusty door, a careless finger had drawn the crossed erect crowbar. She arrived at the threshold of her mother's room. The faint ray of the sun, like a yellow butterfly, was crucified on the bedspread. She nimbly passed through the narrow door and entered her own room. On the edge of the sink, a half-used cake of soap was decomposing in the mass of fog. She turned on the faucet and washed her hands. She ran her finger over the wall before her. They had taken away the copy of the picture of the female saint, and a faded rectangle identified the borders of the picture. She put her palms together and recited some prayers. She was reciting the sentences in the wrong order, chaotic and meaningless. A combination of the stretched-out sounds of the letter S and the cacophonous Z resonated like the buzzing of summer bees under the ceiling. She turned her head and blinked. In the corner, between two walls, an object was shining on the floor. She knelt, picked it up, and examined it. The carnelian surface of the bottle flashed and a colorless liquid moved inside. Leqa opened the red lid and sniffed it. It was Kaveh's inexpensive cologne, mixed with water. She stood up and placed the bottle on the small shelf under the empty space of the picture of the female saint. A gust of wind blew hard, and the gable roof roared. She ran to the window and stuck out her head. From the edge of the cornice, a chimney fell into the courtyard. The feet of the ladder were raised toward the sky. The strands of shade moss were shaking in the wind. Leqa left the room. She stood on the top of the staircase and braided her damp hair. She walked past the landing and sat on the third step. Her thin lips twisted. She knotted her uneven eyebrows. She stared at the doors of the entrance hall with dazed crossed eyes. Herds of sheep were coming in, one after another, pulling the twisting rings of the fog into the building. Water dripped from their intertwined wool. They shook their heads and necks, entered the parlor, and, after a pause in front of the flames, they turned around and went to the entrance hall, spinning and bleating. The light from the glass skylight waved on their wet white wool, igniting it with bright colors. They gathered around the staircase. On the completely empty floor, the wall clock alone was left with its decorative top covered with images of birds and flowers, and the golden pendulum swayed inside the glass box. The tick-tock sound resonated in the fog. The sheep listened. The clock struck ten times. Leqa looked at her wristwatch. She adjusted the time and leaned her head on the banister. Steam was rising from the damp wool of the sheep. The smell of wet soil, fresh milk, alfalfa, and sheep droppings made a halo around her head. Under the humid ceiling, her frozen heart was blossoming. The soft breathing of the herd harmonized with her sporadic breathing. White lambs were climbing the bare staircase, leaning down along the wood, and holding their wet snouts toward the steaming light.

She leaned her chin on her hand. The harsh lines of her face lit up. The scent of her nanny's rice pudding filled her nose. Her dark eyes shone behind the moisture of her tears. In the fireplace, a blue fire flamed up.

October 3, 1990

List of Characters

Members of Edrisi Household

Arsalan: deceased son of Mrs. Edrisi, Vahab's father

Leqa: old-maid daughter of Mrs. Edrisi, older aunt of Vahab

Luba: deceased cousin of Mrs. Edrisi; died when young

Mrs. Edrisi: Zoleykha, matriarch of Edrisi family

Rahila: deceased daughter of Mrs. Edrisi, younger sister of Leqa, favorite aunt of Vahab

Rana: deceased mother of Vahab

Vahab: grandson of Mrs. Edrisi; son of her son, Arsalan; British-educated, lover of books

Yavar: only remaining servant of family

Heroes

Borzu: hot-headed student, revolutionary; idealizes Showkat

Haddadiyan: former mayor of city during previous regime; later given the title of "Neo-Hero"

Kaveh: previously a ladies' man; has been traveling the world

Kowkab: Yusef and Golrokh's mother; assigned to wash clothes for Heroes

Kukan: tailor; used to work for rich people

Moayyad: ugly rich man who turned to Heroes; purposely gave everything to them to gain power; had been betrothed to Rahila

Pari: formerly a hospital nurse, literate; assigned to wash clothes for Heroes

Qadir: house painter

Qobad: old leader of uprising that has led to government of the Heroes

Rakhov: female head of main members of House of Fire
Rashid: factory worker
Riyakhovski: military commander of the House of Fire
Roxana: famous stage actress
Rokhsareh: former servant
Showkat: female boss of revolutionaries that have taken over Edrisi house
Teymur: old man, former gardener of National Paek of city
Torkan: assigned to wash clothes for Heroes
Yunos: poet-sorcerer; left his own city to travel around the world
Yusef: educated son of Kowkab, aspires to be a revolutionary poet

Others

Aslan: Torkan's son
Bakhshi: son of Kowkab, twin brother of Sakhi, brother of Golrokh and
   Yusef
Golrokh: Kowkab's daughter
Gowhar: Pari's daughter
Saber: Gowhar's mute cousin
Sakhi: twin son of Kowkab
Shirin: Torkan's sickly young daughter

Poet, novelist, and short-story writer Ghazaleh Alizadeh (1947–1996) was born in Mashhad to an affluent family. Her father was a merchant, and, like herself, her mother was a writer and poet. After graduating from the University of Tehran with a degree in law and political science, she studied philosophy and film in France for a few years. Her first novel, *The House of the Edrisis*, was awarded a prize for the best novel in "Twenty Years of Fiction Writing" by Iran's Ministry of Islamic Culture and Guidance in 1999.

M. R. Ghanoonparvar is Professor Emeritus of Persian and Comparative Literature at The University of Texas at Austin. He is the recipient of the 2008 Lois Roth Prize for Literary Translation, a Lifetime Achievement Award from the American Association of Teachers of Persian, as well as a Lifetime Achievement Award from *Encyclopædia Iranica*. His recent books include *From Prophets of Doom to Chroniclers of Gloom* and *Iranian Cities in Persian Fiction*. His most recent translations include Shahrokh Meskub's, *Leaving, Staying, Returning*; Moniro Ravanipour's *The Drowned* and *These Crazy Nights*; Ghazaleh Alizadeh's *The Nights of Tehran* and *Two Views and Trial*; and Shahrnush Parsipur's *Blue Logos*. His forthcoming translations include Hossein Atashparvar's *From the Moon to the Well*, and Reza Julai's *Jujube Blossoms*.

www.ingramcontent.com/pod-product-compliance
Lightning Source LLC
Chambersburg PA
CBHW020719020225
21231CB00014B/92